Quicksilver
The Boy With No Skid to His Wheel

by

George Manville Fenn

Double9
BOOKS

Quicksilver
The Boy With No Skid to His Wheel
by George Manville Fenn

Copyright © 2024

All Rights reserved.

ISBN: 978-93-64285-71-1

Published by

DOUBLE 9 BOOKS

2/13-B, Ansari Road
Daryaganj, New Delhi – 110002
info@double9books.com
www.double9books.com
Tel. 011-40042856

ABOUT THE AUTHOR

George Manville Fenn was a very productive author of novels, a writer, an editor, and an educator from England. He was born on January 3, 1831, in Pimlico, London. He mostly learned on his own; he taught himself Italian, French, and German. During the years 1851–1854, he went to Battersea Training College for Teachers and then became the head of a state school in Alford, Lincolnshire. In the early 1850s, Fenn started to write short stories and pieces for newspapers and magazines. The Old Forest Ranger, his first book, came out in 1856. Afterward, he wrote more than 100 books, many of them for teenagers and young adults. He was one of the most famous writers of his time, and his books were well-liked and read by many people. He also worked as a reporter and writer for Fenn. Among the newspapers and magazines, he worked for was The Boy's Own Paper, which he ran from 1866 to 1874. He worked hard to make children's books better and was a strong supporter of education and reading. The Englishman Fenn passed away on August 26, 1909, in Isleworth.

CONTENTS

Chapter One
A Very Strange Pair

He was very grubby, and all about his dark grey eyes there were the marks made by his dirty fingers where he had rubbed away the tickling tears. The brownish red dust of the Devon lanes had darkened his delicate white skin, and matted his shiny yellow curls.

As to his hands, with their fat little fingers, with every joint showing a pretty dimple, they looked white and clean, but that was due to the fact that he was sitting in a bed of moss by the roadside, where the water came trickling down from the red rocks above, and dabbling and splashing the tiny pool, till the pearly drops hung among his dusty curls, and dotted, as if with jewels, the ragged old blue jersey shirt which seemed to form his only garment.

This did not fit him, in spite of its elasticity, for it was what a dealer would have called "man's size," and the wearer was about two and a half, or at the most three; but the sleeves had been cut so that they only reached his elbows, and the hem torn off the bottom and turned into a belt or sash, which was tied tightly round the little fellow's waist, to keep the jersey from slipping off.

Consequently the plump neck was bare, as were his dirty little legs, with their dimpled, chubby knees.

While he splashed and dabbled the water, the sun flashed upon the drops, some of which jewelled the spreading ferns which drooped over the natural fount, and even reached as high as the delicate leafage of stunted overhanging birch, some of whose twigs kept waving in the soft summer breeze, and sweeping against the boy's curly hair.

When the little fellow splashed the water, and felt it fly into his face, he laughed—burst after burst of silvery, merry laughter; and in the height of his enjoyment he threw back his head, his ruddy lips parted, and two rows of pearly teeth flashed in the bright sunshine.

As dirty a little grub as ever made mud-pies in a gutter; but the water, the ferns, moss, and flowers around were to his little soul the most delightful of toys, and he seemed supremely happy.

After a time he grew tired of splashing the water, and, drawing one little foot into his lap, he pursed up his lips, an intent frown wrinkled his shining forehead, and he began, in the most serio-comic manner, to pick the row of tiny toes, passing a chubby finger between them to get rid of the dust and grit.

All this while the breeze blew, the birch-tree waved, and the flowers nodded, while from out of a clump of ling and rushes there came, at regular intervals, a low roar like the growl of a wild beast.

After a few minutes there was the *pad, pad—pad, pad* of a horse's hoofs on the dusty road; the rattle of wheels; and a green gig, drawn by a sleepy-looking grey horse, and containing a fat man and a broad woman, came into sight, approached slowly, and would have passed had not the broad woman suddenly laid her hand upon the reins, and checked the grey horse, when the two red-faced farming people opened their mouths, and stared at the child.

"Sakes alive, Izick, look at that!" said the woman in a whisper, while the little fellow went on picking his toes, and the grey horse turned his tail into a live chowry to keep away the flies.

"Well, I am!" said the fat man, wrinkling his face all over as he indulged in a silent laugh. "Why, moother, he's a perfeck picter."

"The pretty, pretty little fellow," said the woman in a genuine motherly tone. "O Izick, how I should like to give him a good wash!"

"Wash! He's happy enough, bless him!" said the man. "Wonder whose he be. Here, what are you going to do?"

"I'm going to give un a kiss, that's what I'm a-going to do," said the woman getting very slowly out of the gig. "He must be a lost child."

"Well," grumbled the man, "we didn't come to market to find lost children."

Then he sat forward, with his arms resting upon his knees, watching his wife as she slowly approached the unconscious child, till she was in the act of stooping over him to lay her fat red hand upon his golden curls, when there was a loud roar as if from some savage beast, and the woman jumped back scared; the horse leaped sidewise; the farmer raised his whip; and the pair of simple-hearted country folks stared at a fierce-looking face which rose out of the bed of ling, its owner having been sleeping face downward, and now glowering at them above his folded arms.

It was not a pleasant countenance, for it was foul without with dirt and more foul within from disease, being covered with ruddy fiery blotch and pimple, and the eyes were of that unnatural hue worn by one who has for years been debased by drink.

"Yah!" roared the man, half-closing his bleared eyes. "Leave the bairn alone."

"O Izick!" gasped the woman.

"Here, none o' that!" cried the farmer fiercely. "Don't you frighten my wife."

"Let the bairn alone," growled the man again.

"How came you by him!" said the woman recovering herself. "I'm sure he can't be your'n."

"Not mine!" growled the man in a hoarse, harsh voice. "You let the bairn be. I'll soon show you about that. Hi! chick!"

The little fellow scrambled to him, and putting his tiny chubby arms about the man's coarse neck, nestled his head upon his shoulder, and turned to gaze at the farmer and his wife.

"Not my bairn!" growled the man; "what d'yer say to that?"

"Lor, Izick, only look," said the woman in a whisper. "My!"

"Well, what are yer starin' at?" growled the man defiantly; "didn't think he were your bairn, did you!"

"Come away, missus," said the farmer; and the woman reluctantly climbed back into the gig.

"It don't seem right, Izick, for him to have such a bairn as that," said the woman, who could not keep her eyes off the child.

"Ah, well! it ar'n't no business of our'n. Go along!"

This was to the horse, who went off directly in a shambling trot, and the gig rattled along the road; but as long as they remained in sight, the farmer's wife stared back at the little fellow, and the rough-looking tramp glared at her from among the heather and ling.

"Must be getting on—must be getting on," he growled to himself; and he kept on muttering in a low tone as he tried to stagger to his feet, but for a time his joints seemed to be so stiff that he could only get to his knees, and he had to set the child down.

"THE PRETTY BARE ARMS CLUNG TIGHTLY ROUND HIS NECK."

Then after quite a struggle, during which he kept on muttering in a strange incoherent manner, he contrived to get upon his feet, and stood holding on by a branch of the birch-tree, while the child stared in his repellent face.

The next minute he staggered into the road and began to walk away, reeling strangely like a drunken man, talking wildly the while; but he seemed to recall the fact that he had left the child behind, and he staggered back to where a block of stone lay by the water-side, and sat down. "Here, chick!" he growled.

His aspect and the tone of his voice were sufficient to frighten the little fellow away, but he did not seem in the least alarmed, and placed his tiny hands in the great gnarled fists extended to him. Then with a swing the man threw the child over his shoulder and on to his back, staggering and nearly overbalancing himself in the act. But he kept his feet, and growled savagely as his little burden uttered a whimpering cry.

"Hold on," he said; and the next minute the pretty bare arms were clinging tightly round his neck, the hands hidden in the man's grizzly tangled beard; and, pig-a-back fashion, he bore him on along the road.

The sun beat down upon the fair curly head; the dust rose, shuffled up by the tramp's uncertain step, while the chats and linnets twittered among the furze, and the larks sang high overhead. This and the heat, combined with the motion, sufficed to lull the tiny fellow to rest, and before long his head drooped sidewise, and he was fast asleep.

But he did not fall. It was as if the natural instinct which enables the young life to maintain its hold upon the old orang-outang was in force here, so that the child clung tightly to the staggering man, who seemed thenceforth oblivious of his existence.

The day passed on: the sun was setting fast, and the tramp continued to stagger on like a drunken man, talking wildly all the time, now babbling of green leaves, now muttering angrily, as if abusing some one near.

Then came the soft evening-time, as he tottered down a long slope towards the houses lying in a hollow, indicating the existence of a goodly town.

And now groups of people were passed, some of whom turned to gaze after the coarse-looking object with disgust, others with wonder; while the more thoughtless indulged in a grin, and made remarks indicating their impressions of where the tramp had been last.

He did not seem to see them, however, but kept on the same incoherent talking in a low growl, and his eyes glared strangely at objects unseen by those he passed.

All at once, though, he paused as he reached the broad marketplace of the town, and said to one of a group of idlers the one word—

"Workus?"

"Eh?"

"Workus!" said the tramp fiercely.

"Oh! Straight avore you. Zee a big wall zoon as yer get over the bridge."

The man staggered on, and crossed the swift river running through the town, and in due course reached the big wall, in which was a doorway with a bell-pull at the side.

A few minutes later the door had been opened, and a stalwart porter seemed disposed to refuse admission, but his experienced eyes read the applicant's state, and the door closed upon the strangely assorted pair.

Chapter Two
The Tramp's Legacy

The doctor shook his head as he stood beside a plain bed in a whitewashed ward where the tramp lay muttering fiercely, and the brisk-looking master of the workhouse and a couple of elderly women stood in a group.

"No, Hippetts," said the doctor; "the machinery is all to pieces and beyond repair. No."

Just then there was a loud cry, consequent upon one of the women taking the child from where it had been seated upon the foot of the bed, and carrying it toward the door.

In a moment the sick man sprang up in bed, glaring wildly and stretching out his hands.

"Quick! take the boy away," said the master; but the doctor held up his finger, watching the sick man the while.

Then he whispered a few words to the master, who seemed to give an unwilling consent, and the boy was placed within the tramp's reach.

The man had been trying to say something, but the words would not come. As he touched the child's hand, though, he gave vent to a sigh of satisfaction, and sank back upon the coarse pillow, while the child nestled to his side, sobbing convulsively, but rapidly calming down.

"Against all rule and precedent, doctor," said the master, in an ill-used tone.

"Yes, my dear Mr Hippetts," said the doctor, smiling; "but I order it as a sedative medicine. It will do more good than anything I can give. It will not be for long."

The master nodded.

"Mrs Curdley," continued the doctor, "you will sit up with him."

"Yes, sir," said one of the old women with a curtsey.

"Keep an eye to the child, in case he turns violent; but I don't think he will—I don't think he will."

"And send for you, sir, if he do!"

"Yes."

The little party left the workhouse infirmary, all but Mrs Curdley, who saw to lighting a fire for providing herself with a cup of tea, to comfort her from time to time during her long night-watch, and then all was very still in the whitewashed place.

The child took the bread and butter the old woman gave him, and sat on the bed smiling at her as he ate it hungrily, quite contented now; and the only sounds that broke the silence after a time were the mutterings of the sick man.

But these did not disturb the child, who finished his bread and butter, and drank some sweet tea which the old woman gave him, after which his little head sank sidewise, his eyes closed, and he fell fast asleep on the foot of the bed.

The night was warm, and he needed no coverlet, while from time to time the hard-faced old woman went to look at her patient, giving him a cursory glance, and then stopping at the bedside to gently stroke the child's round cheek with her rough finger, and as the little fellow once broke into a crowing laugh in his sleep, it had a strange effect upon the old nurse, who slowly wiped the corners of her eyes with her apron, and bent down and kissed him.

Hour after hour was chimed and struck by the great clock in the centre of the town; and as midnight passed, the watchful old nurse did her watching in a pleasant dream, in which she thought that she was once more young, and that boy of hers who enlisted, went to India, and was shot in an encounter with one of the hill tribes, was young again, and that she was cutting bread and butter from a new loaf.

It was a very pleasant dream, and lasted a long time, for the six o'clock bell was ringing before she awoke with a start and exclaimed—

"Bless me! must have just closed my eyes. Why, a pretty bairn!" she said softly, as her hard face grew soft. "Sleeping like a top, and—oh!"

She caught the sleeping child from the bed, and hurried out of the place to lay him upon her own bed, where about an hour after he awoke, and cried to go to the tramp.

But there was no tramp there for him to join. The rough man had gone on a long journey, where he could not take the child, who cried bitterly, as if he had lost the only one to whom he could cling, till the old woman returned from a task she had had to fulfil, and with one of her pockets in rather a bulgy state.

Her words and some bread and butter quieted the child, who seemed to like her countenance, or read therein that something which attracts the very young as beauty does those of older growth, and the addition of a little brown sugar, into which he could dip a wet finger from time to time, made them such friends that he made no objection to being washed.

"Yes, sir; went off quite quiet in his sleep," said the old nurse in answer to the doctor's question.

"And the child?"

"Oh, I gave him a good wash, sir, which he needed badly," said the woman volubly.

"Poor little wretch!" muttered the doctor as he went away. "A tramp's child—a waif cast up by the way. Ah, Hippetts, I was right, you see: it was not for long."

Chapter Three
Doctor Grayson's Theory

"I want some more."

"Now, my dear Eddy, I think you have had quite as much as is good for you," said Lady Danby, shaking her fair curls at her son.

"No, I haven't, ma. Pa, may I have some pine-apple!"

"Yes, yes, yes, and make yourself ill. Maria, my dear, I wish you wouldn't have that boy into dessert; one can hardly hear one's-self speak."

"Sweet boy!" muttered Dr Grayson of the Manor House, Coleby, as he glanced at Sir James Danby's hopeful fat-faced son, his mother's idol, before which she worshipped every day.

The doctor glanced across the table at his quiet lady-like daughter, and there was such a curious twinkle in his eye that she turned aside so as to keep her countenance, and began talking to Lady Danby about parish work, the poor, and an entertainment to be given at the workhouse.

Dr Grayson and his daughter were dining at Cedars House that evening, greatly to the doctor's annoyance, for he preferred home.

"But it would be uncivil not to go," said Miss Grayson, who had kept her father's house almost from a child. So they went.

"Well, doctor," said Sir James, who was a comfortable specimen of the easy-going country baronet and magistrate, "you keep to your opinion, and I'll keep to mine."

"I will," said the doctor; "and in two years' time I shall publish my book with the result of my long studies of the question. I say, sir, that a boy's a boy."

"Oh yes, we all agree to that, doctor," said Lady Danby sweetly. "Edgar, my dear, I'm sure you've had enough."

"Pa, mayn't I have half a glass of Madeira!"

"Now, my dear boy, you have had some."

"But that was such a teeny weeny drop, ma. That glass is so thick."

"For goodness' sake, Maria, give him some wine, and keep him quiet," cried Sir James. "Don't you hear that Dr Grayson and I are discussing a point in philosophy!"

"Then you mustn't ask for any more, Eddy dear," said mamma, and she removed the decanter stopper, and began to pour out a very thin thread of wine, when the young monkey gave the bottom of the decanter a tilt, and the glass was nearly filled.

"Eddy, for shame!" said mamma. "What will Miss Grayson think?"

"I don't care," said the boy, seizing the glass, drinking some of the rich wine, and then turning to the thick slice of pine-apple his mother had cut.

The doctor gave his daughter another droll look, but she preserved her calm.

"To continue," said the doctor: "I say a boy's a boy, and I don't care whose he is, or where he came from; he is so much plastic clay, and you can make of him what you please."

"You can't make him a gentleman," said Sir James.

"I beg your pardon."

"And I beg yours. If the boy has not got breed in him—gentle blood—you can never make him a gentleman."

"I beg your pardon," said the doctor again. "I maintain, sir, that it is all a matter of education or training, and that you could make a gentleman's son a labourer, or a labourer's son a gentleman."

"And are you going to put that in your book, doctor?"

"Yes, sir, I am: for it is a fact. I'm sure I'm right."

Sir James laughed.

"And I'm sure you are wrong. Look at my boy, now. You can see in an instant that he has breed in him; but if you look at my coachman's son, you will see that he has no breeding at all."

Crork, crork, crork, crork.

"Oh!" from her ladyship, in quite a scream.

"Good gracious!" cried Sir James; and the doctor and Helen Grayson both started to their feet, while Master Edgar Danby kept on making the most unearthly noises, kicking, gasping, turning black in the face, and rolling his eyes, which threatened to start from their sockets.

"What is it?" cried Sir James.

Crash went a glass. A dessert-plate was knocked off the table, and Master Edgar kept on uttering his hoarse guttural sound of *crork, crork, crork!*

He was choking, and the result might have been serious as he sat struggling there, with papa on one side, and mamma on the other, holding his hands, had not Dr Grayson come behind him, and given him a tremendous slap on the back which had a beneficial effect, for he ceased making the peculiar noise, and began to wipe his eyes.

"What was it, dear? what was it, my darling?" sobbed Lady Danby.

"A great piece of pine-apple stuck in his throat," said the doctor. "I say, youngster, you should use your teeth."

"Edgar, drink some water," said Sir James sternly.

Master Edgar caught up his wine-glass, and drained it.

"Now, sir, leave the room!" said Sir James.

"Oh, don't, don't be harsh with him, James," said her ladyship pathetically. "The poor boy has suffered enough."

"I say he shall leave the room," cried Sir James in a towering fury; and Master Edgar uttered a howl.

"Really, James, I—"

Here her ladyship had an hysterical fit, and had to be attended to, what time Master Edgar howled loudly till the butler had been summoned and he was led off like a prisoner, while her ladyship grew worse, but under the ministrations of Helen Grayson, suddenly becoming better, drank a glass of water, and wiped her eyes.

"I am so weak," she said unnecessarily, as she rose from the dessert-table and left the room with Helen Grayson, who had hard work once more to keep her countenance, as she encountered her father's eye.

"Spoils him, Grayson," said Sir James, as they settled down to their port. "Noble boy, though, wonderful intellect. I shall make him a statesman."

"Hah!" ejaculated the firm-looking grey-haired doctor, who had taken high honours at his college, practised medicine for some years, and since the death of his wife lived the calm life of a student in the old Manor House of Coleby.

"Now, you couldn't make a statesman of some boys whom you took out of the gutter."

"Oh yes, I could," said the doctor. "Oh yes, sir."

"Ah, well; we will not argue," said Sir James good-humouredly.

"No," said the doctor, "we will not argue."

But they did argue all the same, till they had had their coffee, when they argued again, and then joined the ladies in the drawing-room, where Master Edgar was eating cake, and dropping currants and crumbs between the leaves of a valuable illustrated book, which he turned over with fingers in a terrible state of stick,—the consequence being that he added illustrations—prints of his fingers in brown.

"Have you settled your debate, Dr Grayson!" said Lady Danby, smiling.

"No, madam; I shall have to prove my theory to your husband, and it will take time."

"My dear James, what is the matter!" said her ladyship as a howl arose.

"Pa says I'm to go to bed, ma, and it's only ten; and you promised me I might sit up as long as I liked."

"How can you make such foolish promises, Maria?" said Sir James petulantly. "There, hold your tongue, sir, and you may stay another half-hour."

"But ma said I might stop up as long as I liked," howled Master Edgar.

"Then for goodness' sake stop up all night, sir," said Sir James impatiently; and Master Edgar stayed till the visitors had gone.

"Enjoyed your evening, my dear?" said the doctor.

"Ye–es, papa," said his daughter; "I—"

"Might have enjoyed it more. Really, Helen, it is absurd. That man opposed my theory tooth and nail, and all the time he kept on proving it by indulging that boy. I say you can make what you like of a boy. Now what's he making of that boy?"

"Sir James said he should make him a statesman," said Helen, smiling.

"But he is making him a nuisance instead. Good-night."

"Good-night, papa."

"Oh, by the way, my dear, I shall have to prove my theory."

"Indeed, papa!"

"Yes. Good-night."

Chapter Four
The Choice of a Boy

Next morning Dr Grayson took his gold-headed cane, and walked down to the workhouse.

Upon dragging at the bell the porter opened the gate obsequiously, and sent a messenger to tell the master Dr Grayson had called.

"Good morning, Hippetts," said the doctor, who being a Poor-Law Guardian, and a wealthy inhabitant of the place, was received with smiles by the important master.

"Good morning, sir. Called to look round."

"No, Hippetts, no," said the doctor, in the tone and manner of one making an inquiry about some ordinary article of merchandise; "got any boys?"

"Boys, sir; the house swarms with them."

"Ah, well, show me some."

"Show you some, sir?"

"Yes. I want a boy."

"Certainly, sir. This way, sir. About what age, sir!"

"Eleven or twelve—not particular," said the doctor. Then to himself: "About the age of young Danby."

"I see, sir," said the master. "Stout, strong, useful boy for a buttons."

"Nonsense!" said the doctor testily, "I want a boy to adopt."

"Oh!" said the master staring, and wondering whether rich philosophical Dr Grayson was in his right mind.

He led the way along some whitewashed passages, and across a gravel yard, to a long, low building, from which came the well-known humming hum of many voices, among which a kind of chorus could be distinguished, and from time to time the sharp striking of a cane upon a desk, followed by a penetrating "Hush! hush!"

As the master opened the door, a hot puff of stuffy, unpleasantly close air came out, and the noise ceased as if by magic, though there were about three hundred boys in the long, open-roofed room.

The doctor cast his eye round and saw a crowd of heads, the schoolmaster, and besides these—whitewash. The walls, the ceiling, the beams were all whitewashed. The floor was hearth-stoned, but it seemed to be whitewashed, and even the boys' faces appeared to have been touched over with a thin solution laid on with the whitewash brush.

Every eye was turned upon the visitor, and the doctor frowned as he looked round at the pallid, wan-looking, inanimate countenances which offered themselves to his view. The boys were not badly fed; they were clean; they were warmly clad; but they looked as if the food they ate did them no good, and was not enjoyed; as if they were too clean; and as if their clothes were not comfortable. Every face seemed to have been squeezed into the same mould, to grow it into one particular make, which was inexpressive, inanimate, and dull, while they all wore the look of being on the high-road to old-manism without having been allowed to stop and play on the way, and be boys.

"Hush! hush!" came from the schoolmaster, and a pin might have been heard to fall.

The boys devoured the doctor with their eyes. He was a stranger. It was something to see, and it was a break in the horrible monotony of their existence. Had they known the object of the visit, a tremendous yell would have arisen, and it would have been formed of two words—"Take me."

It was considered a model workhouse school, too, one of which the guardians were proud. There was no tyranny, no brutality, but there was endless drill and discipline, and not a scrap of that for which every boy's heart naturally yearns;—"Home, sweet home."

No amount of management can make that and deck it with a mother's love; and it must have been the absence of these elements which made the Coleby boys look like three hundred white-faced small old men.

"Now, let me see, sir," said the master; "of course the matter will have to be laid before the Board in the usual form, but you will make your selection now. Good light, sir, to choose."

Mr Hippetts did not mean it unkindly; but he too spoke as if he were busy over some goods he had to sell.

"Let me see. Ah! Coggley, stand out."

Coggley, a very thin boy of thirteen, a little more whitewashy than the rest, stood out, and made a bow as if he were wiping his nose with his right hand, and then curving it out at the doctor.

He was a nice, sad-looking boy, with railways across his forehead, and a pinched-in nose; but he was very thin, and showed his shirt between the top of his trousers and the bottom of his waistcoat, instead of upon his chest, while it was from growth, not vanity, that he showed so much ankle and wrist.

"Very good boy, sir. Had more marks than any one of his age last year."

"Won't do," said the doctor shortly.

"Too thin," said Mr Hippetts to himself. "Bunce!" he shouted.

Bunce stood out, or rather waddled forth, a stoutly-made boy with short legs,—a boy who, if ever he had a chance, would grow fat and round, with eyes like two currants, and a face like a bun.

Bunce made a bow like a scoop upside down.

"Another excellent boy, sir," said Mr Hippetts. "I haven't a fault to find with him. He is now twelve years old, and he—"

"Won't do," said the doctor crossly.

"Go back, Bunce," cried the master. "Pillett, stand out. Now here, sir, is a lad whom I am sure you will like. Writes a hand like copperplate. Age thirteen, and very intelligent."

Pillett came forward eagerly, after darting a triumphant look at Coggley and Bunce. He was a wooden-faced boy, who seemed to have hard brains and a soft head, for his forehead looked nubbly, and there were rounded off corners at the sides.

"Let Dr Grayson hear you say—"

"No, no, Hippetts; this is not an examination," cried the doctor testily. "That is not the sort of boy I want. He must be a bright, intelligent lad, whom I can adopt and take into my house. I shall treat him exactly as if he were my own son, and if he is a good lad, it will be the making of him."

"Oh! I see, sir," said Mr Hippetts importantly. "Go back, Pillett. I have the very boy. Gloog!"

Pillett went back, and furtively held up his fist at triumphant Gloog, who came out panting as if he had just been running fast, and as soon as he had made the regulation bow, he, from old force of habit, wiped his nose on his cuff.

"No, no, no, no," cried the doctor, without giving the lad a second glance, the first at his low, narrow forehead and cunning cast of features being quite enough.

"But this is an admirably behaved boy, sir," protested Mr Hippetts. "Mr Sibery here can speak very highly of his qualifications."

"Oh yes, sir," put in the schoolmaster with a severe smile and a distant bow, for he felt annoyed at not being consulted.

"Yes, yes," said the doctor; "but not my style of boy."

"Might I suggest one, sir!" said Mr Sibery deferentially, as he glanced at the king who reigned over the whole building.

"To be sure," said the doctor. "You try."

Mr Hippetts frowned, and Mr Sibery wished he had not spoken; but the dark look on the master's brow gave place to an air of triumph as the schoolmaster introduced seven boys, one after the other, to all of whom the visitor gave a decided negative.

"Seems a strange thing," he said, "that out of three hundred boys you cannot show one I like."

"But all these are excellent lads, sir," said the master deprecatingly.

"Humph!"

"Best of characters."

"Humph!"

"Our own training, sir. Mr Sibery has spared no pains, and I have watched over the boys' morals."

THE DOCTOR'S CHOICE OF A BOY.

"Yes, I dare say. Of course. Here, what boy's that?"

He pointed with his cane to a pair of round blue eyes, quite at the back.

"That, sir—that lame boy!"

"No, no; that young quicksilver customer with the curly poll."

"Oh! that, sir! He wouldn't do," cried the two masters almost in a breath.

"How do you know!" said the doctor tartly.

"Very bad boy indeed, sir, I'm sorry to say," said the schoolmaster.

"Yes, sir; regular young imp; so full of mischief that he corrupts the other boys. Can't say a word in his favour; and, besides, he's too young."

"How old?"

"About eleven, sir."

"Humph! Trot him out."

"Obed Coleby," said the master in a severe voice.

"Coleby, eh?"

"Yes, sir. Son of a miserable tramp who died some years ago in the House. No name with him, so we called him after the town."

"Humph!" said the doctor, as the little fellow came, full of eagerness and excitement, after kicking at Pillett, who put out a leg to hinder his advance.

The doctor frowned, and gazed sternly at the boy, taking in carefully his handsome, animated face, large blue eyes, curly yellow hair, and open forehead: not that his hair had much opportunity for curling—the workhouse barber stopped that.

The boy's face was as white as those of his companions, but it did not seem depressed and inanimate, for, though it was thin and white, his mouth was rosy and well-curved, and the slightly parted lips showed his pearly white teeth.

"Humph!" said the doctor, as the bright eyes gazed boldly into his.

"Where's your bow, sir?" said the master sternly.

"Oh! I forgot," said the boy quickly; and he made up for his lapse by bowing first with one and then the other hand.

"A sad young pickle," said the master. "Most hopeless case, sir. Constantly being punished."

"Humph! You young rascal!" said the doctor sternly. "How dare you be a naughty boy!"

The little fellow wrinkled his white forehead, and glanced at the schoolmaster, and then at Mr Hippetts, before looking back at the doctor.

"I d'know," he said, in a puzzled way.

"You don't know, sir!"

"No. I'm allus cotching it."

"Say *sir*, boy," cried the master.

"Allus cotching of it, sir, and it don't do me no good."

"Really, Dr Grayson—"

"Wait a bit, Mr Hippetts," said the doctor more graciously. "Let me question the boy."

"Certainly, sir. But he has a very bad record."

"Humph! Tells the truth, though," said the doctor. "Here, sir, what's your name?"

"Obed Coleby."

"*Sir*!" cried the master.

"Obed Coleby, *sir*," said the boy quickly, correcting himself.

"What a name!" ejaculated the doctor.

"Yes, ain't it? I hates it, sir."

"Oh! you do?"

"Yes; the boys all make fun of it, and call me Bed, and Go-to-bed, and Old Bedstead, and when they don't do that, they always call me Old Coal bag or Coaly."

"That will do, sir. Don't chatter so," said Mr Sibery reprovingly.

"Please, sir, he asked me," said the boy in protest; and there was a frank, bluff manner in his speech which took with the doctor.

"Humph!" he said. "Would you like to leave this place, and come and live with me!"

The boy puckered up his face, took a step forward, and the master made a movement as if to send him back; but the doctor laid his hand upon his arm, while the boy gazed into his eyes for some moments with wonderfully searching intentness.

"Well?" said the doctor. "Will you?"

The boy's face smoothed; a bright light danced in his eyes; and, as if full of confidence in his own judgment, he said eagerly —

"Yes; come along;" and he held out his hand.

"And leave all your schoolfellows!" said the doctor.

The boy's bright face clouded directly, and he turned to gaze back at the crowd of closely cropped heads.

"He'll be glad enough to go," said the schoolmaster.

"Yes," said Mr Hippetts; "a most ungrateful boy."

The little fellow — stunted of his age — swung sharply round; and they saw that his eyes were brimming over as he looked reproachfully from one to the other.

"I didn't want to be a bad un, sir," he said. "I did try, and—and—and—I'll stop here, please, and—"

He could say no more, for his face was working, and, at last, in shame and agony of spirit, he covered his face with his hands, and let himself drop in a heap on the stone floor, sobbing hysterically.

"Coleby! Stand up, sir!" cried the master sternly.

"Let him be, Mr Hippetts, if you please," said the doctor, with dignity; and he drew in a long breath, and remained for some moments silent, while the whole school stared with wondering eyes, and the two masters exchanged glances.

"Strange boy," said Mr Hippetts.

Then the doctor bent down slowly, and laid his hand upon the lad's shoulder.

The little fellow started up, flinching as if from a blow, but as soon as he saw who had touched him, he rose to his knees, and caught quickly at the doctor's extended hand, while the look in the visitor's eyes had so strange an influence upon him that he continued to gaze wonderingly in the stern but benevolent face.

"I think you'll come with me?" said the doctor.

"Yes, I'd come. But may I?"

"Yes; I think he may, Mr Hippetts?" said the doctor.

"Yes, sir; of course, sir, if you wish it," said the master, with rather an injured air; "but I feel bound to tell you the boy's character."

"Yes; of course."

"And to warn you, sir, that you will bring him back in less than a week."

"No, Mr Hippetts," said the doctor quietly; "I shall not bring him back."

"Well, sir; if you are satisfied I have nothing to say."

"I am satisfied, Mr Hippetts."

"But he is not so old as you said, sir."

"No."

"And you wanted a boy of good character."

"Yes; but I recall all I said. That is the boy I want. Can I take him at once?"

"At once, sir!" said the master, as the little fellow, with his face a study, listened eagerly, and looked from one to the other. "I shall have to bring your proposal before the Board."

"That is to say, before me and my colleagues," said the doctor, smiling. "Well, as one of the Guardians, I think I may venture to take the boy now, and the formal business can be settled afterwards."

"Oh yes, sir; of course. And I venture to think, sir, that it will not be necessary to go on with it."

"Why, Mr Hippetts?"

"Because," said the master, with a peculiar smile which was reflected in the schoolmaster's face; "you are sure to bring him back."

"I think I said before I shall not bring him back," replied the doctor coldly.

The master bowed, and Mr Sibery cleared his throat and frowned at the boys.

"Then I think that's all," said the doctor, laying his hand upon the boy's head.

"Do I understand you, sir, to mean that you want to take him now?"

"Directly."

"But his clothes, sir; and he must be—"

"I want to take him directly, Mr Hippetts, with your permission, and he will need nothing more from the Union."

"Very good, sir; and I hope that he will take your kindness to heart. Do you hear, Coleby? And be a very good boy to his benefactor, and—"

"Yes, yes, yes, Mr Hippetts," said the doctor, cutting him short. "I'm sure he will. Now, my man, are you ready?"

"Yes, sir," cried the boy eagerly; "but—"

"Well?" said the doctor kindly.

"I should like to say good-bye to some of the chaps, and I've got something to give 'em."

"Indeed! what?"

"Well, sir; I want to give Dick Dean my mouse, and Tommy Robson my nicker, and share all my buttons among the chaps in my dormitory; and then I've six pieces of string and a pair of bones, and a sucker."

"Go and share them, and say good-bye to them all," said the doctor, drawing a breath full of satisfaction; and the boy darted away full of excitement.

"May I say a word to the boys, Mr Sibery?" said the doctor, smiling.

"Certainly, sir."

"Will you call for silence?"

The master called, and the doctor asked the lads to give their old schoolfellow a cheer as he was going away.

They responded with a shout that made the windows rattle.

"And now," said the doctor, "I'm going to ask Mr Hippetts to give you all a holiday, and I am leaving threepence a piece to be distributed among you, so that you may have a bit of fun."

Mr Hippetts smiled as he took the money, and the boys cheered again, in the midst of which shouts the doctor moved off with his charge, but only for his *protégé* to break away from him, and run to offer his hand to Mr Sibery, who coughed slightly, and shook hands limply, as if he were conferring a great favour.

The boy then held out his hand to the master, and he also shook hands in a dignified way.

"Shall I send the boy on, sir?" said Mr Hippetts.

"Thanks, no, Hippetts; I'll take him with me."

"Would you like a fly, sir?"

"No, Hippetts; I'm not ashamed for people to see what I do. Come along, my lad."

"Please, sir; mayn't I say good-bye to Mother Curdley?"

"Mother Curdley? Who is she!"

"Nurse, sir."

"The woman who had charge of him when he was a tiny fellow."

"Ah! to be sure. Yes, certainly," said the doctor. "He may, of course?"

"Oh! certainly, sir. Run on, boy, and we'll follow."

"No larks," said the boy sharply, as he looked at the doctor.

"No; I shall not run away, my man."

The boy darted down a long whitewashed passage, and the doctor said:—

"I understand you to say that he has no friends whatever!"

"None, sir, as far as we know. Quite a foundling."

"That will do," said the doctor; and while the boy was bidding good-bye to the old woman who had tended the sick tramp, the master led the way to the nursery, where about a dozen children were crawling about and hanging close to a large fire-guard. Others were being nursed on the check aprons of some women, while one particularly sour creature was rocking a monstrous cradle, made like a port-wine basket, with six compartments, in every one of which was an unfortunate babe.

"Which he's a very good affectionate boy, sir," said a woman, coming up with the doctor's choice clinging to her apron; "and good-bye, and good luck, and there, God bless you, my dear!" she said, as she kissed the boy in a true motherly way, he clinging to her as the only being he had felt that he could love.

That burst of genuine affection won Mother Curdley five shillings, which she pocketed with one hand, as she wiped her eyes with the other, and then had a furtive pinch of snuff, which made several babies sneeze as if they had bad colds.

"Very eccentric man," said Mr Hippetts.

"Very," assented Mr Sibery.

"But he'll bring the young ruffian back."

The doctor did not hear, for he was walking defiantly down the main street, waving his gold-headed cane, while the boy clung to his hand, and walked with bent head, crying silently, but fighting hard to keep it back.

The doctor saw it, and pressed the boy's hand kindly.

"Yes," he said to himself; "I'll show old Danby now. The very boy I wanted. Ah," he added aloud; "here we are."

Chapter Five
A "Reg'lar" Bad One

Maria, the doctor's maid, opened the door, and as she admitted her master and his charge, her countenance was suggestive of round O's.

Her face was round, and her eyes opened into two round spots, while her mouth became a perfectly circular orifice, as the doctor himself took off the boy's cap, and marched him into the drawing-room, where Helen Grayson was seated.

On his way to the house, and with his young heart swelling at having to part from the only being who had been at all kind to him—for the recollection of the rough tramp had become extremely faint—the boy had had hard work to keep back his tears, but no sooner had he passed the doctor's door than the novelty of all he saw changed the current of his thoughts, and he was full of eagerness and excitement.

The first inkling of this was shown as his eyes lit upon Maria's round face, and it tickled him so that he began to smile.

"Such impidence!" exclaimed Maria. "And a workus boy. My! what's master going to do with him?"

She hurried to the housekeeper's room, where Mrs Millett, who had kept the doctor's house, and attended to the cooking as well, ever since Mrs Grayson's death, was now seated making herself a new cap.

"A workhouse boy, Maria?" she said, letting her work fall upon her knees, and looking over the top of her spectacles.

"Yes; and master's took him into the drawing-room."

"Oh! very well," said Mrs Millett tartly. "Master's master, and he has a right to do what he likes; but if there's anything I can't abear in a house it's a boy in buttons. They're limbs, that's what they are; regular young imps."

"Going to keep a page!" said Maria, whose eyes looked a little less round.

"Why, of course, girl; and it's all stuff."

"Well, I don't know," said Maria thoughtfully. "There's the coal-scuttles to fill, and the door-bell to answer, a deal more than I like."

"Yes," said Mrs Millett, snipping off a piece of ribbon viciously; "I know. That boy to find every time you want 'em done, and a deal less trouble to do 'em yourself. I can't abear boys."

While this conversation was going on in the housekeeper's room, something of a very different kind was in progress in the drawing-room, where the daughter looked up from the letter she was writing, and gazed wonderingly at the boy. For her father pushed the little fellow in before him, and said: "There!" in a satisfied tone, and looked from one to the other.

"Why, papa!" said Helen, after looking pleasantly at the boy.

"Yes, my dear, that's him. There he is. From this hour my experiment begins."

"With this boy?" said Helen.

"Yes, my dear, shake hands with him, and make him at home."

The doctor's sweet lady-like daughter held out her hand to the boy, who was staring about him at everything with wondering delight, till he caught sight of an admirably drawn water-colour portrait of the doctor, the work of Helen herself, duly framed and hung upon the wall.

The boy burst into a hearty laugh, and turned to Helen, running to her now, and putting his hand in hers. "Look there," he cried, pointing with his left hand; "that's the old chap's picture. Ain't it like him!"

The doctor frowned, and Helen looked troubled, even though it was a compliment to her skill; and for a few moments there was a painful silence in the room.

This was however broken by the boy, who lifted Helen's hand up and down, and said in a parrot-like way—

"How do you do?"

Helen's face rippled over with smiles, and the boy's brightened, and he too smiled in a way that made him look frank, handsome, and singularly attractive.

"Oh, I say, you are pretty," he said. "Ten times as pretty as Miss Hippetts on Sundays."

"Hah! yes. Never mind about Miss Hippetts. And look here, my man, Mr Hippetts said that you were anything but a good boy, and your schoolmaster said the same."

"Yes; everybody knows that I am a reg'lar bad boy. The worst boy in the whole school."

Helen Grayson's face contracted.

"Oh, you are, are you!" said the doctor drily.

"Yes, Mr Sibery told everybody so."

"Well, then, now, sir, you will have to be a very good boy."

"All right, sir."

"And behave yourself very nicely."

"But, I say: am I going to stop here, sir?"

"Yes; always."

"What, in this room?"

"Yes."

"And ain't I to go back to the House to have my crumbs!"

"To have your what?"

"Breakfasses and dinners, sir?"

"No, you will have your meals here."

"But I shall have to go back to sleep along with the other boys?"

"No, you will sleep here; you will live here altogether now."

"What! along of you and her?" cried the boy excitedly.

"Yes, always, unless you go to a good school."

"But live here along o' you, in this beautiful house with this nice lady, and that gal with a round face."

"Yes, of course."

"Ra-ra-ra-ra-ra-ra-ra-ra-ri-i-kee!" cried the boy in a shrill, piercing voice; and, to the astonishment of the doctor and his daughter, he made a bound, and then, with wonderful skill and rapidity, began turning the wheel, as it is called, going over and over on hands and feet, completely round the room.

"Here, stop, sir, stop!" cried the doctor, half-angry and half-amused.

"I can do it t'other way too," cried the boy; and, as he had turned before commencing upon his left hand, he began with his right, and completed the circuit of the room in the opposite direction.

"There!" he cried, as he stopped before the doctor and his daughter, flushed and proud. "There isn't a chap in the House can do it as quick as I can. Mr Sibery caught me one day, and didn't I get the cane!"

There was such an air of innocent pride displayed by the boy, that after for the moment feeling annoyed, Helen Grayson sat back in her chair and laughed as much at the boy as at her father's puzzled look, of surprise.

"That's nothing!" cried the boy, as he saw Helen's smiles. "Look here."

He ducked down and placed his head on the hearthrug, his hands on either side in front, and threw his heels in the air, to the great endangerment of the chimney ornaments.

"Get down, sir! get down!" cried the doctor. "I mean, get up."

"It don't hurt," cried the boy, "stand on my head longer than you will for a penny."

"Will you get up, sir!"

The boy let his feet go down into their normal position upon the carpet, and rose up with his handsome young face flushed, and a look of proud delight in his eyes.

"I can walk on my hands ever so far," he shouted boisterously.

"No, no; stop!"

"You look, miss, and see me run like a tomcat."

Before he could be stopped, he was down on all-fours running, with wonderful agility, in and out among the chairs, and over the hearthrug.

"That's what I do to make the boys laugh, when we go to bed. I can go all along the dormitory, and jump from one bed to the other. Where's the dormitory? I'll show you."

"No, no; stop!" cried the doctor, and he caught hold of the boy by the collar. "Confound you, sir: are you full of quicksilver!"

"No. It's skilly," said the boy, "and I ain't full now I'm ever so hungry."

The doctor held him tightly, for he was just off again.

Helen Grayson tried to look serious, but was compelled to hold her handkerchief before her mouth, and hide her face; but her eyes twinkled with mirth, as her father turned towards her, and sat rubbing his stiff grey hair.

The doctor's plan of bringing up a boy chosen from the workhouse had certainly failed, she thought, so far as this lad was concerned; and as the little prisoner stood tightly held, but making all the use he could of his eyes, he said, pointing to a glass shade over a group of wax fruit—

"Is them good to eat!"

"No," said Helen, smiling.

"I say, do you have skilly for breakfast!"

"I do not know what skilly is," replied Helen.

"Then, I'll tell you. It's horrid. They beats up pailfuls of oatmeal in a copper, and ladles it out. But it's better than nothing."

"Ahem!" coughed the doctor, who was thinking deeply.

The boy glanced at him sharply, and then turned again to Helen—

"You mustn't ask for anything to eat at the House if you're ever so hungry."

"Are you hungry?" said Helen.

"Just!"

"Would you like a piece of cake!"

"Piece o' cake? Please. Here, let go."

He shook himself free from the doctor and ran to Helen.

"Sit down on that cushion, and I'll ring for some."

"What, have you got a big bell here? Let me pull it, will you?"

"It is not a big bell, but you may pull it," said Helen, crossing to the fireplace. "There, that will do."

She led the way back to the chair where she had been seated, and in spite of herself felt amused and pleased at the way in which the boy's bright curious eyes examined her, for, outside of his school discipline, the little fellow acted like a small savage, and was as full of eager curiosity.

"I say," he said, "how do you do your hair like that? It is nice."

Just then Maria entered the room.

"Bring up the cake, Maria, and a knife and plate—and—stop—bring a glass of milk."

"Yes, miss," said Maria, staring hard at the boy with anything but favourable eyes.

"I say, do you drink milk?" said the boy.

"Sometimes. This is for you."

"For me? Oh, I say! But you'll put some water to it, won't you!"

"No; you can drink it as it is. No, no! Stop!"

Helen Grayson was too late; in the exuberance of his delight the boy relieved his excited feelings by turning the wheel again round the room, stopping, though, himself, as he reached the place where the doctor's daughter was seated. "Well, why do you look at me like that?"

"I d'know. Feels nice," said the boy. "I say, is that round-face gal your sister?"

"Oh no; she's the servant."

"I'm glad of that," said the boy thoughtfully; "she won't eat that cake, will she!"

Helen compressed her lips to control her mirth, and glanced at her father again, where he sat with his brow knit and lips pursed up thinking out his plans.

Maria entered now with the cake and milk, placing a tray on a little table, and going out to return to the housekeeper, saying—

"Pretty pass things is coming to when servants is expected to wait on workus boys."

In the drawing-room the object of her annoyance was watching, with sparkling eyes, the movements of the knife with which Helen Grayson cut off a goodly wedge of the cake.

"There," she said; "eat that, and sit quite still."

The boy snatched the piece wolfishly, and was lifting it to his mouth, but he stopped suddenly and stretched out his hand—

"Here; you have first bite," he said.

Helen shook her head, but felt pleased.

"No," she said. "It is for you."

"Do," said the boy, fighting hard with the longing to begin.

"No; eat it yourself."

"Would he have a bit if I asked him!" said the boy, torturing himself in his generous impulse.

"No, no. You eat it, my boy."

Once more the cake was within an inch of the bright sparkling teeth, but the bite was not taken. Instead of eating, the boy held out the cake to his hostess.

"Cut it in half, please," he said; "fair halves."

"What for?"

"I'm going to eat one bit; t'other's for Billy Jingle. He's had measles, and been very bad, and he's such a good chap."

"You shall have a piece to send to your schoolfellow," said Helen, with her eyes a little moist now, for the boy's generous spirit was gaining upon her, and she looked at him with more interest than she had displayed a few minutes before.

The boy took a tremendous bite, and began to munch as he sat upon a velvet-covered hassock; but he jumped up directly, and held out the bitten cake again, to say, with his mouth full—

"Oh, do have a bit. It's lovely."

Helen smiled, and laid her hand upon the boy's shoulder, as she shook her head, when to her surprise he caught the soft white hand in his left, gazed hard at it, and then pressed it against his cheek, making a soft purring noise, no bad imitation of a cat.

Then he sat eating and holding the hand which was not taken away, till, as the little stranger munched on in the full enjoyment of the wondrous novelty, the doctor said sharply, "Helen, come here."

The boy stared, but went on eating, and the doctor's daughter crossed the room to where her father sat.

Chapter Six
A Quicksilver Globule

"Well, papa?" she said, looking into his face in a half-amused way.

"Well, Helen," said the doctor, taking her hand and drawing her to him; "about this boy?"

"Yes, dear. You have made up your mind to adopt and bring one up," she said, in a low tone which the lad could not hear.

"Yes," said the doctor, taking his tone from her, "to turn the raw material into the polished cultured article."

"But of course you will take this one back, and select another!"

"And pray why!" said the doctor sharply.

"I thought—I thought—" faltered Helen.

"Oh, nonsense! Better for proving my theory."

"Yes, papa, but—"

"A little wild and rough, that's all; boy-like; high-spirited; right stuff in him."

"No doubt, papa; but he is so very rough."

"Then we'll use plenty of sand-paper and make him smooth. Moral sand-paper. Capital boy, my dear. Had a deal of trouble in getting him—by George! the young wolf! He has finished that cake."

"Then you really mean to keep him, papa?" said Helen, glancing at the boy, where he sat diligently picking up a few crumbs and a currant which he had dropped.

"Mean to keep him? Now, my dear Helen, when did you ever know me undertake anything, and not carry it out!"

"Never, papa."

"Then I am not going to begin now. There is the boy."

"Yes, papa," said Helen rather sadly; "there is the boy."

"I mean to make him a gentleman, and I must ask you to help me with the poor orphan—"

"He is an orphan, then!" said Helen quickly.

"Yes. Son of some miserable tramp who died in the casual ward."

"How dreadful!" said Helen, glancing once more at the boy, who caught her eye, and smiled in a way which made his face light up, and illumined the sallow cheeks and dull white pinched look.

"Dreadful? Couldn't be better for my theory, my dear."

"Very well, papa," said Helen quietly; "I will help you all I can."

"I knew you would, my dear," said the doctor warmly; "and I prophesy that you will be proud of your work, and so shall I. Now, then, to begin," he added loudly.

"All in—all in—all in!" shouted the boy, jumping up like a grasshopper, and preparing to go through some fresh gymnastic feat.

"Ah! ah! Sit down, sir. How dare you!" shouted the doctor; and the boy dropped into his seat again, and sat like a mouse.

"There!" said the doctor softly; "there's obedience. Result of drilling. Now, then, what's the first thing? He must have some clothes."

"Oh yes; at once," said Helen.

"And, look here, my dear," said the doctor testily; "I never use anything of the kind myself, but you girls rub some stuff—pomade or cream—on your hair to make it grow, do you not?"

"Well, yes, papa."

"Then, for goodness' sake, let a double quantity be rubbed at once upon that poor boy's head. Really it is cut so short that he is hardly fit to be seen without a cap on."

"I'm afraid you will have to wait some time," said Helen, with a smile.

"Humph! yes, I suppose so," said the doctor gruffly. "That barber ought to be flogged. Couldn't put the boy in a wig, of course."

"O papa! no."

"Well, I said no," cried the doctor testily. "Must wait, I suppose; but we can make him look decent."

"Are you—are you going—" faltered Helen.

"Going? Going where!"

"Going to have him with us, papa, or to let him be with the servants?" said Helen rather nervously; but she regretted speaking the next moment.

"Now, my dear child, don't be absurd," cried the doctor. "How am I to prove my theory by taking the boy from the lowest station of society and making him, as I shall do, a gentleman, if I let him run wild with the servants!"

"I—I beg your pardon, papa."

"Humph! Granted. Now, what's to be done first? The boy is clean?"

"Oh yes."

"Can't improve him then, that way; but I want as soon as possible to get rid of that nasty, pasty, low-class pallor. One does not see it in poor people's children, as a rule, while these Union little ones always look sickly to me. You must feed him up, Helen."

"I have begun, papa," she said, smiling.

"Humph! Yes. Clothes. Yes; we must have some clothes, and—oh, by the way, I had forgotten. Here, my boy."

The lad jumped up with alacrity, and came to the doctor's side boldly—looking keenly from one to the other.

"What did you say your name was!"

"Bed—Obed Coleby."

"Hah!" cried the doctor; "then we'll do away with that at once. Now, what shall we call you!"

"I d'know," said the boy, laughing. "Jack?"

"No, no," said the doctor thoughtfully, while Helen looked on rather amused at her father's intent manner, and the quick bird-like movements of their visitor.

For the boy, after watching the doctor for a few moments, grew tired, and finding himself unnoticed, dropped down on the carpet, took four pebbles from his pocket, laid them on the back of his right hand, and throwing them in the air, caught them separately by as many rapid snatches in the air.

"Do that again," cried the doctor, suddenly becoming interested.

The boy showed his white teeth, threw the stones in the air, and caught them again with the greatest ease.

"That's it, Helen, my dear," cried the doctor triumphantly. "Cleverness of the right hand—dexterity. Capital name."

"Capital name, papa?"

"Yes; Dexter! Good Latin sound. Fresh and uncommon. Dexter—Dex. Look here, sir. No more Obed. You shall be called Dexter."

"All right," said the boy.

"And if you behave yourself well, perhaps we shall shorten it into Dex."

"Dick's better," said the boy sharply.

"No, it is not, sir; Dex."

"Well, Dix, then," said the boy, throwing one stone up high enough to touch the ceiling, and in catching at it over-handed, failing to achieve his object, and striking it instead, so that it flew against the wall with a loud rap.

"Put those stones in your pocket, sir," cried the doctor to the boy, who ran and picked up the one which had fallen, looking rather abashed. "Another inch, and it would have gone through that glass."

"Yes. Wasn't it nigh!" cried the boy.

"Here, stop! Throw them out of that window."

The boy's brow clouded over.

"Let me give them to some one at the school; they're such nice round ones."

"I said, throw them out of the window, sir."

"All right," said the boy quickly; and he threw the pebbles into the garden.

"Now, then; look here, sir—or no," said the doctor less sternly. "Look here, my boy."

The doctor's manner influenced the little fellow directly, and he went up and laid his hand upon his patron's knee, looking brightly from face to face.

"Now, mind this: in future you are to be Dexter."

"All right: Dexter Coleby," said the boy.

"No, no, no, no!" cried the doctor testily. "Dexter Grayson; and don't keep on saying 'All right.'"

"All—"

The boy stopped short, and rubbed his nose with his cuff.

"Hah! First thing, my dear. Twelve pocket-handkerchiefs, and mark them 'Dexter Grayson.'"

"What? twelve handkerchies for me—all for me?"

"Yes, sir, all for you; and you are to use them. Never let me see you rub your nose with your cuff again."

The boy's mouth opened to say, "All right," but he checked himself.

"That's right!" cried the doctor. "I see you are teachable. You were going to say 'all right.'"

"You told me not to."

"I did; and I'm very pleased to find you did not do it."

"I say, shall I have to clean the knives?"

"No, no, no."

"Nor yet the boots and shoes?"

"No, boy; no."

"I shall have to fetch the water then, shan't I?"

"My good boy, nothing of the kind. You are going to live with us, and you are my adopted son," said the doctor rather pompously, while Helen sighed.

"Which?" queried the boy.

"Which what?" said the doctor.

"Which what you said?"

"I did not say anything, sir."

"Oh my! what a story!" cried the boy, appealing to Helen. "Didn't you hear him say I was to be his something son?"

"Adopted son," said the doctor severely; "and, look here, you must not speak to me in that way."

"All—" Dexter checked himself again, and he only stared.

"Now, you understand," said the doctor, after a few minutes' hesitation; "you are to be here like my son, and you may call me—yes, father, or papa."

"How rum!" said the boy, showing his white teeth with a remarkable want of reverence. "I say," he added, turning to Helen; "what am I to call you!"

Helen turned to her father for instructions, her brow wrinkling from amusement and vexation.

"Helen," said the doctor, in a decided tone. "We must have no half measures, my dear; I mean to carry out my plan in its entirety."

"Very well, papa," said Helen quietly; and then to herself, "It is only for a few days."

"Now, then," said the doctor, "clothes. Ring that bell, Dexter."

The boy ran so eagerly to the bell that he knocked over a light chair, and left it on the floor till he had rung.

"Oh, I say," he exclaimed; "they go over a deal easier than our forms."

"Never mind the forms now, Dexter. I want you to forget all about the old school."

"Forget it?" said the boy, with his white forehead puckering up.

"Yes, and all belonging to it. You are now going to be my son."

"But I shall want to go and see the boys sometimes."

"No, sir; you will not."

"But I must go and see Mother Curdley."

"Humph!" ejaculated the doctor. "Well, we shall see. Perhaps she will be allowed to come and see you."

"Hooray!" cried the boy excitedly; and turning to Helen he obtained possession of her hand. "I say, save her a bit of that cake."

"She shall have some cake, Dexter," said Helen kindly, for she could not help, in spite of her annoyance, again feeling pleased with the boy's remembrance of others.

"And I say," he cried, "when she does come, we'll have a ha'porth o' snuff screwed up in a bit o' paper, and—has he got any gin?"

"Hush, hush!" whispered Helen.

"But she's so fond of a drop," said the boy earnestly.

"And now," said the doctor; "the next thing is clothes. Ah, Maria, send Cribb to ask Mr Bleddan to come here directly."

"Yes, sir," said Maria; and after a glance at the boy she closed the door.

In less than a quarter of an hour Mr Bleddan, the tailor of Coleby, was there; and Dexter stood up feeling tickled and amused at being measured for some new clothes which the tailor said should be ready in a week.

"A week!" said the doctor; "but what am I to do now? The boy can't go like that."

"Ready-made, sir? I've plenty of new and fashionable suits exactly his size."

"Bring some," said the doctor laconically; "and shirts and stockings and boots. Everything he wants. Do you understand!"

Mr Bleddan perfectly understood, and Dexter stood with his eyes sparkling as he heard the list of upper and under garments, boots, caps, everything which the tailor and clothier considered necessary.

The moment the man had gone, Dexter made a dash to recommence his Ixion-like triumphal dance, but this time Helen caught his hand and stopped him.

"No, no, not here," she said quietly; and not in the least abashed, but in the most obedient way, the boy submitted.

"It was because I was so jolly glad: that's all."

"Hah!" said the doctor, smiling. "Now, I like that, Helen. Work with me, and all that roughness will soon pass away."

"I say, will that chap be long?" cried Dexter, running to the window and looking out. "Am I to have all those things for my own self, and may I wear 'em directly?"

"Look here, my lad; you shall have everything that's right and proper for you, if you are a good boy."

"Oh, I'll be a good boy—least I'll try to be. Shall you give me the cane if I ain't?"

"I—er—I don't quite know," said the doctor. "I hope you will not require it."

"Mr Sibery said I did, and he never knew a boy who wanted it worse, but it didn't do me no good at all."

"Well, never mind that now," said the doctor. "You will have to be very good, and never want the cane. You must learn to be a young gentleman."

"Young gentleman?" said Dexter, holding his head on one side like a bird. "One of them who wears black jackets, and turn-down collars, and tall hats, and plays at cricket all day? I shall like that."

"Humph! Something else but play cricket, I hope," said the doctor quietly. "Helen, my dear, I shall begin to make notes at once for my book, so you can take Dexter in hand, and try how he can read."

The doctor brought out a pocket-book and pencil, and Helen, after a moment's thought, went to a glass case, and took down an old gift-book presented to her when she was a little girl.

"Come here, Dexter," she said, "and let me hear you read."

The boy flushed with pleasure.

"Yes," he said. "I should like to read to you. May I kneel down and have the book on your knees!"

"Yes, if you like," said Helen, who felt that the boy was gaining upon her more and more: for, in spite of his coarseness, there was a frank, merry, innocent undercurrent that, she felt, might be brought to the surface, strengthened and utilised to drive the roughness away.

"Read here!" said the boy, opening the book at random. "Oh, here's a picture. What are these girls doing?"

"Leave the pictures till afterwards. Go on reading now."

"Here?"

"Yes; at the beginning of that chapter."

"I shall have to read it all, as there's no other boy here. We always stand up in a class at the House, and one boy reads one bit, and another boy goes on next, and then you're always losing your place, because it's such a long time before it comes round to your turn, and then old Sibery gives you the cane."

"Yes, yes; but go on," said Helen, with a feeling of despair concerning her father's *protégé*.

Dexter began to read in a forced, unnatural voice, with a high-pitched unpleasant twang, and regardless of sense or stops—merely uttering the words one after the other, and making them all of the same value.

At the end of the second line Helen's face was a study. At the end of the fourth the doctor roared out—

"Stop! I cannot stand any more. Saw-sharpening or bag-pipes would be pleasant symphonies in comparison."

At that moment Maria entered.

"Lunch is on the table, if you please, sir."

"Ah, yes, lunch," said the doctor. "Did you put a knife and fork for Master Dexter?"

"For who, sir!" said Maria, staring.

"For Master Dexter here," said the doctor sharply. "Go and put them directly."

Maria ran down to her little pantry, and then attacked Mrs Millett.

"Master's going mad, I think," she said. "Why, he's actually going to have that boy at the table to lunch."

"Never!"

"It's a fact," cried Maria; "and I've come down for more knives and forks."

"And you'd better make haste and get 'em, then," said the housekeeper; "master's master, and he always will have his way."

Maria did make haste, and to her wonder and disgust Dexter was seated at the doctor's table in his workhouse clothes, gazing wonderingly round at everything: the plate, cruets, and sparkling glass taking up so much of his attention that for the moment he forgot the viands.

The sight of a hot leg of lamb, however, when the cover was removed, made him seize his knife and fork, and begin tapping with the handles on either side of his plate.

"Errum!" coughed the doctor. "Put that knife and fork down, Dexter, and wait."

The boy's hands went behind him directly, and there was silence till Maria had left the room, when the doctor began to carve, and turned to Helen—

"May I give you some lamb, my dear?"

"There, I knowed it was lamb," cried Dexter excitedly, "'cause it was so little. We never had no lamb at the House."

"Hush!" said the doctor quietly. "You must not talk like that."

"All right."

"Nor yet like that, Dexter. Now, then, may I send you some lamb!"

"May I say anything?" said the boy so earnestly that Helen could not contain her mirth, and the boy smiled pleasantly again.

"Of course you may, my boy," said the doctor. "Answer when you are spoken to, and try and be polite."

"Yes, sir, I will; I'll try so hard."

"Then may I send you some lamb!"

"Yes; twice as much as you give her. It does smell nice."

The doctor frowned a little, and then helped the boy pretty liberally.

"Oh, I say! Just look at the gravy," he cried. "Have you got plenty, Miss!"

"Oh yes, Dexter," said Helen. "May I—"

"Don't give it all to me, Mister," cried the boy. "Keep some for yourself. I hate a pig."

"Errum!" coughed the doctor, frowning. "Miss Grayson was going to ask if you would take some vegetables!"

"What? taters? No thankye, we got plenty o' them at the House," cried the boy; and he began cutting and devouring the lamb at a furious rate.

"Gently, gently!" cried the doctor. "You have neither bread nor salt."

"Get's plenty o' them at the House," cried the boy, with his mouth full; "and you'd better look sharp, too. The bell'll ring directly, and we shall have to—no it won't ring here, will it!" he said, looking from one to another.

"No, sir," said the doctor sternly; "and you must not eat like that. Watch how Miss Grayson eats her lunch, and try and imitate her."

The boy gave the doctor a sharp glance, and then, in a very praiseworthy manner, tried to partake of the savoury joint in a decent way.

But it was hard work for him. The well-cooked succulent meat was so toothsome that he longed to get to the end of it; and whenever he was not watching the doctor and his daughter he kept glancing at the dish, wondering whether he would be asked to have any more.

"What's that rum-looking stuff?" he said, as the doctor helped himself from a small tureen.

"Mint sauce, sir. Will you have some?"

"I don't know. Let's taste it."

The little sauce tureen was passed to him, and he raised the silver ladle, but instead of emptying it upon his plate he raised it to his lips, and drank with a loud, unpleasant noise, suggestive of the word *soup*.

The doctor was going to utter a reproof, but the sight of Helen's mirth checked him, and he laughed heartily as he saw the boy's face full of disgust.

"I don't like that," he said, pushing the tureen away. "It ain't good."

"But you should—"

"Don't correct him now, papa; you will spoil the poor boy's dinner," remonstrated Helen.

"He said it was lunch," said Dexter.

"Your dinner, sir, and our lunch," said the doctor. "There, try and behave as we do at the table, and keep your elbows off the cloth."

Dexter obeyed so quickly that he knocked a glass from the table, and on leaving his seat to pick it up he found that the foot was broken off.

The doctor started, and uttered a sharp ejaculation.

In an instant the boy shrank away into a corner, sobbing wildly.

"I couldn't help it. I couldn't help it, sir. Don't beat me, please. Don't beat me this time. I'll never do so any more."

"Bless my soul!" cried the doctor, jumping up hastily; and the boy uttered a wild cry, full of fear, and would have dashed out of the open window into the garden had not Helen caught him, the tears in her eyes, and her heart moved to pity as she read the boy's agony of spirit. In fact that one cry for mercy had done more for Dexter's future at the doctor's than a month's attempts at orderly conduct.

"Hush, hush!" said Helen gently, as she took his hands; and, with a look of horror in his eyes, the boy clung to her.

"I don't mind the cane sometimes," he whispered, "but don't let him beat me very much."

"Nonsense! nonsense!" said the doctor rather huskily. "I was not going to beat you."

"Please, sir, you looked as if you was," sobbed the boy.

"I only looked a little cross, because you were clumsy and broke that glass. But it was an accident."

"Yes, it was; it was," cried the boy, in a voice full of pleading, for the breakage had brought up the memory of an ugly day in his young career. "I wouldn't ha' done it, was it ever so; it's true as goodness I wouldn't."

"No, no, Maria, not yet," cried Helen hastily, as the door was opened. "We will ring."

Maria walked out again, and the boy clung to Helen as he sobbed.

"There, there," she said. "Papa is not cross. You broke the glass, and you have apologised. Come: sit down again."

If some one had told Helen Grayson two hours before that she would have done such a thing, she would have smiled incredulously, but somehow she felt moved to pity just then, and leading the boy back to his chair, she bent down and kissed his forehead.

In a moment Dexter's arms were about her neck, and he was clinging to her with passionate energy, sobbing now wildly, while the doctor got up and walked to the window for a few moments.

"There, there," said Helen gently, as she pressed the boy down into his seat, and kissed him once again, after seeing that her father's back was turned. "That's all over now. Come, papa."

The doctor came back, and as he was passing the back of the boy's chair, he raised his hand quickly, intending to pat him on the head.

The boy flinched like a frightened animal anticipating a blow.

"Why, bless my soul, Dexter! this will not do," he said huskily. "Here, give me your hand. There, there, my dear boy, you and I are to be the best of friends. Why, my dear Helen," he added in French, "they must have been terribly severe, for the little fellow to shrink like this."

The boy still sobbed as he laid his hand in the doctor's, and then the meal was resumed; but Dexter's appetite was gone. He could not finish the lamb, and it was only with difficulty that he managed a little rhubarb tart and custard.

"Why, what are you thinking about, Dexter!" said Helen after the lunch; and somehow her tone of voice seemed to indicate that she had forgotten all about the workhouse clothes.

"Will he send me back to the House?" the boy whispered hoarsely, but the doctor heard.

"No, no," he said quickly; and the boy seemed relieved.

That night about eleven, as she went up to bed, Helen Grayson went softly into a little white bedroom, where the boy's pale face lay in the full moonlight, and something sparkled.

"Poor child!" she said, in a voice full of pity; "he has been crying."

She was quite right, and as she bent over him, her presence must have influenced his dreams, for he uttered a low, soft sigh, and then smiled, while, forgetting everything now but the fact that this poor little waif of humanity had been stranded, as it were, at their home, she bent over him and kissed him.

Then she started, for she became aware of the fact that her father was at the door.

The next moment she was in his arms.

"Bless you, my darling!" he said. "This is like you. I took this up as a whim as well as a stubborn belief; but somehow that poor little ignorant fellow, with his rough ways, seems to be rousing warmer feelings towards him, and, please God, we'll make a man of him of whom we shall not be ashamed."

Poor Dexter had cried himself to sleep, feeling in his ignorant fashion that he had disgraced himself, and that the two harsh rulers were quite right,—that he was as bad as ever he could be; but circumstances were running in a way he little thought.

Chapter Seven
Taming the Wild

"Ah!" said the doctor, laying down his pen and rubbing his hands. "That's better;" and he took off his spectacles, made his grey hair stand up all over his head like tongues of silver fire, and looked Dexter over from top to toe.

Thanks to Helen's supervision, the boy looked very creditable. His hair was of course "cut almost to the bone," and his face had still the Union look—pale and saddened, but he was dressed in a neat suit which fitted him, and his turn-down collar and black tie seemed to give his well-cut features quite a different air.

"What did I say, Helen!" said the doctor, with a chuckle. "You see what we have done already. Well, sir, how do you feel now!"

"Not very jolly," said the boy, with a writhe.

"Hem!" coughed the doctor; "not very comfortable you mean!"

"Yes, that's it," said Dexter. "Boots hurts my feet, and when the trousers ain't rubbin' the skin o' my legs, this here collar feels as if it would saw my head off."

"Humph!" ejaculated the doctor stiffly. "You had better put on the old things again."

"Eh? No, thankye," cried Dexter eagerly. "I like these here ever so much. Please may I keep 'em!"

"Of course," said the doctor; "and take care of them, like a good boy."

"Yes. I'm going to be a very good boy now, sir. She says I am to."

He nodded his head in the direction of Helen, and stood upon one leg to ease the foot which the shoe pinched.

"That's right, but don't say *she*. You must look upon Miss Grayson now as if she were your sister."

"Yes, that I will," said the boy warmly.

Helen flushed a little at her father's words, and a serious look came into her sweet face; but at that moment she felt Dexter steal his hand into hers, and then it was lifted and held against the boy's cheek, as, in feline fashion, he rubbed his face against it, and a smile came into her eyes again, as she laid the hand at liberty upon the closely cropped head.

"I say, ain't she pretty, and don't she look nice?" said Dexter suddenly; and his free and easy way made the doctor frown: but he looked at the boy's appearance, and in the belief that he would soon change the manners to match, he nodded, and said, "Yes."

Helen looked at her father, as if asking him what next, but the doctor joined his finger-tips and frowned, as if thinking deeply.

"Dexter and I have been filling his drawers with his new clothes and linen," she said.

"Yes; such a lot of things," cried the boy; "and is that always to be my bedroom?"

"Yes; that's to be your room," said the doctor.

"And I've got three pairs of boots. I mean two pairs of boots, and one pair of shoes," cried Dexter. "One pair on, and two in the bedroom; and I shall get up at six o'clock every morning, and clean 'em, and I'll clean yours too."

"Hem!" coughed the doctor. "No, my boy, your boots will be cleaned for you, and you will not have to dirty your hands now."

The boy stared wonderingly, as the doctor enunciated a matter which was beyond his grasp. But all the time his eyes were as busy as those of a monkey, and wandering all over the study, and taking in everything he saw.

"May I leave Dexter with you now!" said Helen, "as I have a few little matters to see to."

"Yes, yes; of course, my dear. We are beginning capitally. Dexter, my boy; you can sit down on that chair, and amuse yourself with a book, while I go on writing."

The boy looked at the chair, then at the doctor, and then at Helen.

"I say, mayn't I go with you?" he said.

"Not now, Dexter, I am going to be very busy. By and by I will take you for a walk."

Helen nodded, and left the room.

"You'll find some books on that shelf," said the doctor kindly; and he turned once more to his writing, while Dexter went to the bookcase, and, after taking down one or two works, found a large quarto containing pictures.

He returned to the chair the doctor had pointed out, opened the book upon his knees, turned over a few leaves, and then raised his eyes to have a good long wondering stare at the doctor, as he sat frowning there very severely, and in the midst of a great deal of deep thought put down a sentence now and again.

Dexter's eyes wandered from the doctor to a dark-looking bust upon the top of a book-shelf. From thence to a brown bust on the opposite shelf, at which he laughed, for though it was meant for Cicero, it put him greatly in mind of Mr Sibery, and he then fell a-wondering what the boys were doing at the workhouse school.

Just then the black marble timepiece on the shelf chimed four quarters, and struck eleven.

"No matter what may be the descent," wrote the doctor, "the human frame is composed of the same element."

"I say," cried Dexter loudly.

"Eh? Yes?" said the doctor, looking up.

"What time are you going to have dinner!"

"Dinner? One o'clock, sir. Why, it's not long since you had breakfast."

"Seems a long time."

"Go on looking at your book."

Dexter obeyed, and the doctor went on writing, and became very interested in his work.

So did not the boy, who yawned, fidgeted in his seat, rubbed his neck impatiently, and then bent down and tried to ease his boot, which evidently caused him pain.

There was a pause during which Dexter closed the book and fidgeted about; now one leg went out, now the other. Then his arms moved about as if so full of life and energy that they must keep on the jerk.

There was another yawn, but the doctor did not hear it, he was too much intent upon the chapter he was writing. Then a happy thought occurred to Dexter, and he raised the heavy quarto book he had upon his knees, placed it upon his head, and balanced it horizontally.

That was too easy, there was no fun or excitement in the feat, so he placed it edgewise.

That was better, but very easy—both topwise and bottomwise. Harder when tried with the front edges upon his crown, for the big book demonstrated a desire to open.

But he dodged that, and felt happier.

He glanced at the doctor, and smiled at his profile, for in his intentness the writer's thick bottom lip protruded far beyond the upper, and seemed to Dexter as if trying to reach the tip of his nose.

What should he do next?

Could he balance that book on its back?

Dexter held it between his hands and cogitated. The back was round, therefore the feat would be more difficult, and all the more enjoyable, but would the book keep shut?

He determined to try.

Up went the book, his hands on either side keeping it close. Then there was a little scheming to get it exactly in equilibrium; this was attained, and as the boy sat there stiff-necked and rigid of spine, with his eyes turned upwards, there was nothing left to do now but to remove his hands.

This he proceeded to do by slow degrees, a finger at a time, till the heavy work was supported only by the left and right forefingers, the rounded back exactly on the highest point of his cranium.

"All right," said Dexter to himself, supremely happy in his success, and with a quick movement he let his hands drop to his lap.

For one solitary moment the great quarto volume remained balanced exactly; then, as a matter of course, it opened all at once.

Flip! flop! bang!

The book had given him two boxes on the sides of the head, and then, consequent upon his sudden effort to save it, made a leap, and came heavily upon the floor.

Dexter's face was scarlet as he dropped upon his knees to pick it up, and found the doctor gazing at him, or, as in his own mind he put it, threatening a similar caning to that which Mr Sibery gave him a year before, when he dropped the big Bible on the schoolroom floor.

"Be careful, my boy, be careful," said the doctor dreamily, for he was half lost in thought. "That damages the bindings. Take a smaller book."

Dexter felt better, and hastily replaced the work on the shelf, taking one of a smaller size, and returning to his seat to bend down and thrust a finger inside his boot.

"How they do hurt!" he thought to himself; and he made a sudden movement.

Then he checked himself.

No; 'twas a pity. They were so new, and looked so nice.

Yes, he would: they hurt so terribly; and, stooping down, he rapidly unlaced the new boots, and pushed them off, smiling with gratification at the relief.

Then he had another good look round for something to amuse himself with, yawned, glanced at the doctor, dropped down on hands and knees, went softly to the other side of the centre table, and began to creep about with the agility of a quadruped or one of the monkey tribe.

This was delightful, and the satisfied look on the boy's face was a study, till happening to raise his eyes, he saw that the doctor had risen, and was leaning over the writing-table, gazing down at him with a countenance full of wonder and astonishment combined.

"What are you doing, sir?" said the doctor sternly. "Have you lost something?"

Dexter might have said, "Yes, a button—a marble;" but he did not; he only rose slowly, and his late quadrupedal aspect was emphasised by a sheepish look.

"Don't do that on the carpet, sir. You'll wear out the knees of your trousers. Why, where are your boots?"

"On that chair, sir," said Dexter confusedly.

"Then put them on again, and get another book."

Dexter put on his boots slowly, laced them up, and then fetched himself another book.

He returned to his seat, yawning, and glanced at the doctor again.

Booz, booz, booz, boom—'m—'m.

A bluebottle had flown in through the open window, bringing with it the suggestion of warm sunshine, fields, gardens, flowers, and the blue sky and waving trees.

"*Booz!*" said the bluebottle, and it dashed away, leaving a profound silence, broken by the scratching of the doctor's pen.

"I say," cried Dexter excitedly; "is that your garden?"

"Yes, my boy, yes," said the doctor, without looking up from his writing.

"May I go out in it?"

"Certainly, my boy. Yes," said the doctor, without looking up, though there was the quick sound of footsteps, and, with a bound, Dexter was through the open French window, and out upon the lawn.

The doctor did not heed the lapse of time, for he was intent upon his writing, and an hour had passed when the door opened and Helen returned.

"Now I am at liberty, papa," she said; "and—where is Dexter?"

"Eh? The boy? Bless me, I thought he was here!"

Smash! Tinkle!

The sound of breaking glass, and the doctor leaped to his feet, just as a loud gruff voice sounded—

"Here, you just come down."

"Copestake!" cried the doctor. "Why, what is the matter out there!"

Chapter Eight
Old Dan'l is Wroth

Mr Grayson's was the best garden for twenty miles round.

The Coleby people said so, and they ought to have known.

But Dan'l Copestake said it was all nonsense. "Might be made a good garden if master wasn't so close," he used to say to everybody. "Wants more money spent on it, and more hands kept. How'm I to keep a place like that to rights with only two—me and a lab'rer, under me, and Peter to do the sweeping?"

Keep it to rights or not, it was to Helen Grayson four acres of delight, and she was to blame for a great deal which offended Dan'l Copestake, the head-gardener.

"Papa," it would be, "did you give orders for that beautiful privet hedge to be cut down!"

"Eh? no, my dear, Copestake said it kept the light off some of those young trees, and I said he might cut it down."

"Oh, do stop him," cried Helen. "It will take years to grow up, and this past year it has been delightful, with its sweet-scented blossom and beautiful black berries."

So it was with scores of things. Helen wanted to see them growing luxuriantly, Dan'l Copestake loved to hash and chop them into miserably cramped "specimints," as he called them, and the doctor got all the blame.

But what a garden! It was full of old-fashioned flowers in great clumps, many of them growing, to Dan'l's disgust, down among the fruit and vegetables.

There were flowering shrubs and beautiful conifers, a great mulberry-tree on the mossy lawn, and a huge red brick wall all round, literally covered with trained trees, which in their seasons were masses of white bloom, or glowing with purple and golden plums, and light red, black, or yellowy pink cherries, and great fat pears, while, facing the south, there were dozens of trees of peaches, nectarines, and downy golden apricots.

As to the apples, they grew by the bushel, almost by the ton; and for strawberries and the other lower fruits there was no such garden near.

Then there was Helen's conservatory, always full of sweet-scented flowers, and the vinery and pits, where the great purple and amber bunches hung and ripened, and the long green cucumber and melon came in their good time.

But Dan'l grumbled, as gardeners will.

"Blights is offle," he said. "It's the blightiest garden I ever see, and a man might spend all his life keeping the birds down with a gun."

But Dan'l did not spend any part of his life, let alone all, keeping the birds down with a gun. The doctor caught him shooting one day, and nearly shot him out of the place.

"How dare you, sir?" he cried. "I will not have a single bird destroyed."

"Then you won't get no peace, sir, nor not a bit of fruit."

"I shall have the place overrun with slugs and snails, and all kinds of injurious blight, sir, if you use that gun. No, sir, you'll put nets over the fruit when it's beginning to ripen. That will do."

The doctor walked away with Helen, and as soon as they were out of sight, behind the great laurustinus clump, Helen threw her arms about his neck, and kissed him for saving her pet birds.

Consequently, in addition to abundance of fruit, and although it was so close in the town, there was always a chorus of song in the season; and even the nightingale came from the woodlands across the river and sang within the orchard, through which the river ran.

That river alone half made the place, for it was one of those useless rivers, so commercial men called it, where the most you could do was pleasure-boating; barges only being able to ascend to Coleby Bridge, a sort of busy colony from the town, two miles nearer the sea.

"Yes, sir," Sir James Danby had been known to say, "if the river could be deepened right through the town it would be the making of the place."

"And the spoiling of my grounds," said the doctor, "so I'm glad it runs over the solid rock."

This paradise of a garden was the one into which Dexter darted, and in which Dan'l Copestake was grumbling that morning—

"Like a bear with a sore head, that's what I say," said Peter Cribb to the under-gardener. "Nothing never suits him."

"Yes, it do," said Dan'l, showing a very red face over a clump of rhododendron. "Master said you was to come into the garden three days a week, and last week I only set eyes on you twice, and here's half the week gone and you've only been once."

"Look here," said Peter Cribb, a hard-looking bullet-headed man of five-and-twenty; and he leaned on his broom, and twisted one very tightly trousered leg round the other, "do you think I can sit upon the box o' that there wagginette, drivin' miles away, and be sweeping this here lawn same time!"

"Master said as it was your dooty to be in this garden three days a week; and t'other three days you was to do your stable-work—there."

"Didn't I go out with the carriage every day this week?"

"I don't know when you went out with the carriage, and when you didn't," said Dan'l; "all I know is as my lawn didn't get swept; and how the doctor expects a garden like this here to be kept tidy without help, I should be glad to know."

"Well, you'd better go and grumble at him, and not worry me, and—pst! Lookye there."

He pointed with his broom, and both men remained paralysed at the sight which met their eyes.

It was not so much from its extraordinary nature as from what Dan'l afterwards spoke of as its "imperence." That last, he said, was what staggered him, that any human boy should, in the very middle of the day, dare to do such a thing in his garden.

He said *his* garden, for when speaking of it the doctor seemed to be only some one who was allowed to walk through it for a treat.

What the two men gazed at was the figure of a boy, in shirt and trousers, going up the vinery roof, between where the early and the late houses joined and there was a sloping brick coping. From this they saw him reach the big wall against which the vinery was built, and there he sat for a few moments motionless.

"Why, who is he?" said Peter, in a whisper. "He went up that vinery just like a monkey."

Peter had never seen a monkey go up the roof of a vinery, but Dan'l did not notice that.

"Hold your row," said Dan'l, in a low voice; "don't speak, and we'll ketch my nabs. Now we know where my peaches went last year."

"But who is he!" whispered Peter.

"I don't know, and I don't care, but I mean to have him as sure as he's there. Now if master hadn't been so precious 'tickler about a gun, I could ha' brought him down like a bird."

"Lookye there," cried Peter. "See that?"

"Oh yes, I see him," said Dan'l, as the figure ran easily along the top of the twelve-foot wall on all-fours. "I see my gentleman. Nice little game he's having. I'll bet a shilling he's about gorged with grapes, and now he's on the look-out for something else. But let him alone; wait a bit and we'll put salt on his tail before he can say what's what. I knowed some grapes was a-going. I could about feel it, like."

"Well, I never!" whispered Peter, peering through the laurustinus, and watching the boy. "See that?"

"Oh yes, I see him. Nice un he is."

This last was consequent upon the boy running a few yards, and then holding tightly with his hands, and kicking both legs in the air two or three times before trotting on along the wall again as easily as a tomcat.

"See that?" said Peter.

"Oh yes, I can see," said Dan'l. "He's so full o' grapes it makes him lively," and he stared at the boy, who had suddenly stopped, and planting his hands firmly, stood up on them, balancing himself, with his legs spread wide in the air.

"He'll break his neck, that's what he'll do," said Peter.

"Good job too, I says," grumbled Dan'l. "Boys like that ought to be done away with. He's one on 'em out o' the town. Now look here, Peter, we've got to get him, that's what we've got to do."

"Ah, that's better," said Peter, who had been nervous ever since a horse ran away with him. "I don't like to see a boy doing dangerous things that how."

"Don't call a thing like that a boy, do yer!" said Dan'l. "I calls it monkey rubbidge. Now you step round the house, and through the stable, and get down that side o' the wall, and I'll go this. Don't you seem to see him till you hear me whistle. Then grab."

"But how am I to grab when he's up there!" said Peter.

"Ah! 'tis high up," said Dan'l. "Wish I'd got one o' them grappling-irons as hangs down by the bridge; I'd fetch him off pretty quick."

"Shall I get a fruit-ladder?" suggested Peter.

"Nay, we don't want no fruit-ladders," grumbled Dan'l. "We'll soon fetch his lordship down. Now then, you be off."

"Stop a moment," said Peter, as he watched the boy intently. "Look at him! Well, I never did!"

It was a very true remark. Peter certainly never did, and very few boys would have cunning enough to perform such a feat with so much ease. For, after running about fifty yards along the top of the wall, the little fellow turned quickly and ran back again, made offers as if he were going to leap down, and then suddenly squatted down in exact imitation of a cat, and began licking his arms, and passing them over his head.

"Well, he caps me!" cried Peter. "I never see a boy do anything like that since I was at a show at Exeter, and then it was a bigger chap than him."

"Look here," said Dan'l; "I've got it. You get a big strong clothes-prop, and I'll get another, and we'll poke him off. If he comes down your side, mind this: he'll be like a rat, and off as quick as quick; but don't you let him go. Drop your prop, and throw yourself on him; we'll ketch him, and take him in to the gov'nor, and he'll know now where the fruit goes. You couldn't net chaps like this."

In happy ignorance of the doctor's plans, Peter and Dan'l each provided himself with a clothes-prop, and in due time made for the appointed sides of the wall; but no sooner did the boy catch sight of his pursuers than he started off on another all-fours run; but this took him away from the house, and before he had gone far he turned and ran back.

Dan'l whistled, and Peter made a poke at the runner from one side of the wall, while Dan'l made a savage poke from the other.

The boy, who seemed as active as a squirrel, dodged them both, ran along toward the vinery, and as fast as the various trees would allow the two men followed.

Peter was soon out of the race, for a lean-to shed on his side of the wall put a stop to further pursuit, and Dan'l, who looked as malicious as a savage after a wild beast, had the hunt all to himself.

"Ah!" he shouted, as he stopped panting, "now I've got you, my fine fellow."

This was untrue, for he was as far off his quarry as ever, he being at the front of the vinery, and the boy on the top of the wall right at the back of the glass slope.

"Now, then, none o' yer nonsense, and down yer come."

Down the boy did not come, for he squatted there at the top, in a sitting position, with his arms round his knees, gazing coolly but watchfully at the gardener.

"D'yer hear? come down!"

The Yankee 'coon in the tree, when he saw the celebrated Colonel Crockett taking aim at him, and in full possession of the hunter's reputation as a dead shot, is reported to have said, "Don't shoot; I'll come down;" and the boy might have said something of the kind to Dan'l Copestake. But he had no faith in the gardener, and it is expecting too much of a boy who is seated in a safe place, to conclude that he will surrender at the first summons, especially to a fierce-looking man, who is armed with a very big stick.

This boy had not the least intention of giving himself up as a prisoner, and he sat and stared at Dan'l, and Dan'l stared at him.

"Do you hear me?" cried Dan'l; but the boy did not move a muscle, he only stared.

"Are you over there, Peter?" shouted Dan'l.

"Ay! All right!"

"You stop there, then, and nip him if he comes your way. I'll get a ladder, and will soon have him down."

"All right!" came from Peter again; and the boy's eyes watched keenly the old gardener's movements.

"Do you hear what I say!" continued Dan'l. "Am I to fetch that ladder, or will you come down without!"

The boy did not move.

"Let's see: I can reach you with this here, though," Dan'l went on. "Not going to have any more of your nonsense, my fine fellow, so now then."

The boy's eyes flashed as he saw the gardener come close up to the foot of the glass slope, and reach toward him with the long ash clothes-prop; but he measured mentally the length of that prop, and sat still, for, as he had quickly concluded, the gardener could not, even with his arm fully extended, reach to within some feet of where he sat.

Dan'l pushed and poked about, and nearly broke a pane of glass, but the boy did not stir.

"Oh, very well: only you'd better get down; you'll have it all the worse if I do fetch that ladder."

Still the boy made no sign. He merely glanced to right and left, and could have dashed along the wall at once, but that would have taken him down the garden, toward the river, and that was the direction in which he did not want to go.

To his left there was a portion of the house, the wall rising a good height, so that there was no escape in that direction. His way was either by the garden wall, or else down the slope of the vinery, as he had gone up.

But, like a lion in his path, there at the foot of this slope stood Dan'l, with the great clothes-prop, and the boy, concluding that he was best where he was, sat and stared at the gardener, and waited.

"Oh, very well then, my fine fellow: ladder it is," cried Dan'l; and, sticking the prop into the ground with a savage dig, he turned and ran off.

It was only a feint, and he turned sharply at the end of a dozen steps, to find, as he expected, that the boy had moved, and begun to descend.

Dan'l ran back, and the boy slipped into his former place, and sat like a monument of stone.

"Oh, that's your game, is it!" said Dan'l. "But it won't do, my fine fellow. Now, are you coming down?"

No reply.

Dan'l reflected.

If he went off to fetch the ladder from the stable-yard, the boy would slide down the top of the vinery and escape.

That would not do.

If he called to Peter to fetch the ladder, the boy would wait till the groom was gone, and slip over the wall, drop, and escape that way.

That would not do either.

Hah! There was the labourer. He could call him.

It was past twelve, and he had gone to his dinner, Dan'l, like Peter, taking his at the more aristocratic hour of one.

Dan'l was in a fix. He meant to have that boy, and make an example of him, but a great difficulty stared him in the face.

There was no one to call, unless he waited till the doctor came. If the doctor came, he would perhaps take a lenient view of the matter, and let the boy go, and, unless Dan'l could first give the prisoner a sound thrashing with a hazel stick, one of a bundle which he had in his tool-shed, all his trouble would have been in vain.

So he would not call the doctor.

He made two or three more feints of going, and each time the boy began to descend, but only to dart back as the gardener turned.

"Oh, that's your game, is it!" said Dan'l. "Very well; come down, but you can't get out of the garden if you do."

The next time, after a few minutes' thought, Dan'l turned and ran as hard as he could, with every appearance now of going right off for the ladder. But he had made his plans with no little calculation of probabilities; and his idea was now to go right on till he had given the boy time to descend, and make for one of the entrances, when he meant to return, run him down, and seize him, before the young scamp, as he called him, had time to clamber up any other place.

Dan'l ran on, and the boy watched him; and as soon as the gardener showed by his movements that he was evidently going away, began to descend.

Hardly, however, had he reached the ground than Dan'l turned, saw him, and made a fresh dash to capture him.

If the gardener had waited a couple more minutes he would have had a better chance. As it was, the boy had time to reach the dividing wall of the vinery wall again, but just as he was scrambling up, Dan'l was upon him, and was in the act of grasping one arm, when it was snatched away.

In the effort the boy lost his composure, and the steady easy-going confidence which had enabled him to trot along with such facility; and the consequence was that as he made a final bound to reach the back wall his right foot slipped, went through a pane of glass, and as this startled him more, he made another ill-judged attempt, and, slipping, went through the top of the vinery, only saving himself from dropping down inside by spreading his arms across the rafters, and hanging, caught as if in a trap.

"Here, just you come down!"

Directly after the doctor appeared in the study window, and, closely followed by Helen, hurried toward the front of the vinery, where the gardener stood.

Chapter Nine
A Release

"Glad you've come, sir," said the old gardener, telling a tremendous fib. "Got one on 'em at last."

"Got one of them?" cried the doctor.

"Why—"

"O papa dear! look!" cried Helen.

"One of them nippers as is always stealing our fruit," continued Dan'l.

"Why, Dexter," cried the doctor; "you there!" He stared wildly at the boy, who, with his legs kicking to and fro in the vinery in search of support, looked down from the roof of the building like a sculptured cherub, with arms instead of wings.

"Yes, it's all right," said the boy coolly. "Ain't much on it broken," while Dan'l stared and scratched his head, as he felt that he had made some mistake.

"You wicked boy!" cried Helen, with a good deal of excitement. "How did you get in such a position!"

"I couldn't help it," said Dexter. "He chivied me all along the top o' the wall with that great stick, and there's another chap t'other side. He was at me too."

"Is this true, Copestake!" cried the doctor angrily.

"Well, yes, sir; I s'pose it is," said the gardener. "Me and Peter see him a-cuttin' his capers atop o' that wall, and when we told him to come down, he wouldn't, and fell through our vinery."

"Who was going to come down when you was hitting at him with that big stick?" said Dexter indignantly.

"You had no business atop of our wall," said the gardener stoutly. "And now look at the mischief you've done."

"Tut—tut—tut—tut!" ejaculated the doctor.

"Please, sir, I didn't know as he was any one you knew."

"No, no, of course not," said the doctor pettishly. "Tut—tut—tut! Dear me! dear me!"

"I say, ain't some one coming to help me down?" said Dexter, in an ill-used tone.

"Yes, yes, of course," said the doctor. "Keep still, sir, or you'll cut yourself."

"I have cut myself, and it's a-bleeding," said the boy. "Look here, if one of you goes inside this place, and holds up that big long prop, I can put my foot in the fork at the end, and climb up again."

"Get a ladder quickly, Copestake, and call the groom."

"Yes, sir," said Dan'l; and he went off grumbling, while the doctor seized the prop, and went into the vinery.

"Are you much hurt, Dexter?" said Helen sympathisingly.

"I d'know," he replied. "It hurts a bit. I slipped, and went through."

"Now, sir, keep your legs still," cried the doctor from inside, as he raised the prop.

"All right," said the boy, and the next moment one of his feet rested in the fork of the ash prop; but, though the prisoner struggled, and the doctor pushed, there was no result.

"I wants some one to lend a hand up here," said Dexter.

"If I try I shall break some more glass. Is that old chap coming back— him as poked me!"

"Yes, yes," cried Helen. "Keep still; there's a good boy."

"No, I ain't," he said, smiling down at her in the most ludicrous way. "I ain't a good boy. I wish I was. Will he give it me very much?"

He tapped with his hand on the glass, as he pointed down at the doctor, who was still supporting the boy's foot with the prop.

Helen did not reply, for the simple reason that she did not know what to say; and the boy, feeling bound, was making a fresh struggle to free himself, when Dan'l came in sight, round the end of the house, with a light ladder, and just behind him came Peter, with a board used when glass was being repaired.

"Here they come," said Dexter, watching the approach eagerly. "I am glad. It's beginning to hurt ever so."

Dan'l laid the ladder against the vinery at some distance from the front, so that it should lie upon the roof at the same angle, and then, holding it steady, Peter, who was grinning largely, mounted with the board, which he placed across the rafters, so that he could kneel down, and, taking hold of Dexter, who clasped his hands about his neck, he bodily drew him out, and would have carried him down had the boy not preferred to get down by himself.

As he reached the foot of the ladder the doctor was standing ready for him, armed with the clothes-prop, which he held in his hand, as if it were a weapon intended for punishment.

The boy looked up in the stern face before him, and the doctor put on a tremendous frown.

"Please, sir, I'm very sorry, sir," said Dexter.

"You young rascal!" began the doctor, seizing his arm.

"Oh, I say, please, sir, don't hit a fellow with a thing like that."

"Bah!" ejaculated the doctor, throwing down the prop, which fell on the grass with a loud thud. "Copestake!—Peter!—take those things away, and send for the glazier to put in those squares. Here, Dexter; this way."

The doctor strode away half a dozen steps, and then stopped and gazed down.

"Where is your jacket, sir? and where are your boots?"

"I tucked 'em under that tree there that lies on the grass," said the boy, pointing to a small cedar.

"Fetch them out, sir."

Dexter went toward the tree, and his first instinct was to make a dash and escape, anywhere, so as to avoid punishment, but as he stooped down and drew his articles of attire from beneath the broad frond-like branches, he caught sight of Helen's eyes fixed upon him, so full of trouble and amusement that he walked back, put his hand in the doctor's, and walked with him into the house.

Helen followed, and as she passed through the window Dan'l turned to Peter with—

"I say, who is he?"

"I dunno. Looks like a young invalid."

"Ay, that's it," said the gardener. "Hair cut short, and looks very white. He's a young luneattic come for the governor to cure. Well, if that's going to be it, I shall resign my place."

"Oh, I wouldn't do that," said Peter, who was moved to say it from the same feeling which induced the old woman to pray for long life to the tyrant—for fear they might get a worse to rule over them. "Doctor'll make him better. Rum-looking little chap."

As they spoke, they were carrying the ladder and board round to the back of the house, and, in doing so, they had to pass the kitchen door, where Maria was standing.

"See that game!" said Peter.

"Oh yes. I saw him out of one of the bedroom windows."

"Young patient, ain't he?" said Peter.

"Patient! Why, he's a young workhouse boy as master's took a fancy to. I never see such games, for my part."

Peter whistled, and the head-gardener repeated his determination to resign.

"And he'll never get another gardener like me," he said.

"That's a true word, Mr Copestake, sir," said Peter seriously. And then to himself: "No, there never was another made like you, you old tyrant. I wish you would go, and then we should have a little peace."

Chapter Ten
Dexter is very Sorry

Dexter walked into the doctor's study, and Helen came as rearguard behind.

"Now, sir," said the doctor sternly, "I suppose you know that I'm very much displeased with you."

"Yes, sir, of course you are," said the boy seriously. "I don't wonder at it."

Dr Grayson bit his lip.

"Are you going to cane me?"

"Wait and see, sir. Now, first thing, you go up to your room and wash your hands, and dress yourself properly. Then come down to me."

Dexter glanced at Helen, but she kept her eyes averted, and the boy went slowly out, keeping his gaze fixed upon her all the time.

"A young scamp!" said the doctor, as soon as they were alone. "I'm afraid I shall have to send him back."

Helen looked at him.

"I expected him to be a little wild," continued the doctor; "but he is beyond bearing. What do you say, my dear? Too bad, is he not?"

Helen was silent for a few moments.

"It is too soon to say that, papa," she replied at last. "There is a great deal in the boy that is most distasteful, but, on the other hand, I cannot help liking the little fellow."

"Yes; that's just it," cried the doctor. "I feel as if I should like to give him a sound thrashing, but, at the same time, I feel that I could not raise a hand against him. What's to be done? Shall I send him back, and choose another?"

"No, no, papa. If you intend to adopt a boy, let us keep this one, and see what he turns out."

Just then the bell rang for lunch, and a minute after Dexter came running down into the room, with a smile, as if nothing was the matter, shining out of his eyes.

"I say, wasn't that the dinner-bell?" he cried. "I am so precious hungry."

"And have you no apologies to make, sir? Aren't you sorry you were so mischievous, and broke the top of my vinery?"

"Yes; I'm very sorry, sir; but it was that old chap's fault. He made me run and slip. I say, what would he have done if he had caught me?"

"Punished you, or brought you in to me, sir. Now, then, I've been talking about sending you back to the workhouse. You are too mischievous for me."

"Send me back!"

"Yes, of course. I want a boy who will be good."

"Well, I will."

"So you said before, but you are not good. You are about as mischievous a young rascal as I ever saw in my life."

"Yes, sir; that's what Mr Sibery used to say," replied the boy quietly. "I don't want to be."

"Then why are you, sir?"

The boy shook his head, and looked up at the doctor thoughtfully.

"I suppose it's in me," he said.

Helen bit her lip, and turned away, while her father gave his head a fierce rub, as if he was extremely vexed.

"Shall you send me back, sir!" said Dexter at last; and his look was full of wistful appeal.

"Well, I shall think about it," said the doctor.

"I don't want to go," said the boy thoughtfully. "You don't want me to go, do you?" he continued, turning to Helen.

"Here, the lunch is getting cold," said the doctor. "Come along."

As he spoke he half-pushed Dexter before him, and pointed to a chair.

The boy hesitated, but a sharp command from the doctor made him scuffle into his place, after which the grace was said, and the dinner commenced for Dexter—the lunch for his patron and friend.

Roast fowl most delicately cooked, with a delicious sauce; in addition to that made with bread; and there was an ornamentation round the dish of tempting sausages.

The odour from the steaming dishes was enough to have attracted any coarsely-fed workhouse boy, just as a flower, brings a bee from afar.

Helen was helped to a couple of choice slices from the breast, and then the doctor, looking stern all the while, carved off the liver wing, with a fine long piece of juicy breast adhering, and laid it on a plate, with the biggest sausage, gravy, and sauce, Maria carrying the plate afterwards to Helen to be well supplied with vegetables.

Then, according to custom, Maria departed with her nose in the air, and her bosom overcharged with indignant remonstrances, which she was going to let off at Mrs Millett.

The meal was commenced in silence, Dexter taking up his knife and fork, and watching by turns the doctor and Helen, to see how they handled theirs. Then he cut the sausage in half, just as the doctor had cut his, and looked hard at him, but the doctor was gazing down at his plate and frowning.

Dexter looked at Helen, but she was gazing at her father, and everything was very still in the dining-room, while from without, faintly heard, there came the rippling song of a lark, far away over the meadow across the river.

That fowl smelt delicious, and looked good in the extreme, but Dexter laid down his knife and fork, and sat perfectly still.

Helen saw everything, but she did not speak, and the annoyance she had felt began to diminish, for the boy was evidently suffering keenly.

"Hallo!" said the doctor. "Don't you like chicken!"

The boy started, and looked up at him with a troubled face.

"I say, don't you like chicken, sir!"

Dexter tried to answer, but the words would not come; and he sat there with the tears gathering in his eyes, though he tried hard to choke his emotion down.

The doctor was very angry, and sadly disappointed; but he said no more, only went on with his lunch.

"Eat your dinner," said Helen, after a time; and she leant over toward the boy, and whispered the words kindly.

He gave her a quick, grateful look, but he could not speak.

"Come, sir, eat your dinner," said the doctor at last.

"Please, sir, I can't," the boy faltered.

"Why not?"

Dexter had to make another fight to keep down his tears before he could say—

"Please, sir, I never could eat my breakfast when I knew I was going to have the cane."

The doctor grunted, frowned, and went on eating, while the boy directed a pitiful appealing look at Helen.

"Yes," she said at last, "what do you want?"

"May I go up to that place where I slept last night?"

Helen glanced at her father, who nodded shortly, and went on with his dinner, while the required permission being given by Helen, the boy rose hastily, and hurried out of the room.

Doctor Grayson was silent for a few minutes, and then he took a glass of sherry.

"A young scoundrel!" he said. "It's not pleasant to have to say so, but I've made a mistake."

"And are you going to give up your project, papa?" said Helen.

"*No*," he thundered. "Certainly not. It's very awkward, for that bullet-headed drill-sergeant Hippetts will laugh at me, and say 'I told you so,' but I shall have to take the boy back."

Helen was silent.

"He told me I should," he continued; "but I would not believe him. The young dog's face attracted me. He looked so frank and ingenuous. But I'll soon pick out another. My theory is right, and if I have ten thousand obstacles, I'll carry it out, and prove to the world that I knew what I was at."

Helen went on slowly with her lunch, thinking deeply the while.

"Well?" said the doctor angrily, "why don't you speak? Are you triumphing over my first downfall!"

Helen looked up at her father, and smiled reproachfully.

"I was thinking about Dexter," she said softly.

"A confounded ungrateful young dog! Taken him from that wretched place, clothed him, offered him a home of which he might be proud, and he turns upon me like that!"

"It was the act of a high-spirited, mischievous boy," said Helen quietly.

"Mischievous! I should think it was. Confound him! But I'll have no more of his tricks. Back he goes to the Union, and I'll have one without so much spirit."

Helen continued her lunch, and the doctor went on with his, but only to turn pettishly upon his child.

"I wish to goodness you'd say something, Helen," he cried. "It's so exasperating to have every one keeping silence like that."

Helen looked up and smiled.

"Yes, and that's just as aggravating," said the doctor. "Now you are laughing at me."

"No, no; I was thinking very seriously about your project."

"One which I mean to carry out, madam."

"Of course, papa," said Helen quietly; "but I would not be damped at the outset."

"What do you mean, Helen?"

"I mean that I should not take that poor boy back to the life from which you have rescued him, just because he has displayed a few pranks, all due to the exuberance of his nature. Coming from such a place, and making such a change, he is sure to feel it strongly. He is, so to speak, bubbling over with excitement and—"

"Here, stop a moment," said the doctor, in astonishment. "I give up. You had better write that book."

"Not I, papa dear," said Helen, smiling. "And if you are really bent upon this experiment—"

"And I am," said the doctor. "Nothing shall change me."

"Then I think you have selected the very boy."

"You do!" said the doctor excitedly.

"Yes. He is just the wild little savage for you to reclaim."

"But—but a little too bad, Helen?"

"No, papa, I think not; and I think you are not justified in saying bad. I believe he is a very good boy."

"You do?"

"Yes; full of mischief as a boy can be, but very, very affectionate."

"Yes. I think he is," assented the doctor.

"I think he will be very teachable."

"Humph!"

"And it was plain to see that he was touched to the heart with grief at our anger."

"Or is it all his artfulness!"

"Oh no, papa! Certainly not that. The boy is frank and affectionate as can be."

"Then you think it is possible to make a gentleman of him?"

"If it is possible of any boy whom you could get from the Union, papa."

"And you really think he is frank and tender-hearted?"

Helen pointed to the boy's untouched plate.

"And you would not exchange him for something a little more tractable?"

"I don't think you could. I really begin to like the mischievous little fellow, and I believe that in a very short time we should see a great change."

"You do?"

"Yes; but of course we must be prepared for a great many more outbreaks of this kind."

"Unless I stop them."

"No, no, you must not stop them," said Helen quietly. "These little ebullitions must not be suppressed in that way—I mean with undue severity."

"Then you really would not take—I mean send him back?"

"No," said Helen. "I think, perhaps, I could help you in all this."

"My dear Helen," cried the doctor eagerly. "My dear child, you don't know how pleased you make me. I felt that for your sake I must take him back."

"For my sake?" exclaimed Helen.

"Yes; that it was too bad to expose you to the petty annoyances and troubles likely to come from keeping him. But if you feel that you could put up with it till we have tamed him down—"

Helen rose from her chair, and went behind her father's, to lay her hands upon his shoulders, when he took them in his, and crossed them upon his breast, so as to draw her face down over his shoulder.

HELEN SOOTHES DEXTER IN HIS SORROW

"My dear father," she said, as she laid her cheek against his, "I don't know—I cannot explain, but this boy seems to have won his way with me very strangely, and I should be deeply grieved if you sent him away."

"My dear Helen, you've taken a load off my mind. There, go and fetch the poor fellow down. He wanted his dinner two hours ago, and he must be starved."

Helen kissed her father's forehead, and went quietly up to Dexter's room, listened for a few moments, heard a low sob, and then, softly turning the handle of the door, she entered, to stand there, quite taken aback.

The boy was crouched in a heap on the floor, sobbing silently, and with his breast heaving with the agony of spirit he suffered.

For that she was prepared, but the tears rose in her eyes as she grasped another fact. There, neatly folded and arranged, just as the Union teaching had prompted him, were the clothes the boy had worn that day, even to the boots placed under the chair, upon which they lay, while the boy had taken out and dressed himself again in his old workhouse livery, his cap lying on the floor by his side.

Helen crossed to him softly, bent over him, and laid her little white hand upon his head.

The boy sprang to his feet as if he had felt a blow, and stood before her with one arm laid across his eyes, as, in shame for his tears, he bent his head.

"Dexter," she said again, "what are you going to do?"

"Going back again," he said hoarsely. "I'm such a bad un. They always said I was."

"And is that the way to make yourself better?"

"I can't help it," he said, half defiantly. "It's no use to try, and I'm going back."

"To grieve me, and make me sorry that I have been mistaken?"

"Yes," he said huskily, and with his arm still across his eyes. "I'm going back, and old Sibery may cut me to pieces," he added passionately. "I don't care."

"Look up at me, Dexter," said Helen gently, as she laid her hand upon the boy's arm. "Tell me," she continued, "which will you do?—go back, or try to be a good boy, and do what you know I wish you to do, and stay!"

He let her arm fall, gazed wildly in her eyes, and then caught her hand and dropped upon his knees, sobbing passionately.

"I will try; I will try," he cried, as soon as he could speak. "Take me down to him, and let him cane me, and I won't cry out a bit. I'll take it all like Bill Jones does, and never make a sound, but don't, don't send me away."

Helen Grayson softly sank upon her knees beside the boy, and took him in her arms to kiss him once upon the forehead.

"There, Dexter," she said gently, as she rose. "Now bathe your eyes, dress yourself again, and come downstairs to me in the dining-room, as quickly as you can."

Helen went to her own room for a few moments to bathe her own eyes, and wonder how it was that she should be so much moved, and in so short a time.

The doctor was anxiously awaiting her return.

"Well!" he said; "where is the young scamp!"

"In his room," replied Helen, "and—"

"Well—well!" said the doctor impatiently.

"Oh no, father dear," said Helen quietly, but with more emotion in her voice than even she knew. "We must not send him back."

Then she told what had passed, and the doctor nodded his head.

"No," he said; "we must not send him back."

Just then there was a knock at the door, and Maria entered to clear away.

"Not yet, Maria," said Helen quietly. "Take that chicken back, and ask Mrs Millett to make it hot again."

"And the vegetables, ma'am!"

"Yes. I will ring when we want them."

Maria took the various dishes away with a very ill grace, and dabbed them down on the kitchen table, almost hard enough to produce cracks, as she delivered her message to Mrs Millett, who looked annoyed.

"You can do as you please, Mrs Millett," said Maria, giving herself a jerk as if a string inside her had been pulled; "but I'm a-going to look out for a new place."

Chapter Eleven
Master Grayson goes for a Walk

"Couldn't have believed it," said the doctor one evening, when a week had passed away. "It's wonderful." Helen smiled.

"A whole week, and the young dog's behaviour has been even better than I could wish. Well, it's very hopeful, and I am extremely glad, Helen, extremely glad."

Helen said nothing, but she thought a good deal, and, among other things, she wondered how Dexter would have behaved if he had been left to himself. Consequently, she felt less sanguine than the doctor.

The fact was that she had given up everything to devote the whole of her time to the boy, thus taking care that he was hardly ever left to himself.

She read to him, and made him read to her, and battled hard to get him out of his schoolboy twang.

Taken by his bright, handsome face, and being clever with her brush, she had made him sit while she painted his likeness; that is, she tried to make him sit, but it was like dealing with so much quicksilver, and she was fain to give up the task as an impossibility after scolding, coaxing, and bribing, coming to the conclusion that the boy could not keep still.

She played games with him; and at last risked public opinion very bravely by taking the boy out with her for a walk, when one of the first persons she met was Lady Danby.

"I say, what did she mean!" said Dexter, as they walked away.

"That lady—Lady Danby!"

"Yes. Why did she look sorry for me, and call me a *protégé*?"

"Oh," said Helen, smiling; "it is only a French word for any one who is adopted or protected, as papa is protecting you."

"But is it a funny word!"

"Funny? Oh dear no!"

"Then why did she laugh, curious like?"

Helen could not answer that question.

"She looked at me," said Dexter, "as if she didn't like me. I've seen ladies look like that when they've come to see the schools, and us boy's used to feel as if we'd like to throw slates at them."

"You have no occasion to trouble yourself about other people's opinions, Dexter," said Helen quietly; "and of course now you couldn't throw stones or anything else at a lady."

"No; but I could at a boy. I could hit that chap ever so far off. Him as was with that Lady Danby."

"Oh, nonsense! come along; we'll go down by the river."

"Yes; come along," cried Dexter excitedly; "but I don't see why he should sneer at me for nothing."

"What? Master Danby!"

"Yes, him. All the time you two were talking, he kept walking round me, and making faces as if I was physic."

"You fancied it, Dexter."

"Oh no, I didn't. I know when anybody likes me, and when anybody doesn't. Lady Danby didn't like me, and she give a sneery laugh when she called me a *protégé*, and when you weren't looking that chap made an offer at me with the black cane he carried, that one with a silver top and black tassels."

"Did he?"

"Didn't he just! I only wish he had. I'd ha' given him such a oner. Why, I could fight two like him with one hand tied behind me."

Helen's face grew cloudy with trouble, but she said nothing then, only hurried the boy along toward the river.

In spite of her determination she avoided the town main street, and struck off by the narrow turning which led through the old churchyard, with its grand lime-tree avenue and venerable church, whose crocketed spire was a landmark for all the southern part of the county.

"Look, look!" cried Dexter. "See those jackdaws fly out? There's one sitting on that old stone face. See me fetch him down."

"No, no," cried Helen, catching his arm. "You might break a window."

"No, I wouldn't. You see."

"But why throw at the poor bird? It has done you no harm."

"No, but it's a jackdaw, and you always want to throw stones at jackdaws."

"And at blackbirds and thrushes and starlings too, Dexter?" said Helen.

The boy looked guilty.

"You didn't see me throw at them?"

"Yes, I did, and I thought it very cruel."

"Don't you like me to throw stones at the birds?"

"Certainly I do not."

"Then I won't," said Dexter; and he took aim with the round stone he carried at the stone urn on the top of a tomb, hitting it with a sounding crack.

"There, wasn't that a good aim!" he said, with a smile of triumph. "It couldn't hurt that. That wasn't cruel."

Helen turned crimson with annoyance, for she had suddenly become aware of the fact that a gentleman, whom she recognised as the Vicar, was coming along the path quickly, having evidently seen the stone-throwing.

She was quite right in her surmise. It was the Vicar; and not recognising her with her veil down, he strode toward them, making up an angry speech.

"Ah, Miss Grayson," he said, raising his hat, and ceasing to make his stick quiver in his hand, "I did not recognise you."

Then followed the customary hand-shakings and inquiries, during which Dexter hung back, and gazed up at the crocketed spire, and at the jackdaws flying in and out of the slits which lit the stone staircase within.

"And who is this?" said the Vicar, raising his glasses to his eyes, but knowing perfectly well all the time, he having been one of the first to learn of the doctor's eccentricity. "Ah, to be sure; Doctor Grayson's *protégé*. Yes, I remember him perfectly well, and I suppose you remember me!"

"Yes, I remember you," said Dexter. "You called me a stupid boy because I couldn't say all of *I desire*."

"Did I? Ah, to be sure, I remember. Well, but you are not stupid now. I dare say, if I asked you, you would remember every word."

"Don't think I could," said the boy; "it's the hardest bit in the Cat."

"But I'm not going to ask you," said the Vicar. "Miss Grayson here will examine you, I'm sure. There, good day. Good day, Miss Grayson;" and, to

Helen's great relief, he shook hands with both. "And I'm to ask you not to throw stones in the churchyard," he added, shaking his stick playfully. "My windows easily break."

He nodded and smiled again, as Helen and her young companion went on, watching them till they had passed through the further gate and disappeared.

"A mischievous young rascal!" he said to himself. "I believe I should have given him the stick if it had been anybody else."

As he said this, he walked down a side path which led past the tomb that had formed Dexter's target.

"I dare say he has chipped the urn," he continued, feeling exceedingly vexed, as a Vicar always does when he finds any wanton defacement of the building and surroundings in his charge.

"No," he said aloud, and in a satisfied tone, "unhurt. But tut—tut—tut—tut! what tiresome young monkeys boys are!"

He turned back, and went thoughtfully toward the town.

"Singular freak on the part of Grayson. Most eccentric man," he continued. "Danby tells me—now really what a coincidence! Sir James, by all that is singular! Ah, my dear Sir James, I was thinking about you. Ah, Edgar, my boy, how are you?"

He shook hands warmly with the magistrate and his son.

"Thinking about me, eh!" said Sir James, rather pompously. "Then I'll be bound to say that I can tell you what you are thinking."

"No, I believe I may say for certain you cannot," said the Vicar, smiling.

"Of calling on me for a subscription."

"Wrong this time," said the Vicar good-humouredly. "No; I have just met Miss Grayson with that boy."

"Indeed!"

"Yes; very eccentric of Grayson, is it not!"

"Whim for a week or two. Soon get tired of it," said Sir James, laughing.

"Think so?"

"Sure of it, sir; sure of it."

"Well, I hope not," said the Vicar thoughtfully. "Fine thing for the poor boy. Make a man of him."

"Ah, but he is not content with that. He means to make a gentleman of him, and that's an impossibility."

"Ah, well," said the Vicar good-humouredly; "we shall see."

"Yes, sir," said Sir James; "we shall see—we shall see; but it's a most unpleasant episode in our midst. Of course, being such near neighbours, I have been on the most intimate terms with the Graysons, and Lady Danby is warmly attached to Helen Grayson; but now they have this boy there, they want us to know him too."

"Indeed!" said the Vicar, looking half-amused, half puzzled.

"Yes, sir," said Sir James; "and they want—at least Grayson does—Edgar here to become his playmate."

"Ah!" ejaculated the Vicar.

"Sent word yesterday that they should be glad if Edgar would go and spend the afternoon. Awkward, sir; extremely awkward."

"Did he go?"

"Go? no, sir; decidedly not. Edgar refused to go, point-blank."

Master Edgar was walking a little way in front, looking like a small edition of his father in a short jacket, for he imitated Sir James's stride, put on his tall hat at the same angle, and carried his black cane with its two silken tassels in front of him, as a verger in church carries a wand.

"I wasn't going," said Master Edgar importantly. "I don't want to know a boy like that."

"What would you do under the circumstances?" said Sir James.

"Do?" said the Vicar; "why I should—I beg your pardon—will you excuse me? I am wanted."

He pointed to a lady who was signalling to him with a parasol, and hurried off.

"How lucky!" he said to himself. "I don't want to offend Sir James; but 'pon my word, knowing what I do of his young cub, I would rather have Grayson's *protégé* on spec."

"Where are we going for a walk, pa!" said Master Edgar importantly.

"Through the quarry there, and by the windmill, and back home."

"*No*; I meant to go down by the river, pa, to see if there are any fish."

"Another day will do for that, Eddy."

"No, it won't. I want to go now."

"Oh, very well," said Sir James; and they took the way to the meadows.

Meanwhile Helen and Dexter had gone on some distance ahead.

"There, you see, Dexter; how easy it is to do wrong," said Helen, as, feeling greatly relieved, she hurried on toward the meadows.

"I didn't know it was doing wrong to have a cockshy," said Dexter. "Seems to me that nearly everything nice that you want to do is wrong."

"Oh no," said Helen, smiling at the boy's puzzled face.

"Seems like it," said Dexter. "I say, he was going to scold me, only he found I was with you, and that made him stop. Wish I hadn't thrown the stone."

"So do I," said Helen quickly. "Come, you have broken yourself off several bad habits this last week, and I shall hope soon to find that you have stopped throwing stones."

"But mayn't I throw anything else?"

"Oh yes; your ball."

"But I haven't got a ball."

"Then you shall have one," said Helen. "We'll buy one as we go back. There, it was a mistake, Dexter, so remember not to do it again."

They were now on the banks of the glancing river, the hay having been lately cut, and the way open right to the water's edge.

"Yes, I'll remember," said Dexter. "Look—look at the fish. Oh, don't I wish I had a rod and line! Here, wait a moment."

He was down on his chest, reaching with his hand in the shallow water.

"Why, Dexter," said Helen, laughing, "you surely did not think that you could catch fishes with your hand!"

"No," said the boy, going cautiously forward and striking an attitude; "but you see me hit one."

As he spoke he threw a large round pebble which he had picked out of the river-bed with great force, making the water splash up, while, instead of sinking, the stone skipped from the surface, dipped again, and then disappeared.

As the stone made its last splash, the reality of what he had done seemed to come to him, and he turned scarlet as he met Helen's eyes.

"Dexter!" she said reproachfully.

The boy took off his cap, looked in it, rubbed his closely cropped head in a puzzled way, and put his cap slowly on again, to stand once more gazing at his companion.

"I can't tell how it is," he said dolefully. "I think there must be something wrong in my head. It don't go right. I never mean to do what you don't like, but somehow I always do."

"Look there, Dexter," said Helen quickly; "those bullocks seem vicious; we had better go back."

She pointed to a drove of bullocks which had been put in the newly-cut meadows by one of the butchers in the town, and the actions of the animals were enough to startle any woman, for, being teased by the flies, they were careering round the field with heads down and tails up, in a lumbering gallop, and approaching the spot where the couple stood.

They were down by the water, both the stile they had crossed and that by which they would leave the meadow about equidistant, while, as the bullocks were making straight for the river to wade in, and try to rid themselves of their torment, it seemed as if they were charging down with serious intent.

"Come: quick! let us run," cried Helen in alarm, and she caught at Dexter's hand.

"What! run away from them!" cried the boy stoutly. "Don't you be afraid of them. You come along."

"No, no," cried Helen; "it is not safe."

But, to her horror, Dexter shook himself free, snatched off his cap, and rushed straight at the leading bullock, a great heavy beast with long horns, and now only fifty yards away, while the drove were close at its heels.

The effect was magical.

No sooner did the great animal see the boy running forward than it stopped short, and began to paw up the ground and shake its head, the drove following the example of their leader, while, to Helen, as she stood motionless with horror, it seemed as if the boy's fate was sealed.

For a few moments the bullock stood fast, but by the time Dexter was within half a dozen yards, he flung his cap right in the animal's face, and, with a loud snort, it turned as on a pivot, and dashed off toward the upper part of the field, now driving the whole of the rest before it.

"Ha, ha, ha!" laughed Dexter, picking up his cap, and coming back panting. "That's the way to serve them. Come along."

Helen was very white, but the colour began to come in her cheeks again as she saw the boy's bright, frank, animated face; and, as they crossed the second stile, and rambled on through the pleasant meads, it began to dawn upon her that perhaps it would not prove to be so unpleasant a task after all to tame the young savage placed in her hands.

Chapter Twelve
A Pleasant Lesson

One minute Helen Grayson was delighted at the freshness of nature, and the genuine delight and enthusiasm displayed by her companion, the next there came quite a cloud over everything, for it seemed to her that here was a bright young spirit corroded and spoiled by the surroundings to which it had been accustomed. 　　　　　　．

"What's that? What flower's this? Oh, look at that butterfly! Here, Miss Grayson, see here—a long thin fly with his body all blue; and such lovely wings. There's another with purple edges to it. Oh, how lovely!"

Helen's eyes brightened, and she began to enjoy her walk, and forget the stone-throwing, when Dexter damped her enjoyment.

"Oh, here's a lark!" he cried, plunging down into a ditch, and reappearing after a hunt in the long wet grass with a large greenish frog.

"What have you found, Dexter!"

"A jolly old frog. Look here; I'll show you how the boys do up there at the House."

"I think you had better not," said Helen, wincing.

"But it's such a game. You get a flat piece of wood, about so long, and you lay it across a stone. Then you set the frog on one end, and perhaps he hops off. If he does, you catch him again, and put him on the end of the wood over and over again till he sits still, and he does when he is tired. Then you have a stick ready, as if you were going to play at cat, and you hit the end of the stick—"

"Oh!" ejaculated Helen.

"I don't mean the end where the frog is," cried Dexter quickly, as he saw Helen's look of disgust; "I mean the other end; and then the frog flies up in the air ever so high, and kicks out his legs as if he was swimming, and—"

Dexter began his description in a bright, animated way, full of gesticulation; but as he went on the expression in his companion's face seemed to chill him. He did not understand what it meant, only he felt that he was doing or saying something which was distasteful; and he gradually trailed off, and stood staring with his narrative unfinished, and the frog in his hand.

"Could you do that now, Dexter!" said Helen suddenly.

"Do it?" he faltered.

"Yes; with the frog."

"I haven't got a bit of flat wood, and I have no stick, and if I had—I—you—I—"

He stopped short, with his head on one side, and his brows puckered up, gazing into Helen's eyes. Then he looked down, at the frog, and back at Helen.

"You don't mean it?" he said sharply. "You don't want me to? I know: you mean it would hurt the frog."

"Would it hurt you, Dexter, if somebody put you on one end of a plank, and then struck the other end!"

The boy took off his cap and scratched his head with his little finger, the others being closed round the frog, which was turned upside down.

"The boys always used to do it up at the House," he said apologetically.

"Why!" said Helen gravely.

"Because it was such fun; but they always made them hop well first. They'd begin by taking great long jumps, and then, as the boys hunted them, the jumps would get shorter and shorter, and they'd be so tired that it was easy to make them sit still on the piece of wood."

"And when they had struck the wood, and driven it into the air, what did they do to the poor thing then?"

"Sent it up again."

"And then?"

"Oh, they caught it—some of the boys did—caught it like a ball."

"Have you ever done so?" Dexter shuffled about from foot to foot, and looked at the prospect, then at the frog, and then slowly up at the clear, searching eyes watching him.

"Yes," he said, with a sigh; "lots of times."

"And was it to save the poor thing from being hurt by the fall on the hard ground!"

Dexter tried hard to tell a lie, but somehow he could not.

"No," he said slowly. "It was to put it back on the stick, so as the other boys could not catch it first."

"What was done then!"

Dexter was silent, and he seemed to be taking a wonderful deal of interest in the frog, which was panting hard in his hot hand, with only its comical face peeping out between his finger and thumb, the bright golden irised eyes seeming to stare into his, and the loose skin of its throat quivering.

"Well, Dexter, why don't you tell me!"

"Am I to?" said the boy slowly.

"Of course."

There were a few more moments of hesitation, and then the boy said with an effort—

"They used—"

He paused again.

"We used to get lots of stones and shy at 'em till they was dead."

There was a long silence here, during which Helen Grayson watched the play in the boy's countenance, and told herself that there was a struggle going on between the good and evil in the young nature, and once more she asked herself how she could hesitate in the task before her.

Meanwhile it was very uncomfortable for the frog. The day was hot; Dexter's hand was hotter still; and though there was the deliciously cool gurgling river close at hand, with plenty of sedge, and the roots of water grasses, where it might hide and enjoy its brief span of life, it was a prisoner; and if frogs can think and know anything about the chronicles of their race, it was thinking of its approaching fate, and wondering how many of its young tadpoles would survive to be as big as its parent, and whether it was worth while after all.

"Dexter," said Helen suddenly, and her voice sounded so clear and thrilling that the boy started, and looked at her in a shame-faced manner. "Suppose you saw a boy—say like—like—"

"That chap we saw with the hat and stick? him who sneered at me?"

Helen winced in turn. She had young Edgar Danby in her mind, but was about to propose some other young lad for her illustration; but the boy had divined her thought, and she did not shrink now from the feeling that above all things she must be frank if she wished her companion to be.

"Yes; young Danby. Suppose you saw him torturing a frog, a lowly reptile, but one of God's creatures, in that cruel way, what would you say, now?"

"I should say he was a beast."

Helen winced again, for the declaration was more emphatic and to the point than she had anticipated.

"And what would you do?" he continued.

"I'd punch his head, and take the frog away from him. Please, Miss Grayson," he continued earnestly; "I didn't ever think it was like that. We always used to do it—we boys always did, and—and—"

"You did not know then what you know now. Surely, Dexter, you will never be so cruel again."

"If you don't want me to, I won't," he said quickly.

"Ah, but I want you to be frank and manly for a higher motive than that, Dexter," she said, laying her hand upon his shoulder. "There, I will not say any more now. What are you going to do!"

"Put him in the river, and let him swim away."

The boy darted to the side of the rippling stream, stooped down, and lowered the hand containing the frog into the water, opened it, and for a moment or two the half-dead reptile sat there motionless. Then there was a vigorous kick, and it shot off into the clear water, diving right down among the water weeds, and disappearing from their view.

"There!" said Dexter, jumping up and looking relieved. "You are not cross with me now!"

"I have not been cross with you," she said; "only a little grieved."

"Couldn't he swim!" cried the boy, who was anxious to turn the conversation. "I can swim like that, and dive too. We learned in our great bath, and— Oh, I say, hark at the bullocks."

Helen listened, and could hear a low, muttering bellow in the next meadow, accompanied by the dull sounds of galloping hoofs, which were near enough to make the earth of the low, marshy bottom through which the river ran quiver slightly where they stood.

Just then there was a piercing shriek, as of a woman in peril, and directly after a man's voice heard shouting for help.

Chapter Thirteen
Rampant Beef

"Here's something the matter!" cried Dexter; and, forgetting everything in the excitement of the moment, he ran back as hard as he could tear to the footpath leading to the stile they had crossed, the high untrimmed hedge between the fields concealing what was taking place.

Helen followed quickly, feeling certain the while that the drove of bullocks in the next meadow were the cause of the trouble and alarm.

Dexter reached the stile far in advance; and when at last Helen attained to the same post of observation, it was to see Sir James Danby at the far side standing upon the next stile toward the town, shouting, and frantically waving his hat and stick, while between her and the stout baronet there was the drove of bullocks, and Dexter approaching them fast.

For a few moments Helen could not understand what was the matter, but directly after, to her horror, she saw that young Edgar Danby was on the ground, with one of the bullocks standing over him, smelling at the prostrate boy, and apparently trying to turn him over with one of its horns.

"Here! Hi!" shouted Dexter; "bring me your stick."

But Sir James, who had been chased by the leading bullock, was breathless, exhausted, and too nervous to attempt his son's rescue. All he seemed capable of doing was to shout hoarsely, and this he did more feebly every moment.

Dexter made a rush at the bullocks, and the greater part of the drove turned tail; but, evidently encouraged by its success, the leader of the little herd stood firm, tossed its head on high, shook its horns, and uttered a defiant bellow.

"Here, I can't do anything without a stick," said Dexter, in an ill-used tone, and he turned and ran toward Sir James, while, still more encouraged by what must have seemed to its dense brain like a fresh triumph, the bullock placed one of its horns under Edgar Danby and cleverly turned him right over.

"Here, give me your stick!" shouted Dexter, as he ran up to Sir James. "You shouldn't be afraid o' them."

"The boy will be killed," cried Sir James, in agony; and he shouted again, "Help! help!"

"No, he won't," cried Dexter, snatching the magistrate's heavy ebony stick from his hand. "I'll make 'em run."

Raising the stick in the air, Dexter ran toward where the whole drove were trotting back, and gathering round their leader, who now began to sing its war-song, throwing up its muzzle so as to straighten its throat, and emitting a bellow that was, in spite of its size, but a poor, feeble imitation of the roar of a lion.

As Dexter ran up, the drove stood firm for a few moments; then the nearest to him arched its back, curved its tail, executed a clumsy gambol, turned, and fled, the rest taking their cues from this, the most timid in the herd, and going off in a lumbering gallop, their heads now down, and their tails rigid, excepting a few inches, and the hairy tuft at the end.

But the leader stood fast, and shaking its head, bellowed, looked threatening, and lowering one of its long horns, thrust it into the earth, and began to plough up the soft, moist soil.

"Oh, you would, would you?" cried Dexter, who did not feel in the slightest degree alarmed, from ignorance probably more than bravery; and, dashing in, he struck out with the ebony stick so heavy a blow upon the end of the horn raised in the air that the ebony snapped in two, and the bullock, uttering a roar of astonishment and pain, swung round, and galloped after its companions, which were now facing round at the top of the field.

"Broke his old stick," said Dexter, as he bent over Edgar. "Here, I say; get up. They're gone now. You ain't hurt."

Hurt or no, Edgar did not hear him, but lay there with his clothes soiled, and his tall hat trampled on by the drove, and crushed out of shape.

"I say," said Dexter, shaking him; "why don't you get up?"

Poor Edgar made no reply, for he was perfectly insensible and cadaverous of hue.

"Here! Hi! Come here!" cried Dexter, rising and waving his hands, first to Helen, and then to Sir James. "They won't hurt you. Come on."

The effect of the boy's shout was to make the spot where he now knelt down by Edgar Danby the centre upon which the spectators sought to gather. Helen set off first; Sir James, feeling very nervous, followed her example;

and the drove of bullocks, with quivering tails and moistening nostrils, also began to trot back, while Dexter got one arm beneath the insensible boy, and tried hard to lift him, and carry him to the stile nearest the town.

But the Union diet had not supplied him with sufficient muscle, and after getting the boy well on his shoulder, and staggering along a few paces, he stopped.

"Oh, I say," he muttered; "ain't he jolly heavy?"

A bellow from the leader of the bullocks made Dexter look round, and take in the position, which was that the drove were again approaching, and that this combined movement had had the effect of making Helen and Sir James both stop some forty yards away.

"Here, come on!" cried Dexter. "I'll see as they don't hurt you." And Helen obeyed; but Sir James hesitated, till, having somewhat recovered his nerve, and moved by shame at seeing a young girl and a boy perform what was naturally his duty, he came on slowly, and with no little trepidation, toward where Dexter was waiting with his son.

"That's right!" cried Dexter. "Come along. You come and carry him. I ain't strong enough. I'll soon send them off."

The situation was ludicrous enough, and Sir James was angry with himself; but all the same there was the nervous trepidation to overcome, and it was a very hard fight.

"Let me try and help you carry him," said Helen quickly.

"No, no; you can't," cried the boy. "Let him. Oh, don't I wish I'd got a stick. Here, ketch hold."

This last was to Sir James, whose face looked mottled as he came up. He obeyed the boy's command, though: took his son in his arms, and began to retreat with Helen toward the stile.

Meanwhile the bullocks were coming on in their customary stupid way.

"That's right; you go, sir," cried Dexter. "I'll talk to them," and, to Helen's horror, he went down on his hands and knees and ran at the drove, imitating the barking of a dog, not very naturally, but sufficiently true to life to make the drove turn tail again and gallop off, their flight being hastened by the flight of Edgar's damaged hat, which Dexter picked up and sent flying after them, and spinning through the air like a black firework till it dropped.

"'Tain't no good now," said the boy, laughing to himself; "and never was much good. Only done for a cockshy. I'll take them back, though."

This last was in allusion to the broken stick, which he picked up, and directly after found Master Edgar's tasselled cane, armed with which he beat a retreat toward the group making for the stile, with Helen beckoning to him to come.

The bullocks made one more clumsy charge down, but the imitation dog got up by Dexter was enough to check them, and the stile was crossed in safety just as a butcher's man in blue, followed by a big rough dog, came in sight.

Sir James was at first too indignant and too much upset to speak to the man.

"It's of no use, Miss Grayson," he said, "but his master shall certainly be summoned for this. How dare he place those ferocious bulls in a field through which there is a right of way? O my poor boy! my poor boy! He's dead!—he's dead!"

"He ain't," said Dexter sharply.

"Shall I carry him, sir?" said the butcher's man, forgetful of the fact that he would come off terribly greasy on the helpless boy's black clothes.

"No, man," cried Sir James. "Go and watch over those ferocious beasts, and see that they do not injure any one else."

"Did they hurt him, sir!" said the man eagerly.

"Hurt him! Look," cried Sir James indignantly.

"He ain't hurt," said Dexter sturdily. "Only frightened. There was a chap at our school used to go like that. He's fainting, that's what he is doing. You lay him down, and wait till I come back."

Dexter ran to the river, and, without a moment's hesitation, plunged in his new cap, and brought it back, streaming and dripping, with as much water as he could scoop up.

Too nervous even to oppose the boy's order, Sir James had lowered his son to the ground, and, as he lay on the grass, Helen bathed and splashed his face with the water, till it was gone.

"I'll soon fetch some more," cried Dexter.

But it was not needed, for just then Edgar opened his eyes, looked wildly round, as if not comprehending where he was, and then exclaimed with a sob—

"Where's the bull?"

"Hush! hush! my boy; you are safe now; thanks to the bravery of this gallant lad."

Dexter puckered up his forehead and stared.

"Where's my hat!" cried Edgar piteously.

"Scrunched," said Dexter shortly. "Bullocks trod on it."

"And my silver-topped cane!"

"There it lies on the grass," said Dexter, stooping down and picking it up.

"Oh, look at my jacket and my trousers," cried Edgar. "What a mess I'm in!"

"Never mind, my boy; we will soon set that right," said Sir James. "There, try and stand up. If you can walk home it will be all the better now."

"The brutes!" cried Edgar, with a passionate burst of tears.

"Do you feel hurt anywhere?" said Helen kindly.

"I don't know," said the boy faintly, as he rose and took his father's arm.

"Can I help you, Sir James?" said Helen.

"No, no, my dear Miss Grayson, we are so near home, and we will go in by the back way, so as not to call attention. I can never thank you sufficiently for your kindness, nor this brave boy for his gallantry. Good-bye. Edgar is better now. Good-bye."

He shook hands warmly with both.

"Shake hands with Miss Grayson, Eddy," said Sir James, while the butcher's man sat on the stile and lit his pipe.

Edgar obeyed.

"Now with your gallant preserver," said Sir James.

Edgar, who looked extremely damp and limp, put out a hand unwillingly, and Dexter just touched it, and let his own fall.

"You shall hear from me again, my man," said Sir James, now once more himself; and he spoke with great dignity. "Good day, Miss Grayson, and thanks."

He went on quickly with his son, while Helen and Dexter took another footpath, leading to a stile which opened upon the road.

As they reached this, Dexter laid his arm upon the top rail, and his forehead upon his wrist.

"What is the matter, Dexter?" cried Helen, in alarm.

"Nothing: I was only laughing," said the boy, whose shoulders were shaking with suppressed mirth.

"Laughing?"

"Yes. What a game! They were both afraid of the bullocks, and you've only got to go right at 'em, and they're sure to run."

"I think you behaved very bravely, Dexter," said Helen warmly; "and as I've scolded you sometimes, it is only fair that when I can I ought to praise. You were very brave indeed."

"Tchah! that isn't being brave," said the boy, whose face was scarlet. "Why, anybody could scare a few bullocks."

"Yes, but anybody would not," said Helen, smiling. "There, let's make haste home. I was very much frightened too."

"Were you!" said Dexter, with wide open eyes.

"Yes; weren't you?"

"No," said Dexter; "there wasn't anything to be frightened about then. But I'm frightened now."

"Indeed! What, now the danger is past?"

"No, not about that."

"What then, Dexter?"

"Look at my new cap."

He held up his drenched head-covering, all wet, muddy at the bottom, and out of shape.

"'Tain't so bad as his chimney-pot hat, but it's awful, ain't it? What will he say?"

"Papa? Only that you behaved exceedingly well, Dexter. He will be very pleased."

"Think he will?"

"Yes; and you shall have a new cap at once."

"Let's make haste back, then," cried the boy eagerly, "for I'm as hungry as never was. But you're sure he won't be cross?"

"Certain, Dexter. I will answer for that."

"All right. Come along. I was afraid I was in for it again."

Chapter Fourteen
Mr Dengate is Indignant, And Dexter wants some "Wums"

Mr Grayson was delighted when he heard the narrative from Helen.

"There! what did I tell you!" he cried. "Proofs of my theory."

"Do you think so, papa?"

"Think, my dear? I'm sure. Why, there it all was; what could have been better? Young Danby has breed in him, and what did he do? Lay down like a girl, and fainted. No, my dear, you cannot get over it. Pick your subject if you will, but you may make what you like of a boy."

"I hope so, papa."

"That's right, my dear. Brave little fellow! Afraid I should scold him about his cap? Thoughtless young dog, but it was all chivalrous. Couldn't have been better. He shall have a hundred caps if he likes. Hah! I'm on the right track, I'm sure."

The doctor rubbed his hands and chuckled, and Helen went to bed that night better pleased with her task.

Sir James Danby, who was the magnate of Coleby, sent a very furious letter to Dengate the butcher, threatening proceedings against him for allowing a herd of dangerous bullocks to be at large in one of his fields, and ordering him to remove them at once.

Dengate the butcher read the letter, grew red in the face, and, after buttoning up that letter in his breast-pocket, he put on his greasy cap, and went to Topley the barber to get shaved.

Dengate's cap was greasy because, though he was a wealthy man, he worked hard at his trade, calling for orders, delivering meat, and always twice a week, to use his own words, "killing hisself."

Topley lathered Dengate's red round face, and scraped it perfectly clean, feeling it all over with his soapy fingers, as well as carefully inspecting it with his eye, to make sure that none of the very bristly stubble was left.

While Topley shaved, Dengate made plans, and as soon as the operation was over he went back home, and what he called "cleaned hisself." That is to say, he put on his best clothes, stuck a large showy flower in his buttonhole, cocked his rather broad-brimmed hat on one side of his head, and went straight to Dr Grayson's.

Maria opened the door, stared at the butcher, who generally came to the back entrance, admitted him, received his message, and went into the study, where the doctor was writing, and Dexter busily copying a letter in a fairly neat round hand, but could only on an average get one word and a half in a line, a fact which looked awkward, especially as Dexter cut his words anywhere without studying the syllables.

Dexter had just left off at the end of a line, and finished the first letters of the word toothache, leaving "toot" as his division, and taking a fresh dip of ink ready for writing "hache."

"Don't put your tongue out, Dexter, my boy."

"All right," said Dexter.

"And I would not suck the pen. Ink is not wholesome."

"All right, I won't," said Dexter; and he put the nibs between his lips.

"Mr Dengate, sir," said Maria.

"Dengate? What does he want, Maria? Let him see Mrs Millett or Miss Helen."

Maria looked scornfully at Dexter, as if he had injured her in some way.

"Which is what I said to him, sir. 'Master's busy writing,' I says; but he says his dooty, sir, and if you would see him five minutes he would be greatly obligated."

The doctor said, "Send him in."

Maria left the room, and there was a tremendous sound of wiping shoes all over the mat, although it was a dry day without, and the butcher's boots were speckless.

Then there was another burst of wiping on the mat by the study door as a finish off, a loud muttering of instructions to Maria, and the door was opened to admit the butcher, looking hot and red, with his hat in one hand, a glaring orange handkerchief in the other, with which he dabbed himself from time to time.

"Good morning, Dengate," said the doctor; "what can I do for you?"

"Good morning, sir; hope you're quite well, sir. If you wouldn't mind, sir, reading this letter, sir. Received this morning, sir. Sir James, sir."

"Read it? ah, yes," said the doctor.

He ran through the missive and frowned.

"Well, Dengate," he said, "Sir James is a near neighbour and friend of mine, and I don't like to interfere in these matters."

"No, sir, of course you wouldn't, sir, but as a gentleman, sir, as I holds in the highest respect—a gentleman as runs a heavy bill with me."

"Hasn't your account been paid, Dengate!" said the doctor, frowning, while Dexter looked hard at the butcher, and wondered why his face was so red, and why little drops like beads formed all over his forehead.

"No, sir, it hasn't, sir," said the butcher, with a chuckle, "and I'm glad of it. I never ask for your account, sir, till it gets lumpy. I always leave it till I want it, for it's good as the bank to me, and I know I've only to give you a hint like, and there it is."

"Humph!" ejaculated the doctor.

"What I have come about is them bullocks, sir, hearing as your young lady, sir, and young shaver here—"

"Mr Dengate," said the doctor, frowning, "this young gentleman is my adopted son."

"Beg pardon, sir, I'm sure," said the butcher obsequiously. "I had heared as you'd had taken a boy from the—"

"Never mind that, Dengate," said the doctor shortly, as the butcher dabbed himself hurriedly,—"business."

"Exactly, sir. Well, sir, it's like this here: I'm the last man in the world to put dangerous beasts in any one's way, and if I knowed that any one o' them was the least bit risky to a human being, he'd be bullock to-day and beef to-morrow. D'yer see?"

"Yes, of course," said the doctor, "and very proper."

"But what I holds is, sir, and my man too says is, that there ain't a bit o' danger in any on 'em, though if there was nobody ought to complain."

"Well, there I don't agree with you, Dengate," said the doctor haughtily, as Dexter came and stood by him, having grown deeply interested.

"Don't you, sir? Well, then, look here," said the butcher, rolling his yellow handkerchief into a cannon ball and ramming it into his hat, as if it were a cannon that he now held beneath his left arm. "There's a path certainly from stile to stile, but it only leads to my farrest medder, and though I never says nothing to nobody who thinks it's a nice walk down there by the river to fish or pick flowers or what not, though they often tramples my medder grass in a way as is sorrowful to see, they're my medders, and the writing's in my strong-box, and not a shilling on 'em. All freehold, seven-and-twenty acres, and everybody as goes on is a trespasser, so what do you say to that?"

The butcher unloaded the imaginary cannon as he said this triumphantly, and dabbed his face with the ball.

"Say?" said the doctor, smiling; "why, that I'm a trespasser sometimes, for I like to go down there for a walk. It's the prettiest bit out of the town."

"Proud to hear you say so, sir," said the butcher eagerly. "It is, isn't it? and I'm proud to have you go for a walk there, sir. Honoured, I'm sure, and if the—er—the young gentleman likes to pick a spot out to keep ground baited for a bit o' fishing, why, he's hearty welcome, and my man shall save him as many maddicks for bait as ever he likes."

"I'll come," cried Dexter eagerly. "May I go?" he added.

"Yes, yes; we'll see," said the doctor; "and it's very kind of Mr Dengate to give you leave."

"Oh, that's nothing, sir. He's welcome as the flowers in May; but what I wanted to say, sir, was that as they're my fields, and people who comes is only trespassers, I've a right to put anything I like there. I don't put danger for the public: they comes to the danger."

"Yes; that's true," said the doctor. "Of course, now you mention it, there's no right of way."

"Not a bit, sir, and I might turn out old Billy, if I liked."

"I say, who is old Billy?" said Dexter.

"Hush, my boy! Don't interpose when people are speaking."

"Oh, let him talk, sir," said the butcher, good-naturedly. "I like to hear a boy want to know. It's what my boy won't do. He's asleep half his time, and I feed him well too."

"Humph!" ejaculated the doctor.

"Billy's my old bull, as I always keeps shut up close in my yard, because he is dangerous."

"And very properly," said the doctor.

"Quite right, sir, quite right; and I want to know then what right Sir James has to come ordering me about. He's no customer of mine. Took it all away and give it to Mossetts, because he said the mutton was woolly, when I give you my word, sir, that it was as good a bit o' mutton as I ever killed."

"Yes, yes, Dengate, but what has all this to do with me?" said the doctor testily.

"Well, sir, begging your pardon, only this: your young lady and young gentleman was there, and I want to know the rights of it all. My man says the beasts are quiet enough, only playful, and I say the same; but I may be making a mistake. I went in the medder this morning, with my boy Ezry, and he could drive 'em anywheres, and he's only ten. Did they trouble your young folks, sir?"

"Well, Dexter: you can answer that," said the doctor.

"Trouble us?—no!" said Dexter, laughing. "Miss Grayson was a bit afraid of 'em, but I ran the big one, and he galloped off across the fields."

"There," said the butcher; "what did I say? Bit playful, that's all."

"And when we heard a noise, and found one of 'em standing over that young Danby, he was only turning him over, that's all."

"Yes; he was running away, and fell down, and the beasts came to look at him," said Dengate, laughing.

"And Sir James was over on the stile calling for help. Why, as soon as I ran at the bullocks they all galloped off, all but the big one, and I give him a crack on the horn, and soon made him go."

"Of course. Why, a child would make 'em run. That's all, sir, I only wanted to know whether they really was dangerous, because if they had been, as I said afore, bullock it is now, but beef it should be. Good morning, sir."

"What are you going to do!" said the doctor.

"Do, sir? I'm a-going to let Sir James do his worst. My beasts ain't dangerous, and they ain't on a public road, so there they stay till I want 'em for the shop. Morning, young—er—gentleman. You're not afraid of a bullock?"

"No," said Dexter quietly, "I don't think I am."

"I'm sure you ain't, my lad, if you'll 'scuse me calling you so. Morning, sir, morning."

The butcher backed out, smiling triumphantly, but only to put his head in again—

"Beg pardon, sir, only to say that if he'd asked me polite like, I'd ha' done it directly; but he didn't, and I'll stand upon my medder like a man."

"Humph!" said the doctor, as soon as they were alone; "and so you were not afraid of the bullocks, Dexter?"

"There wasn't anything to be afraid of," said the boy. "I'm ever so much more afraid of you."

"Afraid?"

"Yes, when you look cross, sir, only then."

"Well, you must not make me look cross, Dexter; and now get on with your copying. When you've done that you may go in the garden if you'll keep out of mischief."

"And when may I go fishing?"

"When you like."

"Down the meadows!"

"Why not fish down the garden; there's a capital place."

"All right," said Dexter. "I'll go there. But I want a rod and line."

"There is an old rod in the hall, and you can buy a line. No, Helen is going out, and she will buy you one."

Dexter's eyes glistened at the idea of going fishing, and he set to work most industriously at the copying, which in due time he handed over to the Doctor, who expressed himself as highly satisfied: though if he really was, he was easily pleased.

Helen had received her instructions, and she soon afterwards returned with the fishing-line, and a fair supply of extra hooks, and odds and ends, which the doctor, as an old angler, had suggested.

"These—all for me!" cried the boy joyfully.

The doctor nodded.

"Recollect: no mischief, and don't tumble in."

"All right, sir," cried the boy, who was gloating over the new silk line, with its cork float glistening in blue and white paint brought well up with varnish.

"Do you know how to fish!"

"Yes, I know all about it, sir."

"How's that? You never went fishing at the workhouse."

"No, sir; but old Dimsted in the House used to tell us boys all about it, and how he used to catch jack and eels, and roach and perch, in the river."

"Very well, then," said the doctor. "Now you can go."

Dexter went off in high glee, recalling divers instructions given by the venerable old pauper who had been a fishing idler all his life, the river always having more attractions for him than work. His son followed in his steps, and he again had a son with the imitative faculty, and spending every hour he could find at the river-side.

It was a well-known fact in Coleby that the Dimsteds always knew where fish was to be found, and the baskets they made took the place of meat that other fathers and sons of families would have earned.

Rod, line, and hooks are prime necessaries for fishing; but a fish rarely bites at a bare hook, so one of Dexter's first proceedings was to obtain some bait.

Mr Dengate had said that his man should save plenty of gentles for him; but Dexter resolved not to wait for them that day, but to try what he could do with worms and paste. So his first proceeding was to appeal to Mrs Millett for a slice or two of bread.

Mrs Millett was not in the kitchen, but Maria was, and on being appealed to, she said sharply that she was not the cook.

Dexter looked puzzled, and he flushed a little as he wondered why it was that the maid looked so cross, and always answered him so snappishly.

Just then Mrs Millett, who was a plump elderly female with a pleasant countenance and expression, appeared in the doorway, and to her Dexter appealed in turn.

Mrs Millett had been disposed to look at Dexter from the point of view suggested by Maria, who had been making unpleasant allusions to the boy's birth and parentage, and above all to "Master's strange goings on," ever since Dexter's coming. Hence, then, the old lady, who looked upon herself as queen of the kitchen, had a sharp reproof on her tongue, and was about to ask the boy why he hadn't stopped in his own place, and rung for what he wanted. The frank happy expression on his face disarmed her, and she smiled and cut the required bread.

"Well, I never!" said Maria.

"Ah, my dear," said Mrs Millett; "I was young once, and I didn't like to be scolded. He isn't such a bad-looking boy after all, only he will keep apples in his bedroom, and make it smell."

"What's looks!" said Maria tartly, as she gave a candlestick she was cleaning a fierce rub.

"A deal, my dear, sometimes," said the old housekeeper. "Specially if they're sweet ones, and that's what yours are not now."

Dexter was not yet armed with all he wanted, for he was off down the kitchen-garden in search of worms.

His first idea was to get a spade and dig for himself; but the stern countenance of Dan'l Copestake rose up before him, and set him wondering what would be the consequences if he were to be found turning over some bed.

On second thoughts he determined to find the gardener and ask for permission, the dread of not succeeding in his mission making him for the moment more thoughtful.

Dan'l did not need much looking for. He had caught sight of Dexter as soon as he entered the garden, and gave vent to a grunt.

"Now, what mischief's he up to now?" he grumbled; and he set to and watched the boy while making believe to be busy cutting the dead leaves and flowers off certain plants.

He soon became aware of the fact that Dexter was searching for him, and this altered the case, for he changed his tactics, and kept on moving here and there, so as to avoid the boy.

"Here! Hi! Mr Copestake!" cried Dexter; but the old man had been suddenly smitten with that worst form of deafness peculiar to those who will not hear; and it was not until Dexter had pursued him round three or four beds, during which he seemed to be blind as well as deaf, that the old man was able to see him.

"Eh!" he said. "Master want me?"

"No. I'm going fishing; and, please, I want some worms."

"Wums? Did you say wums!" said Dan'l, affecting deafness, and holding his hand to his ear.

"Yes."

"Ay, you're right; they are," grumbled Dan'l. "Deal o' trouble, wums. Gets inter the flower-pots, and makes wum castesses all over the lawn, and they all has to be swept up."

"Yes; but I want some for fishing."

"'Ficient? Quite right, not sufficient help to get 'em swep' away."

"Will you dig a few worms for me, please?" shouted Dexter in the old man's ear.

"Dig wums? What for? Oh, I see, thou'rt going fishing. No; I can't stop."

"May I dig some!" cried Dexter; but Dan'l affected not to hear him, and went hurriedly away.

"He knew what I wanted all the time," said the boy to himself. "He don't like me no more than Maria does."

Just then he caught sight of Peter Cribb, who, whenever he was not busy in the stable, seemed to be chained to a birch broom.

"Will you dig a few worms for me, please?" said Dexter; "red ones."

"No; I'm sweeping," said the groom gruffly; and then, in the most inconsistent way, he changed his tone, for he had a weakness for the rod and line himself. "Going fishing!"

"Yes, if I can get some worms."

"Where's old Copestake!"

"Gone into the yard over there," said Dexter.

"All right. I'll dig you some. Go behind the wall there, by the cucumber frames. Got a pot!"

Dexter shook his head.

"All right. I'll bring one."

Dexter went to the appointed place, and in a few minutes Peter appeared, free from the broom now, and bearing a five-pronged fork and a small flower-pot; for the fact that the boy was a brother angler superseded the feeling of animosity against one who had so suddenly been raised from a lowly position and placed over his head.

Peter winked one eye as he scraped away some of the dry straw, and then turned over a quantity of the moist, rotten soil, displaying plenty of the glistening red worms suitable for the capture of roach and perch.

"There you are," he said, after putting an ample supply in the flower-pot, whose hole he had stopped with a piece of clay; "there's as many as you'll want; and now, you go and fish down in the deep hole, where the wall ends in the water, and I wish you luck."

Chapter Fifteen
Dexter makes a Friend

"I like him," said Dexter to himself, as he hurried down the garden, found the place, and for the next ten minutes he was busy fitting up his tackle, watching a boy on the other side of the river the while, as he sat in the meadow beneath a willow-tree fishing away, and every now and then capturing a small gudgeon or roach.

The river was about thirty yards broad at this spot, and as Dexter prepared his tackle and watched the boy opposite, the boy opposite fished and furtively watched Dexter.

He was a dark, snub-nosed boy, shabbily-dressed, and instead of being furnished with a bamboo rod and a new line with glistening float, he had a rough home-made hazel affair in three pieces, spliced together, but fairly elastic; his float was a common quill, and his line of so many hairs pulled out of a horse's tail, and joined together with a peculiarly fast knot.

Before Dexter was ready the shabby-looking boy on the other side had caught two more silvery roach, and Dexter's heart beat fast as he at last baited his hook and threw in the line as far as he could.

He was pretty successful in that effort, but his cork float and the shot made a loud splash, while the boy opposite uttered a chuckle.

"He's laughing at me," said Dexter to himself; and he tried the experiment of watching his float with one eye and the boy with the other, but the plan did not succeed, and he found himself gazing from one to the other, always hurriedly glancing back from the boy to the float, under the impression that it bobbed.

He knew it all by heart, having many a time drunk in old Dimsted's words, and he remembered that he could tell what fish was biting by the way the float moved. If it was a bream, it would throw the float up so that it lay flat on the water. If it was a roach, it would give a short quick bob. If it was a perch, it would give a bob, and then a series of sharp quick bobs, the last of which would be right under, while if it was a tench, it would glide slowly away.

But the float did nothing but float, and nothing in the way of bobbing, while the shabby boy on the other side kept on striking, and every now and then hooking a fish.

"Isn't he lucky!" thought Dexter, and he pulled out his line to find that the bait had gone.

He began busily renewing it in a very *nonchalant* manner, as he was conscious of the fact that the boy was watching him keenly with critical eyes.

Dexter threw in again; but there was no bite, and as the time went on, it seemed as if all the fish had been attracted to the other side of the river, where the shabby-looking boy, who fished skilfully and well, kept on capturing something at the rate of about one every five minutes.

They were not large, but still they were fish, and it was most tantalising to one to be patiently waiting, while the other was busy landing and rebaiting and throwing in again.

At last a happy thought struck Dexter, and after shifting his float about from place to place, he waited till he saw the boy looking at him, and he said—

"I say?"

"Hullo!" came back, the voices easily passing across the water.

"What are you baiting with?"

"Gentles."

"Oh!"

Then there was a pause, and more fishing on one side, waiting on the other. At last the shabby boy said—

"You're baiting with worms, ain't you?"

"Yes."

"Ah, they won't bite at worms much this time o' day."

"Won't they?" said Dexter, putting out his line.

"No. And you ain't fishing deep enough."

"Ain't I!"

"No. Not by three foot."

"I wish I'd got some gentles," said Dexter at last.

"Do you!"

"Yes."

"Shall I shy some over in the box?"

"Can you throw so far?"

"Yers!" cried the shabby boy. "You'll give me the box again, won't you?"

"Yes; I'll throw it back."

The boy on the other side divided his bait by putting some in a piece of paper. Then putting a stone in his little round tin box, he walked back a few yards so as to give himself room, stepped forward, and threw the box right across, Dexter catching it easily.

"Now, you try one o' them," said the donor of the fresh bait.

Dexter eagerly did as was suggested, and five minutes after there was a sharp tug, which half drew his float below the surface.

"Why, you didn't strike," said the boy sharply.

"Well, you can't strike 'em till you've got hold of them," retorted Dexter; and the shabby-looking boy laughed.

"Yah!" he said; "you don't know how to fish."

"Don't I! Why, I was taught to fish by some one who knows all about it."

"So it seems," said the boy jeeringly. "Don't even know how to strike a fish. There, you've got another bite. Look at him; he's running away with it."

It was no credit to Dexter that he got hold of that fish, for the unfortunate roach had hooked itself.

As the float glided away beneath the surface, Dexter gave a tremendous snatch with the rod, and jerked the fish out of the water among the branches of an overhanging tree, where the line caught, and the captive hung suspended about a foot below a cluster of twigs, flapping about and trying to get itself free.

Dexter's fellow-fisherman burst into a roar of laughter, laid down his rod, and stamped about on the opposite bank slapping his knees, while the unlucky fisherman stood with his rod in his hand, jigging the line.

"You'll break it if you don't mind," cried the shabby boy.

"But I want to get it out."

"You shouldn't have struck so hard. Climb up the tree, get out on that branch, and reach down."

Dexter looked at the tree, which hung over the water to such an extent that it seemed as if his weight would tear it from its hold in the bank, while the water looked terribly deep and black beneath.

"I say," cried the shabby boy jeeringly; "who taught you how to fish!"

"Why, old Dimsted did, and he knew."

"Who did!" cried the boy excitedly.

"Old Dimsted."

"Yah! That he didn't. Why, he's been in the House these ten years—ever since I was quite a little un."

"Well, I know that," shouted back Dexter. "He taught me all the same."

"Why, how came you to know grandfather!" cried the shabby boy.

Dexter ceased pulling at the line, and looked across at his shabbily-dressed questioner. For the first time he glanced down at his well-made clothes, and compared his personal appearance with that of the boy opposite, and in a curiously subtle way he began to awake to the fact that he was growing ashamed of the workhouse, and the people in it.

"MY NAME'S DIMSTED—BOB DIMSTED."

"Yah! you didn't know grandfather," cried the boy mockingly; "and you don't know how to fish. Grandfather wouldn't have taught you to chuck a fish up in the tree. You should strike gently, like that."

He gave the top of his rod a slight, quick twitch, and hooked a good-sized roach. Dexter grinning to see him play it till it was feeble enough to be drawn to the side and lifted out.

"That's the way grandfather taught me how to fish," continued the boy, as he took the hook from the captive's mouth, "I say, what's your name!"

"Dexter Grayson," was the answer, for the boy felt keenly already that the names Obed Coleby were ones of which he could not be proud.

"Ever been in the workus!"

"Yes."

"Ever see grandfather there!"

"Yes, I've seen him," said Dexter, who felt no inclination to enlighten the boy further.

"Ah, he could fish," said the boy, baiting and throwing in again. "My name's Dimsted—Bob Dimsted. So's father's. He can fish as well as grandfather. So can I," he added modestly; "there ain't a good place nowheres in the river as we don't know. I could take you where you could ketch fish every swim."

"Could you?" said Dexter, who seemed awed in the presence of so much knowledge.

"Course I could, any day."

"And will you?" said Dexter eagerly.

"Ah dunno," said the boy, striking and missing another fish. "You wouldn't care to go along o' me?"

"Yes, I should—fishing," cried Dexter. "But my line's fast."

"Why don't you climb up and get it then? Ain't afraid, are you!"

"What, to climb that tree?" cried Dexter. "Not I;" and laying the rod down with the butt resting on the bank, he began to climb at once.

"Mind yer don't tumble in," cried Bob Dimsted; "some o' them boughs gets very rotten—like touchwood."

"All right," said Dexter; and he climbed steadily on in happy ignorance of the fact that the greeny lichen and growth was not good for dark cloth trousers and vests. But the bole of the tree was short, for it had been pollarded, and in a minute or two he was in a nest of branches, several of which protruded over the water, the one in particular which had entangled the fishing-line being not even horizontal, but dipping toward the surface.

"That's the way," shouted Bob Dimsted. "Look sharp, they're biting like fun."

"Think it'll bear?" said Dexter.

"Bear? Yes; half a dozen on yer. Sit on it striddling, and work yourself along till you can reach the line. Got a knife?"

"Yes."

"Then go right out, and when you git far enough cut off the little bough, and let it all drop into the water."

"Why, then, I should lose the fish."

"Not you. Ain't he hooked? You do as I say, and then git back, and you can pull all out together."

Dexter bestrode the branch, and worked himself along further and further till an ominous crack made him pause.

"Go on," shouted the boy from the other side.

"He'll think I'm a coward if I don't," said Dexter to himself, and he worked himself along for another three feet, with the silvery fish just before him, seeming to tempt him on.

"There, you can reach him now, can't you?" cried the boy.

"Yes; I think I can reach him now," said Dexter. "Wait till I get out my knife."

It was not so easy to get out that knife, and to open it, as it would have been on land. The position was awkward; the branch dipped at a great slope now toward the water, and Dexter's trousers were not only drawn half-way up his legs, but drawn so tightly by his attitude that he could hardly get his hand into his pocket.

It was done though at last, the thin bough in which the line was tangled seized by the left hand, while the right cut vigorously with the knife.

It would have been far easier to have disentangled the line, but Bob Dimsted was a learned fisher, and he had laid down the law. So Dexter cut and cut into the soft green wood till he got through the little bough all but one thin piece of succulent bark, dancing up and down the while over the deep water some fifteen feet from the bank.

Soss!

That last vigorous cut did it, and the bough, with its summer burden of leaves, dropped with a splash into the water.

"There! What did I tell you!" cried Dexter's mentor. "Now you can get back and pull all out together. Fish won't bite for a bit after this, but they'll be all right soon."

Dexter shut up his knife, thrust it as well as he could into his pocket, and prepared to return.

This was not so easy, for he had to go backwards. What was more, he had to progress up hill. But, nothing daunted, he took tight hold with his hands, bore down upon them, and was in the act of thrusting himself along a few inches, when—*Crack!*

One loud, sharp, splintering crack, and the branch, which was rotten three parts through, broke short off close to the trunk, and like an echo to the crack came a tremendous—*Plash!*

That water, as already intimated, was deep, and, as a consequence, there was a tremendous splash, and branch and its rider went down right out of sight, twig after twig disappearing leisurely in the eddying swirl.

Chapter Sixteen
"Them as is born to be hanged"

It might have been presumed that Bob Dimsted would either have tried to render some assistance or else have raised an alarm.

Bob Dimsted did nothing of the kind.

For certain reasons of his own, and as one who had too frequently been in the hot water of trouble, Master Bob thought only of himself, and catching his line in his hand as he quickly drew it from the water, he hastily gathered up his fishing paraphernalia, and ran off as hard as he could go.

He had time, however, to see Dexter's wet head rise to the surface and then go down again, for the unwilling bather had one leg hooked in the bough, which took him down once more, as it yielded to the current, and the consequence was that when Dexter rose, breathless and half-strangled, he was fifty yards down the stream.

But he was now free, and giving his head a shake, he trod the water for a few moments, and then struck out for the shore, swimming as easily as a frog.

A few sturdy strokes took him out of the sharp current and into an eddy near the bank, by whose help he soon reached the deep still water, swimming so vigorously that before long he was abreast of the doctor's garden, where a group beneath the trees startled him more than his involuntary plunge.

For there, in a state of the greatest excitement, were the doctor and Helen, with Peter Cribb, with a clothes-prop to be used for a different purpose now.

Further behind was Dan'l Copestake, who came panting up with the longest handled rake just as Dexter was nearing the bank.

"Will he be drowned?" whispered Helen, as she held tightly by her father's arm.

"No; he swims like a water-rat," said the doctor.

"No, no," shouted Dexter, beginning to splash the water, and sheering off as he saw Dan'l about to make a dab at him with the rake.

There was more zeal than discretion in the gardener's use of this implement, for it splashed down into the water heavily, the teeth nearly catching the boy's head.

"Here, catch hold of this," cried Peter Cribb.

"No, no; let me be," cried Dexter, declining the offer of the clothes-prop, as he had avoided it before when he was on the top of the wall. "I can swim ashore if you'll let me be."

This was so self-evident that the doctor checked Dan'l as he was about to make another skull-fracturing dash with the rake; and the next minute Dexter's hand clutched the grass on the bank, and he crawled out, with the water streaming down out of his clothes, and his short hair gummed, as it were, to his head.

"Here!" he cried; "where's my fish?"

"Fish, sir!" cried the doctor; "you ought to be very thankful that you've saved your life."

"O Dexter!" cried Helen.

"I say, don't touch me," cried the boy, as she caught at his hand. "I'm so jolly wet."

He was like a sponge just lifted out of a pail, and already about him there was a pool.

"Here, quick, sir; run up to the house and change your clothes," cried the doctor.

"But I must get my fish, sir."

"Fish!" cried the doctor angrily; "that's not the way to fish."

"Yes, it was, sir; and I caught one."

"You caught one!"

"Yes, sir; a beauty."

"Look here, Dexter," cried the doctor, catching him by his wet arm; "do you mean to tell me that you dived into the river like that and caught a fish!"

"No, sir; I fell in when I was getting my line out of the tree."

"Oh, I see."

"Beg pardon, sir," said Dan'l sourly; "but he've broke a great branch off this here tree."

"Well, I couldn't help it," said Dexter, in an ill-used tone. "I caught my line in the tree, and was obliged to get up and fetch it, and—stop a minute. I can see it. All right."

He ran off along the river-bank till they saw him stoop just where the wall dipped down into the river. There he found the rod floating close to the edge, and, securing it, he soon after drew in the loose branch he had cut off the tree, and disentangled his line, with the little roach still on the hook.

"There!" he cried in triumph, as he ran back with rod, line, and fish; "look at that, Miss Grayson, isn't it a beauty, and— What are you laughing at!"

This was at Peter Cribb, who was grinning hugely, but who turned away, followed by Dan'l.

"Them as is born to be hanged'll never be drowned," grumbled the old gardener sourly, as the two men went away.

"No fear of him being drowned," said Peter. "Swims like a cork."

"It's disgusting; that's what I say it is," growled Dan'l; "disgusting."

"What's disgusting?" said Peter.

"Why, they cuddles and makes a fuss over a boy as is a reg'lar noosance about the place, just as any other varmint would be. Wish he had drowned himself. What call was there for me to come and bring a rake!"

"Ah, he's a rum un, that he is," said Peter. "And master's a rum un; and how they can take to that boy, Miss Helen specially, and have him here's more'n I can understand. It caps me, that it do."

"Wait a bit, my lad, and you'll see," cried the old gardener. "He's begun his games just as such a boy would, and afore long this here garden will be turned into such a wreck as'll make the doctor tear his hair, and wish as he'd never seen the young rascal. He's a bad un; you can see it in his eye. He's got bad blood in him, and bad blood allus comes out sooner or later. Peter Cribb, my lad—"

"Yes."

"We're getting old fellow-servants, though you're only young. Peter, my lad, I'm beginning to tremble for my fruit."

"Eh?"

"Yes; that I am, my lad," said Dan'l in a whisper. "Just as I expected—I was watching of him—that rip's took up with bad company, Poacher Dimsted's boy; and that means evil. They was talking together, and then young Dimsted see me, and run away."

"Did he?"

"Did he? Yes, he just did; and you mark my words, Peter Cribb, it will not be long before the gov'ner gets rid of him."

"Oh yes; it's a very beautiful fish," said the doctor testily; "but make haste in. There, run and get all your wet things off as quickly as you can."

Dexter was so deeply interested in the silvery scales and graceful shape of his fish that he hardly heard the doctor's words, which had to be repeated before the boy started, nodded shortly, and ran off toward the house, while his patron walked to a garden chair, sat down, and gazed up at Helen in a perplexed way.

Helen did not speak, but gazed back at her father with a suppressed laugh twinkling about the corners of her lips.

"You're laughing at me, my dear," said the doctor at last; "but you mark my words—what I say is true. All this is merely the froth of the boy's nature, of which he is getting rid. But tut, tut, tut! All this must be stopped. First a new cap destroyed by being turned into a bucket, and now a suit of clothes gone."

"They will do for a garden suit, papa," said Helen, speaking as if she had had charge of boys for years.

"Well, yes: I suppose so," said the doctor. "But there: I am not going to worry myself about trifles. The cost of a few suits of clothes are as nothing compared to the success of my scheme. Now let's go in and see if the young dog has gone to work to change his things."

The doctor rose and walked up the garden, making comments to his daughter about the course of instruction he intended to pursue with Dexter, and on reaching the house and finding that the object of his thoughts was in his bedroom, he went on to the study just as Maria came from the front door with a letter.

"Letter, eh? Oh, I see. From Lady Danby!"

The doctor opened the letter.

"Any one waiting!" he said.

"Yes, sir. Groom waiting for an answer."

"I'll ring, Maria," said the doctor, and then he smiled and looked pleased. "There, my deaf," he cried, tossing the note to his daughter. "Now I call that very kind and neighbourly. You see, Sir James and Lady Danby feel and appreciate the fine manly conduct of Dexter over that cattle, and they very wisely think that he not only deserves great commendation, but that the present is a favourable opportunity for beginning an intimacy and companionship."

"Yes, papa," said Helen, with rather a troubled look.

"Danby sees that he was wrong, and is holding out the right hand of good fellowship. Depend upon it that we shall have a strong tie between those two boys. They will go to a public school together, help one another with their studies, and become friends for life. Hah! Yes. Sit down, my dear," continued the doctor, rubbing his hands. "My kind regards to Sir James and Lady Danby, that I greatly appreciate their kindness, and that Dexter shall come and spend the day with Edgar on Friday."

Helen wrote the note, which was despatched, and the doctor smiled, and looked highly satisfied.

"You remember how obstinate Sir James was about boys?"

"Yes, papa. I heard a part of the conversation, and you told me the rest."

"To be sure. You see my selection was right. Dexter behaved like a little hero over that adventure."

"Yes," said Helen; "he was as brave as could be."

"Exactly. All justification of my choice. I don't want to prophesy, Helen, but there will be a strong friendship between those boys from that day. Edgar, the weak, well-born boy, will always recognise the manly confidence of Dexter, the er—er, well, low-born boy, who in turn will have his sympathies aroused by his companion's want of—er—well, say, ballast."

"Possibly, papa."

"My dear Helen, don't speak like that," said the doctor pettishly. "You are so fond of playing wet blanket to all my plans."

"Oh no, papa; I am sure I will help you, and am helping you, in all this, but it is not in my nature to be so sanguine."

"Ah, well, never mind that. But you do like Dexter!"

"Yes; I am beginning to like him more and more."

"That's right. I'm very, very glad, and I feel quite grateful to the Danbys. You must give Dexter a few hints about behaving himself, and, so to speak, keeping down his exuberance when he is there."

"May I say a word, papa!"

"Certainly, my dear; of course."

"Well, then, I have an idea of my own with respect to Dexter."

"Ah, that's right," said the doctor, smiling and rubbing his hands. "What is it!"

"I have been thinking over it all a great deal, dear," said Helen, going to her father's side and resting her hand upon his shoulder; "and it seems to me that the way to alter and improve Dexter will be by example."

"Ah yes, I see; example better than precept, eh!"

"Yes. So far his life has been one of repression and the severest discipline."

"Yes, of course. Cut down; tied down, and his natural growth stopped. Consequently wild young shoots have thrust themselves out of his nature."

"That is what I mean."

"Quite right, my dear; then we will give him as much freedom as we can. You will give him a hint or two, though."

"I will do everything I can, papa, to make him presentable."

"Thank you, my dear. Yes, these boys will become great companions, I can see. Brave little fellow! I am very, very much pleased."

The doctor forgot all about the broken branch, and Dexter's spoiled suit of clothes, and Helen went to see whether the boy had obeyed the last command.

Chapter Seventeen
Dan'l is too Attentive

Things were not quite so smooth as Dr Grayson thought, for there had been stormy weather at Sir James's.

"Well, my dear, you are my husband, and it is my duty to obey," said Lady Danby; "but I do protest against my darling son being forced to associate with a boy of an exceedingly low type."

"Allow me, my dear," said Sir James importantly. "By Dr Grayson's act, in taking that boy into his house, he has wiped away any stigma which may cling to him; and I must say that the lad displayed a great deal of animal courage—that kind of brute courage which comes from an ignorance of danger."

"Is it animal courage not to be afraid of animals, ma?" said Master Edgar.

"Yes, my dear, of course," said Lady Danby.

"I wish Edgar would display courage of any kind," said Sir James.

"Why, you ran away from the bulls too, papa," said Master Edgar.

"I am a great sufferer from nervousness, Edgar," said Sir James reprovingly; "but we were not discussing that question. Dr Grayson has accepted the invitation for his adopted son. It is his whim for the moment, and it is only becoming on my part to show that we are grateful for the way in which the boy behaved. By the time a month has gone by, I have no doubt that the boy will be back at the—the place from which he came; but while he is at Dr Grayson's I desire that he be treated as if he were Dr Grayson's son."

"Very well, James," said Lady Danby, in an ill-used tone of voice. "You are master here, and we must obey."

The day of the invitation arrived. Dexter was to be at Sir James's in time for lunch, and directly after breakfast he watched his opportunity and followed Helen into the drawing-room.

"I say," he said; "I can't go there, can I?"

"Why not?" said Helen.

"Lookye here."

"Why, Dexter!" cried Helen, laughing merrily; "what have you been doing!"

"Don't I look a guy!"

There was a change already in the boy's aspect; his face, short as the time had been, was beginning to show what fresh air and good feeding could achieve. His hair had altered very slightly, but still there was an alteration for the better, and his eyes looked brighter, but his general appearance was comical all the same.

Directly after breakfast he had rushed up to his room and put on the clothes in which he had taken his involuntary bath. These garments, as will be remembered, had been obtained in haste, and were of the kind known in the trade as "ready-mades," and in this case composed of a well-glazed and pressed material, containing just enough wool to hold together a great deal of shoddy.

The dip in the river had been too severe a test for the suit, especially as Maria had been put a little more out of temper than usual by having the garments handed to her to dry.

Maria's mother was a washerwoman who lived outside Coleby on the common, and gained her income by acting as laundress generally for all who would intrust her with their family linen; but she called herself in yellow letters on a brilliant scarlet ground a "clear starcher."

During Maria's early life at home she had had much experience in the ways of washing. She knew the smell of boiled soap. She had often watched the steam rising from the copper, and played among the clouds, and she well knew that the quickest way to dry anything that has been soaked is to give it a good wringing.

She had therefore given Dexter's new suit a good wringing, and wrung out of it a vast quantity of sticky dye which stained her hands. Then she had—grumbling bitterly all the time—given the jacket, vest, and trousers a good shake, and hung them over a clothes-horse as near to the fire as she could get them without singeing.

Mrs Millett told her to be sure and get them nice and dry, and Maria did get them "nice and dry."

And now Dexter had put them on and presented himself before Helen, suggesting that he looked a guy.

Certainly his appearance was suggestive of the stuffed effigy borne about on the fifth of November, for the garments were shrunken so that his arms and legs showed to a terrible extent, and Maria's wringing had given them curves and hollows never intended by the cutter, the worst one being in the form of a hump between the wearer's shoulders.

"The things are completely spoiled. You foolish boy to put them on."

"Then I can't go to that other house."

"Nonsense! You have the new clothes that came from the tailor's—those for which you were measured."

"Yes," said Dexter reluctantly; "but it's a pity to put on them. I may get 'em spoiled."

"Then you do not want to go, Dexter," said Helen, smiling.

"No," he cried eagerly. "Ask him to let me stop here."

"No, no," said Helen kindly. "Papa wishes you to go there; it is very kind of the Danbys to ask you, and I hope you will go, and behave very nicely, and make great friends with Edgar Danby."

"How?" said Dexter laconically.

"Well, as boys generally do. You must talk to him."

"What about?"

"Anything. Then you must play with him."

"What at?"

"Oh, he'll be sure to suggest something to play at."

"I don't think he will," said Dexter thoughtfully. "He don't look the sort of chap to."

"Don't say chap, Dexter; say boy."

"Sort of boy to play any games. He's what we used to call a soft Tommy sort of a chap—boy."

"Oh no, no, no! I don't suppose he will be rough, and care for boisterous sports; but he may prove to be a very pleasant companion for you."

Dexter shook his head.

"I don't think he'll like me."

"Nonsense! How can you tell that? Then they have a beautiful garden."

"Can't be such a nice one as this," said Dexter.

"Oh yes, it is; and it runs down to the river as this one does, and Sir James has a very nice boat."

"Boat!" cried Dexter, pricking up his ears. "And may you go in it!"

"Not by yourselves, I suppose. There, I'm sure you will enjoy your visit."

Dexter shook his head again.

"I say, you'll come too, won't you?" he cried eagerly.

"No, Dexter; not this time."

The boy's forehead grew wrinkled all over.

"Come, you are pretending that you do not want to go."

"I don't," said the boy, hanging his head. "I want to stay here along with you."

"Perhaps I should like you to stay, Dexter," said Helen; "but I wish you to go and behave nicely, and you can tell me all about it when you come back."

"And how soon may I come back?"

"I don't suppose till the evening, but we shall see. Now, go and change those things directly. What would papa say if he saw you?"

Dexter went slowly up to his room, and came down soon after to look for Helen.

He found her busy writing letters, so he went off on tiptoe to the study, where the doctor was deep in his book, writing with a very severe frown on his brow.

"Ah, Dexter," he said, looking up and running his eye critically over the boy, the result being very satisfactory. "Let's see, you are to be at Sir James's by half-past twelve. Now only ten. Go and amuse yourself in the garden, and don't get into mischief."

Dexter went back into the hall, obtained his cap, and went out through the glass door into the verandah, where the great wisteria hung a valance of lavender blossoms all along the edge.

"He always says don't get into mischief," thought the boy. "I don't want to get into mischief, I'm sure."

Half-way across the lawn he was startled by the sudden appearance of Dan'l, who started out upon him from behind a great evergreen shrub.

"What are you a-doing of now?" snarled Dan'l.

"I wasn't doing anything," said Dexter, staring.

"Then you were going to do something," cried the old man sharply. "Look here, young man; if you get meddling with anything in my garden there's going to be trouble, so mind that. I know what boys is, so none of your nonsense here."

He went off grumbling to another part of the garden, and Dexter felt disposed to go back indoors.

"He's watching me all the time," he thought to himself; "just as if I was going to steal something. He don't like me."

Dexter strolled on, and heard directly a regular rustling noise, which he recognised at once as the sound made by a broom sweeping grass, and sure enough, just inside the great laurel hedge, where a little green lawn was cut off from the rest of the garden, there was Peter Cribb, at his usual pursuit, sweeping all the sweet-scented cuttings of the grass.

Peter was a sweeper who was always on the look-out for an excuse. He was, so to speak, chained to that broom so many hours a day, and if he had been a galley slave, and the broom an oar, it is morally certain that he would have been beaten with many stripes, for he would have left off rowing whenever he could.

"Well, squire," he said, laying his hands one over the other on the top of the broom-handle.

"Well, Peter. How's the horse?"

"Grinding his corn, and enjoying himself," said Peter. "He's like you: a lucky one—plenty to eat and nothing to do."

"Don't you take him out for exercise?" said Dexter.

"Course I do. So do you go out for exercise."

"Think I could ride?" said Dexter.

"Dersay you could, if you could hold on."

"I should like to try."

"Go along with you!"

"But I should. Will you let me try!"

Peter shook his head, and began to examine his half-worn broom.

"I could hold on. Let me go with you next time!"

"Oh, but I go at ha'-past six, hours before you're awake. Young gents don't get up till eight."

"Why, I always wake at a quarter to six," said Dexter. "It seems the proper time to get up. I say, let me go with you."

"Here, I say, you, Peter," shouted Dan'l; "are you a-going to sweep that bit o' lawn, or am I to come and do it myself. Gawsiping about!"

"Hear that?" said Peter, beginning to make his broom swing round again. "There, you'd better be off, or you'll get me in a row."

Dexter sighed, for he seemed to be always the cause of trouble.

"I say," said Peter, as the boy was moving off; "going fishing again?"

"No; not now."

"You knows the way to fish, don't you? Goes in after them."

Dexter laughed, and went on down to the river, examined the place where the branch had broken off, and then gazed down into the clear water at the gliding fish, which seemed to move here and there with no more effort than a wave of the tail.

His next look was across the river in search of Bob Dimsted; but the shabby-looking boy was not fishing, and nowhere in sight either up or down the stream.

Dexter turned away with another sigh. The garden was very beautiful, but it seemed dull just then. He wanted some one to talk to, and if he went again to Peter, old Dan'l would shout and find fault.

"It don't matter which way I go," said Dexter, after a few minutes, during which time he had changed his place in the garden again and again; "that old man is always watching me to see what I am going to do."

He looked round at the flowers, at the coming fruit, at everything in turn, but the place seemed desolate, and in spite of himself he began thinking of his old companions at the great school, and wondering what they were doing.

Then he recalled that he was to go to Sir James Danby's soon, and he began to think of Edgar.

"I shan't like that chap," he said to himself. "I wonder whether he'll like me."

He was standing thinking deeply and gazing straight before him at the high red brick wall when he suddenly started, for there was a heavy step on the gravel.

Dan'l had come along the grass edge till he was close to the boy, and then stepped off heavily on to the path.

"They aren't ripe yet," he said with an unpleasant leer; "and you'd best let them alone."

Dexter walked quickly away, with his face scarlet, and a bitter feeling of annoyance which he could not master.

For the next quarter of an hour he was continually changing his position in the garden, but always to wake up to the fact that the old gardener was carrying out a purpose which he had confided to Peter.

This the boy soon learned, for after a time he suddenly encountered the groom, still busy with the broom.

"Why, hullo, youngster!" he said; "what's the matter!"

"Nothing," said Dexter, with his face growing a deeper scarlet.

"Oh yes, there is; I can see," cried Peter.

"Well, he's always watching me, and pretending that I'm getting into mischief, or trying to pick the fruit."

"Hah!" said Peter, with a laugh; "he told me he meant to keep his eye on you."

Just then there was a call for Dan'l from the direction of the house, and Mrs Millett was seen beyond a laurel hedge.

Directly after the old man went up to the house, and it seemed to Dexter as if a cloud had passed from across the sun. The garden appeared to have grown suddenly brighter, and the boy began to whistle as he went about in an aimless way, looking here and there for something to take his attention.

He was not long in finding it, for just at the back of the dense yew hedge there were half a dozen old-fashioned round-topped hives, whose occupants were busy going to and fro, save that at the hive nearest the cross-path a heavy cluster, betokening a late swarm, was hanging outside, looking like a double handful of bees.

Dexter knew a rhyme beginning—

"How doth the little busy bee—"

and he knew that bees made honey; but that was all he did know about their habits, save that they lived in hives; and he stood and stared at the cluster hanging outside.

"Why, they can't get in," he said to himself. "Hole's stopped up."

He stood still for a few minutes, and then, as he looked round, he caught sight of some bean-sticks—tall thin pieces of oak sapling, and drawing one of these out of the ground he rubbed the mould off the pointed end, and, as soon as it was clean, took hold of it, and returned to the hive, where he watched the clustering bees for a few minutes, and then, reaching over, he inserted the thin end of the long stick just by the opening to the hive, thrust it forward, and gave it a good rake to right and left.

There was a tremendous buzz and a rush, and the next moment Dexter, stick in hand, was running down the path toward the river, pursued by quite a cloud of angry bees.

Dexter ran fast, of course, and as it happened, right down one of the most shady paths, beneath the densely growing apple-trees, where the bees could not fly, so that by the time he reached the river-side he was clear of his pursuers, but tingling from a sting on the wrist, and from two more on the neck, one being among the hair at the back, and the other right down in his collar.

"Well, that's nice," he said, as he rubbed himself, and began mentally to try and do a sum in the Rule of Three—if three stings make so much pain, how much pain would be caused by the stings of a whole hiveful of bees?

"Bother the nasty vicious little things!" he cried, as he had another rub, and he threw the bean-stick angrily away.

"Don't hurt so much now," he said, after a few minutes' stamping about. Then his face broke up into a merry smile. "How they did make me run!"

Just then there was a shout—a yell, and a loud call for help.

Dexter forgot his own pain, and, alarmed by the cries, ran as hard as he could back again towards the spot from whence the sounds came, and to his horror found that Old Dan'l was running here and there, waving his arms, while Peter had come to his help, and was whisking his broom about in all directions.

For a few moments Dexter could not comprehend what was wrong, then, like a flash, he understood that the bees had attacked the old gardener, and that it was due to his having irritated them with the stick.

Dexter knew how a wasp's nest had been taken in the fields by the boys one day, and without a moment's hesitation he ran to the nearest shrub, tore off a good-sized bough, and joined in the task of beating down the bees.

It is pretty sport to fight either bees or wasps in this way, but it requires a great deal of courage, especially as the insects are sure to get the best of it, as they did in this case, putting their enemies to flight, their place of refuge being the tool-house, into whose dark recesses the bees did not attempt to come.

"Much stung, Dan'l!" said Peter.

"Much stung, indeed! I should think I am. Offle!"

"You got it much, youngster?" said Peter.

"I've got three stings," replied Dexter, who had escaped without further harm.

"And I've got five, I think," said Peter. "What was you doing to 'em, Dan'l!"

"Doin' to 'em!" growled Dan'l, who was stamping about and rubbing himself, and looking exceedingly like the bear in the old fable. "I wasn't doin' nothin' to 'em. One o' the hives have been threatenin' to swarm again, and I was just goin' by, when they come at me like a swarm o' savidges, just as if some one had been teasing them." Dexter was rubbing the back of his neck, and feeling horribly guilty, as he asked himself whether he had not better own to having disturbed the hive; but there was something so unpleasantly repellent about the old gardener, and he was looking so suspiciously from one to the other, that the boy felt as if he could not speak to him.

If it had been Peter, who, with all his roughness, seemed to be tolerant of his presence, he would have spoken out at once; but he could not to Dan'l, and he remained silent.

"They stings pretty sharp," said Peter, laughing. "Blue-bag's best thing. I shall go up and get Maria to touch mine up. Coming?"

"Nay, I'm not coming," growled Dan'l. "I can bear a sting or two of a bee without getting myself painted up with blue-bags. Dock leaves is good enough for me."

"And there aren't a dock left in the garden," said Peter. "You found fault with me for not pulling the last up."

So Peter went up to the house to be blue-bagged, Dan'l remained like a bear in his den, growling to himself, and Dexter, whose stings still throbbed, went off across the lawn to walk off the pain, till it was time to go to Sir James's.

"Who'd have thought that the little things could hurt so much!"

Then the pain began to diminish till it was only a tingle, and the spots where the stings went in were round and hard, and now it was that Dexter's conscience began to prick him as sharply as the bees' stings, and he walked about the garden trying to make up his mind as to whether he should go and confess to Dan'l that he stirred the bees up with a long stick.

But as soon as he felt that he would do this, something struck him that Dan'l would be sure to think he had done it all out of mischief, and he knew that he could not tell him.

"Nobody will know," he said to himself; "and I won't tell. I didn't mean to do any harm."

"Dexter! Dexter!"

He looked in the direction from whence the sounds came, and could see Helen waving her handkerchief, as a signal for him to come in.

"Time to go," he said to himself as he set off to her. "Nobody will know, so I shan't tell him."

And then he turned cold.

Only a few moments before he had left Dan'l growling in his den, and now here he was down the garden, stooping and picking up something.

For a few moments Dexter could not see what the something was, for the trees between them hindered the view, but directly after he made out that Dan'l had picked up a long stick, which had been thrown among the little apple-trees, and was carefully examining it.

The colour came into Dexter's cheeks as he wondered whether Dan'l would know where that stick came from.

The colour would have been deeper still had he known that Dan'l had a splendid memory, and knew exactly where every stick or plant should be. In fact, Dan'l recognised that stick as having been taken from the end of the scarlet-runner row.

"A young sperrit o' mischief! that's what he is," muttered the old man, giving a writhe as he felt the stinging of the bees. "Now what's he been up to with that there stick? making a fishing-rod of it, I s'pose, and tearing my rows o' beans to pieces. I tell him what it is—"

Dan'l stopped short, and stared at the end of the stick—the thin end, where there was something peculiar, betraying what had been done with it.

It was a sight which made him tighten his lips up into a thin red line, and screw up his eyes till they could be hardly seen, for upon the end of that stick were the mortal remains of two crushed bees.

Chapter Eighteen
Dexter spends a pleasant Afternoon

Dexter went up to where Helen was waiting for him, and found her dressed. "Going out!" he said.

"Yes; I thought I would walk up to Sir James's with you," she said; and she cast a critical eye over him, and smiled upon seeing that he only needed a touch with a brush to make him presentable.

This was given, and they set off together, the doctor only giving Dexter a friendly nod in accordance with a promise made not to upset the boy with a number of hints as to how he was to behave.

"It must come by degrees, papa," Helen said; "and any advice given now would only make him more conscious."

Dexter's hair still looked horribly short, but his face did not quite resemble now that of a boy who had just risen from a sick-bed. He looked brighter and more animated, and in nowise peculiar; but all the same, in their short walk, Helen was conscious of the fact that they were being observed by every one they passed, and that plenty of remarks were made.

All at once she noticed that Dexter as she was speaking to him gave quite a start, and following the direction of his eyes, she saw that he was looking at a rough-looking boy, who was approaching them with a fishing-rod over his shoulder, and a basket in his hand.

The boy's mouth widened into a grin as he passed, and Helen asked Dexter if he knew him, the friendly look he had given speaking volumes of a new difficulty likely to be in their way.

"I don't know whether I know him—or not," said Dexter. "I've spoken to him."

"Where? At the schools!"

"No; he was fishing on the other side of the river that day I tumbled in."

"Oh!" said Helen coldly. "Here we are."

She turned through a great iron gate, walked up a broad flight of steps, and knocked.

"There, Dexter," she said, as the door was opened. "I hope you will enjoy yourself."

"Ain't you going in with me!" he whispered excitedly, as a footman in a blue and yellow livery opened the door.

"No; good-bye."

She nodded pleasantly, and went down the steps, leaving Dexter face to face with the footman, who had become possessed of the news of the young guest's quality from no less a personage than Master Edgar himself.

"Will you come in, please," he said, drawing back, and holding the door open with an air that should have made him gain for wages—kicks.

Dexter said, "Yes, sir," as respectfully as if he were the workhouse porter, and took off his cap and went in.

"This way, hif you please," said the supercilious gentleman. "You may leave your cap here."

Dexter put down his cap, and followed the man to a door at the further end of the hall.

"What name!" said the footman.

Dexter stared at him.

"What name shall I announce?" said the man again with chilling dignity.

"Please, I don't know what you mean," said the boy, feeling very much confused.

The man smiled pityingly, and looked down with a most exasperating kind of condescension at the visitor,—in a way, in fact, that stamped him mentally as a brother in spirit, if not in flesh, of Maria, the doctor's maid.

"I 'ave to announce your name to her ladyship," said the footman.

"Oh, my name," cried Dexter, "Obed Cole—I mean Dexter Grayson."

He turned more red than ever in his confusion, and before he could say another word to add to his correction the door was thrown open.

"Master Obed Cole Dextry Grayson," said the footman, in a loud voice; and the boy found himself standing in a large handsomely furnished room in the presence of Lady Danby, who rose with a forced smile, and looked very limp.

"How do you do, Master Grayson!" she said sadly, and she held out her hand.

Dexter in his confusion made a dash at it, and caught it tightly, to find that it felt very limp and cold, but the sensation did not last long, for the thin white fingers were snatched away.

"Eddy, dear," said Lady Danby.

There was no answer, and Dexter stood there, feeling very uncomfortable, and staring hard at the tall lady, who spoke in such an ill-used tone of voice.

"Eddy, my darling," she said a little more loudly, as she turned and looked toward a glass door opening into a handsome conservatory; "come and shake hands with Master Grayson."

There was no reply, but a faint rustling sound fell upon Dexter's quick ears, telling plainly enough that some one was in the conservatory.

Lady Danby sighed, and there was a very awkward pause.

"Perhaps you had better sit down, Master Grayson," she said. "My son will be here soon."

Just at that moment there was a loud important sounding cough in the hall, the handle of the door rattled loudly, and Sir James entered, walking very upright, and smiling with his eyes half-closed.

"Aha!" he exclaimed. "Here you are, then. How do you do—how do you do—how do you do!"

He shook hands boisterously, nodding and smiling the while, and Dexter wondered whether he ought to say, "Quite well, thank you, sir," three times over, but he only said it once.

"That's right," said Sir James. "Quite safe here, eh? No bullocks to run after us now."

"No, sir," said Dexter uneasily.

"But where's Eddy!" cried Sir James.

"He was here a little while ago, my dear," said Lady Danby uneasily. "I think he has gone down the garden."

"No; I think not," said Sir James. "Here, Eddy! Eddy!"

"Yes, pa," came out of the conservatory.

"Why, where are you, sir? Come and shake hands with our young friend."

Master Edgar came slowly into sight, entered the drawing-room, and stood still.

"Well; why don't you welcome your visitor? Come here."

Master Edgar came a little more forward.

"Now, then, shake hands with your friend."

Master Edgar slowly held out a white thin hand in the direction of Dexter, who caught it eagerly, and felt as if he were shaking hands with Lady Danby again.

"That's better," said Sir James. "Now the ice is broken I hope you two will be very great friends. There, we shall have an early dinner for you at three o'clock. Better leave them to themselves, my dear."

"Very well, my love," responded Lady Danby sadly.

"Take Dexter Grayson and show him your games, and your pony, and then you can take him round the garden, but don't touch the boat."

"No, pa," said Edgar slowly.

"He's a little shy, Dexter," said Sir James.

"No, I ain't, ma," said Edgar, in a whisper.

"We are very glad to see you, Dexter," continued Sir James. "There, now, go and enjoy yourself out in the garden, you'll find plenty to see. Come, Eddy."

Master Edgar looked slowly and sulkily up at his father, and seemed to hesitate, not even glancing at his visitor.

"Well!" said Sir James sharply. "Why are you hesitating? Come: run along. That way, Dexter, my lad. You two will soon be good friends."

Dexter tried to smile, but it was a very poor apology for a look of pleasure, while Sir James, who seemed rather annoyed at his son's shrinking, uncouth conduct, laid his hand upon the boy's shoulder and led him into the conservatory.

"Come, Eddy," he said bluffly.

"Must I go, ma!" whispered Eddy.

"Yes, my dear, certainly. Papa wishes it, and you must behave like a young gentleman to your guest."

"Come, Eddy," shouted Sir James from the conservatory.

Master Edgar went out sidewise in a very crabby way, and found Sir James waiting.

"There, no more shyness," said Sir James bluffly. "Go out and enjoy yourselves till dinner-time."

He nodded and smiled at them, gave his son a push toward Dexter, and returned to where Lady Danby was seated, with her brow all in wrinkles.

"They will soon make friends," said Sir James. "It's Grayson's whim, of course, and really, my dear, this seems to be a decent sort of boy. Very rough, of course, but Eddy will give him polish. This class of boy is very quick at picking up things; and if, after a few weeks, Grayson is disappointed and finds out his mistake, why, then, we have behaved in a neighbourly way to him and Helen, and there's an end of it."

"But it seems so shocking for poor Eddy, my dear," remonstrated Lady Danby.

"Fish! pooh! tchah! rubbish! not at all!"

"Eddy may pick up bad language from him, and become rude."

"He had better not!" said Sir James. "He knows differently. The other young dog will learn from him. Make him discontented, I'm afraid; but there—it is not our doing."

Lady Danby sighed.

"They'll come back in an hour or two quite companions," continued Sir James. "Boys like that are a little awkward at their first meeting. Soon wear off. I am going to write letters till three. After their dinner perhaps I shall take them in the boat down the river."

Lady Danby sighed again, and Sir James went to see to his letters for the post.

By this time Master Edgar had walked softly out on to the lawn, with his right hand in his pocket, and his left thumb playing about his mouth, looking the while in all directions but that occupied by Dexter, who followed him slowly, waiting for his young host to speak.

But Eddy did not seem to have the slightest intention of speaking. He only sidled away slowly across the lawn, and then down one of the winding paths among the shrubs and ornamental trees.

This went on for about ten minutes, during which they got to be further and further from the house, not a word being spoken; and though Dexter looked genial and eager as he followed his young host, the silence chilled him as much as did the studied way in which his companion avoided his eyes.

"What a beautiful garden you've got!" said Dexter at last.

There was no reply.

Eddy picked up a stone, and threw it at a thrush.

"It's bigger than Dr Grayson's," said Dexter, after a pause.

Eddy picked a flower, gave a chew at the stalk; then picked it to pieces, and threw it away.

Then he began to sidle along again in and out among the trees, and on and on, never once looking at his companion till they were at the bottom of the garden. A pleasant piece of lawn, dotted with ornamental trees, sloped down to the river where, in a Gothic-looking boat-house, open at either end, a handsome-looking gig floated in the clear water.

"That your boat?" said Dexter eagerly, as his eyes ran over the cushioned seats, and the sculls of varnished wood lying all ready along the thwarts.

Edgar made no reply, only moved nearer to the water, and threw himself on a garden seat near the edge.

"Isn't this a good place for fishing?" said Dexter, trying another tack.

No answer, and it was getting very monotonous. But Dexter took it all good-humouredly, attributing the boy's manner more to shyness than actual discourtesy.

"I say, don't you fish sometimes!"

No reply.

"Have you got any rods and lines!"

Eddy gave a contemptuous sniff, which might have meant anything.

"There's lots at Dr Grayson's," said Dexter eagerly, for the sight of the roach gliding about in the clear water in the shade of the boat-house excited the desire to begin angling. "Shall I go and fetch the rods and lines?"

Eddy leaned back in the garden seat, and rested his head upon his hand.

In despair Dexter sighed, and then recalled Sir James's words about their enjoying themselves.

It was a lovely day; the garden was very beautiful; the river ran by, sparkling and bright; but there was very little enjoyment so far, and Dexter sat down upon the grass at a little distance from his young host.

But it was not in Dexter's nature to sit still long, and after staring hard at the bright water for a few minutes, he looked up brightly at Edgar.

"I say," he cried; "that bullock didn't hurt you the other day, did it?"

Edgar shifted himself a little in his seat, so that he could stare in the other direction, and he tried to screw up his mouth into what was meant to be a supercilious look, though it was a failure, being extremely pitiful, and very small.

Dexter waited for a few minutes, and then continued the one-sided conversation—

"I never felt afraid of bullocks," he said thoughtfully. "If you had run after them with your stick—I say, you got your stick, didn't you?"

No reply.

"Oh, well," said Dexter; "if you don't want to talk, I don't."

"I don't want to talk to a boy like you," said Edgar, without looking.

Dexter started, and stared hard.

"I'm not accustomed to associate with workhouse boys."

Dexter flinched.

Not long back the idea of being a workhouse boy did not trouble him in the least. He knew that there were plenty of boys who were not workhouse boys, and seeing what freedom they enjoyed, and how much happier they seemed, something of the nature of envy had at times crept into his breast, but, on the whole, he had been very well contented till he commenced his residence at the doctor's; and now all seemed changed.

"I'm not a workhouse boy," he said hotly.

"Yes, you are," retorted Edgar, looking at him hard, full in the face, for the first time. "I know where you came from, and why you were fetched."

Dexter's face was burning, and there was an angry look in his eyes, as he jumped up and took a couple of steps toward where Edgar sat back on the garden seat. But his pleasant look came back, and he held out his hand.

"I'm not ashamed of it," he said. "I used to be at the workhouse. Won't you shake hands!"

Edgar sniffed contemptuously, and turned his head away.

"Very well," said Dexter sadly. "I don't want to, if you don't."

Edgar suddenly leaped up, and went along by the side of the river, while Dexter, after a few moments' hesitation, began to follow him in a lonely, dejected way, wishing all the time that he could go back home.

Following out his previous tactics, Edgar sidled along path after path, and in and out among the evergreen clumps, all the while taking care not to come within sight of the house, so that his actions might be seen; while, feeling perfectly helpless and bound to follow the caprices of his young host, Dexter continued his perambulation of the garden in the same unsatisfactory manner.

"Look here," cried Edgar at last; "don't keep following me about."

"Very well," said Dexter, as he stood still in the middle of one of the paths, wondering whether he could slip away, and return to the doctor's.

That seemed a difficult thing to do, for Sir James might see him going, and call him back, and then what was he to say? Besides which, when he reached the doctor's there would be a fresh examination, and he felt that the excuse he gave would not be satisfactory.

Dexter sighed, and glanced in the direction taken by Edgar.

The boy was not within sight, but Dexter fancied that he had hidden, and was watching him, and he turned in the other direction, looking hopelessly about the garden, which seemed to be more beautiful and extensive than the doctor's; but, in spite of the wealth of greenery and flowers, everything looked cheerless and cold.

Dexter sighed. Then a very natural boyish thought came into his head.

"I wonder what's for dinner," he said to himself; but at the same time he knew that it must be a long while yet to dinner-time, and, sighing once more, he walked slowly down the path, found himself near the river again, and went and sat on a stump close to the boat-house, where he could look into the clear water, and see the fish.

It was very interesting to him to watch the little things gliding here and there, and he wished that he had a rod and line to try for some of them, when all at once he started, for a well-aimed stone struck him upon the side of the head, and as it reached its goal, and Dexter started up angrily, there was a laugh and a rustle among the shrubs.

As the pain went off, so did Dexter's anger, and he reseated himself upon the stump, thinking, with his young wits sharpened by his early life.

"I don't call this coming out to enjoy myself," he said drily. "Wonder whether all young gentleman behave like this?"

Then he began thinking about Sam Stubbs, a boy at the workhouse school, who was a terrible bully and tyrant, knocking all his companions about.

But the sight of the clean-looking well-varnished boat, floating so easily in the shade of the roof of its house, took his attention, and he began thinking of how he should like a boat like that to push off into the stream, and go floating along in the sunshine, looking down at the fish, and fastening up every now and then to the overhanging trees. It would be glorious, he thought.

"I wish Dr Grayson had a boat," he thought. "I could learn to row it, and—"

Whack!

Dexter jumped up again, tingling with pain; and then with his face scarlet he sat down once more writhing involuntarily, and drawing his breath hard, as there was a mocking laugh.

The explanation was simple. Master Edgar was dissatisfied. It was very pleasant to his spoiled, morbid mind to keep on slighting and annoying his guest by making him dance attendance upon him, and dragging him about the garden wherever he pleased to go; but it was annoying and disappointing to find that he was being treated with a calm display of contempt.

Under these circumstances Master Edgar selected a good-sized stone — one which he thought would hurt — and took excellent aim at Dexter, where he sat contemplating the river.

The result was most satisfactory: Dexter had winced, evidently suffered sharp pain, but only submitted to it, and sat down again twisting himself about.

Edgar laughed heartily, in fact the tears stood in his eyes, and he retreated, but only to where he could watch Dexter attentively.

"He's a coward," said Edgar to himself. "All that sort of boys are." And with the determination of making his visitor a kind of captive to his bow and spear, or, in plainer English, a slave to his caprices, he went to one of the beds where some sticks had lately been put to some young plants, and selecting one that was new, thin, and straight, he went back on tiptoe, watched his opportunity, and then brought the stick down sharply across Dexter's back.

He drew back for a few moments, his victim's aspect being menacing; but Dexter's young spirit had been kept crushed down for a good many years, and his custom had been under many a blow to sit and suffer patiently, not even crying aloud, Mr Sibery objecting to any noise in the school.

Dexter had subsided again. The flashes that darted from his eyes had died out, and those eyes looked subdued and moist.

For the boy was mentally, as well as bodily hurt, and he wondered what Helen would say, and whether Sir James would correct his son if he saw him behaving in that manner to his visitor.

"Hey: get up!" said Edgar, growing more bold, as he found that he could ill-use his guest with impunity; and as he spoke he gave him a rough poke or two with the sharp end of the stick, which had been pointed with the gardener's pruning-knife.

His treatment of Dexter resembled that which he had been accustomed to bestow upon an unfortunate dog he had once owned—one which became so fond of him that at last it ran away.

"Do you hear!" cried Edgar again. "Get up."

"Don't: you hurt."

"Yes: meant to hurt," said Edgar, grinning. "Get up."

He gave Dexter so sharp a dig with the stick that the latter jumped up angrily, and Edgar drew back; but on seeing that the visitor only went on a few yards to where there was a garden seat, and sat down again, the young tyrant became emboldened, and went behind the seat with a malicious look of satisfaction in his eyes.

"Don't do that," said Dexter quietly. "Let's have a game at something. Do you think we might go in that boat?"

"I should think not indeed," cried Edgar, who now seemed to have found his tongue. "Boats are for young gentlemen, not for boys from the Union."

Dexter winced a little, and Edgar looked pleased.

"Get up!" he shouted; and he made another lunge with the stick.

"I'm always getting into trouble," thought Dexter, as the result of the last few days' teachings, "and I don't want to do anything now."

"Do you hear, blackguard? Get up!"

There was another sharp poke, a painful poke, against which, as he moved to the other end of the seat, Dexter uttered a mild protest.

"Did you hear me say, 'Get up'?" shouted Edgar.

Dexter obeyed, and moved a little nearer to the water's edge.

"I wish it was time to go," he said to himself. "I am so miserable here."

"Now, go along there," said Edgar sharply. "Go on!"

The boy seemed to have a donkey in his mind's eye just then, for he thrust and struck at Dexter savagely, and then hastily threw down the stick, as an angry glow was gathering in his visitor's countenance. For just then there was a step heard upon the gravel.

"Ah, Eddy, my darling," said a voice; and Lady Danby walked languidly by, holding up a parasol. "At play, my dear?"

She did not glance at Dexter, who felt very solitary and sad as the lady passed on, Master Eddy throwing himself on the grass, and picking it off in patches to toss toward the water till his mother was out of sight, when he sprang up once more, and picked the stick from where he had thrown it upon a bed.

As he did this he glanced sidewise, and then stood watching for a few minutes, when he made a playful kind of charge at his visitor, and drove the point of the stick so vigorously against his back that the cloth gave way, making a triangular hole, and causing the owner no little pain.

"Don't," cried Dexter appealingly; "you hurt ever so. Let's play at some game."

"I'm going to," cried Edgar, with a vicious laugh. "I'm going to play at French and English, and you're the beggarly Frenchman at Waterloo. That's the way to charge bayonets. How do you like that, and that, and that!"

"Not at all," said Dexter, trying hard to be good-humoured.

"Then you'll have to like it, and ever so much more, too. Get up, blackguard. Do you hear?"

Dexter rose and retreated; but, with no little agility, Edgar got before him, and drove him toward the water, stabbing and lunging at him so savagely, that if he had not parried some of the thrusts with his hands his face must have been torn.

Edgar grew more and more excited over his work, and Dexter received a nasty dig on one hand, another in the cheek, while another grazed his ear.

This last was beyond bearing. The hurt was not so bad as several which he had before received; but, perhaps from its nearness to his brain, it seemed to rouse Dexter more than any former blow, and, with an angry cry, he snatched at and caught the stick just as it came near his face.

"Let go of that stick! Do you hear?" cried Edgar.

For response Dexter, who was now roused, held on tightly, and tried to pull the stick away.

"Let go," cried Edgar, tugging and snatching with all his might.

Dexter's rage was as evanescent as it was quick. It passed away, and as his enemy made another furious tug at the stick Dexter suddenly let go, and the consequence was the boy staggered back a few yards, and then came down heavily in a sitting position upon the grass.

Edgar sat and stared for a few moments, the sudden shock being anything but pleasant; but, as he saw Dexter's mirthful face, a fit of rage seized him, and, leaping up, he resumed his attack with the stick.

This time his strokes and thrusts were so malicious, and given with so decided a desire to hurt his victim as much as was possible, that, short of running away, Dexter had to do everything possible to avoid the blows.

For the most part he was successful; but at last he received so numbing a blow across the arm that he quivered with pain and anger as he sprang forward, and, in place of retreating, seized the stick, and tried to wrest it away.

There was a brief struggle, but pretty full of vigour.

Rage made Edgar strong, and he fought well for his weapon, but at the end of a minute's swaying here and there, and twistings and heavings innumerable, Edgar's arms felt as if they were being torn from his body, the stick was wrenched away, and as he stood scarlet with passion, he saw it whirled into the air, to fall with a loud splash into the river.

Edgar ground his teeth for a moment or two, and then, as white with anger as his adversary was red, he flew at him, swaying his arms round, and then there was a furious encounter.

Edgar had his own ideas about fighting manoeuvres, which he had tried again and again upon his nurse in bygone times, and upon any of the servants with whom he had come in contact. His arms flew round like flails, or as if he had been transformed into a kind of human firework, and for the next five minutes he kicked, scratched, bit, and tore at his adversary; the next five minutes he was seated upon the grass, howling, his nose bleeding terribly, and the crimson stains carried by his hands all over his face.

For Dexter was not perfect: he had borne till it was impossible to bear more, and then, with his anger surging up, he had fought as a down-trodden English boy will sometimes fight; and in this case with the pluck and steadiness learned in many a school encounter, unknown to Mr Sibery or Mr Hippetts, the keen-eyed and stern.

Result: what might be expected. Dexter felt no pain, only an intense desire to thrash the virulent little tyrant who had scratched his face, kicked his shins, torn at his hair—it was too short still for a good hold—and, finally, made his sharp, white teeth meet in his visitor's neck.

"Served you right!" muttered Dexter, as he knelt down by the river, and bathed his hands and face before dabbing them dry with his pocket-handkerchief. "No business to treat me like that."

Then, as he stood rubbing his face—very little the worse for the encounter—his anger all passed away, and the consequences of his act dawned upon him.

SIR JAMES ARRIVES ON THE SCENE OF THE FIGHT

"Look here," he said; "it was all your fault. Come to the water; that will soon stop bleeding."

He held out his hand, as he bent over the fallen tyrant, meaning to help him to rise, when, quick as lightning, Edgar caught the hand proffered to him and carried it to his teeth.

Dexter uttered a cry of pain, and shook him off, sending him backwards now upon the grass, just as a shadow fell across the contending boys, and Sir James stood frowning there.

Chapter Nineteen
Master Eddy "Hollers Wahoo!"

"What is the meaning of this!" cried Sir James furiously.

Dexter was speechless, and he shrank back staring.

Edgar was ready with an answer. "He's knocking me about, pa. He has done nothing but knock me about ever since he came."

"Oh!" cried Dexter in a voice full of indignant astonishment. "I didn't. He begun it, and I didn't, indeed."

"Silence, sir!" cried Sir James, in his severest magisterial tones. "How dare you tell me such a falsehood? I saw you ill-using my son as you held him down."

"Why, he had got hold of my hand!" cried Dexter indignantly.

"Got hold of your hand, sir? How dare you? How dare you, sir, I say? I've a great mind to—"

Sir James did not finish his speech, but made a gesture with the walking-cane he carried; and just then there was a loud hysterical shriek.

For Lady Danby had realised the fact that something was wrong from the part of the garden where she was promenading, parasol in hand, and she came now panting up, in the full belief that some accident had happened to her darling, and that he was drowned.

"Eddy, Eddy!" she cried, as she came up; and then as soon as she caught sight of his anything but pleasant-looking countenance, she shrieked again wildly, and flung herself upon her knees beside him. "What is it? What is it, my darling?" she sobbed, as she caught him to her heart.

"That horrid boy! Knocking me about," he cried, stopping his howling so as to deliver the words emphatically; and then looking at his stained hands, and bursting into a howl of far greater power than before.

"The wretch! The wretch!" cried Lady Danby. "I always knew it. He has killed my darling."

At this dire announcement Edgar shook himself free from his mother's embrace, looked at his hands again, and then in the extremity of horror, threw himself flat upon his back, and shrieked and kicked.

"O my darling, my darling!" cried Lady Danby.

"He isn't hurt much," cried Dexter indignantly.

"How dare you, sir!" roared Sir James.

"He's killed; he's killed!" cried Lady Danby, clasping her hands, and rocking herself to and fro as she gazed at the shrieking boy, who only wanted a cold sponge and a towel to set him right.

"Ow!" yelled Edgar, as he appreciated the sympathy of his mother, but believed the very worst of his unfortunate condition. The lady now bent over him, said that he was killed, and of course she must have known.

Edgar had never read *Uncle Remus*. All this was before the period when that book appeared; but his conduct might very well be taken as a type of that of the celebrated Brer Fox when Brer Rabbit was in doubt as to whether he was really dead or only practising a ruse, and proceeded to test his truth by saying, as he saw him stretched out—

"Brer Fox look like he dead, but he don't do like he dead. Dead fokes hists up de behime leg, en hollers *wahoo!*"

Edgar, according to Brer Rabbit's ideas, was very dead indeed, for he kept on "histing up de behime leg, en hollering *wahoo!*" with the full power of his lungs.

By this time the alarm had spread, and there was the sound of steps upon a gravel walk, which resulted in the appearance of the supercilious footman.

"Carry Master Edgar up to the house," said Sir James, in his severest magisterial tones.

"Carefully—very carefully," wailed her ladyship piteously; and she looked and spoke as if she feared that as soon as the boy was touched he would tumble all to pieces.

Dexter looked on, with his eyes turning here and there, like those of some captured wild animal which fears danger; and as he looked he caught sight of the footman gazing at him with a peculiar grin upon his countenance, which seemed to be quite friendly, and indicated that the man rather enjoyed the plight in which his young master was plunged.

Master Edgar howled again as he was raised, and directly after began to indulge in what the plantation negroes used to call "playing 'possum"—

that is to say, he suddenly became limp and inert, closing his eyes, and letting his head roll about, as if there were no more bone left in his body, while his mother wrung her hands, and tried then to hold the head steady, as the footman prepared to move toward the house.

"Now, sir," said Sir James sternly, "come here. We will have a few words about this in my library."

Accustomed for years past to obey, Dexter took a step forward to accompany the stern-looking man before him to the house; but such a panorama of troublous scenes rose before his mind's eye directly, that he stopped short, gave one hasty glance round, and then, as Sir James stretched forth his hand, he made one bound which landed him in a clump of hollyhocks and dahlias; another which took him on to the grass; and then, with a rush, he dashed into a clump of rhododendrons, went through them, and ran as hard as he could go toward the house.

For a few moments Sir James was too much astounded to speak. This was something new. He was accustomed to order, and to be obeyed.

He had ordered Dexter to come to him, and for answer the boy had dashed away.

As soon as Sir James could recover his breath, taken away in his astonishment, he began to shout—

"Stop, sir! Do you hear? How dare you?"

If a hundred Sir Jameses had been shouting it would not have stayed Dexter, for he had only one idea in his head just then, and that was to get away.

"Put down Master Edgar, and go and fetch that boy back."

"Carefully! Oh, pray, put him down carefully," cried Lady Danby passionately.

Just then Master Edgar uttered a fresh cry, and his mother wailed loudly.

"No, never mind," cried Sir James, "carry him up to the house; I will fetch that young rascal."

He strode off angrily, evidently believing in his own mind that he really was going to fetch Dexter back; but by that time the boy had reached the house, ran round by the side, dashed down the main street, and was soon after approaching the bridge over the river, beyond which lay the Union and the schools.

Chapter Twenty
An Explanation

For a few moments Dexter's idea was to go to the great gates, ring the porter's bell, and take sanctuary there, for he felt that he had disgraced himself utterly beyond retrieving his character. Certainly, he never dared go back to the doctor's.

He felt for a moment that he had some excuse, for Edgar Danby had brought his punishment upon himself; but no one would believe that, and there was no hope for the offender but to give up everything, and go back to his former life.

But, as the boy reached the gloomy-looking workhouse entrance, and saw the painted bell-pull, through whose coating the rust was eating its way, he shivered.

For there rose up before him the stern faces of Mr Hippetts and Mr Sibery, with the jeering crowd of schoolfellows, who could laugh at and gibe him for his downfall, and be sure to call him Gentleman Coleby, as long as they were together, the name, under the circumstances, being sure to stick.

No, he could not face them there, and beside, though it had never seemed so before, the aspect of the great building was so forbidding that he shrank away, and walked onward toward the outskirts of the town, and on, and on, till he found himself by the river.

Such a sensation of misery and despair came over him, that he began walking along by the bank, seeing nothing of the glancing fish and bright insects which danced above the water. He had room for nothing but the despondent thoughts of what he should do now.

"What would the doctor think of him? What would Helen say?" He had been asked out to spend the day at a gentleman's house, and he had disgraced himself, and—

"Hullo!"

Dexter looked up sharply, and found that he had almost run against his old fishing friend of the opposite side of the river.

"Hullo!" stammered Dexter in reply.

"Got dry again?" said the boy, who was standing just back from the water's edge, fishing, with his basket at his side, and a box of baits on the grass.

"Got dry?" said Dexter wonderingly.

"Yes! My!" cried the boy, grinning, "you did have a ducking. I ran away. Best thing I could do."

"Yes," said Dexter quietly; "you ran away."

"Why, what yer been a-doing of? Your face is scratched, and your hands too. I know: you've been climbing trees. You'll ketch it, spoiling your clothes. That's got him."

He struck and landed a small fish, which he took from the hook and dropped into his basket, where there were two more.

"They don't bite to-day. Caught any down your garden!"

"No," said Dexter, to whom the company of the boy was very cheering just then. "I haven't tried since."

"You are a fellow! Why, if I had a chance like you have, I should be always at it."

"I say, what did you say your name was?"

"Bob Dimsted—Bob," said the fisher, throwing in again. "I know what yours is. You come out of the workus."

"Yes," said Dexter sadly, as he wondered whether he did not wish he was there now. "I came out of the workus—workhouse," he added, as he remembered one of Helen's teachings.

"Why don't you get your rod some day, and a basket of something to eat, and come right up the river with me, fishing? There's whackers up there."

"I should like to," said Dexter thoughtfully, for the idea of the fishing seemed to drive away the troubles from which he suffered.

"Well, come then. I'd go any day, only you must let me have all you caught."

"All?" said Dexter, as he began to think of trophies.

"Yes. As I showed you the place where they're caught, I should want to take them home."

"All right," said Dexter. "You could have them."

"Ah, it's all very well," said the boy, "but there wouldn't be many that you caught, mate. Ah! No, he's off again. Keep a little furder back."

Dexter obeyed, and sat down on the grass, feeling in a half-despairing mood, but as if the company of this rough boy was very pleasant after what he had gone through, and that boys like this were more agreeable to talk to than young tyrants of the class of Edgar Danby.

"Fish don't half bite to-day," said Bob Dimsted. "I wish you'd got a rod here, I could lend you a line—single hair."

"But I haven't got a rod."

"Well, run home and fetch it," said Bob.

"Run home and fetch it?" How could he run home and fetch it? How could he ever go back to the doctor's again?

"No," he said at last, as he shook his head. "I can't go and fetch it."

"Then you can't fish," said the boy, "and 'tain't much use. It's no fun unless they bite, and some days it don't matter how you try, they won't."

"Won't they?" said Dexter, and then he started to his feet, for a familiar voice had spoken close to his ear—

"Why, Dexter!"

The voice was as full of astonishment as the pleasant face which looked in his.

"I thought you were at Sir James Danby's! Is Edgar out here, in the meadows!"

"No—no," faltered Dexter; and Bob Dimsted began to gather up his tackle, so as to make a strategic movement, there being evidently trouble in the rear.

"But what does this mean?" said Helen firmly. "Who is that boy?"

"Bob—Bob Dimsted."

"And do you know him?"

"He—he was fishing opposite our—your—garden the day I fell into the river," faltered Dexter; and he looked longingly at Bob, who was quickly moving away, and wished that those eyes did not hold him so firmly, and keep him from doing the same.

"Was he at your school?"

"No," faltered Dexter.

"Then I am sure papa would not like you to be making acquaintance with boy's like that. But come, Dexter. What is the meaning of all this? I left you at Sir James Danby's."

"Yes," said Dexter, shuffling from foot to foot.

"Then why are you not there now—playing with Edgar?"

Dexter did not answer, but seemed to be admiring the prospect.

"Why, Dexter, your face is all scratched!"

Dexter looked up at her, with the scratched face scarlet.

"How is that!" continued Helen sternly.

"Fighting," said Dexter grimly.

"Fighting? Oh, shame! And with that rough boy!"

"No!" cried Dexter quickly. "He didn't knock me about."

"Then who did!"

"That young Danby."

Dexter's lips were well opened now, and he went on talking rapidly.

"I never did anything to him, but he went on for an hour walking all round the garden, and wouldn't speak; and when I was tired and sat down, he got a stick and knocked me about, and poked me with the point. I stood it as long as I could, and then, when he got worse and worse, I pitched into him, and I'm sure you would have done the same."

Helen did not look as if she would have done the same, but stood gazing at the young monkey before her, wondering whether he was deserving of her sympathy, or had really misbehaved himself, and was trying to palliate his conduct.

"There, Dexter," she said at last. "I really do not know what to do with you. You had better come on and see papa at once."

She took a step toward the town, and then waited, but Dexter stood firm, and cast a glance toward the country.

"Dexter, did you hear what I said!"

The boy looked at her uneasily, and then nodded sullenly.

"Come home with me, then, at once," said Helen quickly.

"It's no use for me to come home along of you," said Dexter surlily. "He'll hit me, and I don't want to go."

Helen hesitated for a few moments, and then laid her hand upon the boy's shoulder.

"I wish you to come, Dexter."

He shook his head.

"Come," she cried, "if you have been in fault confess it frankly."

"But I haven't," cried the boy angrily. "I couldn't help fighting when he knocked me about as he did. He bit me too. Look there!"

He hastily drew up his sleeve, and displayed a ruddy circle on his white skin, which bore pretty strong witness to the truth of his words.

"Then, if you were not to blame, why should you shrink from coming to papa?"

"'Cause he mightn't believe me. Mr Sibery never would, neither," muttered Dexter.

"Tell the truth and papa will be sure to believe you," cried Helen indignantly.

"Think he would!" said Dexter.

"I am sure of it, sir."

"All right then," cried the boy quickly. "I'll come. Oh, I say!"

"What is the matter?"

"Look! Here he comes!"

He pointed quickly in the direction of the town, and, wresting himself from Helen's grasp, set off at a sharp run.

But he had not gone a dozen yards before he turned and saw Helen gazing after him.

He stopped directly, and came slowly and reluctantly back.

"Did you call me!" he said sheepishly.

"No, Dexter; I think it must have been your conscience spoke and upbraided you for being such a coward."

"Yes, it was cowardly, wasn't it?" cried the boy. "I didn't mean to run away, but somehow I did. I say, will he hit me!"

"No, Dexter."

"Will he be very cross with me?"

"I am afraid he will, Dexter; but you must submit bravely, and speak the simple truth."

"Yes, I'm going to," said Dexter, with a sigh; and he glanced behind him at the pleasant stretch of meadows, and far away down among the alders and willows, with Bob Dimsted fishing, and evidently quite free from the care which troubled him.

The doctor strode up, looking very angry.

"So you are there, are you, sir?" he cried austerely. "Do you know of this disgraceful business!"

"Dexter has been telling me," said Helen gravely.

"Humph!" grunted the doctor. "I knew you had come down here, so I thought I would come and tell you of the terrible state of affairs."

"Terrible, papa!"

"Ah! then you don't know. It was not likely he would tell you. Sir James came straight to me, and told me everything. It seems that the two boys were sent down the garden together to play, and that as soon as they were alone, Dexter here began to annoy and tease Edgar."

"Here, just say that again, will you?" cried Dexter sharply.

"I repeat that Dexter here began to annoy and tease Edgar."

"Oh!" ejaculated Dexter.

"And at last, after the poor boy had tried everything to keep his companion from the line of conduct he had pursued, he resolved to go down and sit by the river, leaving Dexter to amuse himself. But unfortunately the spirit of mischief was so strong in him that this boy took out a dahlia-stick with a sharp point—Sir James showed it to me—and then, after stabbing at him for some time, began to use his fists, and beat Edgar in the most cruel way."

"Oh, my!" ejaculated Dexter; and then, giving his right foot a stamp, "Well, of all the— Oh, my! what a whopper!"

The low slangy expression was brought out with such an air of indignant protest that Helen was unable to keep her countenance, and she looked away, while the doctor, who was quite as much impressed, frowned more severely to hide the mirth aroused by the boy's ejaculations, and turned to him sharply—

"What do you mean by that, sir!" he cried.

"Mean?" cried Dexter indignantly, and without a shade of fear in his frank bold eyes; "why there isn't a bit of it true. He didn't like me because I came from over yonder, and he wouldn't speak to me. Then he kept on hitting me, and I wouldn't hit him back, because I thought it would make her cross; but, last of all, he hurt me so that I forgot all about everything, and then we did fight, and I whipped—and that's all."

"Oh, that's all, is it, sir!" said the doctor, who was angry and yet amused.

"Yes, that's all," said Dexter; "only I've got a bite on my arm, and one on my neck, and one on my shoulder. They didn't bleed, though, only pinched and hurt. I only hit him one good un, and that was on the nose, and it made it bleed."

"Humph!" ejaculated the doctor. "Now, look here, Dexter, is every word of that true!"

"Yes, sir, every bit," cried the boy eagerly. "You will see if it ain't."

The doctor's face wrinkled a little more, as to conceal a smile he turned to his daughter—

"Now," he said, "do you think this is true?"

"I feel sure it is," said Helen. "I am convinced that Dexter would not tell either of us a falsehood."

"There!" cried the boy, smiling triumphantly, as he crept to Helen's side and laid his hand in hers. "Hear that? Of course I wouldn't. I wanted to be all right, but—I say, does my head bleed there?"

He took off his cap, and held down his head, while Helen looked at the spot he pointed out, and shuddered slightly.

"That's where he stuck his nails into my head, just like a cat. It did hurt ever so, but I soon forgot it."

"Let's go home," said the doctor gravely. "It is unfortunate, but of course Dexter could not submit to be trampled upon by any boy."

"I say, you do believe me, don't you!" said Dexter quickly.

"Yes, my boy. I believe you on your honour."

"On my honour," said Dexter quickly.

"That will do," said the doctor. "It is unfortunate, but unavoidable. Let us go home to lunch."

"And you will not send me back to the—you know!"

"Certainly not," said the doctor.

"And may I come out here to fish by and by!"

"Certainly," said the doctor. "If you are a good boy."

"No, I think not," said Helen, making a shadow cross the boy's countenance. "Dexter cannot come out fishing alone; I will come with him."

Dexter gave her a meaning look, as he understood why she had said that; and then walked quietly home with the doctor and his daughter to a far more agreeable meal than he would have enjoyed at the baronet's house.

Chapter Twenty One
A Record of Cares

"Hang his impudence!" said the doctor. "What do you think he told me?"

"Sir James?"

"Yes, my dear. Told me I was a regular modern Frankenstein, and that I had made a young monster to worry me to death. Such insolence! Dexter's growing a very nice lad, and I feel as if I could make a nobleman of him if I liked, but I think I'll send him to a good school for a bit. You see, he's full of promise, Helen."

"Yes, papa," said Helen, suppressing her mirth.

"Ah! now you are laughing at me. I mean full of the promise that will some day mean performance. But—yes, I will send him to a good school."

A good school was selected, and Dexter duly sent down to it, leaving Helen very unwillingly, but holding up manfully, and the doctor said he would come back at the holiday-time vastly improved.

In six weeks Dr Grayson received a letter asking him to fetch Dexter away to save him from being expelled.

The Doctor looked very angry as he went down to Cardley Willows, and the inquiries took a stern, rather bitter turn.

"Has the boy been a young blackguard?" he said.

"No," said the principal.

"Dishonest?"

"Oh dear no!"

"Well, what is it then—disobedient!"

"Oh dear no! He'll promise anything."

"Humph! yes," said the doctor to himself.

"I'm very sorry, Dr Grayson," continued the principal; "but the boy is incorrigible, and you must take him away."

The doctor took the boy away, and he had a very stern talking-to at home.

Two months passed away.

"There, Helen," said the doctor one morning; "what do you say to him now? Wonderfully improved, has he not? Good natural boy's colour in his cheeks—better blood, you see, and nice curly hair. Really he is not like the same."

"No, papa; he is greatly changed," said Helen, as she followed the direction of her father's eyes to where Dexter was out on the lawn watching old Dan'l, while old Dan'l, in a furtive manner, was diligently watching him in return.

"Greatly changed," said the doctor thoughtfully, as he scratched the side of his nose with his penholder, "in personal appearance. Sir James seems very sore still about that little affair. Says I ought to have thrashed Dexter, for he behaved brutally to young Edgar."

"And what did you say, papa?"

"Well, not exactly all I thought. Dreadful young limb that Edgar. Spoiled boy, but I could not tell Danby so with such a catalogue of offences as Master Dexter has to show on my black list. You see, Helen, we do not get any further with him."

Helen shook her head sadly.

"There's something wrong in his brain; or something wanting. He'll promise amendment one hour, and go and commit the same fault the very next."

"It is very sad," replied Helen thoughtfully; "but I'm sure he means well."

"Yes, my dear; of course," said the doctor, looking perplexed; "but it's a great drawback to one's success. But there: we must persevere. It seems to me that the first thing to do is to wean him from that terrible love of low companions."

"Say companion," said Helen, smiling.

"Well, a companion, then. I wish we could get that young fishing scoundrel sent away; but of course one cannot do that. Oh, by the way, what about Maria? Is she going away?"

"No," said Helen. "I had a long talk to her about her unreasoning dislike to Dexter, and she has consented to stay."

"Well, it's very kind of her," said the doctor testily. "I suppose Mrs Millett will be giving warning next."

"Oh no," said Helen; "she finds a good deal of fault, but I think, on the whole, she feels kindly toward the poor boy."

"Don't!" cried the doctor, giving the writing-table so angry a slap with his open hand that a jet of ink shot out of the stand and made half a dozen great splashes. "Now, look there, what you've made me do," he continued, as he began hastily to soak up the black marks with blotting-paper. "I will not have Dexter called 'the poor boy.' He is not a poor boy. He is a human waif thrown up on life's shore. No, no: and you are not to call him a human waif. I shall well educate him, and place him on the high-road toward making his way properly in life as a gentleman should, and I'll show the whole world that I'm right."

"You shall, papa," said Helen merrily; "and I will help you all I can."

"I know you will, my dear, and you are helping me," cried the doctor warmly; "and it's very good of you. But I do wish we could make him think before he does anything. His mischievous propensities are simply horrible. And now, my dear, about his education. We must do something more, if it is only for the sake of keeping him out of trouble. You are doing nobly, but that is not enough. I did mean to read classics with him myself, but I have no time. My book takes too much thought. Now, I will not send the poor boy—"

"'Poor boy,' papa!" said Helen merrily.

"Eh? Did I say 'poor boy'!" cried the doctor, scratching his nose again.

"Yes."

"Ah, well; I did not mean it. I was going to say I will not send him to another school. He would be under too many disadvantages, so I think we will decide upon a private tutor."

"Yes, papa; a very excellent arrangement."

"Yes, I think it is; and—well, Maria, what is it!"

"Dan'l, sir," said that young lady, who spoke very severely, as if she could hardly contain her feelings; "and he'd be glad to know if you could see him a minute."

"Send him in, Maria," said the doctor; and then, as the housemaid left the room, "Well, it can't be anything about Dexter now, because he is out there on the—"

The doctor's words were delivered more and more slowly as he rose and walked toward the open window, while Helen felt uneasy, and full of misgivings.

"Why, the young dog was here just now," cried the doctor angrily. "Now, really, Helen, if he has been at any tricks this time, I certainly will set up a cane."

"O papa!"

"Yes, my dear, I certainly will, much as I object to corporal punishment. Well, Daniel, what is it!"

Old Dan'l had a straw hat in his hand—a hat that was rather ragged at the edge, and with which, as if it was to allay some irritation, he kept sawing one finger.

"Beg pardon, sir—pardon, Miss," said Dan'l apologetically; "but if I might speak and say a few words—"

"Certainly, Daniel; you may do both," said the doctor.

"Thanky, sir—thanky kindly, Miss," said the gardener, half-putting his hat on twice so as to have it in the proper position for making a bow; "which I'm the last man in the world, sir, to make complaints."

"Humph!" ejaculated the doctor.

"Serving you as I have now for over twenty year, and remembering puffickly well, Miss, when you was only a pink bit of a baby, as like one o' my tender carnations as could be, only more like a Count dee Parish rose."

"Well, what's the matter, Daniel?" said the doctor hastily, for he wanted to bring the old man's prosings to an end.

"Well, sir, heverythink, as you may say, is the matter. Look at me, sir; I've suffered more in that garden than mortal man would believe!"

"Oh, have you!" said the doctor, taking off his glasses. "You don't look so very bad, Daniel, for a man of sixty-five."

"Sixty-four and three-quarters, begging your pardon, sir; but I have suffered. I've laid awake nights and nights thinking of what was best for planting them borders with s'rubs, as is now a delight to the human eye; and I've walked that garden hundreds o' nights with a lanthorn in search o' slugs, as comes out o' they damp meadows in in counted millions; and I've had my cares in thrips and red spider and green fly, without saying a word about scale and them other blights as never had no name. But never in my life—never in all my born days—never since I was first made a gardener, have I suffered anythink like as I've suffered along o' that there boy."

"Nonsense, Daniel! nonsense!" cried the doctor pettishly.

"Well, sir, I've served you faithful, and took such a pride in that there garden as never was, and you may call it nonsense, sir, but when I see things such as I see, I say it's time to speak."

"Why, you are always coming to me with some petty complaint, sir, about that boy."

"Petty complaint, sir!" cried Dan'l indignantly. "Is Ribstons a petty complaint—my chycest Ribstons, as I want for dessert at Christmas? And is my Sturmer pippins a petty complaint—them as ought to succeed the Ribstons in Febbery and March?"

"Why, what about them?" cried the doctor.

"Oh, nothing, sir; only as half the town's t'other side o' the river, and my pippins is being shovelled over wholesale."

The doctor walked out into the hall and put on his hat, with Dan'l following him; and, after a moment's hesitation, Helen took up a sunshade, and went down the garden after her father.

She overtook him as he was standing by a handsome espalier, dotted with the tawny red-streaked Ribstons, while Dan'l was pointing to a couple of newly-made footmarks.

"Humph! Not all gone, then?" said the doctor, frowning.

"Not yet!" growled Dan'l. "And see there, Miss; there was four stunners on that there little branch this mornin', and they're all gone!"

"Where is Master Dexter?" said the doctor.

Dan'l made a jerking motion with his thumb over his right shoulder, and the doctor walked on over the grass toward the bottom of the grounds.

The little party advanced so noiselessly that they were unheard, and in another minute they were near enough to hear Dexter exclaim—

"Now, then; this time—catch!"

The doctor stopped short in time to see, according to Dan'l's version, the Ribstons and Sturmers thrown across the river to half the town.

"Half the town," according to Dan'l, consisted of Bob Dimsted, who had laid down his rough fishing-rod, and was holding half an apple in one hand, munching away the while, as he caught another deftly; and he was in the act of stuffing it into his pocket as he caught sight of the doctor, and stood for a few moments perfectly motionless. Then, stooping quickly, he gathered up his tackle and ran.

"What's the matter!" cried Dexter.

Bob made no reply, but ran off; and as he did so, Dexter laughingly took another apple from his pocket—a hard green Sturmer pippin, which he threw with such force and accuracy that it struck Bob right in the middle of the back, when the boy uttered a cry of alarm, ran more swiftly, and Dexter stood for a moment roaring with laughter, and then turned to find himself face to face with the trio who had come down the garden.

"And them pippins worth twopence apiece at Christmas, sir!" cried Dan'l.

"What are you doing, Dexter!" cried the doctor sternly.

"I was only giving him an apple or two," said the boy, after a few moments' hesitation.

"Come in, sir," cried the doctor.

"A month's notice, if you please, sir, from to-day," said Dan'l, frowning angrily; but no one paid any heed to him, for the doctor had laid his hand upon Dexter's shoulder, and marched him off.

"And I've never said nothing yet about our bees," grumbled Dan'l. "A young tyke! Raddled 'em up with a long stick on purpose to get me stung to death, he did, as is a massy I warn't. Well, a month to-day. Either he goes or I do. Such whims, to have a boy like that about the place. Well, I'm glad I've brought it to a head, for the doctor won't part with me."

"Now, sir," said the doctor, as he seated himself in his chair, and Helen took up her work, carefully keeping her eyes off Dexter, who looked at her appealingly again and again. "Now, sir, what have you to say for yourself?"

Dexter looked at the doctor, and his countenance was so unpleasantly angry that the ceiling, the floor, and the various objects around seemed preferable, and were carefully observed in turn.

"Do you hear, sir? What have you to say for yourself!"

"What about?" faltered Dexter at last.

"What about, sir? Just as if you did not know! Weren't you forbidden to touch those apples!"

"Only by Daniel, sir; and he said I was never to touch any fruit at all; but you said I might."

"Yes—I did. I said you might have some fruit."

"Apples is fruit," said Dexter.

"*Are* fruit—*are* fruit, sir," cried the doctor, in an exasperated tone.

"Apples *are* fruit," said Dexter.

"But I did not tell you to pick my choice pippins and throw them across the river to every blackguard boy you see."

"But he hasn't got a beautiful garden like we have," protested Dexter.

"What has that got to do with it, sir?" cried the doctor angrily. "I don't grow fruit and keep gardeners on purpose to supply the wants of all the little rascals in the place."

"He asked me to get him some apples, sir."

"Asked you to get him some, indeed! Look here, sir; I've tried very hard to make you a decent boy by kindness, but it does no good. You were told not to associate with that boy any more."

"Please, sir, I didn't," cried Dexter. "I didn't, indeed, sir."

"What? Why, I saw you talking to him, and giving him fruit."

"Please, sir, I couldn't help it. I didn't 'sociate with him; he would come and 'sociate with me."

"Bah!" ejaculated the doctor.

"And he said if I didn't give him some apples and pears he'd come and stand in front of the windows here and shout 'workus' as loud as he could."

"I shall have to send the police after him," said the doctor fiercely; "and as for you, sir, I've quite made up my mind what to do. Kind words are thrown away. I shall now purchase a cane—and use it."

"Oh, I say, don't," cried Dexter, giving himself a writhe, as he recalled sundry unpleasant interviews with Mr Sibery. "It does hurt so, you don't know; and makes black marks on you afterwards, just as if it had been dipped in ink."

Helen bent down over the work she had taken up.

"Don't?" said the doctor sharply. "Then what am I to do, sir? Words are of no use. I did hope that you were going to be a better and more tractable boy."

"Well, but ain't I?" said Dexter, looking puzzled, and rubbing his curly head.

"Better? No, sir; much worse."

Dexter rubbed his head again thoughtfully.

"I haven't torn my clothes this week, and I haven't been down on my knees; and I haven't been on the top of the wall, and I did want to ever so badly."

"No, Dexter; but you climbed right to the top of the big pear-tree," said Helen quickly; "and it was a terribly dangerous thing to do."

"Now you've begun at me!" said the boy in a lachrymose tone. "I'm afraid I'm a regular bad one, and you'd better send me back again."

The doctor looked at Helen, and she returned the glance with a very serious aspect, but there was a merry light in her eyes, as she saw her father's discomfiture.

He read her looks aright, and got up from his seat with an impatient ejaculation.

"I'm going out, my dear," he said shortly.

"Are you going to get a cane!" cried Dexter excitedly. "I say, don't, and I will try so hard to do what you want."

"I was not going to buy a cane, sir," said the doctor, who was half-angry, half-amused by the boy's earnestness. "One of my walking-sticks would do very well when I give you a good sound thrashing. Here, Helen, my dear, you can speak to Dexter a bit. I will have another talk to him to-night."

The doctor left the room, and Dexter stood listening as his step was heard in the hall. Then the door closed, and Helen bent thoughtfully over her work, while the boy stood first on one foot, then on the other, watching her. The window was open, the sun shone, and the garden with its lawn and bright flowers looked wonderfully tempting, but duty and the disgrace he was in acted as two chains to hold the boy there.

"I say," he said at last.

"Yes, Dexter," said Helen, looking up at him sadly.

"Oh, I say, don't look at me like that," he cried.

"You force me to, Dexter," she said gravely.

"But ain't you going to talk to me!"

"If I talk to you, it will only be to scold you very severely."

Dexter sighed.

"Well," he said, after a pause, during which he had been gazing intently in the earnest eyes before him; "you've got to do it, so let's have it over. I was always glad when I had been punished at school."

"Glad, Dexter?"

"Yes, glad it was over. It was the worst part of it waiting to have your whack!"

"Do you want to oblige me, Dexter?" said Helen, wincing at the boy's words.

"Yes, of course I do. Want me to fetch something?"

"No. Once more I want you to promise to leave off some of those objectionable words."

"But it's of no use to promise," cried the boy, with a look of angry perplexity. "I always break my word."

"Then why do you!"

"I dunno," said Dexter. "There's something in me I think that makes me. You tell me to be a good boy, and I say I will, and I always mean to be; but somehow I can't. I think it's because nobody likes me, because—because—because I came from there."

"Do I behave to you as if I did not like you?" said Helen reproachfully.

The boy was on his knees beside her in a moment, holding her hand against his cheek as he looked up at her with his lip working, and a dumb look of pitiful pleading in his eyes.

"I do not think I do, Dexter."

He shook his head, and tried to speak. Then, springing up suddenly, he ran out of the study, dashed upstairs, half-blind with the tears which he was fighting back, and then with his head down through the open door into his bedroom, when there was a violent collision, a shriek followed by a score more to succeed a terrific crash, and when in alarm Helen and Mrs Millet ran panting up, it was to find Dexter rubbing his head, and Maria seated in the middle of the boy's bedroom with the sherds of a broken toilet pail upon the floor, and an ewer lying upon its side, and the water soaking into the carpet.

"What is the matter?" cried Helen.

"I won't—I won't—I declare I won't put up with it no longer!" cried the maid in the intervals of sundry sobs and hysterical cries.

"But how did it happen!" said Mrs Millet.

"It's—sit's—sit's—sit's—sit's—sit's—his tricks again," sobbed Maria.

"Dexter!" cried Helen.

"Yes—es—Miss—es—ma'am," sobbed Maria. "I'd dide—I'd dide—I'd—just half—half—half filled the war—war—war—ter—jug, and he ran—ran—ran at me with his head—dead in the chest—and then—then—then—then knocked me dud—dud—dud—down, and I'll go at once, I will—there."

"Dexter," said Helen sternly; "was this some trick?"

"I don't know," said the boy sadly. "I s'pose so."

"But did you run at Maria and try to knock her down?"

"No," said Dexter. "I was going into my room in a hurry, and she was coming out."

"He did it o' purpose, Miss," cried Maria viciously.

"That will do, Maria," said Helen with dignity. "Mrs Millet, see that these broken pieces are removed. Dexter, come down to the drawing-room with me."

Dexter sighed and followed, feeling the while that after all the Union School was a happy place, and that he certainly was not happy here.

"It is very unfortunate that you should meet with such accidents, Dexter," said Helen, as soon as they were alone.

"Yes," he said piteously, "ain't it? I say—"

"Well, Dexter!"

"It's no good. I know what he wants to do. He said he wanted to make a gentleman of me, but you can't do it, and I'd better be 'prenticed to a shoemaker, same as lots of boys have been."

Helen said nothing, but looked at the boy with a troubled gaze, as she wondered whether her father's plan was possible.

"You had better go out in the garden again, Dexter," she said after a time.

The trouble had been passing off, and Dexter leaped up with alacrity; but as he reached the window he saw Dan'l crossing the lawn, and he stopped short, turned, and came back to sit down with a sigh.

"Well, Dexter," said Helen, "why don't you go?"

He gave her a pitiful look which went right to her heart, as he said slowly—

"No. I shan't go. I should only get into trouble again."

Chapter Twenty Two
The Beginning of Trouble

"I say," said Dexter, a few days later, as he followed Helen into the drawing-room. "What have I been doing now!"

"I hope nothing fresh, Dexter. Have you been in mischief!"

"I don't know," he said; "only I've been in the study, and there's a tall gent."

"Say gentleman, Dexter."

"Tall gentleman with a white handkerchief round his neck, and he has been asking me questions, and every time I answered him he sighed, and said, 'Dear me!'"

"Indeed!" said Helen, smiling. "What did he ask you?"

"If I knew Euclid; and when I said I didn't know him, he said, 'Oh dear me!' Then he asked me if I knew Algebra, and I said I didn't, and he shook his head at me and said, 'Dear me! dear me!' and that he would have to pull me up. I say, what have I done to be pulled up!"

"Don't you know that Euclid wrote a work on Geometry, and that Algebra is a study by which calculations are made!"

"No," said Dexter eagerly. "I thought they were two people. Then why did he say he would have to pull me up?"

"He meant that you were very much behind with, your studies, and that he would have to teach you and bring you forward."

"Oh, I see! And is he going to teach me?"

"Yes, Mr Limpney is your private tutor now; and he is coming every day, so I hope you will be very industrious, and try hard to learn."

"Oh yes, I'll try. Mr Limpney; I don't think he much liked me, though."

"Nonsense, Dexter; you should not think such things."

"All right. I won't then. It will be like going to school again, won't it?"

"Much pleasanter, I hope."

Time glided rapidly on after its usual fashion, and Dexter grew fast.

There was a long range of old stabling at the doctor's house, with extensive lofts. The first part was partitioned off for a coachman's room, but this had not been in use for half a century, and the whole place was ruinous and decayed. Once upon a time some one with a love of horses must have lived there, for there were stalls for eight, and a coach-house as well, but the doctor only kept two horses, and they occupied a new stable built in front of the old.

The back part was one of Dexter's favourite hunting-grounds. Here he could be quite alone, and do pretty well as he liked. Peter the groom never noticed his goings-out and comings-in, and there was no one to find fault with him for being untidy.

Here then he had quite a little menagerie of his own. His pocket-money, as supplied by the doctor, afforded him means for buying any little thing he fancied, and hence he had in one of the lofts a couple of very ancient pigeons, which the man of whom he bought them declared to be extremely young; a thrush in a cage; two hedge-sparrows, which were supposed to be linnets, in another; two mice in an old cigar-box lined with tin; and a very attenuated rat, which had been caught by Peter in a trap, and which was allowed to live *minus* one foreleg that had been cut short off close to the shoulder, but over which the skin had grown.

No one interfered with Dexter's pets, and in fact the old range of stabling was rarely visited, even by the gardeners, so that the place became not only the boy's favourite resort in his loneliness, but, so to speak, his little kingdom where he reigned over his pets.

There was plenty of room, especially in the lofts with their cross-beams and ties; and here, with his pets, as the only spectators, Dexter used to go daily to get rid of the vitality which often battled for exit in the confinement of the house. Half an hour here of the performance of so many natural gymnastic tricks seemed to tame him down—these tricks being much of a kind popular amongst caged monkeys, who often, for no apparent object, spring about and hang by hands or feet, often by their tail.

But he had one piece of enjoyment that would have driven a monkey mad with envy. He had discovered among the lumber a very large old-fashioned bottle-jack, and after hanging this from a hook and winding it up, one of his greatest pleasures was to hang from that jack, and roast till he grew giddy, when he varied the enjoyment by buckling on a strap, attaching himself with a hook from the waist, and then going through either a flying or swimming movement as he spun slowly round.

Then he had a rope-trick or two contrived by means of a long piece of knotted together clothes-line, doubled, and hung from the rafters to form a swing or trapeze.

Dexter had paid his customary morning visit to his pets, and carefully fed them according to his wont; his plan, a very regular one among boys, being to give them twice as much as was good for them one day, and a starving the next—a mode said to be good with pigs, and productive of streaky bacon, but bad for domestic pets. Then he had returned to the house to go through his lessons, and sent long-suffering Mr Limpney, BA, almost into despair by the little progress he had made, after which he had gone down the garden with the expectation of meeting Dan'l at some corner, but instead had come upon Peter, busy as usual with his broom.

"Yer needn't look," said the latter worthy; "he's gone out."

"What! Dan'l has?"

"Yes; gone to see a friend who's a gardener over at Champney Ryle, to buy some seeds."

It was like the announcement of a holiday, and leaving the groom making the usual long stretches with his broom, Dexter went on aimlessly to the river-side, where, for the first time for many months, he found Bob Dimsted fishing.

"Hullo, old un!" was the latter's greeting, "how are you!"

Dexter gave the required information, and hesitated for a few moments, something in the way of a collection of Helen's warnings coming vaguely to his hand; but the volunteered information of the boy on the other side of the river, that he had got some "glorious red wums," and that the fish were well on the feed, drove everything else away, and in a few minutes Dexter was sitting upon the crown of a willow pollard, ten feet out over the river, that much nearer to the fisher, and in earnest conversation with him as he watched his float.

Once more the memory of words that had been spoken to him came to Dexter, but the bobbing of the float, and the excitement of capturing a fish, drove the thoughts away—the fascination of the fishing, and the pleasant excitement of meeting a companion of near his own age, cut off, as he was, from the society of boys, being too much for him; and he was soon eagerly listening, and replying to all that was said.

"Ever go fishing in a boat?" said Bob, after a time.

"No."

"Ah! you should go in a boat," said Bob. "You sit down comfortable, with your feet all dry, and you can float over all the deep holes and best places in the river, and catch all the big fish. It's lovely!"

"Did you ever fish out of a boat?" asked Dexter.

"Did I ever fish out of a boat? Ha! ha! ha! Lots of times. I'm going to get a boat some day, and have a saucepan and kettle and plate and spoon, and take my fishing-tackle, and then I shall get a gun or a pistol, and go off down the river."

"What for!"

"What for? Why, to live like that, catching fish, and shooting wild ducks and geese, and cooking 'em, and eating 'em. Then you have a 'paulin and spread it over the boat of a night, and sleep under it—and there you are!"

Dexter looked at the adventurous being before him in wonder, while he fished on and talked.

"I should make myself a sail, too, and then I shouldn't have to row so much; and then I could go right on down to the end of the river, and sail away to foreign countries, and shoot all kinds of wonderful things. And then you could land sometimes and kill snakes, and make yourself a hut to live in, and do just as you liked. Ah, that is a fine life!"

"Yes," said Dexter, whose eager young mind rapidly painted an illustration to everything his companion described.

"A man I know has been to sea, and he says sometimes you come to places where there's nothing but mackerel, and you can almost ladle 'em out with your hands. I should boil 'em over a fire. They are good then."

Dexter's eyes grew more round.

"Then out at sea you have long lines, and you catch big cod-fish, and soles almost as big as the boat."

"And are you going to have a boat?"

"To be sure I am. I get tired of always coming out to catch little roach and dace and eels. I mean to go soon."

Dexter sighed.

"That man says when you go far enough away, you come to islands where the cocoa-nuts grow; and then, all you've got to do is go ashore and pull your boat up on the sands, and when you are hungry you climb a tree and get a cocoa-nut; and every one has got enough meat and drink in it for a meal."

"Do you?"

"Yerrrs! That you do. That's the sort of place to go and live at. I'm tired o' Coleby."

"Why don't you go and live there, then!" said Dexter.

"I'm going to, some day. It's no use to be in too much of a hurry; I want to save a little money first, and get some more tackle. You see, you want big hooks for big fish, and some long lines. Then you must have a boat."

The idea of the unknown countries made Dexter thrill, and he listened eagerly as the boy went on prosing away while he fished, taking out his line from time to time, and dropping the bait in likely places.

"Haven't made up my mind what boat I shall have yet, only it must be a good one."

"Yes," said Dexter; "you'd want a good big boat."

"Not such a very big un," said Bob. "I should want a nice un with cushions, because you'd have to sit in it so long."

"And sleep in it too?"

"Oh yes; you'd have to sleep in it."

"Should you light the fire, and cook in it!" said Dexter innocently.

"Yah! No, o' course not. You'd go ashore every time you wanted to cook, and light a fire there with a burnin'-glass."

"But suppose the sun didn't shine!"

"Sun always shines out there," said Bob. "That sailor chap told me, and the birds are all sorts of colours, and the fish too, like you see in glass globes. I mean to go."

"When shall you go?"

"Oh, some day when I'm ready. I know of a jolly boat as would just do."

"Do you?"

"Yes; I dessay you've seen it. Belongs to Danby's, down the river. Lives in a boat-house."

"Yes, I've seen it," said Dexter eagerly. "It is a beauty!"

"Well, that's the sort of boat I mean to have. P'r'aps I shall have that."

"You couldn't have that," cried Dexter.

"Why not? They never use it, not more'n twice a year. Dessay they'd lend it."

"That they wouldn't," cried Dexter.

"Well, then, I should borrow it, and bring it back when I'd done with it. What games you could have with a boat like that!"

"Yes," sighed Dexter; "wish we had one!"

"Wouldn't be such a good one as that if you had. That's just the boat I've made up my mind to have."

"And shall you sail right away to a foreign country!" said Dexter, from his nest up in the willow.

"Why, how can you sail away to another place without a mast and sail, stoopid!" cried Bob.

"If you call me stupid," said Dexter sharply, "I'll come and punch your head."

"Yah! Yer can't get at me."

"Can't I? I could swim across in a minute, and I would, if it wasn't for wetting my clothes."

"Yah!" cried Bob scoffingly. "Why, I could fight yer one hand."

"No, you couldn't."

"Yes, I could."

"Well, you'd see, if I came across."

"But yer can't get across," laughed Bob. "I know of a capital mast."

Dexter looked sulky.

"It's part of an old boat-hook my father found floating in the river. I shall smooth it down with my knife if I can't borrow a spokeshave."

"And what'll you do for a sail?" said Dexter, his interest in the expedition chasing away his anger.

"Oh, I shall get a table-cloth or a sheet. Sheets make beautiful sails. You just hoists 'em up, and puts an oar over the stern to steer with, and then away you go, just where you like. Sailing along in a boat's lovely!"

"Ever been in a boat sailing?" asked Dexter.

"No; but I know it is. That sailor told me. He says when you've got all sail set, you just cruises along."

"Do you?"

"Yes. I know; and I mean to go some day; but it's no use to be in a jolly hurry, and you ought to have a mate."

"Ought you?"

"Yes, so as he could steer while a chap went to sleep; because sometimes you'd be a long way from the shore."

Dexter sat very thoughtful and still, dreaming of the wonders of far-off places, such as could be reached by Bob Dimsted and his companion, the impracticability of such a journey never once occurring to him. Bob had been about all his life free to go and come, while he, Dexter, seemed to have been always shut up, as it were, in a cage, which had narrowed his mind.

"Some chaps would be glad of such a chance," said Bob. "It'll be a fine time. My, what fishing I shall have!"

"Shall you be gone long!" said Dexter, after a time.

"Long? Why, of course I shall; years and years. I shan't come back till I've made a fortune, and am a rich man, with heaps of money to spend. Some chaps would be glad to go."

"Yes, of course," said Dexter dreamily.

"I want to get a mate who isn't afraid of anything. Dessay we should meet lions sometimes, and big snakes."

"What! in England!"

"England! Yah! Who's going to stop in England? I'm going to sail away to wonderful places all over the world."

"But would the boat be big enough to cross the great sea?"

"Who's going to cross the great sea?" cried Bob. "Of course I shouldn't. I should only go out about six miles from shore, and keep close in, so as to land every night to get grub, or anything else. P'r'aps to go shooting. My father's got an old gun—a fine un. Think I don't know what I'm about? Shoots hares with it, and fezzans.

"There's another!" he exclaimed, as he hooked and landed an unfortunate little perch, which he threw into his basket with a look of disgust. "I'm sick of ketching such miserable little things as these. I want to get hold of big sea-fish of all kinds, so as to fill the boat. Some chaps would be glad to go," he said again, as he threw his line in once more.

"Yes," said Dexter thoughtfully; "I should like to go."

"You!" said Bob, with a mocking laugh. "You! Why, you'd be afraid. I don't believe you dare go in a boat!"

"Oh yes, I dare," said Dexter stoutly.

"Not you. You're afraid of what the doctor would say. You daren't even come fishing with me up the river."

"They said I was not to go with you," said Dexter quietly; "so I couldn't."

"Then what's the use of your saying you'd like to go. You couldn't."

"But I should like to go," said Dexter excitedly.

"Not you. I want a mate as has got some pluck in him. You'd be afraid to be out all night on the water."

"No, I shouldn't. I should like it."

"Well, I don't know," said Bob dubiously. "I might take you, and I mightn't. You ain't quite the sort of a chap I should want; and, besides, you've got to stay where you are and learn lessons. Ho! ho! ho! what a game, to be obliged to stop indoors every day and learn lessons! I wonder you ain't ashamed of it."

Dexter's cheeks flushed, and he looked angrily across the river with his fists clenched, but he said nothing.

"You wouldn't do. You ain't strong enough," said Bob at last.

"I'm as strong as you are."

"But you daren't come."

"I should like to come, but I don't think they'd let me."

"Why, of course they wouldn't, stoopid. You'd have to come away some night quietly, and get in the boat, and then we'd let her float down the river, and row right away till morning, and then we could set the sail, and go just wherever we liked, because we should be our own masters."

"Here's some one coming after you," said Bob, in a low voice; and he shrank away, leaving Dexter perched up in the crown of the tree, where he stopped without speaking, as he saw Helen come down the garden, and she walked close by him without raising her eyes, and passed on.

Chapter Twenty Three
The Trouble Grows

Dexter got down out of the willow-tree with a seed in his brain.

Bob Dimsted had dropped that seed into his young mind, and there it had struck root directly, and continued to grow. A hard fight now commenced.

So long as he was with Helen or the doctor, he could think of nothing but the fact that they were so kind to him, and took so much interest in his welfare, that it would be horribly ungrateful to go away without leave, and he vowed that he would not go.

But so sure as he was alone, a series of dissolving views began to float before his vivid imagination, and he saw Sir James Danby's boat managed by Bob Dimsted and himself, gliding rapidly along through river and along by sunlit shores, where, after catching wonderfully tinted fish, he and the boy landed to light a fire, cook their food, and partake of it in a delightful gipsy fashion. Then they put to sea again, and glided on past wondrous isles where cocoa-nut palms waved in the soft breeze.

Try how he would, Dexter could not keep these ideas out of his head, and the more he thought, the brighter and more attractive they became; and day after day found him, whenever he had an opportunity, waiting about by the river-side in the expectation of seeing Bob Dimsted.

Bob did not come, but as Dexter climbed up into his nest in the willow pollard his vivid imagination supplied the words he had said, and he seemed to see himself sailing away, with the boy for his companion, down the river, and out into the open sea; a portion of this globe which he formed out of his own fancy, the result being wonderfully unlike the truth.

Bob did not come, but Helen noticed how quiet and thoughtful the boy seemed, and also how he affected that portion of the garden.

"Why don't you fish, Dexter?" she said to him one day, as she saw him gazing disconsolately at the river.

He had not thought of this as an excuse for staying down by the river, but he snatched at the idea now, and for the next week, whenever he could get away from his lessons or their preparation, he was down on the bank, dividing his time between watching his float and the opposite shore.

But still Bob Dimsted did not come; and at last Dexter began to settle down seriously to his fishing, as the impressions made grew more faint.

Then all at once back they came; for as he sat watching his float one day, a voice said sharply—

"Now then! why don't you strike!"

But Dexter did not strike, and the fish went off with the bait as the holder of the rod exclaimed—

"Why haven't you been fishing all this time!"

"What was the good?" said Bob, "I was getting ready to go, and talking to my mate, who's going with me."

"Your mate!" exclaimed Dexter, whose heart sank at those words.

"Yes, I know'd you wouldn't go, so. I began to look out for a chap who would."

"But I didn't say that I really would not go," said Dexter, as he laid his tackle under the bushes.

"Oh yes, you did; I could see what you meant. Do they bite to-day!"

"I don't know," said Dexter dolefully. "But, I say, you couldn't have that boat if you wanted to."

"Oh yes, I could if I liked."

"But it isn't yours."

"Tchah! couldn't you borrow it!"

Dexter did not see how, and he climbed into the willow, while Bob went on fishing.

"I hate a chap who is always trying to find out things to stop a fellow from doing anything. Why don't you say you won't go and ha' done with it?"

Dexter sighed as he thought of the wonderful fish to be caught, and the great nuts on the trees, each of which nuts would make a meal. Then of the delight of sailing away in that beautiful boat down the river, and then out to sea, where they could land upon the sands and light their fire; and it seemed to him that such a life would be one long time of delight.

He sat in his nest picking the buds off the willow twigs, and bending and lacing them together, furtively glancing at grubby-looking Bob Dimsted, whose appearance was not attractive; but what were appearances to a boy who possessed such gifts of knowledge in fishing and managing a boat, and had learned so much about foreign lands?

Dexter sighed again, and Bob gave him a furtive look, as with evident enjoyment he took a red worm out of some moss and stuck his sharp hook into it, drew the writhing creature over the shank, and then passed the point through again and again.

So to speak, he had impaled Dexter on a moral hook as well, the barb had gone right in so that it could not be drawn out without tearing; and Dexter writhed and twined, and felt as if he would have given anything to get away.

Bob went on fishing, throwing the twisting worm just down among the roots of a willow-tree, and the float told directly after that the cast was not without avail, for there was a quick bobbing movement, then a sharp snatch, Bob struck, and, after a good deal of rushing about and splashing, a good-sized perch was landed, with its sharp back fin erect, and its gilded sides, with their black markings, glistening in the sunshine.

"What a beauty!" cried Dexter enthusiastically, as for the moment the wonders of the boating expedition were forgotten.

But they were brought back directly.

"Pooh!" exclaimed Bob contemptuously. "That's nothing; only a little perch. Why, if we went off fishing in that boat, you'd chuck a fish like that in again."

But Bob did not "chuck" that perch in again; he placed it in his basket, and directly after caught up his various articles of fishing-gear and ran off.

Dexter was about to speak, but just then he heard a harsh cough, and, glancing through the screen of willow twigs which surrounded him, he saw old Dan'l coming hastily down over the grass path towards the tree.

"Yes, I can see yer," he shouted, as he reached the water's edge; and, to Dexter's surprise, he found that it was not he the old gardener was addressing. "You come over there fishing again, I'll send the police arter yer."

Bob, safe at a distance, made a derisive gesture.

"None of your sarse, you poaching young vagabond. I know what you came there for. Be off with you."

"Shan't," cried Bob, as he settled down to fish a hundred yards away.

"Always coming here after that boy," grumbled Dan'l. "If I could have my way I'd bundle 'em both out of the town together. Young robbers,— that's what they are, the pair of 'em."

Dexter's face flushed, and he was about to respond, but the old gardener began to move away.

"Doctor ought to be ashamed of himself," he grumbled, as he stood for a moment or two looking round in search of Dexter, but never looking above the brim of his broad straw hat, and the next moment Dexter was left alone seated in the crown of the old willow, very low-spirited and thoughtful, as he came down from his perch, brushed the bits of green from his clothes, and then walked slowly up toward the house, taking the other side of the garden; but of course coming right upon Dan'l, who followed him about till he took refuge in the doctor's study, with a book whose contents seemed to be a history of foreign lands, and the pictures records of the doings of one Dexter Grayson and his companion Bob. For the old effervescence consequent upon his having been kept down so long was passing off, and a complete change seemed to be coming over the boy.

MR. LIMPNEY TRIES TO TEACH EUCLID TO DEXTER

Chapter Twenty Four
The Pleasant Ways of Learning

"Now, Master Grayson," said Mr Limpney, "what am I to say to the doctor!"

The private tutor threw himself back in his seat in the study, vacated by the doctor, while Dexter had his lessons, placed his hands behind his head, and, after wrinkling his forehead in lines from his brow to right on the top, where the hair began, he stared hard at his pupil.

"I say again, sir, what am I to tell the doctor!"

"I don't know," said Dexter dolefully. Then, plucking up a little spirit: "I wrote out all my history questions, and did the parsing with a little help from Miss Grayson, and I did the sum you set me all by myself."

"Yes; but the Algebra, the Classics, and the Euclid! Where are they?"

"There they are," said Dexter, pointing dismally to some books on the table.

"Yes, sir, there they are—on that table, when they ought to be in your head."

"But they won't go in my head, sir," cried Dexter desperately.

"Nonsense, sir! you will not let them, and I warn you plainly, that if we do not make better progress, I shall tell the doctor that I will not continue to take his payment for nothing."

"No; I say; don't do that," said Dexter piteously. "He wouldn't like it."

"I cannot help that, sir. I have my duty to perform. Anybody can do those childish history and grammatical questions; it is the classical and mathematical lessons in which I wish you to excel. Now, once more. No, no, you must not refer to the book. 'In any right-angled triangle, the square of the side—' Now, go on."

Dexter took up a slate and pencil, wrinkled up his forehead as nearly like the tutor's as he could, and slowly drew a triangle.

"Very good," said Mr Limpney. "Now, go on."

Dexter stared at his sketch, then helplessly at his instructor.

"I ought to write *ABC* here, oughtn't I, sir?"

"Yes, of course. Go on."

Dexter hesitated, and then put a letter at each corner.

"Well, have it that way if you like," said Mr Limpney.

"I don't like it that way, sir," said Dexter. "I'll put it your way."

"No, no. Go on your way."

"But I haven't got any way, sir," said Dexter desperately.

"Nonsense, nonsense! Go on."

"Please, sir, I can't. I've tried and tried over and over again, but the angles all get mixed up with the sides, and it is all such a muddle. I shall never learn Euclid. Is it any use?"

"Is it any use!" cried the tutor scornfully. "Look at me, sir. Has it been any use to me!"

Dexter looked at the face before him, and then right up the forehead, and wondered whether learning Euclid had made all the hair come off the top of his head.

"Well, go on."

"I can't, sir, please," sighed the boy. "I know it's something about squares, and *ABC*, and *BAC*, and *CAB*, and—but you produce the lines."

"But you do not produce them, sir," cried Mr Limpney angrily; "nor anything else! You ought to be ashamed of yourself, sir!"

"I am," said Dexter innocently. "I'm a dreadfully stupid boy, sir, and I don't think I've got any brains."

"Are you going through that forty-seventh problem this morning, sir?"

Dexter made a desperate attempt, floundered on a quarter of a minute, and broke down in half.

"Tut—tut—tut!" ejaculated Mr Limpney. "I'm sure you have not looked at it since I was here."

"That I have, sir," cried Dexter, in a voice full of eager protest. "Hours and hours, sir, I walked up and down the garden with it, and then I took the book up with me into my loft, and made a chalk triangle on the floor, and kept on saying it over and over, but as fast as I said it the words slipped out of my head again. I can't help it, sir, I am so stupid."

"Algebra!" said Mr Limpney, in a tone of angry disgust.

"Am I not to try and say the Euclid, sir?"

"Algebra!" cried Mr Limpney again, and he slapped the table with a thin book. "Now then, where are these simple equations?"

Dexter drew a half-sheet of foolscap paper from a folio, and rather shrinkingly placed it before his tutor, who took a pair of spectacles from his pocket, and placed them over his mild-looking eyes.

"Let me see," he said, referring to a note-book. "The questions I gave you were: 'A spent 2 shillings and 6 pence in oranges, and says that three of them cost as much under a shilling as nine of them cost over a shilling. How many did he buy?'"

Mr Limpney coughed, blew his nose loudly, as if it were a post-horn, and then went on—

"Secondly: 'Two coaches start at the same time for York and London, a distance of 200 miles, travelling one at nine and a half miles an hour, the other at nine and a quarter miles; where will they meet, and in what time from starting?'"

He gave his nose a finishing touch with his handkerchief, closed his note-book, and turned to Dexter.

"Now then," he said. "Let us see."

He took the sheet of paper, looked at one side, turned it over and looked at the other, and then raised his eyes to Dexter's, which avoided his gaze directly.

"What is this?" he cried.

"The equations, sir," said Dexter humbly.

"Tut—tut—tut!" ejaculated Mr Limpney. "Was there ever such a boy? *plus* where it ought to be *minus*, and—why, what's this!"

"This, sir?" said Dexter. "Half-crowns."

"But it was to be oranges. How many did he buy? and here you say he bought ninety-seven half-crowns. I don't know how you arrived at it, or what you mean. A man does not go to a shop to buy half-crowns. He spent half a crown in oranges."

"Yes, sir."

"I believe it's sheer obstinacy. You do not want to do these equations—simple equations too, mind you! Now then, about the stage-coaches. When did they meet, and in what time from starting? Now then—there are your figures, where did they meet? Look and tell me."

Dexter took the half-sheet of paper, stared at it very doubtfully, and then looked up.

"Well!" said Mr Limpney. "Where did they meet?"

"Peterborough, sir."

"Where!" cried Mr Limpney in astonishment.

"Peterborough, sir."

"Now, will you have the goodness to tell me how you found out that?"

"On the map, sir."

"Bless my soul!" exclaimed the tutor. "Well, go on. At what time from starting!"

"About ten o'clock, sir."

"Better and better," said the tutor sarcastically. "Now, will you kindly explain—no, no, don't look at your figures— Will you kindly explain how you arrived at this sapient conclusion?"

Dexter hesitated, and shifted one foot over the other.

"Well, sir, I am waiting," cried Mr Limpney, in a tone of voice which made Dexter think very much resembled that of Mr Sibery when he was angry.

"I—I—"

"Don't hesitate, sir. Have I not told you again and again that a gentleman never hesitates, but speaks out at once? Now then, I ask you how you arrived at this wonderful conclusion?"

"I tried over and over again, sir, with the a's and b's, and then I thought I must guess it."

"And did you guess it?"

"No, sir, I suddenly recollected what you said."

"And pray, what did I say!"

"Why, sir, you always said let x represent the unknown quantity, and— and x stands for ten—ten o'clock."

Mr Limpney snatched the paper from the boy's hand, and was about to tear it up, when the door opened and Dr Grayson entered.

"Well," he said pleasantly, "and how are we getting on?"

"Getting on, sir?" said Mr Limpney tartly. "Will you have the goodness to ask my pupil!"

"To be sure—to be sure," said the doctor. "Well, Dexter, how are you getting on? Eh? what's this? Oh, Algebra!" he continued, as he took the half-sheet of paper covered with the boy's calligraphy. "Oh, Algebra! Hah! I never was much of a fist at that."

"Only simple equations, sir," said the tutor.

"Ah, yes. Simple equations. Well, Dexter, how are you getting on?"

"Very badly, sir."

"Badly? Nonsense!"

"But I am, sir. These things puzzle me dreadfully. I'm so stupid."

"Stupid? Nonsense! Nothing of the kind. Scarcely anybody is stupid. Men who can't understand some things understand others. Now, let's see. What is the question? H'm! ah! yes, oranges. H'm! ah! yes; not difficult, I suppose, when you know how. And—what's this? London and York—stage-coaches. Nine and a half miles, nine and a quarter miles, and—er—h'm, yes, of course, where would they meet?"

"Peterborough, sir," said Mr Limpney sarcastically, and with a peculiar look at Dexter.

"H'm! would they now?" said the doctor. "Well, I shouldn't have thought it! And how is he getting on with his Latin, Mr Limpney!"

"Horribly, sir!" exclaimed the tutor sharply. "I am very glad you have come, for I really feel it to be my duty to complain to you of the great want of diligence displayed by my pupil."

"Dear me! I am very sorry," exclaimed the doctor. "Why, Dexter, my boy, how's this? You promised me that you would be attentive."

"Yes, sir, I did."

"Then why are you not attentive?"

"I do try to be, sir."

"But if you were, Mr Limpney would not have cause to complain. It's too bad, Dexter, too bad. Do you know why Mr Limpney comes here?"

"Yes, sir," said the boy dismally; "to teach me."

"And you do not take advantage of his teaching. This is very serious. Very sad indeed."

"I am sure, Dr Grayson, that no tutor could have taken more pains than I have to impart to him the various branches of a liberal education; but after all these months of teaching it really seems to me that we are further behind. He is not a dull boy."

"Certainly not. By no means," said the doctor.

"And I do not give him tasks beyond his powers."

"I hope not, I am sure," said the doctor.

"And yet not the slightest progress is made. There is only one explanation, sir, and that is want of diligence."

"Dear me! dear me! dear me!" exclaimed the doctor. "Now, Dexter, what have you to say?"

"Nothing, sir!" said the boy sadly; "only I think sometimes that my brains must be too wet."

"Good gracious! boy: what do you mean!"

"I mean too wet and slippery, sir, so that they will not hold what I put into them."

The doctor looked at the tutor, and the tutor looked at the doctor, as if he considered that this was impertinence.

"I am very sorry—very sorry indeed, Dexter," said the doctor. "There, sir, you can go now. I will have a talk to Mr Limpney. We must see if we cannot bring you to a better frame of mind."

Chapter Twenty Five
Dexter's Dumb Friends

Dexter went out into the hall feeling exceedingly miserable, for he had left the occupants of the study talking about him, and, as the saying goes, it made his ears burn. "I couldn't help it," he said dolefully: "I did try. I'll go and tell Miss Grayson all about it, and ask her to take my part."

He went into the drawing-room, but Helen was not there, so he ran upstairs, and was in the act of tapping at her bedroom door, when Maria came out of another room.

It was a curious fact, but there it was: Dexter always had the effect upon Maria that a dog has upon a cat. The dog may be of the most amiable disposition, and without the slightest desire to fight or worry, but as soon as he is seen, up goes the cat's back in an arch, the tail becomes plumose and the fur horrent, while, with dilated eyes and displayed teeth glistening, puss indulges in the bad language peculiar to cats.

Maria being of a different physique did not display these signs of aggression exactly, but she invariably became vicious and metaphysically showed her teeth.

"It's of no use your knocking there, Master Dexter. Miss Helen isn't at home, and I'm quite sure if she was that she wouldn't approve of your trapesing up out of the garden in your muddy and dirty shoes. I've got enough to do here without cleaning up after you."

"But I haven't been in the garden, Maria," said Dexter, apologetically. "I have just come out of the study."

"Don't I tell you she ain't at home," said Maria spitefully.

"Do you know when she will be back!"

"No, I don't," said Maria, and then sarcastically: "I beg your pardon, *sir*—no I don't, *sir*."

Maria went along the passage like a roaring wind, she made so much noise with her skirts, and then hurried downstairs, as if in great haste to get hold of a door that she could bang; and as soon as she did reach one, she made so much use of her opportunity that a picture in the hall was blown sidewise, and began swinging to and fro like a great square pendulum.

Dexter sighed, and felt very miserable as he stole downstairs again, and past the study door, where the murmur of voices talking, as he knew, about him made him shiver.

He was obliged to pass that door to get his cap, and then he had to pass it again to get to the garden door.

Mr Limpney was talking, and Mr Limpney, being accustomed to lecture and teach, spoke very loudly, so that Dexter heard him say —

"I must have more authority, sir, and —" Dexter heard no more, for he fled into the garden, but he knew that having authority meant the same as it meant with Mr Sibery, and it sounded like going backwards.

He felt more miserable as he went out into the garden.

"Nobody hardly seems to like me, or care for me here," he said dolefully; and, led by his inclination, he began to make his way down the long green path toward the river, half fancying that Bob Dimsted might be fishing.

But before he had gone far he saw Dan'l, who was busy doing up a bed, and his appearance seemed to be the signal for the old man to put down his tools and take out his great pruning-knife, as if he meant mischief, but only to stoop from time to time to cut off a dead flower as an excuse, so it seemed, for following Dexter wherever he went.

It was impossible to go about the garden under these circumstances, so Dexter went down a little way, passed round a large *Wellingtonia*, and walked slowly back toward the house, but, instead of entering, went by the open window of the study, where the voice of Mr Limpney could still be heard talking loudly, and, as it seemed to the listening boy, breathing out threatenings against his peace of mind. The voice sounded so loud as he went by that he half-expected to hear himself called in, and in great dread he hurried on by the conservatory, and round the house to the old stable-yard.

As he reached this he could hear a peculiar hissing noise — that which Peter always made when he was washing the carriage, or the horses' legs — to blow away the dust, so he said.

For a moment Dexter felt disposed to go into the new stable and talk to Peter, but the opportunity was not tempting, and, hurrying on, the boy reached the old buildings, looked round for a moment, and, thus satisfied that he was not observed, he made a spring up to a little old window, caught the sill, scrambled up directly, and, passing through, disappeared inside.

He uttered a sigh as of relief, and crossing the damp stones of the gloomy old place he reached a crazy flight of steps, which led up to a loft, on either side of which were openings, through which, when the stable had been in use, it had been customary to thrust down the stored-up hay.

Dexter stopped here in the darkness for a few minutes listening, but no one was following him, and he walked along to a second ladder which led to a trap-door through which he passed, closed the trap, and then, in the long roof a place greatly resembling in shape the triangle over whose problem of squares he had that day stumbled, he seemed once more himself.

His first act was to run quietly along some boards laid over the loft ceiling, and, making a jump that would not have disgraced an acrobat, he caught at a rope, pendent from the highest portion of the rafters, twisted his legs about it, and swung easily to and fro.

The motion seemed to give him the greatest satisfaction, and as the impetus given died out, he dropped one foot, and with a few vigorous thrusts set himself going again till he was tired.

But that was not very soon, and he did not leave off till there were sundry scratchings and squeakings, which drew his attention to his pets, all of which were eager for food.

They were a heterogeneous collection, but, for the most part, exceedingly tame, and ready to allow themselves to be handled, constant familiarity with the gentle hand so often thrust into their boxes or cages having robbed it of its terrors.

Dexter's happiest moments were passed here, saving those which Helen continued to make pleasant to the boy; and as soon as his pets had drawn his attention, he took off his jacket and vest, rolled up his sleeves, and began to attend to their wants.

His rabbits—two which he had bought through Bob Dimsted, who made a profit of a hundred per cent, by the transaction—were lifted out of the packing-case they occupied, and in which they were kept by the lid being closed within half an inch, by their pink ears, and immediately stood up on their hind-legs, with drooping fore-paws, their pink noses twitching as they smelt their owner's legs, till he gave them a couple of red carrots, a portion of Dan'l's last year's store.

The next to be taken out was a hedgehog, a prize of his own discovering, and captured one day asleep and tightly rolled up beneath one of the Portugal laurels.

The minute before its box was open, the hedgehog was actively perambulating its dark prison, but the moment it was touched it became a ball, in which form it was rolled out on to the rough floor close to a flower-pot saucer of bread and milk, smuggled up directly after breakfast each morning.

Next came the large grey rat, captured originally in the steel trap, and whose first act might have been anticipated. It did not resent its owner's handling; but the moment it was set down it darted under the loose boards, and remained there until tempted forth by the smell of the bread and milk, and a tempting piece of candle-end, the former of which it helped the hedgehog to eat.

The mice, which lived in the old cigar-box—not white mice, nor those furry little sleepers given to hiding away in nooks and corners for elongated naps, but the regular grey cheese-nibblers—next, after a good deal of scratching, took Dexter's attention. As soon as the lid was open, and the boy's hand thrust in, they ran up his fingers, and then along his arm to his shoulder, wonderfully active and enterprising with their sharp little noses, one even venturing right up the boy's head after a pause by one ear, as if it looked like the cavernous entrance to some extremely snug hiding-place.

"Quiet! Don't tickle," cried Dexter, as he gently put up one hand for the mouse to run upon; and every movement was made so gently that the little creatures were not alarmed, but rested gently upon the boy's hand, as he lifted them down to where he had placed some scraps of cheese and a biscuit, all articles of provender being derived from the stores situated in his trousers-pockets, and that of his jacket.

The list was not yet complete, for an old wire trap had been turned into a cage, and here dwelt Dexter's greatest favourite—about the shabbiest-looking squirrel that ever exhibited bare patches upon its skin, and a tail from which the plume-like hair had departed.

It cost five shillings, all the same, at a little broker's shop down in the most poverty-stricken part of Coleby. It had been bought by the broker at a sale in company with a parrot, a cockatoo, and a canary, all being the property of a lady lately deceased. The canary died before he reached home, and the parrot and cockatoo, on the strength of being able to screech and say a few words, soon found owners, but the squirrel, being shabby-looking, hung on hand, or rather outside the little shop, in a canary's cage, to which it had been promoted after its own revolving wire home had been sold, the purchaser declining to buy the squirrel because he was so shabby.

The poor little brute did not improve afterwards, for he rubbed the hair off his face by constantly trying to get through either the seed or water hole, and every time he—for the sake of exercise—whisked round the cage, it was to the disadvantage of his tail, which daily grew more and more like that of Dexter's rat.

This little unfortunate might have been bought for a shilling by such a boy as Bob Dimsted, but the superfine broadcloth of Dexter's jacket and trousers sent it up to five, and pocket-money had to be saved for weeks before it finally came into the boy's possession, to be watched with the greatest attention to see if its hair would grow.

The squirrel's nose was thrust between the bars of the old wire rat-trap, and when this was not the case, the active little animal performed a kind of evolution suggestive of its trying to make the letters SS in its prison, as skaters contrive them upon the ice, till the wire door was open, and with one bound it was upon its owner's shoulder, then up in the rafters, along one beam and down another, till the first wild excitement of freedom was over, when it dropped upon the floor, and began to forage for food.

DEXTER FINDS COMFORT AMONG HIS PETS.

Dexter was so truly happy among his little subjects that he sat down upon the edge of an old box, forgetful of other claimants while he attended to the wants of these, calling them by endearing names, giving the rabbits oats from his pockets, a handful of which grain came now and then from Peter.

The boy had intuitively discovered the way to tame his various pets. Fear will accomplish a great deal with dumb animals, but the real secret of winning their confidence is quietness, the art of never alarming them, but by perfectly passive behaviour, and the most gentle of movements, accustom the timid creatures to our presence. The rest was merely habituating them to the fact that their owner was the sole source from which food was to be obtained.

No one told Dexter all this; he learned it in his solitary communings with the animal world. For somehow it seems to be the law of nature that every moving thing goes about in dread of losing its life from something else which either preys upon or persecutes it. The house-sparrow, the most domestic of wild birds, gives a look-out for squalls between every peck, but it will soon learn to distinguish the person who does not molest and who feeds it, even to coming at his call, while fish, those most cold-blooded of creatures, which in an ordinary way go off like a silver flash at the sight of a shadow, will grow so familiar that they will rise to the surface and touch the white finger-tips placed level with the water.

So Dexter sat smiling and almost without movement among his subjects, with the rabbits begging, the mice coming and going, now feeding and now taking a friendly walk up his legs and about his chest, and the squirrel bounding to him from time to time after nuts, which were carried up to the beam overhead, and there rasped through with its keen teeth, the rat the while watching it from the floor till furnished with another nut, as it had pounced upon one the squirrel dropped.

There was yet another pet—one which had been very sluggish all through the winter, but now in fine sunshiny days fairly active, and ready upon this occasion to come forth and be fed.

Dexter rose very slowly, talking gently the while to the mice, which he coaxed to his hand with a piece of cheese, and then placed them upon the floor, while he went to a corner where, turned upside down upon a slate, stood one of Dan'l's large flower-pots, the hole being covered with a piece of perforated zinc.

The pot was lifted, slate and all, turned over, and the slate lifted off, to display quite a nest of damp moss, which, as the boy watched, seemed for a few minutes uninhabited, but all at once it began to heave in one part; there was an increasing movement, as if something was gliding through it, and then from among the soft moss a smooth glistening head with two bright eyes appeared, and a curious little tongue darted out through an opening between the tightly-closed jaws.

There was no doubt of the nature of the creature, which glided forth more and more till it developed itself into a snake of a bright olive green, about thirty inches long, its singular markings and mottlings looking as bright as if it had been varnished.

Dexter watched the curious horizontal undulating movement of the little serpent for some time before he touched it, and then taking it up very gently, its tail hung swinging to and fro, while the front portion curved and undulated, and searched about for a place to rest till it found one upon the boy's arm, up which it began to glide as if the warmth were pleasant, ending by nestling its head in the hollow of the elbow-joint.

Meanwhile there was another rustling and movement of the moss, but nothing showed for a time.

Dexter smoothed and stroked the snake, which seemed to be perfectly content when it was moved, but soon after began to insinuate its blunt rounded head here and there, as if in search of something, till its owner bore it to a large pickle-jar standing upon a beam nearly level with the floor, and upon his placing the reptile's head on a level with the mouth, it glided in at once, inch by inch, over the side, and through Dexter's hands, till it disappeared, the finely-graduated tail passing over the edge, and it was gone, the jar being its larder, in which were stored, ready for consumption, half a dozen of Dan'l's greatest enemies—the slugs.

As Dexter turned to the heap of moss once more, at which one of the rabbits was sniffing, there was another heaving movement, followed by a sharp rap on the boards, the alarm signal of the rabbit which bounded away, while a blunt, broad head and two glistening eyes slowly appeared; then what looked like a short sturdy arm with outstretched fingers pressed down the moss, then another arm began to work, and by slow degrees a huge toad, which seemed to be as broad as it was long, extricated itself from the soft vegetable fibre, and crept away on to the boards, all in the most deliberate manner, as if it was too fat to move fast.

"Hallo, Sam!" said Dexter, laughing. "Why, you've been asleep for a month."

The toad seemed to be looking up at him in an unblinking fashion, but did not move, and Dexter stooped down to touch it, but the moment his hand approached, the reptile rose on its legs, arched its back, lowered its head, swelled itself up, and uttered a low, hissing sound.

Dexter waited for a moment, and then softly began to scratch its side, the result evidently being so satisfactory to the toad that it began by leaning over toward the rubbing fingers, and then more and more, as if the sensation were agreeable in the extreme.

A little coaxing then induced it to crawl slowly into its master's hand, which it more than filled, sitting there perfectly contented till it was placed in another pickle-jar to feed, this one being furnished with wood-lice, pill millipedes, and other luxuries dear to a toad.

The striking of a clock roused Dexter from his communings with his pets, and hastily restoring them to their various habitations, he resumed his jacket, and after a quick glance round descended the steps.

"I couldn't take them with me," he said sadly, as he stood for a few minutes in the old dark stable; "and if I left them without setting them at liberty they would all die."

Chapter Twenty Six
The Growing Cloud

"Dexter, I want to talk to you," said Helen, a few weeks later. The boy sighed.

"Ah! you are afraid I am going to scold you," she said.

"I don't mind you scolding me," he replied; "but I don't think I have done anything this time, except—"

"Except what?" said Helen, for the boy paused.

"Except talk to Bob Dimsted."

"Have you been out to meet him?"

"No, that I haven't," cried Dexter. "He came to the bottom of the river to fish, and he spoke to me; and if I had not answered, it would have seemed so proud."

Helen was silent for a few moments, not knowing what to say.

"It was not about that," she said, at last, "but about your lessons. Mr Limpney has again been complaining very bitterly to papa about your want of progress."

"Yes," said Dexter, "and he is always scolding me."

"Then why don't you try harder?"

"I do, but I am so stupid."

"You are not, Dexter. You always learn easily enough with me."

"Yes, with you," said the boy quickly, "but you don't want me to say angle ABC is equal to the angle CBA, and all such stuff as that."

"Don't call it stuff," said Helen, smiling in spite of herself; "it is Geometry."

"But it is rum stuff all the same. What's the use of my learning about straight lines and squares and angles?"

"But you are behind with your Algebra too."

"Yes," sighed Dexter, "I'm just as stupid over that."

"Now, Dexter!"

"But I am, quite. Why can't I go on finding out things by Arithmetic, as we used at the schools? It was bother enough to learn that. Oh, what a lot of caning I had over nine times!"

"Over nine times!" said Helen.

"Over a hundred, I should say," cried Dexter. "I mean with strokes on the hand, and taps on the head, and over the shoulders—counting 'em altogether; and wasn't I glad when I knew it all, and twelve times too, and somebody else used to get it instead of me."

"Dexter, papa wishes you to learn these things."

"Do you?" said the boy.

"Yes, very much. I should like to see you master them all."

"Then I will. See if I don't," he cried.

"That's right. Try and please Mr Limpney by being energetic."

"Yes, I'll try," said Dexter; "but I don't think he'll be pleased."

"I shall be. Now, get out your last lessons over which you failed so dismally, and I'll try and help you."

"Will you?" cried the boy, in delighted tones, and he hurriedly obtained his folio, pens, and ink, feeling in such high spirits that if Bob Dimsted had been at hand to continue his temptations they would have been of no avail.

The orange question was first debated, and tried in two or three different ways without success. Then it was laid aside for the time being, while the stage-coaches were rolled out and started, one from London to York, the other from York to London.

"Look here," said Dexter, "I'll try the one that starts from London, while you try the one from York."

That was only another simple equation, but in its novelty to Helen Grayson, as difficult as if it had been quadratic, and for a time no sound was heard but the busy scratching of two pens.

"It's of no good," said Dexter suddenly, and with a look of despair upon his face. "I'm so terribly stupid."

"I'm afraid, Dexter," said Helen merrily, "if you are stupid, I am too."

"What! can't you do it!"

"No."

"Are you sure?"

"Yes, Dexter. Algebra is beyond me."

"Hooray!" cried the boy, leaping from his seat, and dancing round the room, ending by relieving his excitement by turning head over heels on the hearthrug.

"Is that to show your delight at my ignorance, Dexter?" said Helen, smiling.

"No," he cried, colouring up, as he stood before her out of breath. "It was because I was glad, because I was not so stupid as I thought."

"You are not stupid, Dexter," said Helen, smiling. "We must go back to the beginning, and try and find out how to do these things. Does not Mr Limpney explain them to you?"

"Yes," said Dexter dismally, "but when he has done, I don't seem to see what he means, and it does make me so miserable."

"Poor boy!" said Helen gently. "There, you must not make your studies a trouble. They ought to be a great pleasure."

"They would be if you taught me," said Dexter eagerly. "I say, do ask Dr Grayson to send Mr Limpney away, and you help me. I will try so hard."

"A pretty tutor I should make," cried Helen, laughing. "Why, Dexter, I am as ignorant, you see, as you!"

Dexter's face was a study. He seemed hurt and pleased at the same time, and his face was full of reproach as he said—

"Ignorant as me! Oh!"

"There, I'll speak to papa about your lessons, and he will, I have no doubt, say a few words to Mr Limpney about trying to make your tasks easier, and explaining them a little more."

"Will you!" cried the boy excitedly, and he caught her hands in his.

"Certainly I will, Dexter."

"Then I will try so hard, and I'll write down on pieces of paper all the things you don't want me to do, and carry 'em in my pockets, and take them out and look at them sometimes."

"What!" cried Helen, laughing.

"Well, that's what Mr Limpney told me to do, so that I should not forget the things he taught me. Look here!"

He thrust his hand into his trousers-pocket, and brought out eagerly a crumpled-up piece of paper, but as he did so a number of oats flew out all over the room.

"O Dexter! what a pocket! Now what could you do with oats?"

"They were only for my rabbits," he said. "There, those are all nouns that end in *us*, feminine nouns. Look, *tribus, acus, porticus*. Isn't it stupid?"

"It is the construction of the language, Dexter."

"Yes; that's what Mr Limpney said. There, I shall put down everything you don't like me to do on a piece of paper that way; and take it out and read it, so as to remember it."

"Try another way, Dexter."

"How?" he said wonderingly.

"By fixing these things in your heart, and not on paper," Helen said, and she left the room.

"Well, that's the way to learn them by heart," said the boy to himself thoughtfully, as with brow knit he seated himself by a table, took a sheet of paper, and began diligently to write in a fairly neat hand, making entry after entry; and the principal of these was—

"Bob Dimsted: not to talk to him."

The next day the doctor had a chat with Mr Limpney respecting Dexter and his progress.

"You see," said the doctor, "the boy has not had the advantages lads have at good schools; and he feels these lessons to be extremely difficult. Give him time."

"Oh, certainly, Doctor Grayson," said Mr Limpney. "I have only one wish, and that is to bring the boy on. He is behind to a terrible extent."

"Yes, yes, of course," said the doctor; "but make it as easy for him as you can—for the present, you know. After a time he will be stronger in the brain."

Mr Limpney, BA, looked very stern. He was naturally a good-hearted, gentlemanly, and scholarly man. He thoroughly understood the subjects he professed to teach. In fact, the ordinary routine of classic and mathematical study had, by long practice, grown so simple to him, that he was accustomed to look with astonishment upon a boy who stumbled over some of the learned blocks.

In addition, year upon year of imparting knowledge to reckless and ill-tempered as well as stupid boys had soured him, and, in consequence, the well-intentioned words of the doctor did not fall on ground ready to receive them quite as it should.

"Complaining about my way of teaching, I suppose," he said to himself. "Well, we shall see."

The result was that Mr Limpney allowed the littleness of his nature to come uppermost, and he laboriously explained the most insignificant portions of the lessons in a sarcastic manner which made Dexter writhe, for he was not slow to find that the tutor was treating him with contempt.

To make matters worse, about that time Dan'l watched him more and more; Peter was unwell and very snappish; there was a little difficulty with Mrs Millett over some very strong camomile-tea which Dexter did not take; and on account of a broken soap-dish which Maria took it into her head Dexter meant to lay to her charge,—that young lady refused even to answer the boy when he spoke; lastly, the doctor seemed to be remarkably thoughtful and stern. Consequently Dexter began to mope in his den over the old stable, and at times wished he was back at the Union Schools.

The wish was momentary, but it left its impression, and the thought that, with the exception of Helen, no one liked him at the doctor's house grew and grew and grew like the cloud that came out of the fisherman's pot when Solomon's seal was removed, and that cloud threatened to become the evil genii that was to overshadow the boy's life.

Chapter Twenty Seven
Dexter writes a Letter

Dexter watched his chance one afternoon when the study was empty, and stole in, looking very guilty.

Maria saw him going in, and went into the kitchen and told Mrs Millett.

"I don't care," she said, "you may say what you like, but it's in him."

"What's in him!" said the old housekeeper, raising her tortoise-shell spectacles so as to get a good look at Maria, who seemed quite excited.

"Master may have tutors as is clergymen to teach him, and Miss Helen may talk and try, but he's got it in him, and you can't get it out."

"Who are you talking about, Maria," said the old lady testily.

"That boy," said Maria, shaking her head. "It's of no good, he's got it in him, and nothing won't get it out."

"Bless my heart!" cried Mrs Millett, thinking first of mustard and water, and then of castor-oil, "has the poor fellow swallowed something?"

"No-o-o-o!" ejaculated Maria, drawing the word out to nearly a foot in length.

"But you said he'd got something in him, Maria. Good gracious me, girl! what do you mean!"

"Sin and wickedness, Mrs Millett. He comes of a bad lot, and Dan'l says he's always keeping bad company."

"Dan'l's a chattering old woman, and had better mind his slugs and snails."

"But the boy's always in mischief; see how he spoiled your silk dress."

"Only spotted it, Maria, and it was clean water. I certainly thought it rained as I went under his window."

"Yes, and you fetched your umbrella."

"I did, Maria. But he's better now. Give him his physic regular, and it does him good."

"Did you find out what was the matter with those salts and senny!"

"No, Maria, I did not. I had to break the glass to get it out; set hard as a stone. It was a good job he did not take it."

Mrs Millett never did find out that Dexter had poured in cement till the glass would hold no more, and his medicine became a solid lump.

"Ah, you'll be tired of him soon," said Maria.

"No, I don't think I shall, Maria. You see he's a boy, and he does behave better. Since I told him not, he hasn't taken my basting-spoon to melt lead for what he calls nickers; and then he hasn't repeated that wicked cruel trick of sitting on the wall."

"Why, I see him striddling the ridge of the old stable, with his back to the weathercock, only yesterday."

"Yes, Maria, but he wasn't fishing over the wall with worms to try and catch Mrs Biggins's ducks, a very cruel trick which he promised me he wouldn't do any more; and he hasn't pretended to be a cat on the roof, nor yet been to me to extract needles which he had stuck through his cheeks out of mischief; and I haven't seen him let himself down from the stable roof with a rope; and, as I told him, that clothes-line wasn't rope."

"Ah, you always sided with the boy, Mrs Millett," said Maria; "but mark my words, some of these mornings we shall get up and find that he has let burglars into the house, and Master and Miss Helen will be robbed and murdered in their beds."

"Maria, you're a goose," said the old housekeeper. "Don't talk such rubbish."

"Ah, you may call it rubbish, Mrs Millett, but if you'd seen that boy just now stealing—"

"Stealing, Maria?"

"Yes 'm, stealing into Master's study like a thief in the night—and after no good, I'll be bound,—you wouldn't be so ready to take his part."

"Gone in to write his lessons," said Mrs Millett. "There, you go and get about your work."

Maria snorted, stuck out her chin, and left the kitchen.

"Yes, she may talk, but I say he's after no good," muttered the housemaid; "and I'm going to see what he's about, or my name ain't what it is."

Meanwhile Dexter was very busy in the study, but in a furtive way writing the following letter in a bold, clear hand, which was, however, rather shaky in the loops of the letters, while the capitals had an inclination to be independent, and to hang away from the small letters of the various words:—

Sir,

Me and a friend have borrowed your boat, for we are going a long journey; but as we may keep it all together, I send to you fourteen shillings and a fourpny piece, which I have saved up, and if that isn't quite quite enough I shall send you some more. I hope you won't mind our taking your boat, but Bob Dimsted says we must have it, or we can't get on.

Yours af—very truly,

Obed Coleby, or To Sir Jhames Danby, Dexter Grayson.

Dexter's spelling was a little shaky here and there, but the letter was pretty intelligible; and, as soon as it was done, he took out his money and made a packet of it, and doubled it up, a task he had nearly finished, when he became aware that the door was partly opened, and as he guiltily thrust the packet into his pocket the door opened widely, and Maria entered, with a sharp, short cough.

"Did I leave my duster here, Master Dexter!" she said, looking round sharply.

Before Dexter could reply, she continued—

"No, I must have left it upstairs."

She whisked out and closed the door with a bang, the very opposite of the way in which she had opened it, and said to herself triumphantly—

"There, I knew he was doing of something wrong, and if I don't find him out, my name ain't Maria."

Dexter hurriedly finished his packet, laying the money in it again after further consideration—in and out amongst the paper, so that the money should not chink, and then placing it in the enclosure with the letter, he tied it up with a piece of the red tape the doctor kept in a little drawer, sealed it, and directed it in his plainest hand to Sir James Danby.

Dexter felt better after this was done, and the jacket-pocket a little bulgy in which his missive was stuffed. He had previously felt a little uneasy about the boat; but though not quite at rest now, he felt better satisfied, and as if this was a duty done.

That same evening, just before it grew dusk, Dexter watched his opportunity, and stole off down the garden, after making sure that he was not watched.

There was no one visible on the other side, and it seemed as if Bob Dimsted was not coming, so after waiting a few minutes Dexter was about to go back to the house, with the intention of visiting his pets, when there was a loud chirping whistle from across the river.

Dexter looked sharply through the gathering gloom; but still no one was visible, and then the chirp came again.

"Are you there, Bob?"

"Why, course I am," said that young gentleman, rising up from where he had lain flat behind a patch of coarse herbage. "I'm not the sort of chap to stay away when I says I'll come. Nearly ready!"

"Ye–es," said Dexter.

"No gammon, you know," said Bob. "I mean it, so no shirking out."

"I mean to come too," said Dexter with a sigh.

"Well, you do sound jolly cheerful; you don't know what a game it's going to be."

"No, not quite—yet," said Dexter. "But how are we going to manage!"

"Well, if ever!" exclaimed Bob. "You are a rum chap, and no mistake. Of course we shall take the boat, and I've got that table-cloth ready for a sail, and a bit of rope to hoist it up."

Dexter winced about that table-cloth, one which he had borrowed at Bob's wish from the housekeeper's room.

"But must we take that boat?"

"Why, of course, but we shall send it back some day as good as new, hanging behind a ship, and then have it sent up the river. I know lots of fellows who'll put it back for me if I ask 'em."

Dexter felt a little better satisfied, and then listened to his companion's plans, which were very simple, but effective all the same, though common honesty did not come in.

The conversation was carried on across the river, and to ensure its not being heard, Dexter lay down on the grass and put his lips close to the water, Bob Dimsted doing the same, when, it being quite a still evening, conversation became easy.

"What are your people doing now?" said Bob, after they had been talking some time.

"Dr Grayson is writing, and Miss Grayson reading."

"Why, we might go now—easy."

"No," said Dexter. "If we did, it would be found out directly, and we should be fetched back, and then, I dare say, they'd send me again to the school."

"And yer don't want to go there again, do you!"

"No," said Dexter, with a shudder. "Don't forget the ball of string I told you about?"

"No, I've got that," replied Bob sharply. "And p'r'aps that won't be long enough. It's very deep in the sea. Now mind, you're here."

"Yes, I'll mind."

"If yer don't come, I won't never forgive you for making a fool of me."

"I won't do that," said Dexter; and then after a little more hesitation as to something he particularly wanted to do, and which he saw no other way of doing, he whispered—

"Bob!"

"Hullo!"

"Will you do something for me before you come!"

"Yes, if I can. But I say, don't you forget to bring a big bundle of your clothes and things, and if you don't want 'em all, I can wear some of 'em."

Dexter was silent.

"And as much money as you can; and, I say, the old un never give you a watch, did he?"

"No."

"You wouldn't like to borrow his, would you!"

"No, of course not," said Dexter indignantly.

"Oh, I don't want you to, unless you like. Only watches is useful at sea. Sailors find out where they are by their watches. I don't quite know how, but we could soon find out. Whatcher want me to do!"

"I want you to take a little parcel to Sir James Danby's."

"I ain't going to carry no parcels," said Bob importantly.

"It's only a very little one, as big as your hand. You know the letter-box in Sir James's big door!"

"I should just think I do," said Bob, with a hoarse laugh. "Me and two more boys put a lighted cracker in last fift' o' November."

"I want you to go there last thing," said Dexter, as he could not help wondering whether the cracker made a great deal of noise in the letter-box; "and to drop the packet in just as if it was a letter. I mean just before you come."

"But what for?"

"Because it must be taken there. I want it taken."

"O very well. Where is it?"

"Here," said Dexter, taking out his carefully tied and sealed packet.

"Chuck it across."

"Get up, then, and be ready to catch it."

"All right! Now then, shy away."

Dexter drew back from the river, and aiming carefully at where he could see Bob's dim figure, he measured the distance with his eye, and threw.

Slap!

"Got it!" cried Bob. And then, "Oh!"

There was a splash.

"Just kitched on the top o' my finger, and bounced off," whispered the boy excitedly.

"O Bob, what have you done!"

"Well, I couldn't help it. I ain't a howl.—How could I see in the dark!"

"Can't you see where it fell in!"

"Why, ain't I a-trying. Don't be in such a fuss."

Dexter felt as if their expedition was at an end, and he stood listening with a breast full of despair as Bob lay down at the edge of the river, and rolling up his sleeve began feeling about in the shallow water.

"It's no good," he said. "It's gone."

"O Bob!"

"Well, what's the good of 'O Bobbing' a fellow? I couldn't help it. It's gone, and— Here: I got it!"

Bob rose up and gave his arm a whirl to drive off some of the moisture.

"It's all right," he said. "I'll wrap it in my hankychy, and it'll soon dry in my pocket, I say, what's inside?"

"Something for Sir James."

"Oh! S'pose you don't know!"

"Is the paper undone?" said Dexter anxiously.

"No, it's all right, I tell yer, and it'll soon get dry."

"And you'll be sure and take it to Sir James's."

"Now?"

"No, no, last thing to-night, just before you come, and don't ring, only drop the thing in the letter-box."

"All right. Didn't I get my arm wet! There, I'm going home to get it dry, and put the rest of my things ready. Mind you bring yours all right."

Dexter did not answer, but his companion's words made him feel very low-spirited, for he had a good deal in his mind, and he stood listening to Bob, as that young worthy went off, whistling softly, to make his final preparations for the journey down the river to sea, and then to foreign lands, and the attempt seemed now to begin growing very rapidly, till it was like a dense dark cloud rising higher and higher, and something seemed to keep asking the boy whether he was doing right.

He felt that he was not, but, at the same time, the idea that he was thoroughly misunderstood, and that he would never be happy at the doctor's, came back as strongly as ever.

"They all look upon me as a workhouse boy," he muttered, "and Bob's right. I'd better go away."

Chapter Twenty Eight
Preparations for Flight

Dexter listened till Bob Dimsted's whistle died away, and then stole from the place of appointment to go back to the house, where he struck off to the left, and made his way into the loft, where he took a small piece of candle from his pocket, lit it, and set it in an old ginger-beer bottle.

The light roused the various occupants of the boxes and cages. That and the step were suggestive of food, and sundry squeakings and scratchings arose, with, from time to time, a loud rap on the floor given by one of the rabbits.

There was a lonely desolate feeling in Dexter's breast as he set the rat at liberty, for the furtive-looking creature to hurry beneath the boards which formed the rough floor.

Then the mice were taken out of their box, and the first movement of the little creatures was to run all over their master, but he hurriedly took them off him, feeling more miserable than ever, and ready to repent of the step he was about to take.

The rabbits were carried downstairs, and turned out into the yard, Dexter having a belief that as they had once grown tame perhaps, many generations back, they might now as easily grow wild, and if in the process they made very free with old Dan'l's vegetables, until they escaped elsewhere, it would not be very serious.

As it was, they crept here and there over the stones for a few moments, and then went off investigating, and evidently puzzled by their freedom.

The hedgehog and squirrel were brought down together, and carried right into the garden, where the former was placed upon one of the flower-beds, and disappeared at once; the latter held up to a branch of the ornamental spruce, into which it ran, and then there was a scuffling noise, and Dexter ran away back to the stable, afraid to stop, lest the little ragged jacketed animal should leap back upon him, and make him more weak than he was.

He climbed again to the loft, hearing a series of tiny squeaks as he mounted—squeaks emanating from his mice, and directly after he nearly crushed the rat, by stepping upon it as the little animal ran up to be fed.

He had come for the toad and snake, and hurriedly plunging his hand into the big pot he found Sam the toad, seated right at the top, evidently eager to start on a nocturnal ramble, but the snake was coiled up asleep.

It was a curious pet, that toad, but somehow, as it sat nestled up all of a squat in the boy's warm hand, he felt as if he should like to take it with him. It was not big, and would take up little room, and cost nothing to feed.

Why not?

He hesitated as he descended and crossed the yard to the garden, and decided that he would not. Bob Dimsted might not like it.

He reached the garden, and crossed the lawn to the sunny verbena bed. That seemed a suitable place for the snake, and he tenderly placed it, writhing feebly, among the thin pegged-down strands.

Then came the other reptile's turn.

They had been friends and even companions together in the big flower-pot, Dexter argued, so they should have the chance of being friends again in the flower-bed.

The toad was in his left hand, and going down on one knee he separated the verbenas a little, and then placed his hand, knuckles downward, on the soft moist earth, opening his fingers slowly the while.

"Good-bye, Sam," he said, in a low voice. "You and I have had some good fun together, old chap, and I hope you will be very happy when I'm gone."

He slowly spread his hand flat, so that his fingers and thumb ceased to form so many posts and rails about the reptile, or a fleshly cage. In imagination he saw the dusky grey creature crawl off his hand gladly into the dewy bed, and it made him more sad to find how ready everything was to be free, and he never for a moment thought about how he was going to play as ungrateful a part, and march off too.

"Good-bye, Sam," he said, as he recalled how he had played with and tickled that toad, and how it had enjoyed it all, and turned over to be rubbed. Then he seemed to see it walk in its heavy, cumbrous way slowly off, with its bright golden eyes glistening, till it sat down in a hollow, and watched him go.

But it was all fancy. The toad did not crawl out of his hand among the verbenas, nor go right away, but sat perfectly motionless where it was, evidently, from its acting, perfectly warm, comfortable, and contented.

"Well, Sam, why don't you go!" said Dexter softly. "Do you hear?"

He gave his hand a jar by striking the back on the earth, but the toad did not move, and when he touched it with his right hand, it was to find the fat squat reptile squeezed up together like a bun.

He stroked it, and rubbed it, as he had rubbed it scores of times before, and the creature once more pressed up against his fingers, while Dexter forgot everything else in the gratification of finding his ugly pet appreciate his attentions.

"Now then! off you go!" he cried quickly; but the creature did not stir.

"Are you going?" said Dexter. "Come: march."

Again it did not stir.

"He don't want to go," cried the boy, changing it from, one hand to the other; and the next moment he was holding it, nose downward, over his jacket-pocket, when the toad, pretty actively for one of its kind, began to work its legs and dived slowly down beneath the pocket-handkerchief crumpled-up there, and settled itself at the bottom.

"It seems to know," cried Dexter. "And it shall go with me after all."

Curious boy! some one may say, but Dexter had had few opportunities for turning his affections in ordinary directions, and hence it was that they were lavished upon a toad.

Indoors, when he stole back after setting all his pets at liberty to shift for themselves, Dexter felt very guilty. He encountered Mrs Millett in the hall, and a thrill ran through him as she exclaimed—

"Ah, there you are, Master Dexter, I just want a few words with you."

"Found out!" thought the guilty conscience, which needs no accuser.

"Now just you look here, sir," said the old housekeeper, in a loud voice, as she literally button-holed the boy, by hooking one thin finger in his jacket, so that he could not get away, "I know all."

"You—you know everything," faltered the boy.

"Yes, sir. Ah, you may well look 'mure. You little thought I knew."

"How—how did you find out?" he stammered.

"Ah! how did I find out, indeed! Now, look here, am I to go straight to the doctor and tell him!"

"No, no, pray don't," whispered Dexter, catching her arm.

"Well, then, I must tell Miss Helen."

"No, no, not this time," cried Dexter imploringly; and his tone softened the old lady, who shook the borders of her cap at him.

"Well, I don't know what to say," said Mrs Millett softly. "They certainly ought to know."

Dexter gazed at her wildly. He knew that everything must come out, but it was to have been in a few hours' time, when he was far away, and deaf to the angry words and reproaches. To hear them now seemed more than he could bear. It could not be. Bob Dimsted must think and say what he liked, and be as angry and unforgiving as was possible. It could not be now. He must plead to the old housekeeper for pardon, and give up all idea of going away.

MRS. MILLETT GIVES DEXTER SOME ADVICE

"Ah!" she said. "I see you are sorry for it, then."

"Yes, yes," he whispered. "So sorry, and—and—"

"You'll take it this time, like a good boy!"

"Take it?"

"Yes, sir. Ah! you can't deceive me. Last time I saw the empty glass I knew as well as could be that you hadn't taken it, for the outside of the glass wasn't sticky, and there were no marks of your mouth at the edge. I always put plenty of sugar in it for you, and that showed."

"The camomile-tea!" thought Dexter, a dose of which the old lady expected him to take about once a week, and which never did him any harm, if it never did him any good.

"And you'll take it to-night, sir, like a good boy!"

"Yes, yes, I will indeed," said Dexter, with the full intention of keeping his word out of gratitude for his escape.

"Now, that's like being a good boy," said the old lady, smiling, and extricating her fingers from his button-hole, so as to stroke his hair. "It will do you no end of good; and how you have improved since you have been here, my dear, your hair's grown so nicely, and you've got such a good pink colour in your cheeks. It's the camomile-tea done that."

Mrs Millett leaned forward with her hands on the boy's shoulder, and kissed him in so motherly a way that Dexter felt a catching of the breath, and kissed her again.

"That's right," said the old lady. "You ain't half so bad as Maria pretends you are. 'It's only a bit of mischief now and then,' I says to her, 'and he's only a boy,' and that's what you are, ain't it, my dear?"

Dexter did not answer.

"I shall put your dose on your washstand, and you mind and take it the moment you get out of bed to-morrow morning."

"Yes," said Dexter dismally.

"No! you'll forget it. You've got to take that camomile-tea to-night, and if you don't promise me you will, I shall come and see you take it."

"I promise you," said Dexter, and the old lady nodded and went upstairs, while the boy hung about in the hall.

How was it that just now, when he was going away, people were beginning to seem more kind to him, and something began to drag at his heart to keep him from going?

He could not tell. An hour before he had felt a wild kind of elation. He was going to be free from lessons, the doctor's admonitions, and the tame regular life at the house, to be off in search of adventure, and with Bob for his companion, going all over the world in that boat, while now, in spite of all he could do, he did not feel so satisfied and sure.

There was something else he knew that he ought to do. He could not bid Helen good-bye with his lips, but he felt that he must bid her farewell another way, for she had always been kind to him from the day he came.

He crept into the study again, this time without being seen.

There was a faint light in the pleasant room, for the doctor's lamp had been turned down, but not quite out.

A touch sent the flame brightly round the ring, and the shade cast a warm glow on the boy's busy fingers as he took out paper and envelope; and then, with trembling hand, sore heart, and a pen that spluttered, he indited another letter, this time to Helen.

> My dear Miss Grayson,
>
> I am afraid you will think me a very ungrateful boy, but I am obliged to go away to seek my fortune all over the world. You have been so kind to me, and so has Doctor Grayson sometimes, but everybody else has hated me, and made game of me because I was a workhouse boy, and I could not bear it any longer, and Bob Dimsted said he wouldn't if he was me, and we are going away together not to come back again any more.—I am,
>
> Your Affec Friend.
>
> Dexter Grayson.
>
> PS—I mean Obed Coleby, for I ought not to call myself Dexter any more, and I would have scratched it out, only you always said it was better not to scratch out mistakes because they made the paper look so untidy.
>
> I like you very much, and Mrs Millett too, but I can't take her fiz—physick to-night.
>
> Is physick spelt with a k?

There was a tear—a weak tear in each of Dexter's eyes as he wrote this letter, for it brought up many a pleasant recollection of kindnesses on Helen's part.

He had just finished, folded and directed this, when he fancied he heard a door open across the hall.

Thrusting the note into his pocket so hastily that one corner went into the toad, he caught up a piece of the doctor's foolscap, and began rapidly to make a triangle upon it, at whose sides and points he placed letters, and then, feeling like the miserable impostor he was, he rapidly let his pen trace a confused line of *A's* and *B's* and *C's*, and these backwards and forwards.

This went on for some minutes, so that there was a fair show upon the paper, when the door softly opened, Helen peered in, and then coming behind him bent down, and, in a very gentle and sisterly way, placed her hands over his eyes.

"Why, my poor hard-working boy," she said gently. "So this is where you are; and, oh dear, oh dear! Euclid again. That Mr Limpney will wear your brains all away. There, come along, I am going to play to papa, and then you and I will have a game at draughts."

Dexter rose with his heart beating, and that strange sensation of something tugging at his conscience. Why were they all so kind to him to-night, just when he was going away?

"Why, you look quite worn out and dazed, Dexter," said Helen merrily. "There, come along."

"Eh? Where was he? In mischief?" said the doctor sharply, as they entered the drawing-room.

"Mischief? No, papa: for shame!" cried Helen, with her arm resting on the boy's shoulders. "In your study, working away at those terrible sides and angles invented by that dreadful old Greek Euclid." "Work, eh? Ha! that's good!" cried the doctor jovially. "Bravo, Dexter! I am glad."

If ever a boy felt utterly ashamed of himself, Dexter did then. He could not meet the doctor's eye, but was on his way to get a book to turn over, so as to have something to look at, but this was not to be.

"No, no, you have had enough of books for one day, Dexter. Come and turn over the music for me. Why! what's that?"

"That?" said Dexter slowly, for he did not comprehend.

"Yes, I felt it move. You have something alive in your pocket."

He felt prompted to lie, but he could not tell a falsehood then, and he stood with his teeth set.

"Whatever have you got alive in your pocket?" said the doctor. "I know. A young rabbit, for a guinea."

"Is it?" cried Helen. "Let me look: they are such pretty little things."

"Yes, out with it, boy, and don't pet those things too much. Kill them with kindness, you know. Here, let me take it out."

"No, no!" cried Dexter hastily.

"Well, take it out yourself."

A spasm of dread had run through the boy, as in imagination he saw the doctor's hand taking out the letter in his pocket.

"It isn't a young rabbit," he faltered.

"Well, what is it, then? Come, out with it."

Dexter hesitated for a few moments, and now met the doctor's eye. He could not help himself, but slowly took out his pocket-handkerchief, as he held the note firmly with his left hand outside the jacket. Then, diving in again, he got well hold of Sam, who was snug at the bottom, and, with burning cheeks, and in full expectation of a scolding, drew the toad slowly forth.

"Ugh!" ejaculated Helen.

The doctor, who was in a most amiable temper, burst into a roar of laughter.

"Well, you are a strange boy, Dexter," he said, as he wiped his eyes. "You ought to be a naturalist by and by. There, open the window, and put the poor thing outside. You can find plenty another time."

Dexter obeyed, glad to be out of his quandary, and this time, as he put Sam down, the reptile crawled slowly away into the soft dark night.

He closed the window, and went back to find the doctor and Helen all smiles, and ready to joke instead of scold. Then he went to the piano, and turned over the music, the airs and songs making him feel more and more sad, and again and again he found himself saying—

"Why are they so kind to me now, just as I am going away?"

"Shall I stop!" he said to himself, after a time.

"No: I promised Bob I would come, and so I will."

Chapter Twenty Nine
An Act of Folly

Bedtime at last, and as Dexter bade the doctor and his daughter "good-night," it seemed to him that they had never spoken so kindly to him, and the place had never appeared to be so pleasant and homelike before.

His heart sank as he went up to his room, and he felt as if he could not go away. The lessons Mr Limpney had given him to write out were not done; but he had better stop and face him, and every other trouble, including the window he had broken, and never owned to yet.

It was impossible to go away and leave everybody who was so kind. A harsh word would have kept him to the point; but now he wavered as he sat down on the edge of his bed, with his mind in a whirl.

Then, as he sat there, he pictured in his own mind the figure of Bob Dimsted, waiting for him, laden with articles of outfit necessary for their voyage, and behind Bob loomed up bright sunny scenes by sea and land; and with his imagination once more excited by all that the boy had suggested, Dexter blinded himself to everything but the object he had in view.

He had planned in his own mind what he would take with him, but now it had come to the point he felt a strange compunction. Everything he possessed seemed to him as if it belonged to the doctor, and, finally, he resolved to take nothing with him but the clothes in which he stood.

He began walking about the room in a listless way, looking about at the various familiar objects that he was to see no more, and one of the first things to strike him was a teacup on the washstand, containing Mrs Millett's infusion, bitter, nauseous, and sweetened to sickliness; and it struck Dexter that the mixture had been placed in a cup instead of a glass, so as to make it less objectionable in appearance.

He could not help smiling as he took up the cup and smelt it, seeing at the same time the old dame's pleasant earnest face—a face that suddenly seemed to have become very loving, now he was to see it no more.

He set down the cup, and shook his head, and then, as if nerving himself for the task, he went to the drawers, took out a key from his pocket, and then, from the place where it lay, hidden beneath his clean linen, brought forth the old clothes-line twisted and knotted together—the line which had done duty in the loft as a swing.

He listened as he crossed to the door, but all was still downstairs, and it was not likely that any one would come near his room that night; but still he moved about cautiously, and taking the line with his hands, about two feet apart, snapped it again and again with all his might, to try if it was likely to give way now beneath his weight.

It seemed firm as ever, but he could not help a shiver as he laid it by the window, and thought of a boy being found in the shrubbery beneath, with a broken leg, or, worse still, neck.

Then as he waited for the time to glide by, so that all might be in bed before he made his escape, a sudden chill ran through him.

He had remembered everything, as he thought; and yet there was one thing, perhaps the simplest of all, forgotten. He was going to take no bundle, no money, nothing which the doctor had in his kindness provided for him; but he could not go without a cap, and that was hanging in the hall, close to the drawing-room door.

The question arose whether he should venture down to get it now, or after the doctor had gone to bed.

It took him some time to make up his mind; but when he had come to a decision he opened his door softly, listened, and stole out on to the landing.

All was very still as he looked over the balustrade to where the lamp shed its yellow rays all round, and to his mind more strangely upon the object he wanted to obtain than elsewhere.

It was a very simple thing to do, and yet it required a great deal of nerve, for if the drawing-room door were opened just as he reached the hat-stand, and the doctor came out, what should he say?

Then there was the risk of being heard, for there were, he knew, two of the old oaken stairs which always gave a loud crack when any one passed down, and if they cracked now, some one would be sure to come out to see what it meant.

Taking a long catching breath he went quickly to the top of the stairs, and was about to descend in a desperate determination to go through with his task, when an idea struck him, and bending over the balustrade he spread his hands, balanced himself carefully, and then slid down the mahogany rail, round curve after curve as silently as could be, and reaching the curl at the bottom dropped upon the mat.

Only five or six yards now to the hat-stand, and going on tiptoe past the entrance to the drawing-room, he was in the act of taking down the cap, when the handle rattled, the door was thrown open, and the hall grew more light.

In his desperation Dexter snatched down the cap, and stood there trying to think of what he should say in answer to the question that would be asked in a moment—

"What are you doing there!"

It was Helen, chamber-candlestick in hand, and she was in the act of stepping out, when her step was arrested by words which seemed to pierce into the listener's brain:—

"Oh, about Dexter!"

"Yes, papa," said Helen, turning.

"What do you think about—"

Dexter heard no more. Taking advantage of Helen's back being turned as she bent over towards the speaker, the boy stepped quickly to the staircase, ran up, and had reached the first landing before Helen came out into the hall, while before she had closed the door he was up another flight, and gliding softly toward his own room, where he stood panting as he closed the door, just as if he had been running a distance which had taken away his breath.

It was a narrow escape, and he was safe; but his ears tingled still, and he longed to know what the doctor had said about him.

As he stood listening, cap in hand, he heard Helen pass his door singing softly one of the ballads he had heard that evening; and once more a curious dull sensation of misery came over him, as he seemed to feel that he would never hear her sing again, never feel the touch of her soft caressing hand; and somehow there was a vague confused sense of longing to go to one who had treated him with an affectionate interest he had never known before, even now hardly understood, but it seemed to him such gentleness and love as might have come from a mother.

For a moment or two he felt that he must open the door, call to her, throw himself upon his knees before her, and confess everything, but at that moment the laughing, mocking face of Bob Dimsted seemed to rise between them, and his words buzzed in his ear—words that he had often said when listening to some account of Dexter's troubles—

"Bother the old lessons, and all on 'em! I wouldn't stand it if I was you. They've no right to order you about, and scold you as they do."

The weak moments passed, and just then there was the doctor's cough heard, and the closing of his door, while directly after came the chiming of the church clock—a quarter past eleven.

Half an hour to wait and think, and then good-bye to all his troubles, and the beginning of a new life of freedom!

All the freedom and the future seemed to be behind a black cloud; but in the fond belief that all would soon grow clear Dexter waited.

Half-past eleven, and he wondered that he did not feel sleepy.

It was time to begin though now, and he took the line and laid it out in a serpentine fashion upon the carpet, so that there should be no kinks in the way; and then the next thing was to fasten one end tightly so that he could safely slide down.

He had well thought out his plans, and, taking one end of the line, he knotted it securely to the most substantial place he could find in the room, passing it behind two of the bars of the grate. Then cautiously opening his window, a little bit at a time, he thrust it higher and higher, every faint creak sending a chill through him, while, when he looked out upon the dark starlight night, it seemed as if he would have to descend into a black gulf, where something blacker was waiting to seize him.

But he knew that the black things below were only great shrubs, and lowering the rope softly down he at last had the satisfaction of hearing it rustle among the leaves.

Then he waited, and after a glance round to see that everything was straight, and the letter laid ready upon the table, he put out the candle.

"For the last time!" he said to himself, and a great sigh came unbidden from his breast.

A quarter to twelve.

Dexter waited till the last stroke on the bell was thrilling in the air before setting his cap on tightly, and passing one leg over the sill.

He sat astride for a few moments, hesitating for the last time, and then passed the other leg, and lowered himself down till he hung by his hands, then twisted his legs about the rope, seized it with first one hand then the other, and hung by it with his whole weight, in the precarious position of one trusting to an old doubled clothes-line, suspended from a second-floor window.

It was hard work that descent, for he could not slide on account of the knots; and, to make his position more awkward, the rope began to untwist—

one line from the other,—and, in consequence, as the boy descended slowly, he bore no small resemblance to a leg of mutton turning before a fire.

That was the only mishap which occurred to him then, for after resting for a few moments upon the first-floor sill he continued his journey, and reached the bottom in the midst of a great laurel, which rustled loudly as he tried to get out, and then tripped over a horizontal branch, and fell flat.

He was up again in an instant, and, trembling and panting, made a couple of bounds which took him over the gravel walk and on to the lawn, where he stood panting and listening.

There was a light in the doctor's room, and one in Helen's; and just then the doctor's shadow, looking horribly threatening, was thrown upon the blind.

He must be coming, Dexter thought, and, turning quickly, he sped down the lawn, avoiding the flower-beds by instinct, and the next minute had reached the kitchen-garden, down whose winding green walk he rapidly made his way.

Chapter Thirty
Dark Deeds

It was very dark among the trees as Dexter reached the grass plot which sloped to the willows by the river-side, but he knew his way so well that he crept along in silence till he had one hand resting upon the trunk he had so often climbed, and stood there gazing across the starlit water, trying to make out the figure of his companion in the boat.

All was silent, save that, now and then, the water as it ran among the tree-roots made a peculiar whispering sound, and once or twice there was a faint plash in the distance, as if from the feeding of a fish.

"Hist! Bob! Are you there!"

"Hullo!" came from the other side. "I was just a-going."

"Going?"

"Yes. I thought you wasn't a-coming, and I wasn't going to stop here all night."

"But you said twelve."

"Well, it struck twelve an hour ago."

"No; that was eleven. There—hark!"

As proof of Dexter's assertion the church clock just then began to chime, and the heavy boom of the tenor bell proclaiming midnight seemed to make the soft night air throb.

"Thought it was twelve long enough ago. Ready!"

"Yes," said Dexter, in an excited whisper. "Got the boat?"

"No: course I haven't. It'll take two to get that boat."

"But you said you would have it ready."

"Yes, I know; but we must both of us do that. I waited till you come."

This was a shock; and Dexter said, in a disappointed tone—

"But how am I to get to you!"

"Come across," said Bob coolly.

"Come across—in the dark!"

"Why, of course. You ain't afraid, are you? Well, you are a chap!"

"But it's too deep to wade."

"Well, who said it wasn't!" growled the boy. "You can swim, can't you?"

"But I shall get so wet."

"Yah!" ejaculated Bob in tones of disgust. "You are a fellow. Take your clothes off, make 'em in a bundle, and swim over."

Dexter was half-disposed to say, "You swim across to me," but nothing would have been gained if he had, so, after a few minutes' hesitation, and in genuine dread, he obeyed the wishes of his companion, but only to pause when he was half-undressed.

"I say, though," he whispered, "can't you get the boat? It's so cold and dark."

"Well, you are a fellow!" cried Bob. "Beginning to grumble afore we start. It's no use to have a mate who's afraid of a drop of water, and don't like to get wet."

"But—"

"There, never mind," grumbled Bob; "we won't go."

"But I didn't say I wouldn't come, Bob," whispered Dexter desperately. "I'll come."

There was no answer.

"Bob." Still silence.

"I say, don't go, Bob. I'm very sorry. I'm undressing as fast as I can. You haven't gone, have you?"

Still silence, and Dexter ceased undressing, and stood there in the cold night air, feeling as desolate, despairing, and forlorn as boy could be.

"What shall I do?" he said to himself; and then, in a despondent whisper, "Bob!"

"Hullo!"

"Why, you haven't gone!" joyfully.

"No; but I'm going directly. It's no use for me to have a mate who hasn't got any pluck. Now then, are you coming, or are you not!"

"I'm coming," said Dexter. "But stop a moment. I'll be back directly."

"Whatcher going to do!"

"Wait a moment and I'll show you."

Dexter had had a happy thought, and turning and running in his trousers to the tool-shed, he dragged out a small deal box in which seeds had come down from London that spring. It was a well-made tight box, and quite light, and with this he ran back.

"Why, what are you doing?" grumbled Bob, as soon as he heard his companion's voice.

"Been getting something to put my clothes in," whispered Dexter. "I don't want to get them wet."

"Oh," said Bob, in a most unconcerned way; and he began to whistle softly, as Dexter finished undressing, tucked all his clothes tightly in the box, and bore it down to the water's edge, where it floated like a little boat.

"There!" cried Dexter excitedly. "Now they'll be all dry when I've got across. Ugh! how cold the water is," he continued, as he dipped one foot. "I wish I'd brought a towel."

"Yah! what does a fellow want with a towel? You soon gets dry if you run about. Going to walk across!"

"I can't," said Dexter; "it's too deep."

"Well, then, swim. I could swim that with one hand tied behind."

"I couldn't," said Dexter, hesitating, for it was no pleasant task to plunge into the little gliding river at midnight, and with all dark around.

"Now then! Look alive! Don't make a splash."

"Oh!"

"What's the matter?"

"It is cold."

"Yah! Then, get back to bed with you, and let me go alone."

"I'm coming as fast as I can," said Dexter, as he lowered himself into the stream, and then rapidly climbed out again, as the cold water caused a sudden catching of the breath; and a nervous shrinking from trusting himself in the dark river made him draw right away from the edge.

"Why, you ain't swimming," said Bob. "Here, look sharp! Why, you ain't in!"

"N–no, not yet," said Dexter, shivering.

"There's a coward!" sneered Bob.

"I'm not a coward, but it seems so dark and horrible to-night, and as if something might lay hold of you."

"Yes, you are a regular coward," sneered Bob. "There, jump in, or I'll shy stones at yer till you do."

Dexter did not speak, but tumbled all of a heap on the short turf, shrinking more and more from his task.

"I shall have to go without you," said Bob.

"I can't help it," said Dexter, in a low, tremulous whisper. "It's too horrid to get in there and swim across in the dark."

"No, it ain't. I'd do it in a minute. There, jump in."

"No," said Dexter sadly. "I must give it up."

"What, yer won't do it!"

"I can't," said Dexter sadly. "We must try some other way. I'm going to dress again. Oh!"

"What's the matter now!"

"My clothes!" *Splash*! *Rush*!

Dexter had rapidly lowered himself into the black deep stream and was swimming hard and fast, for as he rose and sought for his garments he suddenly recalled the fact that he had turned the box into a tiny barge, laden it with his clothes, and placed them in the river, while now, as he went to take them out, he found that the stream had borne the box away, and it was going down toward the sea.

"Try if you can see them, Bob," said Dexter, as he panted and struggled on through the water.

"See what?"

"My clothes. They're floating down the river."

Bob uttered a low chuckling laugh, and trotted along by the edge of the river; but it was too dark for him to see anything, and Dexter, forgetting cold and dread, swam bravely on, looking well to right and left, without avail, till all at once, just in one of the deepest eddies, some fifty yards down below the doctor's house, and where an unusually large willow spread its arms over the stream, he caught sight of something which blotted out the starlight for a moment, and then the stars' reflection beamed out again.

Something was evidently floating there, and he made for it, to find to his great joy that it was the floating box, which he pushed before him as he swam, and a couple of minutes later he was near enough to the edge on the meadow-side to ask Bob's help.

"Ain't got 'em, have you?" the latter whispered.

"Yes; all right. I'll come out there. Give me a hand."

Dexter swam to the muddy overhanging bank, and seized the hand which Bob extended toward him.

"Now then, shall I duck yer!" said Bob, who had lain down on the wet grass to extend his hand to the swimmer.

"No, no, Bob, don't. That would be cowardly," cried Dexter. "Help me to get out my clothes without letting in the wet. It is so cold."

"But you swam over," said Bob sneeringly.

"Yes; but you don't know how chilly it makes you feel. Mind the clothes."

Bob did mind, and the next minute Dexter and the barge of dry clothes were upon the grass together.

"Oh, isn't it cold?" said Dexter, with his teeth chattering.

"Cold? no. Not a bit," said Bob. "Here, whatcher going to do!"

"Do? Dress myself. Here, give me my shirt. Oh, don't I wish I had a towel!"

"You leave them things alone, stoopid. You can't dress yet."

"Not dress!"

"No," cried Bob loudly.

"What do you mean!"

"You come along and I'll show yer. Why, we haven't got the boat."

"No, but—"

"Well, you're all ready, and you've got to swim across and get it."

"I've got to get it!" cried Dexter in dismay. "Why, you said you would get the boat."

"Yes, but I didn't know then that you were going to swim across."

"But you said it would take two to get it," protested Dexter.

"Yes, I thought so then, but you're all ready and can swim across, and get it directly. Here, come along!"

"But—but," stammered Dexter, who was shivering in the chill night air.

"What, you're cold? Well, come along. I'll carry the box. Let's run. It'll warm yer."

Dexter was ready with another protest, but he did not utter it. His companion seemed to carry him along with the force of his will, but all the same there was a troublous feeling forcing itself upon him that he had made a mistake, and he could not help a longing for his room at the doctor's with its warm bed, comfort, safety, and repose.

But he knew it was too late, and he was too much hurried and confused to do more than try to keep up with Bob Dimsted as he ran by his side carrying the box till they had reached the meadow facing Sir James Danby's garden; and there, just dimly seen across the river, was the low gable-end of the boat-house beneath the trees.

"Hush! don't make a row," whispered Bob. "Now then, slip in and fetch it. Why, you could almost jump it."

"But, Bob—I—I don't like to go. I'm so cold."

"I'll precious soon warm yer if you don't look sharp," cried Bob fiercely. "Don't you try to make a fool of me. Now then, in with you!"

He had put the box down and gripped Dexter fiercely by the arm, causing him so much pain that instead of alarming it roused the boy's flagging spirit, and he turned fiercely upon his assailant, and wrested his arm free.

"That's right," said Bob. "In with you. And be sharp, and then you can dress yerself as we float down."

Dexter's instinct was to resist and give up, but he felt that he had gone too far, and feeling that his companion might consider him a coward if he refused to go, he lowered himself down into the water.

"That's yer sort," said Bob, in a loud whisper. "You'll soon do it."

"But suppose the chains are locked!"

"They won't be locked," said Bob. "You go acrost and see."

In the eager desire to get an unpleasant task done, Dexter let himself glide down into the swift stream about a dozen yards above the boat-house, and giving himself a good thrust off with his feet, he swam steadily and easily across, the river there being about thirty yards wide, and in a very short time he managed to touch the post at the outer corner of the long low boat-house. Then, hardly knowing how he managed it, he found bottom as his hand grasped the gunwale of the boat, and walking along beside it he soon reached the chain which moored it to the end.

Here in his excitement and dread it seemed as if his mission was to fail. It was dark enough outside, but in the boat-house everything seemed to be of pitchy blackness, and try how he would he could find no way of unfastening the chain.

He tried toward the boat, then downwards, then upwards, and in the boat again, and again. His teeth were chattering, his chest and shoulders felt as if they were freezing, and his hands, as they fumbled with the wet chain, began to grow numbed, while, to add to his excitement and confusion, Bob kept on from time to time sending across the river a quick hissing—

"I say; look sharp."

Then he heard a sound, and he splashed through the water in retreat toward the river, for it seemed that they were discovered, and some one coming down the garden.

But the sound was repeated, and he realised the fact that it was only the side of the boat striking against a post.

"I say, are you a-coming?" whispered Bob.

"I can't undo the chain," Dexter whispered back.

"Yer don't half try."

Just then the clock chimed half-past twelve, and Dexter stopped involuntarily; but a fresh summons from his companion roused him to further action, and he passed once more along to the prow of the boat, and seizing the chain felt along it till this time he felt a hook, and, wondering how it was that he had missed it before, he began with trembling fingers to try and get it out from the link through which it was thrust.

It was in very tightly, though, for the point being wedge-shaped the swaying about and jerking to and fro of the boat had driven it further and further in, so that it was not until he had been ready over and over again to give up in despair that the boy got the iron free.

Then panting with dread and excitement he found the rest easy; the chain was passed through a ring-bolt in one of the posts at the head of the boat-house, and through this he drew it back slowly and cautiously on account of the rattling it made.

It seemed of interminable length as he drew and drew, piling up the chain in the bows of the boat till he thought he must have obtained all, when there was a sudden check, and it would come no further.

Simple enough in broad daylight, and to a person in the boat, but Dexter was standing waist deep in the water, and once more he felt that the case was hopeless.

Another call from Bob roused him, and he followed the chain with his hand till he had waded to the post, and found that the hook had merely caught in the ring, and only needed lifting out, and the boat was at liberty.

But just at this moment there was a furious barking, and a dog seemed to be tearing down the garden toward the boat-house.

In an agony of horror Dexter climbed into the boat, and feeling the side of the long shed he thrust and thrust with so much effect that he sent the light gig well out into the stream and half-across the river. Then seizing an oar, as the dog was now down on the bank, snapping and barking more furiously than ever, he got it over into the water, and after a great deal of paddling, and confused counter-action of his efforts, forced the boat onward and along, till it touched the shore where Bob was waiting with the box.

"No, no, don't come out," he whispered. "Here, help me get these in."

Dexter crept to the stern of the boat, and in his effort to embark the box nearly fell overboard, but the treasure was safe. Then Bob handed in a basket, and a bundle of sticks, evidently his rod, and leaping in directly after, gave the boat sufficient impetus to send it well out into the stream, down which it began to glide.

"Ah, bark away, old un," said Bob contemptuously, as the sound of the dog's alarm notes grew more distant, and then more distant still, for they were going round a curve, and the garden side of the river was thick with trees.

"Is that Danby's dog!" whispered Bob.

"I don't know," said Dexter, with his teeth chattering from cold and excitement.

"Why! you're a-cold," said Bob coolly. "Here, I'll send her along. You look sharp and dress. I say, where's your bundle of things?"

"Do you mean my clothes?"

"No! Your bundle."

"I didn't bring anything," said Dexter, hurriedly slipping on his shirt.

"Well, you are a chap!" said Bob sourly, but Dexter hardly heard him, for he was trying to get his wet body covered from the chill night air; and he could think of nothing but the fact that he had taken a very desperate step, and the boat was bearing them rapidly away from what seemed now to have been a very happy home—further out, further away from the doctor and from Helen, downward toward the sea, and over that there was a great black cloud, beyond which, according to Bob Dimsted, there were bright and glorious lands.

At that moment, chill with the cold and damp, Dexter would have given anything to have been back in his old room, but it was too late, the boat was gliding on, and Bob had now got out the sculls. The town lights were receding, and they were going onward toward that dark cloud which Dexter seemed to see more dimly now, for there was a dumb depressing sensation of despair upon him, and he turned his eyes toward the river-bank, asking himself if he could leap ashore.

Chapter Thirty One
Times of Delight!

"Here we are!" said Bob Dimsted, as he sat handling the sculls very fairly, and, as the stream was with them, sending the boat easily along. "I think we managed that first-rate."

Dexter made no reply, for he had his teeth fast set, and his lips pressed together to keep the former from chattering, but he thought a great deal, and found himself wondering what Bob had done toward getting the boat.

With the covering up of his goose-skinned body, and the return of some of his surface heat, the terrible fit of despondency began to pass away, and Dexter felt less ready to sit down in helpless misery at the bottom of the boat.

"Getting nice and warm, ain'tcher?"

"Not very, yet."

"Ah, you soon will be, and if you ain't you shall take one of these here oars. That'll soon put you right. But what a while you was!"

"I—I couldn't help it," shivered Dexter, drawing in his breath with a quick hissing sound; "the chain was so hard to undo."

"Ah, well, never mind now," said Bob, "only, if we'd got to do it again I should go myself."

Dexter made no protest, but he thought it sounded rather ungrateful. He was too busy, though, with buttons, and getting his fingers to work in their regular way, to pay much heed, and he went on dressing.

"I say, what a jolly long while you are!" continued Bob. "Oh, and look here! I'd forgot again: why didn't you bring your bundle with all your clothes and things, eh!"

"Because they weren't mine."

"Well, you are a chap! Not yourn? Why, they were made for you, and you wore 'em. They can't be anybody else's. I never see such a fellow as you are! I brought all mine."

It was an easy task, judging from the size of the bundle dimly seen in the bottom of the boat, but Dexter said nothing.

"How much money have you got?" said Bob, after a pause.

"None at all."

"What?"

There was utter astonishment in Bob Dimsted's tones as he sat motionless, with the sculls balanced on the rowlocks, staring wildly through the gloom, as Dexter now sat down and fought hard with an obstinate stocking, which refused to go on over a wet foot—a way stockings have at such times.

"Did you say you hadn't got any money?" cried Bob.

"Yes. I sent it all in a letter to pay for the boat in case we kept it."

"What, for this boat?" cried Bob.

"Yes."

"And you call yourself a mate?" cried Bob, letting the scull blades drop in the water with a splash, and pulling hard for a few strokes. "Well!"

"I felt obliged to," said Dexter, whose perseverance was rewarded by a complete victory over the first stocking, when the second yielded it with a better grace, and he soon had on his shoes, and then began to dry his ears by thrusting his handkerchief-covered finger in the various windings of each gristly maze.

"Felt obliged to?"

"Yes, of course. We couldn't steal the boat."

"Yah, steal it! Who ever said a word about stealing? We've only borrowed it, and if we don't send it back, old Danby's got lots of money, and he can buy another. But, got no money! Well!"

"But we don't want money, do we!" said Dexter, whom the excitement as well as his clothes now began to make comparatively warm. "I thought we were going where we could soon make our fortunes."

"Yes, of course we are, stoopid; but you can't make fortunes without money. You can't ketch fish if yer ain't got no bait."

This was a philosophical view of matters which took Dexter aback, and he faltered rather as he spoke next, this time with his ears dry, his hair not so very wet, and his jacket buttoned up to his chin.

"I'm very sorry, Bob," he said gently.

"Sorry! Being sorry won't butter no parsneps," growled Bob.

"No," said Dexter mildly, "but we haven't got any parsneps to butter."

"No, nor ain't likely to have," growled Bob, and then returning to a favourite form of expression: "And you call yourself a mate! Here, come and kitch holt of this scull."

Dexter sat down on the thwart, and took the scull after Bob had contrived to give him a spiteful blow on the back with it before he extricated it from its rowlock.

Dexter winced slightly, but he bore the pain without a word, and began rowing as well as a boy does row who handles a scull for the first time in his life. And there he sat, gazing to right and left at the dark banks of the river, and the stars above and reflected below, as they went slowly on along the bends and reaches of the little river, everything looking strangely distorted and threatening to the boy's unaccustomed eyes.

The exercise soon began to bring a general feeling of warmth to his chilled frame, and as the inward helplessness passed away it began to give place to an acute sense of fear, and his eyes wandered here and there in search of Sir James Danby, the doctor, and others more terrible, who would charge them with stealing the boat in spite of his protests and the money he had left behind.

And all the time to make his trip more pleasant he had to suffer from jarring blows upon the spine, given by the top of Bob's oar.

In nearly every case this was intentional, and Bob chuckled to himself, as with the customary outburst of his class he began to abuse his companion.

"Why don't yer mind and keep time!" he cried. "Who's to row if you go on like that? I never see such a stoopid."

"All right, Bob, I'll mind," said Dexter, with all the humility of an ignorance which kept him from knowing that as he was rowing stroke Bob should have taken his time from him.

The blows on the back had two good effects, however: they gratified Bob, who had the pleasure of tyrannising over and inflicting pain upon his comrade, while Dexter gained by the rapid increase of warmth, and was most likely saved from a chill and its accompanying fever.

Still that night trip was not pleasant, for when Bob was not grumbling about the regularity of Dexter's stroke, he had fault to find as to his pulling too hard or not hard enough, and so sending the head of the boat toward the right or left bank of the stream. In addition, the young bully kept up a running fire of comment on his companion's shortcomings.

"I never see such a mate," he said. "No money and no clothes. I say," he added at the end of one grumbling fit, "what made you want to run away!"

"I don't know," said Dexter sadly. "I suppose it was because you persuaded me."

"Oh, come, that's a good un," said Bob. "Why, it was you persuaded me! You were always wanting to go away, and you said we could take Danby's boat, and go right down to the sea."

"No!" protested Dexter; "it was you said that."

"Me!" cried Bob. "Oh, come, I like that, 'pon my word I do. It was you always begging of me to go, and to take you with me. Why, I shouldn't never have thought of such a thing if you hadn't begun it."

Dexter was silent, and now getting thoroughly warm he toiled on with his oar, wondering whether Bob would be more amiable when the day came, and trying to think of something to say to divert his thoughts and make him cease his quarrelsome tone.

"I never see such a mate," growled Bob again. "No money, no clothes! why, I shall have to keep yer, I s'pose."

"How long will it take us to get down to the sea, Bob?" said Dexter at last.

"I d'know. Week p'r'aps."

"But we shall begin fishing before then, shan't we!"

"Fishing! How are you going to fish without any rod and line? Expects me to find 'em for yer, I s'pose!"

"No, but I thought you would catch the fish, and I could light a fire and cook them."

"Oh, that's what yer thought, was it? Well, p'r'aps we shall, and p'r'aps we shan't."

"Do you think they will come after us!" ventured Dexter, after a time.

"Sure to, I should say; and if they do, and they kitches us, I shall say as it was you who stole the boat."

"No, you won't," said Dexter, plucking up a little spirit now he was getting more himself. "You wouldn't be such a sneak."

"If you call me a sneak, I'll chuck you out of the boat," cried Bob angrily.

"I didn't call you a sneak, I only said you wouldn't be such a sneak," protested Dexter.

"I know what you said: yer needn't tell me, and I won't have it, so now then. If you want to quarrel, you'd better get out and go back."

"But I don't want to quarrel, Bob; I want to be the best of friends."

"Then don't yer call me a sneak, because if you do it'll be the worse for you."

"Oh, I say, Bob," protested Dexter, as he tugged away at his oar, "don't be so disagreeable."

"And now he says I'm disagreeable!" cried Bob. "Well of all the chaps as ever I see you're about the nastiest. Look here, do you want to fight? because if you do, we'll just go ashore here and have it out."

"I don't want to fight indeed, Bob."

"Yes, you do; you keep egging of me on, and saying disagreeable things as would have made some chaps give you one for yourself ever so long ago. Lookye here, only one on us can be captain in this here boat, and it is going to be either me or you. I don't want to be, but I ain't going to be quite jumped upon, so we'll get ashore here, and soon see who it's going to be."

As Bob Dimsted spoke in a low snarling way, he gave his scull so hard a pull that he sent the boat's head in toward the bank.

"First you want one thing, and then you want another, and then you try to make out that it was me who stole the boat."

"I only said it wasn't me."

"There," cried Bob, "hark at that! Why, who was it then?" Didn't you take yer clothes off and swim over while I stood t'other side?

Dexter did not answer, but went on rowing with a hot feeling of anger rising in his breast.

"Oh, so now you're sulky, are you? Very well, my lad, we'll soon see to that. If you don't know who's best man, I'm going to show you. It's dark, but it's light enough for that, so come ashore and—"

Whish! rush! crash!

"Row! pull! pull!" whispered Bob excitedly, as there was a loud breaking of the low growth on the bank close by them, followed by the loud clap given by a swing-gate violently dashed to.

Dexter pulled, but against the bank, for they were too close in for them to get a dip of the oar in the water; but what he did was not without some effect, and, as Bob backed, the boat's head gradually glided round, shot into the stream, and they went swiftly on again, pulling as hard as they could.

"Did you see him!" whispered Bob at last.

"No, did you?"

"No, but I nearly did. He has been creeping along the bank for ever so long, and he nearly got hold of the boat."

"Who was it?" whispered Dexter.

"Pleeceman, but pull hard, and we shall get away from him yet."

They both pulled a slow stroke for quite an hour, and by that time the horse that had been feeding upon the succulent weedy growth close to the water's edge had got over its fright, and was grazing peaceably once more.

Bob was quiet after that. The sudden alarm had cut his string of words in two, and he was too much disturbed to take them up again to join. In fact he was afraid to speak lest he should be heard, and he kept his ill-temper— stirred up by the loss of a night's rest—to himself for the next hour, when suddenly throwing in his oar he said—

"Look here, I'm tired, and I shall lie down in the bottom here and have a nap. You keep a sharp look-out."

"But I can't row two oars," said Dexter.

"Well, nobody asked you to. You've got to sit there with the boat-hook, and push her off if ever she runs into the bushes. The stream'll take her down like it does a float."

"How far are we away from the town!"

"I d'know."

"Well, how soon will it be morning!"

"How should I know? I haven't got a watch, have I? If I'd had one I should have sold it so as to have some money to share with my mate."

"Have you got any money, Bob?"

"Course I have. Don't think I'm such a stoopid as you, do yer!"

Dexter was silent, and in the darkness he laid in his oar after the fashion of his companion, and took up the boat-hook, while Bob lifted one of the cushions from the seat, placed it in the bottom of the boat, and then curled up, something after the fashion of a dog, and went off to sleep.

Dexter sat watching him as he could dimly make out his shape, and then found that the stern of the boat had been caught in an eddy and swung round, so that he had some occupation for a few moments trying to alter her position in the water, which he did at last by hooking the trunk of an overhanging willow.

This had the required effect, and the head swung round once more; but in obtaining this result Dexter found himself in this position—the willow refused to give up its hold of the boat-hook. He naturally, on his side, also refused, and, to make matters worse, the current here was quite a race, and the boat was going rapidly on.

He was within an ace of having to leave the boat-hook behind, for he declined to try another bath—this time in his clothes. Just, however, at the crucial moment the bark of the willow gave way, the hook descended with a splash, and Dexter breathed more freely, and sat there with the boat-hook across his knees looking first to right and then to left in search of danger, but seeing nothing but the low-wooded banks of the stream, which was gradually growing wider as they travelled further from the town.

It was a strange experience; and, comparatively happy now in the silence of the night, Dexter kept his lonely watch, thinking how much pleasanter it was for his companion to be asleep, but all the time suffering a peculiar sensation of loneliness, and gazing wonderingly at the strange, dark shapes which he approached.

Men, huge beasts, strange monsters, they seemed sometimes right in front, rising from the river, apparently as if to bar his way, but always proving to be tree, bush, or stump, and their position caused by the bending of the stream.

Once there was a sudden short and peculiar grating, and the boat stopped short, but only to glide on again as he realised that the river was shallow there, and they had touched the clean-washed gravelly bottom.

There was enough excitement now he was left to himself to keep off the depression he had felt, for now the feeling that he was gliding away into a new life was made more impressive by the movement of the boat, which seemed to him to go faster and faster among dimly seen trees, and always over a glistening path that seemed to be paved with stars.

Once, and once only, after leaving the town behind was there any sign of inhabited building, and that was about an hour after they started, when a faint gleam seemed to be burning steadily on the bank, and so near that the light shone down upon the water. But that was soon passed, and the river ran wandering on through a wild and open district, where the only inhabitants were the few shepherds who attended the flocks.

On still, and on, among the low meadows, through which the river had cut its way in bygone times. Serpentine hardly expressed its course, for it so often turned and doubled back over the ground it had passed before; but still it, on the whole, flowed rapidly, and by slow degrees mile after mile was placed between the boys and the town. Twice over a curious sensation of drowsiness came upon Dexter, and he found himself hard at work trying to hunt out some of his pets, which seemed to him to have gone into the most extraordinary places.

For instance, Sam the toad had worked himself down into the very toe of the stocking he had been obliged to take off when he went into the water, and the more he tried to shake it out, the more tightly it clung with its little hands.

Then he woke with a start, and found out that he had dozed off.

Pulling himself together he determined not to give way again, but to try and guide the boat.

To properly effect this he still sat fast with the boat-hook across his knees, and in an instant he was back at the doctor's house in Coleby, looking on while Helen was busy reading the letter which had been brought down from the bedroom.

Dexter could see her perfectly plainly. It seemed a thoroughly realistic proceeding, and she was wiping her eyes as she read, while, at the same moment, the doctor entered the room with the willow pollard from the bottom of the garden; and lifting it up he called him an ungrateful boy, and struck him a severe blow on the forehead which sent him back on to the carpet.

But it was not on to the carpet, but back into the bottom of the boat, and certainly it was a willow branch which had done the mischief, though not in the doctor's hand.

Dexter got up again, feeling rather sore and confused, for the boat had drifted under a projecting bough, just on a level with the boy's head, but his cap had saved him from much harm.

Dexter's first thought was that Bob would jump up and begin to bully him for going to sleep. But Bob was sleeping heavily, and the bump, the fall, and the rocking of the boat only acted as a lullaby to his pleasant dreams.

And then it seemed that a tree on the bank—a tall poplar—was very much plainer than he had seen any tree before that night. So was another on the other bank, and directly after came a sound with which he was perfectly familiar at the doctor's—a sound that came beneath his window among the laurustinus bushes.

Chink—chink—chink—chink.

A blackbird—answered by another. And then all at once it seemed to be so cold that it was impossible to help shivering; and to ward off the chilling sensation Dexter began to use the boat-hook as a pole, thrusting it down first on one side of the boat and then on the other as silently as he could, so as not to wake Bob. Sometimes he touched bottom, and was able to give the boat a good impetus, but as often as not he could not reach the river-bed. Still the exercise made his blood circulate, and drove away the dull sense of misery that had been coming on.

As he toiled on with the pole, the trees grew plainer and plainer, and a soft pearly dawn seemed to be floating over the river. The birds uttered their calls, and then, all at once, in a loud burst of melody, up rose a lark from one of the dewy meadows on his right. Then further off there was another, and right away high up in the east one tiny speck of dull red.

Soon this red began to glow as if gradually getting hotter. Then another and another speck appeared—then scores, fifties, hundreds—and Dexter stood bathed in the rich light which played through the curling river mists, as the whole of the eastern heavens became damasked with flecks of gold.

In a comparatively short time these faded, and a warm glow spread around the meadows and wild country on either side, where empurpled hills rose higher and higher, grew more and more glorious, and the river sparkled and danced and ran in smooth curves, formed eddies, and further in advance became one wonderful stretch of dancing golden ripples, so beautiful that Dexter stood on the thwart with the pole balanced in his hand wondering whether everything could be as beautiful at Coleby as he saw it now.

Then there was a sudden shock, so sharp that he could not save himself, but took a kind of header, not into the water, but right on to Bob Dimsted, landing with his knees in Bob's softest portion, and the pole right across his neck, just as Bob tried to rise, and uttered a tremendous yell. The wonder was that the end of the boat-hook had not gone through the bottom of the boat.

Chapter Thirty Two
Master and Slave

"Eee! I say! Whatcher doing of!" roared Bob, beginning to struggle, as Dexter contrived to get his feet once more.

"I—I couldn't help it, Bob," he said, in a shame-faced way.

"Couldn't help it! Here, don'tcher try to wake me again that way."

"I didn't. I—"

"Coming jumping on a fellow."

"I didn't, Bob. The boat stopped all at once, and I tumbled forward."

"Then just you tumble on to some one else next time," growled Bob, sitting up rubbing himself, and then yawning loudly. "Why, hulloa! Whatcher been doing of now?"

"I? Nothing Bob."

"Yes, you have. You've got the boat aground."

"I—I didn't indeed, Bob. It went like that all of itself," stammered Dexter.

"Went all of itself! You are a fellow to leave to manage a boat. I just shut my eyes a few minutes and you get up to them games. Here, give us holt!"

He snatched at the boat-hook, and began to thrust with all his might: but in vain.

"Don't stand staring like that," he cried, becoming all at once in a violent hurry to get on. "Come and help. D'yer want them to come and ketch us!"

Dexter went to his help, and by dint of thrusting together the boat was pushed off the shallows, and gliding once more into deep water began to float gently on.

There was a few minutes' silence, during which Bob took the sculls and began to pull, looking, with his eyes red and swollen up, anything but a pleasant companion; and in spite of himself Dexter began to think that Bob as a conversational friend across the water was a very different being to

Bob as the captain of their little vessel, armed with authority, and ready to tyrannise over his comrade to the fullest extent.

Suddenly a thought occurred to Dexter as he ran his eye over the handsome cushions of the well-varnished boat.

"Bob!" he said.

There was no answer.

"Bob, did you take that parcel and drop it in Sir James's letter-box!"

"What parcel!" said Bob sourly.

"That one I threw over to you last night."

"Oh! that one as fell in the water?"

"Yes: did you take it?"

"Why, didn't you tell me to!"

"Yes: but did you?"

"Why, of course I did."

"That's right. I say, where are we now?"

"I d'know. Somewhere down the river."

"Hadn't we better begin to fish?"

"Fish? What for?"

"Because I'm getting so hungry, and want my breakfast."

"Yes, you're a nice fellow to wantcher bragfuss. Got no money and no clothes. I s'pose I shall have to keep yer."

"No, no, Bob. I'll work, or fish, or do anything."

"Yes, so it seems," said Bob sarcastically; "a-sitting there like a gent, and letting me do everything."

"Well, let me pull one oar."

"No, I can do it, and you shall have some bragfuss presently. I don't want to be took, because you've stole a boat."

Dexter turned pale, and then red with indignation, but he did not say anything, only waited till his lord should feel disposed to see about getting a meal.

This happened when they were about a couple of miles lower down the stream, which steadily opened out and became more beautiful, till at last it seemed to be fully double the size it was at Coleby.

Here they came abreast of a cluster of cottages on the bank, one of which, a long whitewashed stone building, hung out a sign such as showed that it was a place for refreshment.

"There," said Bob, "we'll land there—I mean you shall, and go in and buy some bread and cheese."

"Bread and cheese," faltered Dexter. "Shan't we get any tea or coffee, and bread and butter?"

"No! of course not. If we both get out they'll be asking us questions about the boat."

Bob backed the boat close to the shore, stern foremost, and then said—

"Now, look here, don't you make no mistake; but you jump out as soon as I get close in, and go and ask for four pen'orth o' bread and cheese. I'll row out again and wait till you come."

Dexter did not like the task, and he could not help thinking of the pleasant breakfast at the doctor's, but recalling the fact that a fortune was not to be made without a struggle, he prepared to land.

"But I haven't got any money," he said. "No, you haven't got any money," said Bob sourly, as he tucked one oar under his knee, so as to get his hand free to plunge into his pocket. "There you are," he said, bringing out sixpence. "Look sharp."

Dexter took the money, leaped ashore, and walked up to the little public-house, where a red-faced woman waited upon him, and cut the bread and cheese.

"Well," she said, looking wonderingly at her customer, "don't you want no beer!"

Dexter shook his head, lifted up his change, and hurried out of the place in alarm, lest the woman should ask him any more questions.

But she did not attempt to, only came to the door to watch the boy as he went back to the boat, which was backed in so that Dexter could jump aboard; but Bob, whose eyes were looking sharply to right and left in search of danger, just as a sparrow scrutinises everything in dread while it is eating a meal, managed so badly in his eagerness to get away, that, as Dexter leaped in, he gave a tug with the sculls, making the boat jerk so sharply that Dexter's feet began to move faster than his body, and the said body came down in a sitting position that was more sudden than agreeable.

"Well, you are a fellow!" cried Bob, grinning. "Any one would think you had never been in a boat before."

Dexter gathered together the portions of food which had been scattered in the bottom of the boat, and then sat looking ruefully at his companion.

"If any of that there's dirty, you've got to eat it," said Bob sourly. "I shan't."

As he spoke he tugged as hard as he could at the sculls, rowing away till they were well round the next bend, and quite out of sight of the woman who stood at the door watching them, and as Bob bent down, and pulled each stroke well home, Dexter sat watching him with a troubled feeling which added to his hunger and discomfort. For once more it began to seem that Bob was not half so pleasant a companion as he had promised to be when he was out fishing, and they sat and chatted on either side of the little river.

But he brightened up again as Bob suddenly began to pull harder with his left-hand scull, turning the boat's head in toward the shore where a clump of trees stood upon the bank with their branches overhanging, and almost touching the water.

"Look out! Heads!" cried Bob, as the bow of the boat touched the leafage, and they glided on through the pliant twigs; and as the sculls were laid in, Bob rose up in his place, seized a good-sized bough, and holding on by it worked the boat beneath, and in a position which enabled him to throw the chain over, and securely moor the little vessel in what formed quite a leafy arbour with the clear water for floor, and the thwarts of the boat for seats.

"There," cried Bob, in a satisfied tone, and with a little of his old manner, "whatcher think o' that? Talk about a place for a bragfuss! Why, it would do to live in."

Dexter said it was capital, but somehow just then he began to think about the pleasant room at the doctor's, with the white cloth and china, and the silver coffee-pot, and the odour from the covered dish which contained ham or bacon, or fried soles.

"Now then!" cried Bob; "I'm as hungry as you, and we're all safe here, so hand over."

Dexter gave him one of the portions of bread and cheese—the better of the two, but Bob turned it over and examined it in a dissatisfied way, scowling at it the while, and casting an occasional glance at that which Dexter had reserved for himself.

"What I says is—play fair," he growled. "I don't want no more than half."

"But that's the bigger half, Bob."

"I dunno so much about that."

"And this is the one which seemed to be a little gritty."

"Oh, is it?" said Bob surlily; and he began eating in a wolfish fashion, making fierce snaps and bites at his food, as he held the bread in one hand, the cheese in the other, and taking alternate mouthfuls.

"Hunger is sweet sauce," and Dexter was not long in following Bob's example, that is as to the eating, but as he sat there munching away at the cakey home-made bread, and the strong cheese, in spite of its being a glorious morning, and the sun showering down in silver pencils through the overhanging boughs—in spite of the novelty of the scene, and the freedom, there did not seem to be so much romance in the affair as had been expected; and try how he would he could not help longing for a good hot cup of coffee.

This was not heroic, but the boy felt very miserable. He had been up all night, going through adventures that were, in spite of their tameness, unusually exciting, and he was suffering from a nervous depression which robbed him of appetite as much as did his companion's words. For instead of being merry, confidential, and companionable, Bob scarcely opened his lips now without assuming the overbearing bullying tone he had heard so often from his elders.

"Come, get on with your bragfuss," said Bob sharply. "We're going on d'rectly, and you've got to pull."

"I can't eat much this morning," said Dexter apologetically; "and I'm thirsty."

"Well, why don't yer drink!" said Bob, grinning, and pointing at the river. "Here, I'll show you how."

He took off his cap, and placing his chest on the side of the boat, leant over till his lips touched the clear flowing stream.

"Hah!" he said at last, rising and passing his hand across his lips; "that's something like water, that is. Better than tea, or drinking water out of a mug."

"Doesn't it taste fishy?" Dexter ventured to say.

"Fishy! Hark at him!" cried Bob mockingly. "You try."

Dexter's mouth felt hot and dry, and laying aside what he had not eaten of his bread and cheese he followed his companion's example, and was drawing in the cool sweet water, when he suddenly felt Bob's hand on the back of his, neck, and before he could struggle up his head was thrust down into the water over and over again.

"Don't, don't!" he panted, as he thrust against the side of the boat and got free. "You shouldn't do that."

There was a flash of anger in his eyes as he faced Bob, and his fists were clenched, but he did not strike out, he contented himself with rubbing the water from his eyes, and then wiping his face upon his handkerchief.

"I shouldn't do that? Why shouldn't I do that?" said Bob threateningly. "Serve yer right, sittin' down to bragfuss without washing yer face. Going to have any more?"

Dexter did not answer; but finished drying his face, and then took up his bread and cheese.

"Oh, that's it, is it!" said Bob. "Sulky, eh? Don't you come none o' them games with me, young fellow, or it will be the worse for yer."

Dexter made no reply, but went on eating, having hard work to swallow each mouthful.

Time back all this would not have made so much impression upon him, but the social education he had been receiving in his intercourse with Helen Grayson had considerably altered him, and his breast swelled as he felt the change in his companion, and began to wish more than ever that he had not come.

Almost as he thought this he received a curious check.

"It won't do for you to be sulky with me," began his tyrant. "You've got to go along o' me now you have come. You couldn't go back after stealing this boat."

"Stealing!" cried Dexter, flushing up. "I didn't steal it. We borrowed it together."

"Oh, did we?" said Bob mockingly; "I don't know nothing about no *we*. It was you stole it, and persuaded me to come."

"I didn't," cried Dexter indignantly. "I only borrowed it, and you helped me do it."

"Oh, did I? We shall see about that. But you can't go back never no more, so don't you think that."

Bob's guess at his companion's thoughts was pretty shrewd; and as Dexter sat looking at him aghast, with the full extent of his delinquency dawning upon him, Bob began to unloose the chain.

"Now then," he said, "finish that there bread and cheese, or else put it in yer pocket. We're going on again, and I want to catch our dinner."

The idea of doing something more in accordance with the object of their trip roused Dexter into action, and, after helping to force the boat from among the branches, he willingly took one of the sculls; and in obedience to the frequently given orders, rowed as well as his inexperience would allow, and they glided swiftly down the stream.

"What are you going to do first, Bob?" said Dexter, who felt more bright and cheerful now out in the sunshine, with the surface all ripple and glow.

"Why, I told yer just now!" said the boy surlily. "Mind what yer doing, or you'll catch a crab."

Dexter did catch one the next moment, thrusting his oar in so deeply that he could hardly withdraw it, and bringing forth quite a little storm of bullying from his companion.

"Here, I shall never make nothing o' you," cried Bob. "Give's that there oar."

"No, no, let me go on pulling," said Dexter good-humouredly, for his fit of anger had passed off. "I'm not used to it like you are, but I shall soon learn."

He tried to emulate Bob's regular rowing, and by degrees managed to help the boat along till toward midday, when, seeing an attractive bend where the river ran deep and dark round by some willows, Bob softly rowed the boat close up to the bank, moored her to the side, and then began to fit together his tackle, a long willow wand being cut and trimmed to do duty for a rod.

This done, a very necessary preliminary had to be attended to, namely, the finding of bait.

Bob was provided with a little canvas bag, into which he thrust a few green leaves and some scraps of moss, before leaping ashore, and proceeding to kick off patches of the bank in search of worms.

Dexter watched him attentively, and then his eyes fell upon a good-sized, greenish-hued caterpillar which had dropped from a willow branch into the boat.

This seemed so suitable for a bait that Dexter placed it in one of Bob's tin boxes, and proceeded to search for more; the boughs upon being shaken yielding six or seven.

"Whatcher doing of?" grumbled Bob, coming back to the boat, after securing a few worms. "Yah! they're no use for bait."

All the same, though, the boy took one of the caterpillars, passed the hook through its rather tough skin, and threw out some distance in front of the boat, and right under the overhanging boughs.

There was a quick bob of the float, and then it began to glide along the top of the water, while, as Bob skilfully checked it, there was a quick rushing to and fro, two or three minutes' hard fight, and a half-pound trout was drawn alongside, and hoisted into the boat.

"That's the way I doos it," said Bob, whose success suddenly turned him quite amiable. "Fish will take a caterpillar sometimes. Give us another!"

The bait was passed along to the fisherman, who threw out, and in five minutes was again successful, drawing in, after a short struggle, a nice little chub.

After that, it was as if the disturbance of the water had driven the fish away, and though Bob tried in every direction, using the caterpillar, a worm, a bit of bread paste, and a scrap of cheese, he could not get another bite.

Bob tried after that till he was tired, but no fish would bite, so he handed the rod to Dexter, who also fished for some time in vain, when a removal was determined upon; but though they tried place after place there were no more bites, and hunger having asserted itself once more, they landed to prepare their dinner.

The place chosen was very solitary, being where the river ran deeply beneath a high limestone cliff, and landing, a few sticks were soon gathered together ready for a fire.

"But we have no matches," said Dexter.

"You mean you ain't got none," sneered Bob, taking a box out of his pocket. "I'm captain, and captains always thinks of these things. Now then, clean them fish, while I lights this fire. Got a knife, ain't yer!"

Dexter had a knife, and he opened it and proceeded to perform the rather disgusting task, while Bob lay down and began blowing at the fire to get it into a blaze.

That fish-cleaning was very necessary, but somehow it did not add to the charm of the *alfresco* preparations; and Dexter could not help thinking once how uncomfortable it would be if it came on to rain and put out the fire.

But it did not come on to rain; the wood burned merrily, and after a piece of shaley limestone had been found it was placed in the fire where the embers were most clear, and the fish laid upon it to cook.

The success was not great, for when the fish began to feel the heat, and hissed and sputtered, the piece of stone began to send off splinters, with a loud crack, from time to time. Then a pocket-knife, though useful, is not a convenient cooking implement, especially when, for want of lard or butter, the fish began to stick to the stone, and refused to be turned over without leaving their skins behind.

"Ain't it fun?" said Bob.

Dexter said it was. He did not know why, for at that moment a piece of green wood had sent a jet of hot, steamy smoke in his eyes, which gave him intense pain, and set him rubbing the smarting places in a way which made them worse.

"Here, don't make such a fuss over a bit o' smoke," said Bob. "You'll soon get used to that. Mind, that one's tail's burning!"

Dexter did mind, but the fish stuck so close to the stone that its tail was burned off before it could be moved, a mishap which drew from Bob the remark—

"Well, you are a chap!"

Before the fish were done, more and more wood had to be collected; and as a great deal of this was green, a great smoke arose, and, whenever a puff of wind came, this was far from agreeable.

"How small they are getting!" said Dexter, as he watched the browning fish.

Bang!

A great piece of the stone splintered off with a report like that of a gun, but, fortunately, neither of the boys was hurt.

"We shall have to buy a frying-pan and a kittle," said Bob, as soon as examination proved that the fish were safe, but stuck all over splinters of stone, which promised ill for the repast. "Can't do everything at once."

"I'm getting very hungry again," said Dexter; "and, I say, we haven't got any bread."

"Well, what o' that?"

"And no salt."

"Oh, you'll get salt enough as soon as we go down to the sea. You may think yourself jolly lucky as you've got fish, and some one as knows how to kitch 'em. They're done now. I'll let you have that one. 'Tain't so burnt as this is. There, kitch hold!"

A fish hissing hot and burnt on one side is not a pleasant thing to take in a bare hand, so Dexter received his upon his pocket-handkerchief, as it was pushed toward him with a piece of stick; and then, following his companion's example, he began to pick off pieces with the blade of his pocket-knife, and to burn his mouth.

"'Lishus, ain't it?" said Bob, making a very unpleasant noise suggestive of pigs.

Dexter made no reply, his eyes were watering, and he was in difficulties with a bone.

"I said 'lishus, ain't it!" said Bob again, after more pig noise.

"Mine isn't very nice," said Dexter.

"Not nice? Well, you are a chap to grumble! I give you the best one, because this here one had its tail burnt off, and now you ain't satisfied."

"But it tastes bitter, and as if it wants some bread and salt."

"Well, we ain't got any, have we? Can't yer wait?"

"Yes," said Dexter; "but it's so full of bones."

"So are you full of bones. Go on, mate. Why, I'm half done."

Dexter did go on, wondering in his own mind whether his companion's fish was as unpleasant and coarse eating as the one he discussed, giving him credit the while for his disinterestedness, he being in happy ignorance of the comparative merits of fresh-water fish when cooked; and therefore he struggled with his miserable, watery, insipid, bony, ill-cooked chub, while Bob picked the fat flakes off the vertebra of his juicy trout.

"Wish we'd got some more," said Bob, as he licked his fingers, and then wiped his knife-blade on the leg of his trousers.

"I don't," thought Dexter; but he was silent, and busy picking out the thin sharp bones which filled his fish.

"Tell you what," said Bob, "we'll— Look out!"

He leaped up and dashed to the boat, rapidly unfastening the chain from where it was secured to a stump.

Dexter had needed no further telling, for he had caught sight of two men at the same time as Bob; and as it was evident that they were running toward the fire, and as Dexter knew intuitively that he was trespassing, he sprang up, leaving half his chub, and leaped aboard, just as Bob sprang from the bank, seized an oar, and thrust the boat away.

It was pretty close, for as the stern of the boat left the shore the foremost man made a dash at it, missed, and nearly fell into the water.

Chapter Thirty Three
The Life of the Free

"Here," cried the man, as he recovered himself, "it's of no use. Come back!"

Dexter was so influenced by the man's words that he was ready to go back at once. But Bob was made of different stuff, and he began now to work the boat along by paddling softly, fish-tail fashion.

"Do you hear!" roared the man, just as the other came trotting up, quite out of breath.

"Yah!" cried Bob derisively, as he began to feel safe. "Come back, you young scoundrel!" roared the man fiercely. "Here, Digges, fetch 'em back."

He was a big black-whiskered man in a velveteen jacket, evidently a gamekeeper, and he spoke to his companion as if he were a dog.

This man hesitated for a moment or two.

"Go on! Fetch 'em back," cried the keeper.

"But it's so wet."

"Wet? Well, do you want me to go? In with you."

The underkeeper jumped off the bank at once into the water, which was about up to his knees; but by this time Bob was working the boat along more quickly, and before the underkeeper had waded out many yards Bob had seated himself, put out the second scull, and, helped by the stream, was able to laugh defiance at his would-be captors.

"Here, I ain't going any further," grumbled the underkeeper. "It will be deep water directly," and he stopped with the current rippling just about his thigh.

"Are you coming back!" cried the keeper, looking round about him and pretending to pick up a big stone.

"No! Come arter us if you want us," cried Bob, while Dexter crouched down watching the man's hand, ready to dodge the missile he expected to see launched at them.

"If you don't come back I'll—"

The man did not finish his speech, but threw himself back as if about to hurl the stone.

"Yah!" cried Bob. "Y'ain't got no stone."

"No, but I've got a boat up yonder."

"Go and fetch it, then," cried Bob derisively.

"You young scoundrels! Landing here and destroying our plantations. I'll send the police after you, and have you before the magistrates, you poaching young vagabonds!"

"So are you!" cried Bob.

"Hush, don't!" whispered Dexter.

"Who cares for them?" cried Bob. "We weren't doing no harm."

"Here, come out, Digges, and you run across and send the men with a boat that way. I'll go and get ours. We'll soon have 'em!"

The man slowly waded out while the keeper trampled on the fire, stamping all over it, to extinguish the last spark, so that it should not spread, and then they separated, going in different directions.

"Row, Bob; row hard," cried Dexter, who was in agony.

"Well, I am a-rowing, ain't I? We warn't doing no harm."

"Let me have an oar."

"Ketch hold, then," cried Bob; and as soon as Dexter was seated they began to row as if for their lives, watching in turn the side of the river and the reach they were leaving behind in expectation of seeing the pursuers and the party who were to cut them off.

Dexter's horror increased. He pictured himself seized and taken before a magistrate, charged with damaging, burning, and trespassing. The perspiration began to stand out in beads upon each side of his nose, his hair grew wet, and his cap stuck to his forehead as he toiled away at his oar, trying hard to obey the injunctions of his companion to pull steady—to keep time—not to dip his scull so deep, and the like.

As for Bob, as he rowed he was constantly uttering derisive and defiant remarks; but all the same his grubby face was rather ashy, and he too grew tremendously hot as he worked away at his scull for quite an hour, during which time they had not seen anything more formidable than half a dozen red oxen standing knee-deep in the water, and swinging their tails to and fro to drive away the tormenting flies.

"They hadn't got no boat," said Bob at last. "I know'd it all the time. Pretended to throw a stone at us when there wasn't one near, only the one we tried to cook with, flee him take hold of it and drop it again!"

"No."

"I did. Burnt his jolly old fingers, and serve him right. We never said nothing to him. He ain't everybody."

"But let's get further away."

"Well, we're getting further away, stream's taking us down. You are a coward."

"You were frightened too."

"No, I wasn't. I laughed at him. I'd ha' give him something if he'd touched me."

"Then why did you run away?"

"'Cause I didn't want no bother. Here, let's find another good place, and catch some more fish."

"It won't be safe to stop yet, Bob."

"Here, don't you talk to me, I know what I'm about. We'll row round that next bend, and I'll show you a game then."

"Hadn't we better go on till we can buy some bread and butter?" said Dexter; and then as he saw some cattle in a field a happy hunger-engendered thought occurred to him,—"And perhaps we can get some milk."

"You're allus thinking of eating and drinking," cried Bob. "All right! We'll get some, then."

They rowed steadily on, with Dexter rapidly improving in the management of his oar, till a farm-house was sighted near the bank; but it was on the same side as that upon which they had had their adventure.

They were afraid to land there, so rowed on for another quarter of a mile before another building was sighted.

This proved to be a farm, and they rowed up to a place where the cattle came down to drink, and a plank ran out on to a couple of posts, evidently for convenience in landing from a boat, or for dipping water.

"Here, I'll go this time," said Bob, as the boat glided up against the posts. "No games, you know."

"What games!"

"No going off and leaving a fellow!"

"Don't be afraid," said Dexter.

"I ain't," said Bob, with a malicious grin. "Why, if a fellow was to serve me such a trick as that I should half-kill him."

Bob landed, and as Dexter sat there in the swift-streamed Devon river gazing at the rippling water, and the glorious green pastures and quickly sloping hills, everything seemed to him very beautiful, and he could not help wishing that he had a pleasanter companion and some dinner.

Bob soon returned with a wine bottle full of milk and half a loaf, and a great pat of butter of golden yellow, with a wonderful cow printed upon it, the butter being wrapped in a rhubarb leaf, and the bread swung in Bob's dirty neckerchief.

"Here y'are!" he cried, as he stepped into the boat and pushed off quickly, as if he felt safer when they were on the move. "We'll go lower down, and then I'll show you such a game."

"Let's have some bread and butter first," said Dexter.

"No, we won't; not till we get further away. We'll get some fish first and light a fire and cook 'em, and—pull away—I'll show yer."

Dexter obeyed; but his curiosity was excited.

"Going to catch some more fish!"

"You wait and you'll see," was the reply; and in the expectation of a hearty meal matters looked more bright, especially as the day was glorious, and the scenery beautiful all round.

No signs of pursuit being seen, Dexter was ready to laugh with his companion now.

"I knew all the time," said Bob, with superior wisdom in every intonation of his voice; "I should only have liked to see them come."

Dexter said nothing, and the next minute, as they were in a curve of the river, where it flowed dark and deep, they ran the boat in once more beside a meadow edged with pollard willows.

"Now then, I'll show you some fishing," cried Bob, as he secured the boat.

"No, not now: let's have something to eat first," protested Dexter.

"Just you look here, young un, I'm captain," cried Bob. "Do you know what cray-fish are!"

Dexter shook his head.

"Well, then, I'm just going to show yer."

The water was about two feet deep, and ran slowly along by a perpendicular clayey bank on the side where they were, and, deliberately undressing, Bob let himself down into the river, and then began to grope along by the side, stooping from time to time to thrust his hand into some hole.

"Here, undo that chain, and let her drift by me," he cried. "I shall fish all along here."

Dexter obeyed—it seemed to be his fate to obey; and taking the boat-hook he held on easily enough by tree after tree, for there was scarcely any stream here, watching intently the while, as Bob kept on thrusting his hand into some hole.

"Oh!" cried Bob suddenly, as he leaned down as far as he could reach, and then rose slowly.

"Got one?"

"No: I missed him. It was an eel; I just felt him, and then he dodged back. Such a big un! They're so jolly hard to hold."

This was exciting, and now Dexter began for the first time to be glad that he had come.

"I've got him now!" cried Bob excitedly; and, rising from a stooping position, in which his shoulder was right underneath, he threw a dingy-looking little fresh-water lobster into the boat.

Dexter examined it wonderingly, and was favoured with a nip from its claws for his attention.

"Here's another," said Bob, and he threw one much larger into the boat, its horny shell rattling on the bottom.

"Are they good to eat?" said Dexter.

"Good to eat? Why, they're lovely. You wait a bit. And, I say, you look how I do it; I shall make you always catch these here, so you've got to learn."

Dexter paid attention to the process, and felt that there was not much to learn: only to find out a hole—the burrow of the cray-fish,—and then thrust in his hand, and, if the little crustacean were at home, pull it out. The process was soon learned, but the temptation to begin was not great.

Bob evidently found the sport exciting, however, for he searched away with more or less success, and very soon there were a dozen cray-fish of various sizes crawling about the bottom of the boat.

"There's thousands of them here," cried Bob, as he searched away all along beneath the steep bank, which was full of holes, some being the homes of rats, some those of the cray-fish, and others of eels which he touched twice over—in one case for the slimy fish to back further in, but in the other, for it to make a rush out into the open water, and swim rapidly away.

The pursuit of the cray-fish lasted till the row of willows came to an end, and with them the steep bank, the river spreading out again, and becoming stony and shallow.

"How many are there?" said Bob, as he climbed out upon the grass, after washing his clayey arm.

"Twenty-one," said Dexter.

"Ah, just you wait a bit till I'm dressed."

Bob said no more, but indulged in a natural towel. That is to say, he had a roll on the warm grass, and then rose and ran to and fro in the glowing sunshine for about five minutes, after which he rapidly slipped on his things, which were handed to him from the boat.

"Now," he cried, as he stepped in once more and seized an oar, "I'll show you something."

They rowed on for some distance, till a suitable spot was found at the edge of a low, scrubby oak wood which ran up a high bank.

The place was extremely solitary. There was plenty of wood, and as soon as the boat had been moored Dexter was set to work collecting the sticks in a heap, close up to where there was a steep bare piece of stony bank, and in a few minutes the dry leaves and grass first collected caught fire, then the twigs, and soon a good glowing fire was burning.

The bread and butter and bottle of milk were stood on one side, and close by them there was a peculiar noise made by the unhappy cray-fish which were tied up in Bob's neckerchief, from which the bread had been released.

"Going to cook 'em!" he said; "in course I am. Wait a bit and I'll show yer. I say! this is something like a place, ain't it!"

Dexter agreed that it was, for it was a sylvan nook which a lover of picnics would have considered perfect, the stream ran swiftly by, a few yards away the stony bank rose up, dotted with patches of brown furze and heath, nearly perpendicularly above their heads, and on either side they were shut in by trees and great mossy stones.

The fire burned brightly, and sent up clouds of smoke, which excited dread in Dexter's breast for a few moments, but the fear was forgotten directly in the anticipation of the coming feast, in preparation for which Bob kept on adding to the central flame the burnt-through pieces of dead wood, while Dexter from time to time fetched more from the ample store beneath the trees, and broke them off ready for his chief.

"What are you going to do, Bob!" he said at last.

"Going to do? You want to know too much."

"Well, I'm so hungry."

"Well, I'll tell yer. I'm going to roast them cray-fish, that's what I'm going to do."

"How are you going to kill them!"

"Going to kill 'em? I ain't going to kill 'em."

"But you won't roast them alive."

"Won't I? Just you wait till there's plenty of hot ashes and you'll see."

Dexter had made pets of so many creatures that he shrank from inflicting pain, and he looked on at last with something like horror as Bob untied his kerchief, shot all the cray-fish out on the heathy ground, and then, scraping back the glowing embers with his foot till he had left a bare patch of white ash, he rapidly thrust in the captives, which began to hiss and steam and whistle directly.

The whistling noise might easily have been interpreted to mean a cry of pain, but the heat was so great that doubtless death was instantaneous, and there was something in what the boy said in reply to Dexter's protests.

"Get out! It don't hurt 'em much."

"But you might have killed them first."

"How was I to kill 'em first?" snarled Bob, as he sat tailor fashion and poked the cray-fish into warmer places with a piece of burning stick.

"Stuck your knife into them."

"Well, wouldn't that have hurt 'em just as much?"

"Let them die before you cooked them."

"That would hurt 'em ever so much more, and took ever so much longer."

"Well I shan't like to eat them," said Dexter.

"More for me, then. I say! don't they smell good?"

Dexter had a whiff just then, and they certainly did smell tempting to a hungry boy; but he made up his mind to partake only of bread and butter, and kept to his determination for quite five minutes after Bob had declared the cookery complete, and picked the tiny lobsters out of the hot ashes with his burnt stick.

"They're too hot to touch yet," he said. "Wait a bit and I'll show you. Cut the bread."

Dexter obeyed with alacrity, and was soon feasting away on what might very well be called "Boy's Delight," the honest bread and butter which has helped to build up our stalwart race.

Bob helped himself to a piece of bread, spread it thickly with butter, and, withdrawing a little way from the fire, hooked a hot cray-fish to his side, calmly picking out the largest; and as soon as he could handle it he treated it as if it were a gigantic shrimp, dividing the shell in the middle by pulling, and holding up the delicate hot tail, which drew easily from its armour-like case.

"Only wants a bit of salt," he cried, smacking his lips over the little *bonne bouche*, and then proceeding to pick out the contents of the claws, and as much of the body as he deemed good to eat.

Dexter looked on with a feeling of disgust, while Bob laughed at him, and finished four of the cray-fish, throwing the shells over his shoulder towards the river.

Then Dexter picked up one, drew off the shell, smelt it, tasted it, and five minutes later he was as busy as Bob, though when they finished the whole cooking he was seven fish behind.

"Ain't they 'lishus?" cried Bob.

"Yes," said Dexter, unconsciously repeating his companion's first remark, "only want a bit of salt."

Chapter Thirty Four
An Awkward Pursuer

It was wonderful how different the future looked after that picnic dinner by the river-side. The bread and butter were perfect, and the cray-fish as delicious as the choicest prawns. The water that glided past the bank was like crystal; the evening sun lit up the scene with orange and gold; and as the two boys lolled restfully upon the bank listening to the murmur of the running water, the twitter of birds, and the distant lowing of some ox, they thoroughly appreciated everything, even the rest after their tiring night's work and toilsome day.

"Are we going on now!" said Dexter at last.

"What for?" asked Bob, as he lay upon his back, with his head in a tuft of heath.

"I don't know."

"What's the good of going on? What's the good o' being in a hurry?"

"I'm not in a hurry, only I should like to get to an island where there's plenty of fruit."

"Ah, we shan't get to one to-day!" said Bob, yawning. Then there was silence; and Dexter lay back watching the beautiful river, and the brown boat as it swung easily by its chain.

Soon a butterfly flitted by—a beautiful orange brown butterfly covered with dark spots, dancing here and there over the sylvan nook, and the next minute Dexter as he lay on his back felt cool, and began wondering while he looked straight up at the stars, fancying he had been called.

He felt as if he had never seen so many stars before glittering in the dark purple sky, and he began wondering how it was that one minute he had been looking at that spotted butterfly, and the next at the stars.

And then it dawned upon him that he must have been fast asleep for many hours, and if he had felt any doubt about this being the right solution of his position a low gurgling snore on his left told that Bob Dimsted was sleeping still.

It was a novel and curious sensation that of waking up in the silence and darkness, with the leaves whispering, and that impression still upon him that he had been called.

"It must have been old Dan'l," he had thought at first. "Perhaps he was in search of them," and he listened intently. Or it might have been the men who had come upon them where they had the first fire, and they had seen this one.

"No, they couldn't see this one, for it was out."

Dexter was about to conclude that it was all imagination, when, from far away in the wood he heard, in the most startling way:—*Hoi hoi—hoo hoo*!

He started to his feet, and was about to waken Bob, when a great ghostly-looking bird came sweeping along the river, turned in at the nook quite low down, and then seemed to describe a curve, passing just over his head, and uttered a wild and piercing shriek that was appalling.

Dexter's blood ran cold, as the cry seemed to thrill all down his spine, and in his horror he made a rush to run away anywhere from the terrible thing which had startled him.

But his ill luck made him once more startle Bob from his slumbers, for, as he ran blindly to reach the shelter of the wood, he fell right over the sleeping boy, and went down headlong.

"Here! I—oh, please sir, don't sir—don't sir,—it was that other boy, sir, it wasn't me, sir. It was—was—it was—why, what games are you up to now!"

"Hush! Bob. Quick! Let's run."

"Run!" said Bob excitedly, as the frightened boy clung to him. "I thought they'd come."

"Yes, they're calling to one another in the wood," whispered Dexter excitedly; "and there was a horrid something flew up, and shrieked out."

"Why, I heerd it, and dreamed it was you."

"Come away—come away!" cried Dexter. "There, hark!"

Hoi hoi—hoi hoi! came from not far away.

"Ha, ha, ha!" laughed Bob. "You are a one!" and putting his hands to his mouth, to Dexter's great astonishment he produced a very good imitation of the cry.

"Why, you'll have them hear us and come," he whispered.

"Yah! you are a coward! Why, it's an old howl."

"Owl! calling like that!"

"Yes, to be sure. I've heerd 'em lots o' times when I've been late fishing up the river."

"But there was a big thing flew over my head, and it shrieked out."

"That was a howl too. Some of 'em shouts, and some of 'em screeches. I say, I hope you've kept a heye on the boat!"

"Are you sure that other was an owl too!" said Dexter excitedly.

"Course I am. Think I've been out in the woods with father after the fezzans, and stopping out all night, without knowing a howl?"

Dexter felt quite warm now.

"I never heard one before, and it frightened me."

"Yes, you're easily frightened," said Bob contemptuously. "You haven't been to sleep, have you!"

"Yes, I have."

"Then you oughtn't to have been. If you've been to sleep and let that boat go, I'll never forgive you."

Bob had hardly uttered the words when Dexter, who had forgotten all about the boat, ran to the water's edge feeling sure that it was gone.

But it was quite safe, and he went back to Bob.

"What shall we do now!" he said.

"Do?" said Bob, yawning. "You sit and keep watch while I go to sleep for a quarter of an hour. Then you may call me, and I'll take my turn."

Bob curled himself up after the fashion of a dog, and went off to sleep directly, while, as Dexter, who felt chilly, began to walk up and down between the water's edge and the steep cliff-like bank, he could not help once more wishing that he was in his comfortable bed at the doctor's.

He waited for long over a quarter of an hour, keeping his lonely watch, but Bob slept on and snored.

At the end of about an hour and a half he thought it would only be fair to call his companion to take his turn, but he called in vain.

Then he tried shaking, but only to elicit growls, and when he persevered Bob hit out so savagely that Dexter was fain to desist.

"I'll let him sleep half an hour longer," he said to himself; and he walked to and fro to keep himself warm.

It must have been after an hour that he called Bob again.

"All right," said that worthy.

"But it isn't all right," cried Dexter. "It ain't fair. Come: get up."

"All right! I'll get up directly. Call me in about ten minutes."

Dexter waited a little while, and called his companion. But in vain.

And so it went on, with the sleeper sometimes apologetic, sometimes imploring, till it was broad daylight; and then Bob rose and shook himself.

"I say, 'tain't fair," said Dexter ill-humouredly.

"Well, why didn't you make me get up!"

"I did try, lots of times."

"But you didn't half try. You should have got me quite awake."

"It's too bad, and I'm as sleepy as can be," grumbled Dexter.

"Here! whatcher going to do?" cried Bob.

"Lie down and sleep till breakfast-time."

"Oh, are yer?" cried Bob. "We've got to go and catch our breakfasts."

"What, now?"

"To be sure. I'm getting hungry. Come along. I'll find a good place, and it's your turn now to get some cray-fish."

"But I'm so cold and sleepy."

"Well, that'll warm yer. There, don't look sulky."

Bob got into the boat and unfastened the chain, so that there was nothing left for Dexter to do but follow; and they rowed away down the river, which was widening fast.

The exercise and the rising sun sent warmth and brighter thoughts into Dexter, so that he was better able to undertake the task of searching the holes for cray-fish when the boat was brought up under a suitable bank, and urged on by Bob he had to undress and take an unwilling bath, and a breakfast-hunt at the same time.

He was clumsy, and unaccustomed to the task, but driven by Bob's bullying tones, and helped by the fact that the little crustaceans were pretty plentiful, he managed to get a dozen and a half in about an hour.

"There, come out, and dress now," said Bob ill-humouredly. "It's more trouble to tell you than to have got 'em myself. I'd ha' found twice as many in the time."

Dexter shivered, and then began to enjoy the warmth of his garments after as good a wipe as he could manage with a pocket-handkerchief. But it was the row afterwards that gave the required warmth—a row which was continued till another farm-house was seen beside a great cider orchard.

Here Dexter had to land with sixpence and the empty bottle.

"I promised to take that there bottle back," said Bob, with a grin, "but I shan't now. Lookye here. You make 'em give you a good lot of bread and butter for the sixpence, and if they asks you any questions, you say we're two gentlemen out for a holiday."

Dexter landed, and went up to the farm-house, through whose open door he could see a warm fire, and inhale a most appetising odour of cooking bacon and hot coffee.

A pleasant-faced woman came to the door, and her ways and looks were the first cheery incidents of Dexter's trip.

"Sixpennyworth of bread and butter, and some milk?" she said. "Yes, of course."

She prepared a liberal exchange for Dexter's coin, and then after filling the bottle put the boy's chivalry to the test.

"Why, you look as if you wanted your breakfast," she said. "Have a cup of warm coffee?"

Dexter's eyes brightened, and he was about to say *yes*. But he said *no*, for it seemed unfair to live better than his comrade, and just then the vision of Bob Dimsted looking very jealous and ill-humoured rose before him.

"I'm in a hurry to get back," he said.

The woman nodded, and Dexter hastened back to the water-side.

"I was just a-going without yer," was his greeting. "What a while you've been!"

"I was as quick as I could be," said Dexter apologetically.

"No, you weren't, and don't give me none of your sarce," said Bob. "Kitch holt o' that scull and pull. D'yer hear!"

Dexter obeyed, and they rowed on for about a mile before a suitable place was found for landing and lighting a fire, when, after a good deal of ogreish grumbling, consequent upon Bob wanting his breakfast, a similar meal to that of the previous day was eaten, and they started once more on their journey down-stream to the sea, and the golden land which would recompense Dexter, as he told himself, for all this discomfort, the rough brutality of his companion, and the prickings of conscience which he felt whenever Coleby occurred to his mind, and the face of Helen looked reproach into the very depth of his inner consciousness.

All that morning, when they again started, he found the river widen and change. Instead of being clear, and the stones visible at the bottom, the banks were further away, so were the hills, and the water was muddy. What was more strange to Dexter was that instead of the stream carrying them along it came to meet them.

At last Bob decided that they would moor by the bank, and begin once more to fish.

They landed and got some worms, and for a time had very fair sport, taking it in turns to catch some small rounded silvery and creamy transparent fish, something like dace, but what they were even Bob did not know. He was never at a loss, however, and he christened them sea-gudgeon.

Dexter was just landing one when a sour-looking man in a shabby old paintless boat came by close to the shore, and looked at them searchingly. But he looked harder at the boat as he went by, turned in, as it seemed, and rowed right into the land.

"There must be a little river there," Bob said. "We'll look presently. I say, didn't he stare!"

Almost as he spoke the man came out again into the tidal river and rowed away, went up some distance, and they had almost forgotten him when they saw him come slowly along, close inshore.

"Bob," whispered Dexter, "he's after us."

To which Bob responded with a contemptuous—

"Yah!"

"Much sport?" said the man, passing abreast of their boat about half a dozen yards away, and keeping that by dipping his oars from time to time.

"Pretty fair," said Bob, taking the rod. "'Bout a dozen."

"What fish are they!" said Dexter eagerly, and he held up one.

"Smelts," said the man, with a peculiar look. "Come fishing?"

"Yes," said Bob sharply. "We've come for a day or two's fishing."

"That's right," said the man, with a smile that was a little less pleasant than his scowl. "I'm a fisherman too."

"Oh, are yer?" said Bob.

"Yes, that's what I am."

"He ain't after us," whispered Bob. "It's all right."

Dexter did not feel as if it was. He had an innate dislike to the man, who looked furtive and underhanded.

"Got a tidy boat there," said the man at last.

"Yes, she's a good un to go along," said Bob.

"Wouldn't sell her, I s'pose!" said the man.

"What should we sell her for?" said Bob, hooking and landing a fish coolly enough.

"I d'know. Thought you might want to part with her," said the man. "I wouldn't mind giving fifteen shillings for a boat like that."

"Yah!" cried Bob mockingly. "Why, she's worth thirty at least."

"Bob!" whispered Dexter excitedly. "You mustn't sell her."

"You hold your tongue."

"I wouldn't give thirty shillings for her," said the man, coming close now and mooring his own crazy craft by holding on to the gunwale of the gig. "She's too old."

"That she ain't," cried Bob. "Why, she's nearly new."

"Not she. Only been varnished up, that's all. I'll give you a pound for her."

"No," said Bob, to Dexter's great relief.

"I'll give you a pound for her, and my old 'un chucked in," said the man. "It's more than she's worth, but I know a man who wants such a boat as that."

"You mustn't sell her, Bob," whispered Dexter, who was now in agony.

"You hold your row. I know what I'm a-doing of."

"Look here," said the man, "I'm going a little farder, and I'll fetch the money, and then if you like to take it we'll trade. It's more'n she's worth, though, and you'd get my little boat in, as is as good a boat as ever swum."

He pushed off and rowed away, while, as soon as he was out of sight, Dexter attacked his companion with vigour.

"We mustn't sell her, Bob," he said.

"Why not? She's our'n now."

"No, she isn't; and we've promised to take her back."

"Look here!" said Bob, "have you got any money?"

"No, but we shan't want any as soon as we get to the island."

"Yes, we shall, and a pound would be no end of good."

"But we would have to give up our voyage."

"No, we shouldn't. We'd make his boat do."

"But it's such a shabby one. We mustn't sell the boat, Bob."

"Look here! I'm captain, and I shall do as I like."

"Then I shall tell the man the boat isn't ours."

"If you do I'll knock your eye out. See if I don't," cried Bob fiercely.

Dexter felt hot, and his fists clenched involuntarily, but he sat very still.

"If I like to sell the boat I shall. We want the money, and the other boat will do."

"I say it won't," said Dexter sharply.

"Why, hullo!" cried Bob, laughing. "Here's cheek."

"I don't care, it would be stealing Sir James's boat, and I say it shan't be done."

"Oh, yer do—do yer!" said Bob, in a bullying tone.

"You won't be happy till I've given you such a licking as'll make yer teeth ache. Now, just you hold your row, and wait till I gets yer ashore, and you shall have it. I'd give it to yer now, only I should knock yer overboard and drown'd yer, and I don't want to do that the first time."

Bob went on fishing, and Dexter sat biting his lip, and feeling as he used to feel when he had had a caning for something he had not done.

"I shall do just as I please," said Bob, giving his head a waggle, as if to show his authority. "So you've got to sit still and look on. And if you says anything about where the boat came from, I shall tell the man you took it."

"And, if you do, I shall tell him it's a lie," cried Dexter, as fiercely as his companion; and just then he saw the man coming back.

Chapter Thirty Five
Bob asks a Question

"Caught any more?" said the man.

"Only one," replied Bob.

"Ah! I could show you a place where you could pull 'em up like anything. I say, though, the boat ain't worth a pound."

"Oh yes, she is," said Bob.

"Not a pound and the boat too."

"Yes, she is," said Bob, watching Dexter the while out of the corner of one eye.

"I wouldn't give a pound for her, only there's a man I know wants just such a boat."

Dexter sat up, looking very determined, and ready to speak when he thought that the proper time had come, and Bob kept on watching him.

"THERE, I'LL GIVE YOU THE TWENTY SHILLINGS FOR THE BOAT."

"Look here!" said the man, "as you two's come out fishing, I'll give you fifteen shillings and my boat, and that's more than yours is worth."

"No, you won't," said Bob.

"Well, sixteen, then. Come, that's a shilling too much."

Bob shook his head, hooked, and took a good-sized smelt off his hook.

"It's more than I care to give," said the man, who grew warm as Bob seemed cold. "There, I'll go another shilling—seventeen."

Bob still shook his head, and Dexter sat ready to burst out into an explosion of anger and threat if his companion sold the boat.

"Nineteen, then," said the man. "Nineteen, and my old un as rides the water like a duck. You won't?"

"No," said Bob.

"Well, then," cried the man, "I'm off."

"All right," said Bob coolly.

"There, I'll give you the twenty shillings, but you'll have to give me sixpence back. Look here! I've got the money."

He showed and rattled the pound's worth of silver he had.

"Come on. You get into my boat, and I'll get into yours."

"No, yer won't," said Bob. "I won't sell it."

"What!" cried the man angrily, and he raised one of his oars from the water.

"I won't sell," cried Bob, seizing the oars as he dropped his rod into the boat.

"You mean to tell me that you're going to make a fool of me like that!"

He began to pull the little tub in which he sat toward the gig, but Bob was too quick for him. The gig glided through the water at double the rate possible to the old craft, and though it was boy against man, the former could easily hold his own.

Fortunately they were not moored to the bank or the event might have been different, for the man had raised his oar as if with the intention of striking the boat in which the boys were seated.

"Here, you, stop!" he shouted.

Bob replied in dumb show with his sculls, dipping them as fast as he could, and looking very pale the while, till they were well out of reach, when he rested for a moment, and yelled back in defiant tones the one word—

"Yah!"

"All right, my lads," shouted the fellow. "I know yer. You stole that boat, that's what you've done!"

"Row hard, Bob!" whispered Dexter.

"It's all very fine to say row hard. You kitch hold and help."

Dexter readily seized the second scull, and began to pull with so much energy and effect that they had soon passed the muddy creek up which the man had gone and come, and before long he was out of sight.

"It was all your fun, Bob," said Dexter, as they went on. "I thought you meant to sell the boat."

"So I did," grumbled Bob; "only you were so disagreeable about it. How are we to get on for money when mine's all done!"

"I don't know," said Dexter dolefully. "Can't we work for some?"

"Yah! How can we work? I say, though, he knew you'd stolen the boat."

"I didn't steal it, and it isn't stolen," said Dexter indignantly. "I wrote and told Sir James that we had only borrowed it, and I sent some money, and I shall send some more if we cannot find a way to get it back."

"See if they don't call it stealing," said Bob grimly. "Look there at the her'ns."

He nodded toward where a couple of the tall birds were standing heel-deep in the shallow water, intent upon their fishing, and so well accustomed to being preserved that they did not attempt to rise from their places.

Dexter was so much interested in the birds that he forgot all about their late adventure.

Then they rowed on for about a couple of hours, and their next proceeding was to look out for a suitable spot for their meal.

There were no high cliff-like banks now, but here and there, alternating with meadows, patches of woodland came down to the water's edge, and at one of these they stopped, fastened the boat to a tree where it was quite out of sight; and now for the first time they began to see boats passing along.

So far the little tub in which the would-be purchaser of their gig was seated was the only one they had seen on the water, but they were approaching a village now, and in low places they had seen high posts a short distance from the water's edge, on which were festooned long nets such as were used for the salmon at the time they run.

As soon as they had landed, a fire was lit, the fish cleaned, and the remainder of the bread and butter left from the last meal brought ashore. After which, as an experiment, it was decided to roast the smelts before the blaze, a task they achieved with more or less success.

As each fish was deemed sufficiently cooked it was eaten at once—a piece of bread forming the plate—and, with the exception of wanting salt, declared to be delicious.

"Ever so much better than chub, Bob," said Dexter, to which for a wonder that young gentleman agreed.

Evening soon came on, and as it was considered doubtful whether they could find as satisfactory a place for their night's rest as that where they were, it was decided to stop, and go on at sunrise next morning.

"We shall get to the sea to-morrow," said Bob, as he began to yawn. "I'm jolly glad of it, for I'm tired of the river, and I want to catch cod-fish and soles, and something big. Whatcher yawning for?"

"I'm tired and sleepy," said Dexter, as he sat upon the roots of an old tree, three or four yards from the water's edge.

"Yah! you're always sleepy," said Bob.

"But I had to keep watch while you slept."

"So you will have to again."

"But that isn't fair," said Dexter, in ill-used tones. "It's your turn to watch now."

"Well, I'll watch half the night, if you watch the other," said Bob. "That's fair, isn't it?"

"Yes."

"Then I shall lie down now, and you can call me when it's twelve o'clock."

"But I shan't know when it is," protested Dexter.

"Well, I ain't particular," said Bob, stretching himself beneath the tree. "Guess what you think's fair half, and I'll get up then."

"But will you get up!" said Dexter.

"Of course I will, if you call loud enough. There, don't bother, I'm ever so tired with rowing, and I shall go to sleep at once."

Bob kept his word as soon as darkness had set in, and Dexter sat listening to the lapping of the water, and wondered whether, if they camped out like this in a foreign land, crocodiles would come out of the rivers and attack them.

He sat down, for he soon grew tired of standing and walking about, and listened to Bob's heavy breathing, for the boy had gone off at once.

It was very dark under the trees, and he could only see the glint of a star from time to time. It felt cold too, but as he drew himself close together with his chin down upon his knees he soon forgot that, and began thinking about the two owls he had heard the past night. Then he thought about the long-legged herons he had seen fishing in the water; then about their own fishing, and what capital fish the smelts were.

From that he began to think about hunting out the cray-fish from the banks, and how one of the little things had nipped his fingers quite sharply.

Next he began to wonder what Helen Grayson thought about him, and what the doctor had said, and whether he should ever see them again, and whether he should like Bob any better after a time, when camping out with him, and how long it would be before they reached one of the beautiful hot countries, where you could gather cocoa-nuts off the trees and watch the lovely birds as they flitted round.

And then he thought about how long it would be before he might venture to call Bob.

And then he began thinking about nothing at all.

When he opened his eyes next it was morning, with the sun shining brightly, and the birds singing, and Bob Dimsted had just kicked him in the side.

"Here, I say, wake up," he cried. "Why, you've been to sleep."

"Have I!" said Dexter sheepishly, as he stared helplessly at his companion.

"Have yer? Yes; of course yer have," cried Bob angrily. "Ain't to be trusted for a moment. You're always a-going to sleep. Whatcher been and done with that there boat!"

Chapter Thirty Six
In Dire Straits

"Done with the boat?"

"I haven't done anything with the boat."

"Then where is it?"

"Fastened up to that old tree."

"Oh, is it!" cried Bob derisively. "I should like to see it, then. Come and show me!"

Dexter ran to the water's edge, and found the place on the bark where the chain had rubbed the trunk, but there was no sign of the boat.

"Now then," cried Bob fiercely, "where is it?"

"I don't know," said Dexter dolefully. "Yes, I do," he cried. "The chain must have come undone, and it's floating away."

"Oh, is it?" said Bob derisively. "Then you'd better go and find it!"

"Go and find it?"

"Yes; we can't go to sea in our boots, can we, stoopid?"

"But which way shall I go, Bob? Sometimes the tide runs up, and sometimes it runs down."

"Yes, and I'll make you run up and down. You're a nice un, you are! I just shet my eyes for a few minutes, and trust you to look after the boat, and when I wake up again you're fass asleep, and the boat gone."

"I'm very sorry, Bob, but I was so tired."

"Tired! You tired! What on? Here, go and find that boat!"

Dexter started off, and ran along the bank in one direction, while Bob went in the other, and at the end of half an hour Dexter came back feeling miserable and despondent as he had never felt before.

"Found it, Bob!" he said.

For answer his companion threw himself down upon his face, and began beating the ground with his fists, as if it were a drum.

"I've looked along there as far as I could go," said Dexter sadly. "What shall we do!"

"I wish this here was your stoopid head," snarled Bob, as he hammered away at the bare ground beneath the tree. "I never see such a chap!"

"But what shall we do?" said Dexter again.

"Do? I dunno, and I don't care. You lost the boat, and you've got to find it."

"Let's go on together and walk all along the bank till we find somebody who has seen it."

"And when we do find 'em d'yer think they'll be such softs as to give it to us back again!" This was a startling question.

"I know 'em," said Bob. "They'll want to know where we got it from, and how we come by it, and all sorts o' nonsense o' that kind. Say we ain't no right to it. I know what they'll say."

"But p'r'aps it's floating about?"

"P'r'aps you're floating about!" cried Bob, with a snarl. "Boat like that don't go floating about without some one in it, and if it does some one gets hold of it, and says it's his."

This was a terrible check to their adventurous voyage, as unexpected as it was sudden, and Dexter looked dolefully up in his companion's face.

"I know'd how it would be, and I was a stoopid to bring such a chap as you," continued Bob, who seemed happiest when he was scolding. "You've lost the boat, and we shall have to go back."

"Go back!" cried Dexter, with a look of horror, as he saw in imagination the stern countenance of the doctor, his tutor's searching eyes, Helen's look of reproach, and Sir James Danby waiting to ask him what had become of the boat, while Master Edgar seemed full of triumph at his downfall.

"Go back?" No he could not go back. He felt as if he would rather jump into the river.

"We shall both get a good leathering, and that won't hurt so very much."

A good leathering! If it had been only the thrashing, Dexter felt that he would have suffered that; but his stay at the doctor's had brought forth other feelings that had been lying dormant, and now the thrashing seemed to him the slightest part of the punishment that he would have to face. No: he could not go back.

"Well, whatcher going to do!" said Bob at last, with provoking coolness. "You lost the boat, and you've got to find it."

"I will try, Bob," said Dexter humbly. "But come and help me."

"Help yer? Why should I come and help yer? You lost it, I tell yer."

Bob jumped up and doubled his fists.

"Now then," he said; "get on, d'yer hear? get on—get on!"

At every word he struck out at Dexter, giving him heavy blows on the arms—in the chest—anywhere he could reach.

Dexter's face became like flame, but he contented himself with trying to avoid the blows.

"Look here!" he cried suddenly.

"No, it's you've got to look here," cried Bob. "You've got to find that there boat."

Dexter had had what he thought was a bright idea, but it was only a spark, and it died out, leaving his spirit dark once more, and he seemed now to be face to face with the greatest trouble of his life. All his cares at the Union, and then at the doctor's, sank into insignificance before this terrible check to their adventure. For without the boat how could they get out of England? They could not borrow another. There was a great blank before him just at this outset of his career, and try how he would to see something beyond he could find nothing: all was blank, hopeless, and full of despair.

Had his comrade been true to him, and taken his share of the troubles, it would have been bad enough; but it was gradually dawning upon Dexter that the boy he had half-idolised for his cleverness and general knowledge was a contemptible, ill-humoured bully—a despicable young tyrant, ready to seize every opportunity to oppress.

"Are you a-going?" cried Bob, growing more brutal as he found that his victim made no resistance, and giving him a blow on the jaw which sent him staggering against one of the trees.

This was too much; and recovering himself Dexter was about to dash at his assailant when he stopped short, for an idea that seemed incontrovertible struck him so sharply that it drove away all thought of the brutal blow he had received.

"I know, Bob," he cried.

"Know? What d'yer know?"

"Where the boat is."

"Yer do?"

"Yes: that man followed us and took it away."

Bob opened his mouth, and half-closed his eyes to stare at his companion, as he balanced this idea in his rather muddy brain.

"Don't you see?" cried Dexter excitedly.

"Come arter us and stole it!" said Bob slowly.

"Yes: he must have watched us, and waited till we were asleep."

"Go on with you!"

"He did. I feel as sure as sure," cried Dexter.

There was a pause during which Bob went on balancing the matter in his mind.

"He has taken it up the river, and he thinks we shall be afraid to go after it."

"Then he just thinks wrong," said Bob, nodding his head a good deal. "I thought something o' that kind a bit ago, but you made me so wild I forgot it again."

"But you see now, Bob."

"See? O' course I do. I'll just let him know—a thief. Here, come on, and we'll drop on to him with a policeman, and show him what stealing boats means."

"No, no, Bob, we can't go with a policeman. Let's go ourselves, and make him give it up."

"But s'pose he won't give it to us!"

"We should have to take it," said Dexter excitedly.

"Come on, then. He's got my fishing-tackle too, and—why just look at that! Did you put them there?"

He darted to where his bundle and rough fishing-rod lay among the trees.

"No; he must have thrown them out. Let's make haste. We know where the boat is now!"

The boys started at once, and began to tramp back along the side of the river in the hope of finding the place where the boat was moored; but before they had gone far it was to find that floating down with the stream, or even rowing against the tide, was much easier work than forcing their way through patches of alder-bushes, swampy meadows, leaping, and sometimes wading, little inlets and ditches and the like.

Their progress was very slow, the sun very hot, and at least a dozen times now they came upon spots which struck both as being the muddy bank off which they had captured the smelts.

It was quite afternoon before they were convinced, for their further passage was stopped by the muddy inlet up which they had seen the man row, and not a hundred yards away was the bank under which they had fished.

"Sure this is the place?" said Bob, as he crouched among some osiers and looked cautiously round.

"Yes," said Dexter; "I'm certain this is the place. I saw him row up here. But—"

"But what?"

"He'd be quite sure not to take the boat up here."

"Why not?"

"For fear we should come after it."

"Get out! Where would he take it, then?"

"He'd hide it somewhere else; perhaps on the other side. Look!"

Dexter pointed up the river to where, about a couple of hundred yards further on, a boat could be seen just issuing from a bed of reeds.

Bob seized Dexter's arm to force him lower down among the osiers, but it was not necessary, for they were both well concealed; and as they continued there watching it was to see the boat come slowly toward them, and in a few minutes they were satisfied that it was the man they sought, propelling it slowly toward where they stooped.

The fellow came along in a furtive manner, looking sharply round from time to time, as if scanning the river to see if he was observed.

He came on and on till he reached the creek at whose mouth the boys were hidden, and as he came so close that they felt it impossible that they could remain unseen he suddenly ceased rowing, and stood up to shade his eyes from the sunshine, and gaze sharply down the river for some minutes.

Then giving a grunt as of satisfaction he reseated himself, and rowed slowly up the creek, till he disappeared among the osiers and reeds which fringed its muddy banks.

As he passed up he disturbed a shoal of large fish which came surging down, making quite a wave in the creek, till they reached the river, where all was still.

"The boat's up there, Bob," said Dexter, after a long silence, so as to give the man time to get well out of hearing.

"Yes, but how are we to get to it?"

"Wade," said Dexter laconically. "'Tain't deep, only muddy."

To cross the creek was necessary, and Bob softly let himself down from the bank till his feet were level with the water, then taking hold of a stout osier above his head he bent it down, and then dropped slowly into the water, which came nearly to his waist.

"Come on!" he said, and after getting to the end of the osier he used his rod as a guide to try the depth, and with some difficulty, and the water very nearly to his chest, he got over.

Dexter did not hesitate, but followed, and began to wade, feeling his feet sink at every step into the sticky mud, and very glad to seize hold of the end of the rod Bob was civil enough to hold to him from the further bank, up which they both crept, dripping like water-rats, and hid among the osiers on the other side.

"Come on," whispered Bob, and with the mud and water trickling from them they crept along through quite a thicket of reeds, osiers, and the red-flowered willow-herb, while great purple patches of loosestrife blossomed above their heads.

Every step took them further from the enemy, but they kept down in their stooping position, and a few yards from the bank of the river, feeling sure that they could not miss their way; and so it proved, for after what seemed to be an interminable journey they found themselves stopped by just such another creek as that which they had left, save and except that the mouth was completely hidden by a bed of reeds some of which showed where a boat had lately passed through.

Whether their boat was there or not they could not tell, but it seemed easy to follow up the creek from the side they were on, and they crept along through the water-growth, which was thicker here than ever, but keeping as close as they could to the side, the scarped bank being about eight feet above the water.

The creek was not above twenty feet wide, and, from the undisturbed state of the vegetation which flourished down its banks to where the tide seemed to rise, it seemed as if it was a rare thing for a boat to pass along.

They stopped at every few yards to make sure that they were not passing that of which they were in search, looking carefully up and down, while the creek twined so much that they could never see any extent of water at a time.

They must have wound in and out for quite three hundred yards, when, all at once, as they stooped there, panting and heated with the exercise, and with the hot sun beating down upon their heads, Dexter, who was in front, stopped short, for on his right the dense growth of reeds suddenly ceased, and on peering out it was to see a broad opening where they had been cut down, while within thirty yards stood a large stack of bundles, and beside it a rough-looking hut, toward which the man they had seen rowing up the other creek was walking.

They had come right upon his home, which seemed to be upon a reedy island formed by the two creeks and the river.

The boys crouched down, afraid to stir, and watching till they saw the man enter the rough reed-thatched hut, when, moving close to the edge of the bank, they crept on again after a few moments' hesitation, connected with an idea of making a retreat.

Their perseverance was rewarded, for not fifty yards further on they looked down upon what seemed to be a quantity of reeds floating at the side of the creek, but one bundle had slipped off, and there, plainly enough, was the gunwale of the boat, the reeds having been laid across it to act as a concealment in case any one should glance carelessly up the creek.

"Come on, Bob," whispered Dexter; and he let himself slide down into the muddy water as silently as he could, and began to tumble the bundles of reeds off into the creek.

Bob followed his example, and, to their great delight, they found that the sculls and boat-hook were still in their places, while the boat-chain was secured to a stake thrust down into the mud.

This was soon unloosed after they had climbed in, dripping, and covering the cushions with mud, but all that was forgotten in the delight of having found the boat.

"Now, Bob, you row softly down and I'll use the boat-hook," whispered Dexter, as he stood up in the stern, while Bob sat down, seized the oars, and laid them in the rowlocks, ready to make the first stroke, when high above them on the bank they heard a quick, rushing noise, and directly after, to their horror, there stood, apparently too much dumbfounded to speak, the man they had seen a few minutes before going into the reed hut.

Chapter Thirty Seven
Second-Hand Stealing

"Here, you, sir! stop!" he roared.

"Pull away, Bob!" whispered Dexter, for Bob had paused, half-paralysed by the nearness of the danger. But he obeyed the second command, and tugged at the oars.

"D'yer hear!" roared the man, with a furious string of oaths. "Hold hard or I'll—"

He did not say what, but made a gesture as if striking with a great force.

"Don't speak, Bob: pull hard," whispered Dexter, bending forward in the boat so as to reach the rower, and encourage him to make fresh efforts, while, for his part, he kept his eyes upon the man.

"D'yer hear what I say?" he roared again. "What d'yer mean by coming here to steal my boat?"

"'Tain't yours," cried Dexter.

"What? Didn't I buy it of yer and pay for it?"

"You came and stole it while we were asleep, you thief!" cried Dexter again.

"Say I stole yer boat and I'll drown'd yer," cried the man, forcing his way through the reeds and osiers so as to keep up with them. "If you don't take that back it'll be the worse for yer. Stop! D'yer hear? Stop!"

Bob stopped again, for the man's aspect was alarming, and every moment he seemed as if he was about to leap from the high bank.

Fortunately for all parties he did not do this, as if he had reached the edge of the boat he must have capsized it, and if he had leaped into the bottom, he must have gone right through.

Bob did not realise all this; but he felt certain that the man would jump, and, with great drops of fear upon his forehead he kept on stopping as the man threatened, and, but for Dexter's urging, the boat would have been given up.

"I can hear yer," the man roared, with a fierce oath. "I hear yer telling him to row. Just wait till I get hold of you, my gentleman!"

"Row, Bob, row!" panted Dexter, "as soon as we're out in the river we shall be safe."

"But he'll be down upon us d'reckly," whispered Bob.

"Go on rowing, I tell you, he daren't jump."

"You won't stop, then, won't yer?" cried the man. "If yer don't stop I'll drive a hole through the bottom, and sink yer both."

"No, he won't," whispered Dexter. "Row, Bob, row! He can't reach us, and he has nothing to throw."

Bob groaned, but he went on rowing; and in his dread took the boat so near the further side that he kept striking one scull against the muddy bank, and then, in his efforts to get room to catch water, he thrust the head of the boat toward the bank where the man was stamping with fury, and raging at them to go back.

This went on for a hundred yards, and they were still far from the open river, when the man gave a shout at them and ran on, disappearing among the low growth on the bank.

"Now, Bob, he has gone," said Dexter excitedly, "pull steadily, and as hard as you can. Mind and don't run her head into the bank, or we shall be caught."

Bob looked up at him with a face full of abject fear and misery, but he was in that frame of weak-mindedness which made him ready to obey any one who spoke, and he rowed on pretty quickly.

Twice over he nearly went into the opposite bank, with the risk of getting the prow stuck fast in the clayey mud, but a drag at the left scull saved it, and they were getting rapidly on now, when all at once Dexter caught sight of their enemy at a part of the creek where it narrowed and the bank overhung a little.

The man had run on to that spot, and had lain down on his chest, so as to be as far over as he could be to preserve his balance, and he was reaching out with his hands, and a malicious look of satisfaction was in his face, as the boat was close upon him before Dexter caught sight of him, Bob of course having his back in the direction they were going.

"Look out, Bob," shouted Dexter. "Pull your right! pull your right!"

Bob was so startled that he looked up over his shoulder, saw the enemy, and tugged at the wrong oar so hard that he sent the boat right toward the overhanging bank.

"I've got yer now, have I, then?" roared the man fiercely; and as the boat drifted towards him he reached down and made a snatch with his hand at Dexter's collar.

As a matter of course the boy ducked down, and the man overbalanced himself.

For a moment it seemed as if he would come down into the boat, over which he hung, slanting down and clinging with both hands now, and glaring at them with his mouth open and his eyes starting, looking for all the world like some huge gargoyle on the top of a cathedral tower.

"Stop!" he roared; and then he literally turned over and came so nearly into the boat that he touched the stern as it passed, and the water he raised in a tremendous splash flew all over the boys.

"Now, Bob, pull, pull, pull!" cried Dexter, stamping his foot as he looked back and saw the man rise out of the water to come splashing after them for a few paces; but wading through mud and water was not the way to overtake a retreating boat, and to Dexter's horror he saw the fellow struggle to the side and begin to scramble up the bank.

Once he slipped back; but he began to clamber up again, and his head was above the edge when, in obedience to Bob's tugging at the sculls, the boat glided round one of the various curves of the little creek and shut him from their view.

"He'll drown'd us. He said he would," whimpered Bob. "Let's leave the boat and run."

"No, no!" cried Dexter; "pull hard, and we shall get out into the river, and he can't follow us."

"Yes, he can," cried Bob, blubbering now aloud. "He means it, and he'll half-kill us. Let's get out to this side and run."

"Pull! I tell you, pull!" cried Dexter furiously; and Bob pulled obediently, sending the boat along fast round the curves and bends, but not so fast but that they heard a furious rustling of the osiers and reeds, and saw the figure of the man above them on the bank.

"There, I told you so," whimpered Bob. "Let's get out t'other side."

"Row, I tell you!" roared Dexter; and to his surprise the man did not stop, but hurried on toward the mouth of the creek.

"There!" cried Bob. "He's gone for his boat, and he'll stop us, and he'll drown'd us both."

"He daren't," said Dexter stoutly, though he felt a peculiar sinking all the time.

"But he will, he will. It's no use to row."

Dexter felt desperate now, for theirs was an awkward position; and to his horror he saw that Bob was ceasing to row, and looking up at the bank on his left.

"You go on rowing," cried Dexter fiercely.

"I shan't," whimpered Bob; "it's of no use. I shan't row no more."

Thud!

Bob yelled out, more in fear than in pain, for the sound was caused by Dexter swinging the boat-hook round and striking his companion a sharp rap on the side of the head.

"Go on rowing," cried Dexter, "and keep in the middle."

Bob howled softly; but, like a horse that has just received an admonition from the whip, he bent to his task, and rowed with all his might, blubbering the while.

"That's right," cried Dexter, who felt astonished at his hardihood. "We can't be far now. Pull—pull hard. There, I can see the river. Hurray, Bob, we're nearly there!"

Bob sobbed and snuffled, and bent down over his oars, rowing as if for life or death. The boat was speeding swiftly through the muddy water, the opening with its deep fringe of reeds was there, and Dexter was making up his mind to try and direct Bob to pull right or left so as to get to the thinnest place that the boat might glide right out, when he saw something.

"No, Bob, only a little way," he had said. "Pull with all your might."

Then he stopped short and stared aghast.

Fortunately Bob was bending down, sobbing, and straining every nerve, as if he expected another blow, otherwise he would have been chilled by Dexter's look of dread, for there, just as if he had dropped from the bank and begun wading, was their enemy, who, as the boat neared, took up his position right in the middle of the creek, where the water was nearly to his chest, and, with the reeds at his back, waited to seize the boat.

Dexter stood holding the boat-hook, half-paralysed for a few moments, and then, moved by despair, he stepped over the thwart toward Bob.

"No, no," cried the latter, ducking down his head. "I will pull—I will pull."

He did pull too, with all his might, and the boat was going swiftly through the water as Dexter stepped right over the left-hand scull, nearly toppled over, but recovered himself, and stood in the bows of the boat, as they were now within twenty yards of the man, who, wet and muddy, stood up out of the creek like some water monster about to seize the occupants of the boat for a meal.

"Pull, Bob, hard!" whispered Dexter, in a low, excited voice; and Bob pulled.

The boat sped on, and the man uttered a savage yell, when, with a cry of horror, Bob ceased rowing.

But the boat had plenty of impetus, and it shot forward so swiftly that, to avoid its impact, the man drew a little on one side as he caught at the gunwale.

Whop!

Dexter struck at him with the light ash pole he held in his hand—struck at their enemy with all his might, and then turned and sat down in the boat, overcome with horror at what he had done, for he saw the man fall backward, and the water close over his head.

Then there was a loud hissing, rustling sound as the boat glided through the reeds, which bent to right and left, and rose again as they passed, hiding everything which followed.

The next moment the force given to the boat was expended, and it stopped outside the reeds, but only to commence another movement, for the tide bore the bows round, and the light gig began to glide softly along.

"I've killed him," thought Dexter; and he turned cold with horror, wondering the while at his temerity and what would follow.

"Was that his head?" said Bob, in rather a piteous voice, as he sat there resting upon his oars.

"Yes," said Dexter, in a horror-stricken whisper. "I hit him right on the head."

"You've been and gone and done it now, then," whimpered Bob. "You've killed him. That's what you've done. Never did see such a chap as you!"

"I couldn't help it," said Dexter huskily.

"Yes, that's what you always says," cried Bob, in an ill-used tone. "I wish I hadn't come with yer, that I do. I say, ought we to go and pick him up? It don't matter, do it?"

"Yes, Bob; we must go back and pull him out," said Dexter, with a shudder. "Row back through the reeds. Quick, or he may be drowned!"

"He won't want any drowning after that whack you give him on the head. I don't think I shall go back. Look! look!"

Dexter was already looking at the frantic muddy figure upon the bank, up which it had climbed after emerging from the reeds. The man was half-mad with rage and disappointment, and he ran along shaking his fists, dancing about in his fury, and shouting to the boys what he would do.

His appearance worked a miraculous effect upon the two boys. Dexter felt quite light-hearted in his relief, and Bob forgot all his sufferings and dread now that he was safely beyond their enemy's reach. Laying the blades of the sculls flat, as the boat drifted swiftly on with the tide, he kept on splashing the water, and shouting derisively—

"Yah! yah! Who cares for you? Yah! Go home and hang yourself up to dry! Yah! Who stole the boat!"

Bob's derision seemed to be like oil poured upon a fire. The man grew half-wild with rage. He yelled, spat at them, shook his fists, and danced about in his impotent fury; and the more he raged, the more delighted Bob seemed to be.

"Yah! Who stole the boat!" he kept on crying; and then added mocking taunts. "Here! hi!" he shouted, his voice travelling easily over the water, so that the man heard each word. "Here! hi! Have her now? Fifteen shillings. Come on. Yah!"

"Quick, Bob, row!" cried Dexter, after several vain efforts to stop his companion's derisive cries.

"Eh?" said Bob, suddenly stopping short.

"Row, I tell you! Don't you see what he's going to do!"

The man had suddenly turned and disappeared.

"No," said Bob. "I've scared him away."

"You haven't," said Dexter, with his feeling of dread coming back. "He's running across to the other creek to get the boat."

Bob bent to his oars directly, and sent the gig rapidly along, and more and more into the swift current. He rowed so as to incline toward the further shore, and soon after they passed the mouth of the other creek.

"Get out with yer," said Bob. "He ain't coming. And just you look here, young un; you hit me offull on the head with that there boat-hook, and as soon as ever I gits you ashore I'll make you go down on your knees and cry *chi—ike*; you see if I don't, and—"

"There he is, Bob," said Dexter excitedly; and looking toward the other creek, there, sure enough, was the man in his wretched little tub of a boat, which he was forcing rapidly through the water, and looking over his shoulder from time to time at the objects of his pursuit.

Bob pulled with all his might, growing pallid and muddy of complexion as the gig glided on. Matters had been bad enough before. Now the map would be ten times worse, while, to make things as bad as they could be, it soon became evident that the tide was on the turn, and that, unless they could stem it in the unequal battle of strength, they would be either swept back into their enemy's arms or else right up the river in a different direction to that which they intended to go, and, with the task before them, should they escape, of passing their enemy's lair once again.

Chapter Thirty Eight
The Crowning Point of the Trip

"Come and lay hold o' one scull," said Bob, whose eyes seemed to be fixed as he stared at the back of their enemy. "Oh, do be quick!"

Dexter slipped into his place, took the scull, and began to row.

"Getting closer, ain't he?" whispered Bob hoarsely. "Yes. I'm afraid so."

"Pull, pull!"

Dexter needed no telling, and he tugged away at the oar as the boat glided a little more swiftly on.

"Ain't leaving him behind, are we!" growled Bob, whose face now grew convulsed with horror. "No; I'm afraid he's coming nearer."

"Oh dear, oh dear!" groaned Bob. "He'll half-kill me, and it's all your fault. Let's stop rowing and give him the boat."

"That we won't," cried Dexter, setting his teeth. "I'll row till I die first."

"But it'll only make him more savage," growled Bob. "I wish I was safe at home."

"You're not half-pulling, Bob."

"It's of no use, matey. He's sure to ketch us, and the furder we rows, the more wild he'll be."

"I don't care," cried Dexter; "he shan't have it if I can help it. Row!"

In his most cowardly moments Bob was obedience itself, and breaking out into a low sobbing whimper, as if it were a song to encourage him in his task, he rowed on with all his might, while only too plainly it could be seen that the man was gaining steadily upon them in spite of the clumsiness of his boat; and consequently it was only a question of time before the boys were overtaken, for the muscles of the man were certain to endure longer than those of Dexter, untrained as they were to such work.

"He's closer, ain't he?" whined Bob.

"Yes, ever so much," replied Dexter, between his set teeth.

"Well, jest you recollect it was you hit him that whack on the head. I didn't do nothing."

"Yes, you did," said Dexter sharply. "You said, *yah!* at him, and called him names."

"No, I didn't. Don't you be a sneak," whined Bob. "You were ever so much worse than me. Is he coming closer?"

"Yes."

It was a fact, closer and closer, and the tide ran so strongly now that the boys had hard work to make much progress. They did progress, though, all the same, for their boat was narrow and sharp. Still the current was dead against them, and their want of movement added to their despair.

Bad as it was for them, however, it was worse for the man in his heavy little broadly-bowed tub; and so it happened that just as Bob began to row more slowly, and burst into a fit of howling, which made Dexter feel as if he would like to turn and hit him over the head with his oar—a contact of scull against skull—the man suddenly ceased rowing, turned in his seat, and sat shaking his fist at them, showing his teeth in his impotent rage.

"There!" cried Bob, who was transformed in an instant. "We've bet him. He can't pull no further. Yah! yah!"

Bob changed back to his state of cowardly prostration, and began to tug once more at his oar, for his derisive yell galvanised the man once more into action, and the pursuit was continued.

"Oh!" howled Bob. "Who'd ha' thought o' that?"

"Who's stupid now?" panted Dexter, as he too rowed with all his might.

Bob did nothing but groan, and the pursuit and flight were once more continued, each moment with despair getting a stronger hold of the fugitives. The oar felt hot in Dexter's blistered hands, a peculiar sensation of heaving was in his chest, his eyes began to swim, and he was just about to cease rowing, when he could hardly believe his starting eyes—their enemy had once more given up the pursuit, and was sitting wrenched round, and staring after them.

"Don't, pray, don't shout at him this time, Bob," panted Dexter.

"I won't if you're afraid," said the young scoundrel.

"Keep on rowing, or he'll come after us again."

Bob's scull was dipped again directly, and the motion of the boat was kept up sufficiently to counteract the drift of the tide, while the man in the little tub was swept rapidly away.

"Let's get over the other side to those trees," said Dexter, as he felt that he could row no further, and the boat's head was directed half-across the stream so as to reach the clump of willows indicated, where, after a much heavier pull than they had anticipated, the gig was made fast, and Bob's first act after laying down his scull was to lean over the side and drink heartily of the muddy water.

Dexter would gladly have lain down to rest, but there was a watch to keep up.

Bob mocked at the idea.

"Yah!" he said; "he won't some any more. I say, are you nearly dry?"

"Nearly," said Dexter, "all but my boots and socks."

These he took off, and put in the sun to dry, as he sat there with his elbows on his knees, and his chin on his hands, watching till Bob was asleep.

He was faint and hungry, and the idea was strong in his mind that the man would steal down upon them when he was not expected. This thought completely drove away all drowsiness, though it did not affect his companion in the slightest degree.

The next thing ought to have been to get some food, but there was no likely place within view, and though several boats and a barge or two passed, the fear of being questioned kept the watcher from hailing them, and asking where he could get some bread and milk.

The hours glided slowly by, but there was no sign of the shabby little boat. The tide ran up swiftly, and the gig swung easily from its chain; and as Dexter sat there, hungry and lonely, he could not keep his thoughts at times from the doctor's comfortable house.

Towards evening the socks and boots were so dry that Dexter replaced them, looking down the while rather ruefully at his mud-stained trousers. He rubbed them and scratched the patches with his nails; but the result was not satisfactory, and once more he sat gazing up the river in expectation of seeing their enemy come round the bend.

It was getting late, and the tide had turned, as Dexter knew at once by the way in which the boat had swung round with its bows now pointing up-stream. And now seemed the time when the man might appear once more in pursuit.

The thought impressed him so that he leaned over and shook Bob, who sat up and stared wonderingly about.

"Hallo!" he said. "What time is it!"

"I don't know, but the tide has turned, and that man may come after us again."

"Nay, he won't come any more," said Bob confidently. "Let's go and get something to eat."

It was a welcome proposal, and the boat being unmoored, Dexter took one of the sculls, and as they rowed slowly down with the tide he kept his eyes busy watching for the coming danger, but it did not appear.

Bob went ashore at a place that looked like a ferry, where there was a little public-house, and this time returned with a small loaf, a piece of boiled bacon, and a bottle of cider.

"I'd ha' brought the bacon raw, and we'd ha' cooked it over a fire," said Bob, "only there don't seem to be no wood down here, and there's such lots of houses."

Dexter did not feel troubled about the way in which the bacon was prepared, but sat in the boat, as it drifted with the tide, and ate his portion ravenously, but did not find the sour cider to his taste.

By the time they had finished, it was growing dark, and lights were twinkling here and there on either bank, showing that they were now in a well-populated part.

"Where are we to sleep to-night, Bob?" said Dexter at last.

"Dunno yet. Can't see no places."

"We must be near the sea now, mustn't we?"

"Yes, pretty handy to it," said Bob, with the confidence of one in utter ignorance. "We shall be there to-morrow, and then we can catch heaps of cod-fish, and soles, and mack'rel, and find oysters. It'll be all right then."

This was encouraging, but somehow Dexter did not feel so much confidence in his companion as of old.

But Bob's rest, and the disappearance of danger had brought him back to his former state, and he was constantly making references to the departed enemy.

"I should just liked to have ketched him touching me!" he said. "I'd ha' give his shins such a kicking as would soon have made him cry 'Leave off.'"

Dexter sat and stared through the gloom at the young Gascon.

"I'd ha' soon let him know what he'd get if he touched me."

"Hi, Bob! look out!"

Bob uttered a cry of dread, and nearly jumped overboard as something still and dark suddenly loomed up above him. Then there was a bump, which nearly finished what the boy had felt disposed to do; and then they were gliding along by the side of a vessel anchored in midstream.

As they swept past the stern the boat bumped again against something black and round, which proved to be a floating tub. With this they seemed to have become entangled, for there was a rasping grating noise, then the boat's chain began to run rapidly over the bows, the boat swung round, and their further progress was checked. A piece of the chain with the hook had been left hanging over, and when they had touched the tub buoy the hook had caught, and they were anchored some little distance astern the large vessel.

"Here's a game!" cried Bob, as soon as he had recovered from his astonishment. "Well, we can't go on in the dark. Let's stop here."

"But we've got to find a place to sleep, Bob," protested Dexter.

"Yah! you're always wanting to go to sleep. There ain't no place to sleep ashore, so let's sleep in the boat. Why, we shall always have to bunk down there when we get out to sea."

"But suppose the boat should sink?"

"Yah! suppose it did. We'd swim ashore. Only mind you don't get outer bed in the night and walk into the water. I don't want to go to sleep at all."

Dexter did not feel drowsy, but again he could not help thinking of his room with the white hangings, and of how pleasant it would be to take off his clothes once more and lie between sheets.

"Some chaps is always thinking about going to bed," said Bob jauntily. "Long as I gets a nap now and then, that's all I want."

Dexter did not know it, but Bob Dimsted was a thorough-paced second-hand boy. Every expression of this kind was an old one, such as he had heard from his father, or the rough men who consorted with him, from the bullying down to the most playful remark. But, as aforesaid, Dexter did not realise all this. He had only got as far as the fact that Bob was not half so nice as he used to be, and that, in spite of his boasting and bullying, he was not very brave when put to the test.

"There, I shan't go to sleep yet. You can have one o' them cushins forward," said Bob at last; and, suffering now from a sudden feeling of weariness, Dexter took one of the cushions forward, placed it so as to be as comfortable as possible, realising as he did this that, in spite of his words, Bob was doing the same with two cushions to his one, and before he had been lying there long, listening to the rippling of the water, and gazing up at the stars, a hoarse, wheezing noise proclaimed the fact that Bob Dimsted was once more fast asleep.

Dexter was weary now in the extreme, the exertion and excitement he had gone through had produced, in connection with the irregular feeding, a state of fatigue that under other circumstances might have resulted in his dropping off at once, but now he could only lie and listen, and keep his eyes dilated and wide open, staring for some danger which seemed as if it must be near.

He did not know what the danger might be, unless it was that man with the boat, but something seemed to threaten, and he could not sleep.

Then, too, he felt obliged to think about Bob and about their journey. Where they were going, what sort of a place it would be, and whether they would be any more happy when they got to some beautiful island; for he was fain to confess that matters were very miserable now, and that the more he saw of Bob Dimsted the less he liked him.

He was in the midst of one of his thoughtful moods, with Bob for his theme, and asking himself what he should do if Bob did begin to thrash him first time they were on shore; and he had just come to the conclusion that he would not let Bob thrash him if he could help it, when Bob suddenly leaped forward and hit him a round-handed sort of blow, right in the back of the neck.

This so enraged him that he forgot directly all about companionship, and the sort of tacit brotherly compact into which they had entered, and springing at his assailant he struck him a blow in the chest, which sent him staggering back.

For a moment or two Bob seemed to be beaten; then he came at him furiously, the turf was trampled and slippery, and they both went down; then they got up again, and fought away, giving and taking blows, every one of which sounded with a loud slap.

That fight seemed as if it would never end, and Dexter felt as if he were getting the worst of it, consequent upon an inherent dislike to inflict pain, and his having passed over again and again opportunities for administering effective blows. At last they joined in what became little more than a wrestle, and Dexter felt the ground giving way beneath his feet; the back of his neck hurt him terribly, and he was about to give in, when the boys began to cheer, Mr Sibery ran up with the cane, and the doctor came looking stern and frowning, while he saw Helen Grayson put her hand to her eyes and turn away.

"It's all Bob Dimsted's fault," he cried passionately; and he woke up with the words upon his lips, and a crick in the back of his neck, consequent upon the awkward cramped-up position in which he had lain.

It was broad daylight, and for a few moments he was too much confused to understand where he was; but as he realised it all, and cast a quick look round in search of danger, he saw that they were hooked on to the slimy buoy, that twenty yards further there was the hull of an old schooner, against which they had been nearly capsized the previous evening, and four or five hundred yards beyond that, slowly paddling along, was their enemy, looking over his shoulder as if he had seen them, and meant to make sure of them now.

Dexter hesitated between wakening Bob and setting the boat adrift.

He decided on doing the latter, and hauling on the chain, he drew the boat right up to the buoy, followed the chain with his hands till he could touch the hook, and after some difficulty, his efforts reminding him of the night when he unfastened the chain in the boat-house—he dragged the hook from where it clung to a great rusty link, and all the time his eyes were as much fixed upon the man in the boat as upon the task he had in hand.

Clear at last, and drifting away again. That was something towards safety, and he now stepped over the thwarts and shook Bob.

Bob was too comfortable to open his eyes, and no matter what his companion did he could get no reply till he bent lower, and, inspired by the coming danger, shouted in his ear—

"I've got yer at last."

Bob sprang up as if electrified, saw who spoke, and was about to burst into a torrent of angry abuse, when he followed the direction of Dexter's pointing hand, caught the approaching danger, and seized an oar.

It was none too soon, for as Dexter seized the other, the man evidently realised that his prey was about to make another effort to escape, and, bending to his work, he sent the little tub-like boat surging through the water.

"Pull, Bob!" said Dexter excitedly, an unnecessary order, for Bob had set his teeth, and, with his face working, was tugging so hard that it needed all Dexter's efforts to keep the boat from being pulled into the right-hand shore.

The chase had begun in full earnest, and for the next hour, with very little alteration in their positions, it kept on. Then the pace began to tell on the boys. They had for some time been growing slower in their strokes, and they were not pulled so well home. Bob engaged every now and then in a dismal, despairing howl, usually just at the moment when Dexter thrust his oar too deeply in the water, and had hard work to get it out.

But their natural exhaustion was not of such grave consequence as might have been imagined, for their pursuer was growing weary too, and his efforts were greatly wanting in the spirit he displayed at first. On the other hand, though the man came on slowly, he rowed with a steady, stubborn determination, which looked likely to last all the morning, and boded ill for those of whom he was in chase.

Bob's face was a study, but Dexter's back was toward him, and he could not study it. The enemy was about two hundred yards behind, and whenever he seemed to flag a little Bob's face brightened; but so sure as the man glanced over his shoulder, and began to pull harder, the aspect of misery, dread, and pitiable helplessness Bob displayed was ludicrous; and at such times he glanced to right and left to see which was the nearest way to the shore.

As Bob rowed he softly pushed off his boots. Soon after he made three or four hard tugs at his oar, and then, by a quick movement, drew one arm out of his jacket. Then rowing with one hand he shook himself quite clear of the garment, so as to be unencumbered when he began to swim, for that was his intention as soon as the man overtook them, and his peril became great.

"He wants most of all to get the boat," he thought to himself; and soon after he opened his heart to Dexter.

"Lookye here!" he said, "he wants to get the boat; and if he can get that he won't come after us. Let's row pretty close to the bank, and get ashore and run."

"What! and leave the boat?" cried Dexter. "That I'm sure I will not."

Dexter pulled all the harder after hearing this proposal, and Bob uttered a moan.

All that morning the flight and pursuit were kept up, till on both sides it became merely a light dipping of the oars, so as to keep the boats' heads straight, the tide carrying them along.

It was plain enough now that they were getting toward the mouth of the river, which was now quite broad. Houses were growing plentiful, barges lay at wharves or moored with other boats in the stream, and care had to be exercised to avoid coming in collision with the many obstacles in their way.

But they kept on; and though at Bob's piteous suggestion they wound in and out among the many crafts in the hope of shaking off their pursuer, it was all in vain, for he kept doggedly on after them, with the matter-of-fact determination of a weasel after a rabbit, sure of its scent, and certain that before long the object of the pursuit would resign itself to its fate.

On still in a dreary mechanical way. Dexter could hardly move his arms, and Bob was, in spite of his long experience, almost as helpless.

"It's of no use," the latter said at last; and he ceased rowing.

"No, no, Bob; don't give in!" cried Dexter excitedly. "We shall soon tire him out now. Row! Row!"

"Can't," said Bob drearily. "I haven't another pull in me."

"Then give me the other scull, and let me try."

"Yah! you couldn't pull both," cried Bob. "There, I'm going to try a hundred more strokes, and then I shall swim ashore. I ain't going to let him catch me."

"Pull, then, a hundred more," cried Dexter excitedly. "Oh, do make it two, Bob! He'll be tired out by then."

"I'm a-going to pull a hundred," grumbled Bob, "and then give it up. Now then!"

The sculls splashed the water almost together, and for a few strokes the boys pulled vigorously and well; but it was like the last bright flashes of an expiring candle, and long before the half-hundred was reached the dippings of the blades grew slower and slower. Then they became irregular, while, to add to the horror of the position, the man in pursuit seemed to have been keeping a reserve of strength ready for such an emergency, and he now came on rapidly.

Bob would have proposed putting ashore once more, but, in avoiding the various crafts, they had now contrived to be about midstream, and in his horror and dread of the coming enemy all thought of scheming seemed to have been driven out of his head.

He uttered a despairing yell, and began to tug at his oar once more; Dexter followed his example, and the distance again increased.

But only for a few minutes, then they seemed to be growing weaker, their arms became like lead; their eyes grew dim, and the end was very near.

"Ah, I've got yer at last, have I?" shouted the man, who was not forty yards away now.

"Not yet," muttered Dexter. "Pull, Bob, pull!"

Bob responded by going through the motion of rowing, but his scull did not dip into the water, and, meeting with no resistance, he went backwards off the seat, with his heels in the air.

Dexter jumped up, seized his companion's scull, and, weary as he was, with all the stubborn English pluck which never knows when it is beaten, he reseated himself, shipped his scull, and bent forward to try, inexperienced as he was, to make another effort for escape.

As he seated himself, breathless and panting hard, he gave one glance at his enemy, then another over his shoulder at a boat on ahead, which it would be his duty to avoid, for it seemed to be going right across his track.

Then he began to row, putting the little strength he had left into his last strokes.

"Ah, it's no good," cried the man triumphantly. "I've got yer at last."

"How—ow!" yelled Bob, with a cry like a Newfoundland dog shut out on a cold night.

"Drop that there rowing, or I'll—"

Dexter heard no more. He was pulling frantically, but making hardly any way. Then he heard voices ahead, glanced round with his sculls raised, and found that he was running right toward the craft just ahead.

Another moment and there was a bump.

The man had driven his little tub right into the stern of the gig, and as he laid hold he snarled out—

"I knew I should ketch yer."

"How—ow!" yelled Bob again, from where he lay on his back in the bottom of the boat, his legs still over the seat.

Bump!

There was another shock, and Dexter started up, saw that he had run into the boat ahead, and that one of the two sailors, who had been rowing, had taken hold of the bows.

He saw that at a glance, but he also saw something else which seemed to freeze the blood in his breast.

For there, seated in the stern of that large boat into which he had run, were the Doctor, Sir James Danby, old Dan'l, and Peter.

Chapter Thirty Nine
Brought to Book

Dexter did not pause a moment. It did not occur to him that he was utterly exhausted, and could hardly move his arms. All he realised was the fact that on the one side was the man whom he had half-killed with the boat-hook, just about to stretch out his hand to seize him, on the other, those whom he dreaded far more, and with one quick movement he stepped on to the thwart of the gig, joined his hands, dived in, and disappeared from sight, in the muddy water.

For a few moments there was the silence of utter astonishment, and then the man who had pursued the boys down the river began to take advantage of the general excitement by keeping hold of the side of the gig and beginning to draw it away; but Bob set up such a howl of dismay that it drew Peter's attention, and he too seized the boat from the other end, caught out the chain, and hooked it on to a ring-bolt of the big boat in which he sat.

"You drop that there, will yer!" cried the man. "It's my boat."

"How—ow!" cried Bob, in the most canine of yelps; and at the same moment the gig was literally jerked from the man's hold, for the two sailors had given a tremendous tug at their oars to force the boat in the direction that Dexter was likely to take after his rise, and the next minute a dozen yards were between the tub and the gig.

"For heaven's sake, mind! stop!" cried the doctor excitedly. "Don't row, men, or you may strike him down."

The men ceased rowing, and every eye began to search the surface of the water, but no sign of Dexter could be seen.

"He could not sink like that," cried Sir James. "He must rise somewhere."

But must or no, Dexter did not rise, and the men began to paddle softly down-stream, while the doctor stood up in the boat gazing wildly round.

"It was all my doing," he said to himself. "Poor boy! poor boy!"

A feeling of horror that was unbearable seemed to be creeping over the occupants of the great boat. Even Dan'l, who looked upon Dexter as his mortal enemy, and who had suggested, in the hope of seeing him sent to prison, that the surest way of capturing the boys was to go down to the mouth of the river—even Dan'l felt the chill of horror as he mentally said—

"'Tain't true. Them as is born to be hanged is sometimes drowned."

But just then there was a tremendous splash, and the big boat rocked to and fro, the captive gig danced, and Bob uttered another of his canine yelps, for Peter had suddenly stepped on to the gunwale, dived in after something he had seen touch the surface of the water twenty yards lower down, where it had been rolled over and over by the rapid tide, and a minute later, as he swam vigorously, he shouted—"I've got him!"

And he was seen holding the boy's head above the water, as he turned to try and stem the current, and swim back to the boat.

The task was not long, for the two sailors sent her down with a few vigorous sweeps of their oars, and Dexter and his rescuer were dragged over the side, as the man with the tub slowly backed away.

No time was lost in reaching the shore, and the insensible boy was carried up to the principal hotel in the port, where quite an hour elapsed before the surgeon whose services were sought was able to pause from his arduous task, and announce that his patient would live.

For it was a very narrow escape, and the surgeon said, as he shook hands with Dr Grayson—

"Some men would have given it up in despair, sir. But there he is, safe and sound, and, I dare say, boy-like, it will not be very long before he gets into some mischief again."

Sir James Danby coughed, and Doctor Grayson frowned as he met his friend's peculiar look. But nothing was said then till the surgeon had been up to see his patient once more, after which he returned, reported that Dexter had sunk into a sound slumber, and then took his leave.

"I suppose we shall not go back to Coleby to-night?" said Sir James.

"I shall not," said the doctor; "but, my dear Danby, pray don't let me keep you."

"Oh! you will not keep me," said Sir James quietly. "I've got to make arrangements about my boat being taken up the river."

"Why not let my men row it back!" said the doctor.

"Because I did not like to impose on your kindness."

"Then they may take it?"

"I shall only be too grateful," said Sir James.

Nothing more was said till they had ordered and sat down to a snug dinner in the hotel, when Sir James opened the ball.

"Now, Grayson," he said, "I happen to be a magistrate."

"Yes, of course," said the doctor uneasily.

"Well, then, I want to have a few words with you about those two boys."

The doctor nodded.

"Your groom is with your *protégé*, and your old gardener has that other young scoundrel in charge."

"In charge?" said the doctor.

"Yes; you may call it so. I told him not to lose sight of the young rascal, and I also told your groom to exercise the same supervision over the other."

"But surely, my dear Danby, you do not mean to—"

"Deal with them as I would with any other offender? Why not?"

The doctor had no answer ready, so Sir James went on—

"I valued that boat very highly, and certainly I've got it back—with the exception of the stains upon the cushions—very little the worse. But this was a serious theft, almost as bad as horse-stealing, and I shall have to make an example of them."

"But one of them has been terribly punished," said the doctor eagerly.

"Pooh! not half enough, sir. Come, Grayson, of course this has completely cured you of your mad folly!"

"My mad folly!" cried the doctor excitedly. "May I ask you what you mean?"

"Now, my dear Grayson, pray don't be angry. I only say, as an old friend and neighbour, surely you must be ready to agree that your wild idea of making a gentleman out of this boy—one of the dregs of our civilisation—is an impossibility?"

"Nothing of the sort, sir," cried the doctor angrily. "I never felt more certain of the correctness of my ideas."

"Tut—tut—tut—tut!" ejaculated Sir James. "Really, Grayson, this is too much."

"Too much, sir? Nothing of the kind. A boyish escapade. Nothing more."

"Well!" said Sir James drily, "when such cases as this are brought before us at the bench, we are in the habit of calling them thefts."

"Theft: pooh! No, no!" cried the doctor stubbornly. "A boyish prank. He would have sent the boat back."

"Would he?" said Sir James drily. "I suppose you think his companion would have done the same?"

"I have nothing to do with the other boy," said the doctor shortly. "It was a most unfortunate thing that Dexter should have made his acquaintance."

"Birds of a feather flock together, my dear Grayson," said Sir James.

"Nothing of the kind, sir. It was my fault," cried the doctor. "I neglected to let the boy have suitable companions of his own age; and the consequence was that he listened to this young scoundrel, and allowed himself to be led away."

"Do I understand aright, from your defence of the boy, that you mean to forgive him and take him back!"

"Certainly!" said the doctor.

"Grayson, you amaze me! But if I prove to you that you are utterly wrong, and that the young dog is an arrant thief, what then?"

"Then," said the doctor, "I'm afraid I should have to— No, I wouldn't. I would try and reform him."

"Well," said Sir James, "if you choose to be so ultra lenient, Grayson, you must; but I feel that I have a duty to do, and as soon as we have had our wine I propose that we have the prisoners here, and listen to what they have to say."

"Prisoners?"

"Yes. What else would you call them?"

Before the doctor could stand up afresh in Dexter's defence a waiter entered the room.

"Beg pardon, sir, but your groom says would you be good enough to step upstairs?"

"Bless my heart!" cried the doctor. "Is it a relapse?"

He hurried up to the room where Dexter had been sleeping, to find that, instead of being in bed, he was fully dressed, and lying on the floor, with Peter the groom holding him down.

"Why, what's the matter!" cried the doctor, as he entered the room hastily, followed by Sir James.

"Matter, sir?" said Peter, "matter enough. If I hadn't held him down like this here I believe he'd 'a' been out o' that window."

"Why, Dexter!" cried the doctor.

The boy struggled feebly, and then, seeing the futility of his efforts, he lay still and closed his eyes.

"Went off fast asleep, sir, as any one would ha' thought," said Peter. "And seeing him like that I thought I'd just go down and fetch myself a cup o' tea; but no sooner was I out o' the room than he must have slipped out and dressed hisself—shamming, you know—and if I hadn't come back in the nick o' time he'd have been gone."

The doctor frowned, and Sir James looked satisfied, as he gave him a nod.

"Going to run away, eh!"

"Yes, Sir James," said the groom; "and it was as much as I could do to hold him."

"Get up, Peter," said the doctor.

The groom rose, and Dexter leapt up like a bit of spring, and darted toward the door.

But Sir James was close to it, and catching the boy by the arm he held him.

"Take hold, of him, my man," he said; "and don't let him go."

Peter obeyed, getting a tight grip of Dexter's wrist.

"Now, you give in," he whispered. "It's no good, for I shan't let go."

"Bring him down," said Sir James sternly.

Peter shook his head warningly at Dexter, and then, as Sir James and the doctor went down to their room, Peter followed with his prisoner, who looked over the balustrade as if measuring the distance and his chance if he made a jump.

"Now," said Sir James, as the boy was led into the room; "stand there, sir, and I warn you that if you attempt to run away I shall have in the police, and be more stern. You, my man, go and tell the gardener to bring up the other boy."

Peter left the room after giving Dexter a glance, and the doctor began to walk up and down angrily. He wanted to take the business into his own hands, but Sir James was a magistrate, and it seemed as if he had a right to take the lead.

There was a painful silence, during which Dexter stood hanging his head, and feeling as if he wished he had been drowned, instead of being brought round to undergo such a painful ordeal as this.

Ten minutes must have elapsed before a scuffling was heard upon the stairs, and Bob Dimsted's voice whimpering—

"You let me alone, will yer? I never done nothing to you. Pair o' great cowards, y'are. Don't knock me about, or it'll be the worse for yer. Hit one o' your own size. I never said nothing to you."

This was continued and repeated right into the room, Dan'l looking very severe and earnest, and holding on by the boy's collar, half-dragging him, while Peter pushed behind, and then closed the door, and stood before it like a sentry.

"You have not been striking the boy, I hope!" said the doctor.

"Strike him, sir? no, not I," said Dan'l; "but I should like to. Been a-biting and kicking like a neel to get away."

Sir James had never seen an eel kick, but he accepted the simile, and turning to Bob, who was whimpering and howling—"knocking me about"—"never said nothing to him"—"if my father was here," etc.

"Silence!" roared Sir James, in his severest tones; and Bob gave quite a start and stared.

"Now, sir," said Sir James. "Here, both of you; stand together, and mind this: it will be better for both of you if you are frank and straightforward."

"I want to go home," whimpered Bob. "Y'ain't no business to stop me here."

"Silence!" roared Sir James; and Bob jumped.

Dexter did not move, but stood with his eyes fixed to the floor.

"Now!" said Sir James, gazing fiercely at Bob; "you know, I suppose, why you are here."

"No! I don't," whimpered Bob. "And y'ain't no business to stop me. I want to go home."

"Silence, sir!" roared Sir James again. "You do not know? Well, then, I will tell you. You are before me, sir, charged with stealing a boat."

"Oh!" ejaculated Bob, in a tone of wondering innocence.

"And I perhaps ought to explain," said Sir James, looking hard at Dr Grayson, and speaking apologetically, "that in an ordinary way, as the boat was my property, I should feel called upon to leave the bench; but as this is only a preliminary examination, I shall carry it on myself. Now, sir," he continued, fixing Bob's shifty eyes, "what have you to say, sir, for stealing my boat?"

"Stealing your boat!" cried Bob volubly; "me steal your boat, sir? I wouldn't do such a thing."

"Why, you lying young dog!"

"No, sir, I ain't, sir," protested Bob, as Dexter slowly raised his head and gazed at him. "It wasn't me, sir. It was him, sir. That boy, sir. I begged him not to, sir; but he would do it."

"Oh, it was Dexter Grayson, was it?" said Sir James, glancing at the doctor, who was gnawing his lip and beating the carpet with his toe.

"Yes, sir; it was him, sir. I was t'other side o' the river one day, sir," rattled off Bob, "and he shouts to me, sir, 'Hi!' he says, just like that, sir, and when I went to him, sir, he says, 'Let's steal the old cock's boat and go down the river for a game.'"

"Well?" said Sir James.

"Well, sir, I wouldn't, sir," continued Bob glibly. "I said it would be like stealing the boat; and I wouldn't do that."

"Oh!" said Sir James.

"Is this true, Dexter!" said the doctor sternly.

"No, sir. He wanted me to take the boat."

"Oh, my!" cried Bob. "Hark at that now! Why, I wouldn't ha' done such a thing."

"No, you look a nice innocent boy," said Sir James.

"Yes, sir; and he was allus at me about that boat, and said he wanted to go to foreign abroad, he did, and the best way, he said, was to steal that there boat and go."

"Oh," said Sir James. "And what more have you to say, sir?"

"It isn't true, sir," said Dexter, making an effort to speak, and he gazed angrily at his companion. "Bob here wanted me to go with him, and he persuaded me to take the boat."

"Oh! only hark at him!" cried Bob, looking from one to the other.

"And I thought it would be like stealing the boat to take it like that."

"Well, rather like it," said Sir James sarcastically.

"And so I sent that letter and that money to pay for it, sir, and I meant to send the rest if it wasn't quite enough."

"Ah!" ejaculated the doctor eagerly.

"What letter? What money?" said Sir James.

"That money I sent by Bob Dimsted, sir, to put in your letter-box."

"I never received any money," cried Sir James. "You sent some money!"

"Yes, sir; before we took the boat, sir."

"Ah!" ejaculated the doctor again.

"And you sent it by this boy?"

"Yes, sir."

"Then where is the money?" cried Sir James, turning upon Bob.

"I dunno, sir. I never had no money."

"You did, Bob, in a letter I gave you," cried Dexter excitedly.

"Oh!" ejaculated Bob, with an astonished look. "Well, if ever!"

"This is getting interesting," said Sir James. "Now, sir, where's that money?"

"He never give me none, sir," cried Bob indignantly. "I never see no letter."

"You did. The one I threw across the river to you!" said Dexter.

"Oh, what a cracker!" cried Bob. "I never had no letter, gen'lemen, and I never see no money. Why don't you tell the truth, and the kind gentlemen won't be so hard on you?"

"I am telling the truth," cried Dexter, "It was you asked me to take the boat."

"Only hark at him!" cried Bob. "Why yer'd better say yer didn't take all yer clothes off and swim acrost and get it."

"I did," said Dexter; "but you made me. You said you'd go."

"Oh, you can tell 'em!" cried Bob.

"And I did give you the money to take."

"Oh, well, I've done," said Bob. "I never did hear a chap tell lies like you can!"

"I think that will do," said Sir James, with a side glance at the doctor, who sat with his brows knit, listening. "Now, you will both go back to the room where you are to sleep, and I warn you that if you attempt to escape, so surely will you be taken by the police, and then this matter will assume a far more serious aspect. You, my men, will have charge of these two boys till the morning. They are not to speak to each other, and I look to you to take them safely back to Coleby by the early train. That will do."

BOB DIMSTED IN THE HANDS OF THE LAW.

Dexter darted one glance at the doctor, but his face was averted.

"Please, sir," he began.

"Silence!" cried Sir James. "I think Dr Grayson understands your character now, and I must say I never heard a more cowardly attempt to fasten a fault upon another. No: not a word. Go!"

Bob Dimsted was already outside with Dan'l's knuckles in the back of his neck.

Peter was more gentle with his prisoner as he led him away.

"You've been and done it now, young fellow," he said. "I would ha' told the truth."

Dexter turned to him with bursting heart, but he could not speak, and as soon as he was in his bedroom he threw himself before a chair, and buried his face in his hands, so as to try and shut out the reproachful face of Helen, which he seemed to see.

"I wish I had not been saved," he cried at last passionately, and then he glanced at the window, and listened, while downstairs Sir James was saying quietly—

"There, Grayson, I think you understand the boy's character now."

"No," said the doctor shortly. "I don't think I do."

"What!"

"And I'd give a hundred pounds," said the doctor, "to know the truth."

"Really," said Sir James, laughing. "You are the most obstinate man I ever knew."

"Yes," said the doctor. "I suppose I am."

Chapter Forty
"Huzza! We're Homeward Bound!"

The first wet day there had been for a month. It seemed as if Mother Nature had been saving up all her rain in a great cistern, and was then letting it out at once.

No glorious sapphire seas and brilliant skies; no golden sunshine pouring down on tawny sands, over which waved the long pinnate leaves of the cocoa-nuts palms; no brilliant-coloured fish that seemed to be waiting to be caught; no glorious life of freedom, with their boat to enable them to glide from isle to isle, where it was always summer; but rain, rain, rain, always rain, pouring down from a lead-black sky.

A dreary prospect, but not half so dreary as Dexter's spirits, as he thought of what was to come.

If ever boy felt miserable, he did that next morning, for they were all going back to Coleby. The romantic adventure was at an end, and he was like a prisoner.

Why had he left the doctor's? What had he gained by it but misery and wretchedness. Bob had turned out one of the most contemptible cowards that ever stepped. He had proved to be a miserable tyrannical bully when they were alone; and in the face of danger a wretched cur; while now that they were caught he was ready to tell any lie to save his own skin.

What would Helen say to him, and think of him? What would Mr Hippetts say—and Mr Sibery?

He would be sent back to the Union of course; and one moment he found himself wishing that he had never left the schools to be confronted with such misery as he felt now.

They were on their way back by rail. The doctor, who had not even looked at him, was in a first-class carriage with Sir James, and the plans being altered, and the boat sent up to Coleby by a trustworthy man, Bob and Dexter were returning in a second-class carriage, with their custodians, Peter and old Dan'l.

They were the sole occupants of the carriage, and soon after starting Bob turned to Dexter—

"I say!" he exclaimed.

Dexter started, and looked at him indignantly—so angrily, in fact, that Bob grinned.

"Yer needn't look like that," he said. "If I forgives yer, and begins to talk to yer, what more d'yer want!"

Dexter turned away, and looked out of the window.

"There's a sulky one!" said Bob, with a coarse laugh; and as he spoke it was as if he were appealing to old Dan'l and Peter in turn. "He would do it. I tried to hold him back, but he would do it, and he made me come, and now he turns on me like that."

"You're a nice un," said Peter, staring hard at the boy.

"So are you!" said the young scamp insolently. "You mind yer own business, and look arter him. He's got to look arter me—ain't yer, sir!"

"Yes," said old Dan'l sourly; "and I'm going to stuff a hankychy or something else into your mouth if you don't hold your tongue."

"Oh, are yer!" said Bob boldly. "I should just like to see yer do it."

"Then you shall if you don't keep quiet."

Bob was silent for a few minutes, and then amused himself by making a derisive grimace at Dan'l as soon as he was looking another way.

"It was all his fault," he said sullenly. "He would take the boat."

"Ah, there was about six o' one of you, and half a dozen of the other," said Peter, laughing. "You'll get it, young fellow. Six weeks hard labour, and then four years in a reformatory. That's about your dose."

"Is it?" said Bob derisively. "That's what he'll get, and serve him right—a sneak."

Dexter's cheeks, which were very pale, began to show spots of red, but he stared out of the window.

"I shouldn't have gone, only he was allus at me," continued Bob. "Allus. Some chaps ain't never satisfied."

Old Dan'l filled his pipe, and began to smoke.

"You'll get enough to satisfy you," said Peter. "I say, Dan'l, you wouldn't mind, would you?"

"Mind what?" grunted Dan'l.

"Giving me one of the noo brooms. One out o' the last dozen—the long switchy ones. I could just cut the band, and make about three reg'lar teasers out of one broom."

"What, birch-rods?" said Dan'l, with a sort of cast-iron knocker smile.

"Yes," said Peter.

"Mind? no, my lad, you may have two of 'em, and I should like to have the laying of it on."

"Yah! would yer!" said Bob defiantly. "Dessay you would. I should like to see yer."

"But you wouldn't like to feel it," said Peter. "My eye, you will open that pretty mouth of yours! Pig-ringing'll be nothing to it."

"Won't be me," said Bob. "It'll be him, and serve him right."

Dexter's cheeks grew redder as he pictured the disgrace of a flogging scene.

"Not it," continued Peter. "You'll get all that. Sir James'll give it you as sure as a gun. Won't he, Dan'l!"

"Ah!" ejaculated the old gardener. "I heerd him say over and over again that ha wouldn't lose that boat for a hundred pounds. You'll get it, my gentleman!"

"No, I shan't, 'cause I didn't do it. He'll give it to him, and sarve him right, leading me on to go with him, and boasting and bouncing about, and then pretending he wanted to buy the boat, and saying he sent me with the money."

"So I did," cried Dexter, turning sharply round; "and you stole it, and then told lies."

"That I didn't," said Bob. "I never see no money. 'Tain't likely. It's all a tale you made up, and—oh!"

Bob burst into a regular bellow of pain, for, as he had been speaking, he had edged along the seat a little from his corner of the carriage, to bring himself nearer Dexter, who occupied the opposite diagonal corner. As Bob spoke he nodded his head, and thrust his face forward at Dexter so temptingly, that, quick as lightning, the latter flung out his right, and gave Bob a back-handed blow in the cheek.

"Oh! *how*!" cried Bob; and then menacingly, "Here, just you do that again!"

Dexter's blood was up. There was a long course of bullying to avenge, and he did that again, a good deal harder, with the result that the yell Bob emitted rose well above the rattle of the carriage.

"Well done, young un," cried Peter delightedly. "That's right. Give it him again. Here, Dan'l, let 'em have it out, and we'll see fair!"

"No, no, no!" growled the old gardener, stretching out one hand, and catching Bob by the collar, so as to drag him back into his corner—a job he had not the slightest difficulty in doing. "None o' that. They'd be blacking one another's eyes, and there'd be a row."

"Never mind," cried Peter, with all the love of excitement of his class.

"No, no," said Dan'l. "No fighting;" and he gave Dexter a grim look of satisfaction, which had more kindness in it than any the boy had yet seen.

"Here, you let me get at him!" cried Bob.

"No, no, you sit still," said Dan'l, holding him back with one hand.

The task was very easy. A baby could have held Bob, in spite of the furious show of struggling that he made, while, on the other hand, Peter sat grinning, and was compelled to pass one arm round Dexter, and clasp his own wrist, so as to thoroughly imprison him, and keep him back.

"Better let 'em have it out, Dan'l," he cried. "My one's ready."

"Let me go. Let me get at him," shrieked Bob.

"Yes, let him go, Dan'l," cried Peter.

But Dan'l shook his head, and as Bob kept on struggling and uttering threats, the old man turned upon him fiercely—

"Hold your tongue, will you?" he roared. "You so much as say another word, and I'll make you fight it put."

Bob's jaw dropped, and he stared in astonishment at the fierce face before him, reading therein so much determination to carry the threat into effect that he subsided sulkily in his corner, and turned away his face, for every time he glanced at the other end of the carriage it was to see Peter grinning at him.

"Ah!" said Peter at last; "it's a good job for us as Dan'l held you back. You made me shiver."

Bob scowled.

"He's thoroughbred game, he is, Dan'l."

Dan'l chuckled.

"He'd be a terrible chap when his monkey was up. Oh, I am glad. He'd ha' been sure to win."

"Let him alone," growled Dan'l, with a low chuckling noise that sounded something like the slow turning of a weak watchman's rattle; and then muttering something about white-livered he subsided into his corner, and solaced himself with his pipe.

Meanwhile Peter sat opposite, talking in a low tone to Dexter, and began to ask him questions about his adventures, listening with the greatest eagerness to the short answers he received, till Dexter looked up at him piteously.

"Don't talk to me, please, Peter," he said. "I want to sit and think."

"And so you shall, my lad," said the groom; and he too took out a pipe, and smoked till they reached Coleby.

Dexter shivered as he stepped out upon the platform. It seemed to him that the stationmaster and porters were staring at him as the boy who ran away, and he was looking round for a way of retreat, so as to escape what was to come, when Sir James and the doctor came up to them.

"You can let that boy go," said the doctor to Dan'l.

"Let him go, sir?" cried the gardener, looking at both the gentlemen in turn.

Sir James nodded.

Bob, whose eyes had been rat-like in their eager peering from face to face, whisked himself free, darted to the end of the platform, and uttered a loud yell before he disappeared.

"Look here, Dexter," said the doctor coldly; "I have been talking to Sir James on our way here. Now sir, will you give me your word not to try and escape?"

Dexter looked at him for a moment or two.

"Yes, sir," he said at last, with a sigh.

"Then come with me."

"Come with you, sir?"

Dexter looked at his stained and muddy clothes.

"Yes," said the doctor; "come with me."

Sir James shrugged his shoulders slightly, and gave the doctor a meaning look.

"Good-bye, Grayson," he said, and he shook hands.

"As for you, sir," he added sternly, as he turned to Dexter, "you and your companion have had a very narrow escape. If it had not been for your good friend here, matters would have gone ill with you—worse perhaps than you think."

Dexter hung his head, and at a sign from the doctor went to his side, and they walked out of the station with Dan'l and Peter behind.

The doctor stopped.

"You have given me your word, sir, that you will come quietly up to the house," he said coldly.

"Yes, sir," said Dexter sadly.

The doctor, signed to Dan'l and Peter to come up to them.

"You can go on first," he said; and the men passed on.

"I don't want you to feel as if you were a prisoner, Dexter," said the doctor gravely. "It is one of the grandest things in a gentleman—his word— which means his word of honour."

Dexter had nothing he could say; and with a strange swelling at the throat he walked on beside the doctor, gazing at the pavement a couple of yards in front of him, and suffering as a sensitive boy would suffer as he felt how degraded and dirty he looked, and how many people in the town must know of his running away, and be gazing at him, now that he was brought back by the doctor, who looked upon him as a thief.

Every house and shop they passed was familiar. There were several of the tradespeople too standing at their doors ready to salute the doctor, and Dexter's cheeks burned with shame. His punishment seemed more than he could bear.

In another ten minutes they would be at the house, where Maria would open the door, and give him a peculiar contemptuous look—the old look largely intensified; and but for the doctor's words, and the promise given, the boy felt that he must have run away down the first side-turning they passed.

Then, as Maria faded from his mental vision, pleasant old Mrs Millett appeared, with her hands raised, and quite a storm of reproaches ready to be administered to him, followed, when she had finished and forgiven him, as he knew she would forgive him, by a dose of physic, deemed by her to be absolutely necessary after his escapade.

The house at last, and everything just as Dexter had anticipated. Maria opened the door, and then wrinkled up her forehead and screwed up her lips in a supercilious smile.

"Your mistress in!" said the doctor.

"Yes, sir, in the drawing-room, sir."

"Hah!" ejaculated the doctor.

"Found him, sir? *And* brought him back!" cried a familiar voice; and Mrs Millett hurried into the hall. "O you bold, bad boy!" she cried. "How dare you? And you never took your medicine that night. Oh, for shame! for shame!"

"Hush, hush, Mrs Millett!" said the doctor sternly. "That will do."

He signed to the old lady, and she left the hall, but turned to shake her head at the returned culprit as she went, while Maria gave him a meaning smile as soon as the doctor's back was turned, and then passed through the baize door.

The doctor stood there silent and frowning for a few minutes, with his eyes fixed upon the floor, while Dexter awaited his sentence, painfully conscious, and longing for the doctor to speak and put him out of his misery.

"Now, sir," he said at last; "you had better go in and speak to Miss Grayson. She is waiting, I suppose, to see you in that room. I sent word we were coming."

"No, no," said Dexter quickly. "Don't send me in there, sir. You'd better send me back to the school, sir. I'm no good, and shall only get into trouble again; please send me back. I shouldn't like to see Miss Grayson now."

"Why not!" said the doctor sternly.

"Because you don't believe me, sir, and she won't, and—and—you had better send me back."

"I am waiting to see you here, Dexter," said Helen gravely, and the boy started away with a cry, for the drawing-room door had opened silently, and Helen was standing on the mat.

Chapter Forty One
How the Doctor punished

Dexter's interview with Helen was long and painful, for at first it seemed as if she had lost all confidence and hope in the boy, till, realising all this, he cried in a wild outburst of grief—"I know how wrong it all was, but nearly everybody here seemed to dislike me, and I did tell the truth about the boat, but no one believes. Do—do ask him to send me away."

There was a long silence here, as, for the first time, in spite of a hard fight, Dexter could not keep back his tears.

The silence was broken by Helen, who took his hand, and said gently—

"I believe you, Dexter. I am sure you would not tell a lie."

In an instant his arms were round her neck, and he was clinging to her unable to speak, but his eyes, his convulsed face, telling the doctor's daughter that she was right.

That evening, feeling very strange and terribly depressed, Dexter had gone to his old bedroom, thinking it must be for the last time, and wondering how Mr Sibery would treat him.

Helen had sat talking to him for quite a couple of hours, winning from him a complete account of his adventures, and in return relating to him how concerned every one had been on the discovery of his evasion, and how bitterly the doctor had been mortified on learning later on that the boat had been taken. Who were the culprits was known in the course of the day, with the result that, acting on the suggestion already alluded to, the doctor had gone down to the mouth of the river to wait the coming of the borrowers of the boat.

Helen had exacted no promises from Dexter. He had made none, but sat there with her, his hand in hers, wondering and puzzled how it was that he could have run away, but the more he thought, the more puzzled he grew.

"Well," said the doctor that evening, as he sat with his daughter, "I told Danby that I was more determined than ever; that it was only a boyish escapade which he must look over to oblige me, and he agreed after making a great many bones about it. But I feel very doubtful, Helen, and I may as well confess it to you."

"Doubtful?" she said.

"Yes, my dear. I could have forgiven everything if the boy had been frank and honest—if he had owned to his fault in a straightforward way; but when he sought to hide his own fault by trying to throw it on another, I couldn't help feeling disgusted."

"But, papa—"

"Let me finish, my dear. I know what you are about to say. Woman-like, you are going to take his part. It will not do. The lying and deceit are such ugly blemishes in the boy's character that I am out of heart."

"Indeed, papa?" said Helen, smiling. "Ah, it's all very well for you to laugh at me because I have failed over my hobby; but I feel I'm right all the same, and I tell you that his ignorance, vulgarity—"

"Both of which are wonderfully changed."

"Yes, my dear, granted, and he does not talk so much about the workhouse. He was a great deal better, and I could have forgiven this mad, boyish prank—though what could have influenced him, I don't know."

"I can tell you," said Helen. "A boy's love of adventure. The idea of going off in a boat to discover some wonderful island where he could live a Robinson Crusoe kind of life."

"A young donkey!" cried the doctor. "But there, it's all off. I could have forgiven everything, but the cowardly lying."

"Then, poor fellow, he is forgiven."

"Indeed, no, my dear. He goes back to the Union to-morrow; but I shall tell Hippetts to apprentice him to some good trade at once, and I will pay a handsome premium. Confound Hippetts! He'll laugh at me."

"No, he will not, papa."

"Yes, he will, my dear. I know the man."

"But you will not be laughed at."

"Why not?"

"Because you will not send Dexter back."

"Indeed, my dear, but I shall. I am beaten, and I give up."

"But you said you would forgive everything but the deceit and falsehood."

"Yes, everything."

"There is no deceit and falsehood to forgive."

"What?"

"Dexter has told me everything. The simple truth."

"But he should have told it before, and said he took the boat."

"He told the truth in every respect, papa."

"My dear Helen," said the doctor pettishly, "you are as obstinate as I am. The lying young dog—"

"Hush, papa, stop!" said Helen gently. "Dexter is quite truthful, I am sure."

"That is your weak woman's heart pleading for him," said the doctor. "No, my dear, no; it will not do."

"I am quite certain, papa," said Helen firmly, "that he spoke the truth."

"How do you know, my dear?"

"Because Dexter told me again and again before he went up to bed."

"And you believe him?"

"Yes, and so will you."

"Wish I could," said the doctor earnestly. "I'd give a hundred pounds to feel convinced."

"You shall be convinced for less than that, papa," said Helen merrily. "Give me a kiss for my good news."

"There's the kiss in advance, my dear. Now, where is the news?"

"Here, papa. If Dexter were the hardened boy you try to make him—"

"No, no: gently. He makes himself one."

"—he would have gone up to bed to-night careless and indifferent after shedding a few fictitious tears—"

"Very likely."

"—and be sleeping heartily by now."

"As he is, I'll be bound," cried the doctor energetically.

"Of course, I may be wrong," said Helen, "but Dexter strikes me as being so sensitive a boy—so easily moved, that, I am ready to say, I am sure that he is lying there half-heartbroken, crying bitterly, now he is alone."

"I'll soon prove that," said the doctor sharply; and, crossing the room in his slippers, he silently lit a candle and went upstairs to Dexter's door, where he stood listening for a few minutes, to find that all was perfectly still. Then turning the handle quietly, he entered, and it was quite half an hour before he came out.

"Well, papa?" said Helen, as the doctor returned to the drawing-room.

"You're a witch, my dear," he said.

"I was right?"

"You always are, my dear."

"And you will not send him back to the Union schools!"

"Send him back!" said the doctor contemptuously.

"Nor have him apprenticed?" said Helen, with a laughing light in her eyes.

"Have him ap— Now that's too bad, my dear," cried the doctor. "Danby will laugh at me enough. You need not join in. Poor boy! I'm glad I went up."

There was a pause, during which the doctor sat back in his chair.

"Do you know, my dear, I don't feel very sorry that the young dog went off."

"Not feel sorry, papa!"

"No, my dear. It shows that the young rascal has plenty of energy and spirit and determination."

"I hope you did not tell him so!"

"My dear child, what do you think me?" cried the doctor testily. "By the way, though, he seems to thoroughly see through his companion's character now. I can't help wishing that he had given that confounded young cad a sound thrashing."

"Papa!"

"Eh? No, no: of course not," said the doctor. "I was only thinking aloud."

Helen sat over her work a little longer, feeling happier than she had felt since Dexter left the house; and then the lights were extinguished, and father and daughter went up to bed.

The doctor was very quiet and thoughtful, and he stopped on the stairs.

"Helen, my dear," he whispered, "see the women-servants first thing in the morning, and tell them I strictly forbid any allusion whatever to be made to Dexter's foolish prank."

Helen nodded.

"I'll talk to the men myself," he said. "And whatever you do, make Mrs Millett hold her tongue. Tut—tut—tut! Now, look at that!"

He pointed to a tumbler on a little papier-maché tray standing at Dexter's door.

"Never mind that, dear," said Helen, smiling. "I dare say it is only camomile-tea, and it shows that the poor boy has not lost his place in dear old Millett's heart."

Helen kissed her father, and stopped at her own door feeling half-amused and half-tearful as she saw the old man go on tiptoe to Dexter's room, where, with the light of the candle shining on his silver hair and beard, he tapped gently with his knuckles.

"Asleep, Dexter?"

There was a faint "No, sir!" from within.

"Make haste and go to sleep," said the doctor. "Good-night, my boy. God bless you!"

Helen saw him smile as he turned away from the door, and it may have been fancy, but she thought she saw a glistening as of moisture in one corner of his eye.

"Poor Dexter!" she said softly, as she entered her room, while the boy, as he lay there in the cool, soft sheets, utterly wearied out, but restless and feverish with excitement, felt the doctor's last words send, as it were, a calm, soothing, restful sensation through his brain, and five minutes later he was sleeping soundly, and dreaming that some one bent over him, and said, "Good-night. God bless you!" once again.

Chapter Forty Two
Bob Dimsted's Medicine

It was some time before Dexter could summon up courage to go down to the breakfast-room. That he was expected, he knew, for Mrs Millett had been to his door twice, and said first that breakfast was ready, and, secondly, that master was waiting.

When he did go in, he could hardly believe that he had been away, for there was a kiss from Helen, and a frank "Good morning," and shake of the hand from the doctor, not the slightest allusion being made to the past till breakfast was nearly over, when Maria brought in a note.

"Hah! From Limpney," said the doctor. "I sent Peter on to say that Dexter was back, and that I should like the lessons to be resumed this morning."

Dexter's eyes lit up. The idea of being busy over lessons once more seemed delightful.

"Confound his impudence!" said the doctor angrily, as he ran through the note. "Hark here, Helen: 'Mr Limpney's compliments, and he begs to decline to continue the tuition at Dr Grayson's house.'"

Helen made a gesture, and glanced at her father meaningly —

"Eh? Oh! Ah! Yes, my dear. Well, Dexter, you'll have to amuse yourself in the garden this morning. Go and have a few hours' fishing."

"If you please, sir, I'd rather stay in here if I might, and read."

"No, no, no," said the doctor cheerily. "Fine morning. Get Peter to dig you some worms, and I'll come and look at you presently. It's all right, my boy. We said last night we'd draw a veil over the past, eh? You go and have a good morning's fishing."

Dexter was at his side in a moment, had thrust his hand in the doctor's, and then fled from the room.

"Want to show him we've full confidence in him again. Bah, no! That boy couldn't look you in the face and tell you a lie. My dear Helen, I'm as certain of my theory being correct as of anything in the world. But hang that

Limpney for a narrow-minded, classic-stuffed, mathematic-bristling prig! We'll have a better."

Dexter felt a strange hesitancy; but the doctor evidently wished him to go and fish, so he took his rod, line, and basket, and was crossing the hall when he encountered Mrs Millett.

"It was very nice of you, my dear, and I'm sure it will do you good. You did take it all now, didn't you?"

"Yes, every drop," said Dexter, smiling; and the old lady went away evidently highly gratified.

Old Dan'l was busy tidying up a flower-bed as he reached the lawn, and, to Dexter's astonishment, he nodded and gave him another of his cast-iron smiles.

Further down the garden Peter was at work.

"Dig you up a few worms, Master Dexter? Course I will. Come round to the back of the old frames."

A curious sensation of choking troubled Dexter for a few moments, but it passed off, and in a short time he was furnished with a bag of red worms, and walking down to the river he sat down and began to fish with his mind going back to the night of his running away, and he seemed to see it all again; the undressing, the hesitation, and the cold plunge after his clothes, and all the rest of the miserable dreary time which had proved so different from what he had pictured in his mind.

Peter had said that the fish would "bite like fun at them worms."

But they did not, for they had no chance. The worms crawled round and round the canvas bag, and played at making Gordian knots with each other, while several fish came and looked at the unbaited hook which Dexter offered for their inspection, but preferred to leave the barbed steel alone.

For quite half an hour Dexter sat there dreamily gazing at his float, but seeing nothing but the past, when he started to his feet, for there was a splash in the water close to his feet, the drops flying over him, and there, across the river, grinning and looking very dirty, was Bob Dimsted.

"Yah! Who stole the boat?" he cried.

Dexter flushed up, but he made no reply. Only took out his line, and this time he baited it and threw in again.

"Yah; who stole the boat!" cried Bob again. "I say, ain't he been licked? Ain't his back sore?"

Dexter set his teeth hard and stared at his float, as Bob baited his own line, and threw in just opposite, to begin fishing just as if nothing had happened.

It was a painful position. To go on fishing was like taking up with Bob again; to go away seemed like being afraid.

But Dexter determined upon this last, drew out his line, and was stooping to pick up his basket, when Bob broke into a derisive war-dance—

"Yah, yah!" he cried. "Yer 'bliged to go. Yah! yer miserable, white-faced sneak! g'ome! g'ome! yah!"

Dexter banged down his basket again, and threw in his line with a big splash, as his eyes flashed defiance across the stream.

"Ah! it's all very fine," said Bob; "but yer dussen't do that if it weren't for the river. Why, if I'd got yer here I'd bung both yer eyes up for yer. Yah! yer sneak!"

"Here, you just be off. D'yer hear!" cried an angry voice; and Peter came up, broom in hand.

"She yarn't," cried Bob? "Who are you? This ain't your field. Stop as long as I like. Yah!"

"Wish I was over the other side and I'd pitch you in, you sarcy young vagabond."

"So are you!" cried Bob. "You dussen't touch me. Fish here as long as I like. Pair o' cowards, that's what you are—pair o' cowards. Fight either of yer one hand."

"Wish we was over there," said Peter; "and we'd make you sing another song, my fine fellow."

"Would yer? Yah! who cares for you!"

"Look here, you've no business to come opposite our place to fish!" cried Peter, "so be off!"

"Yah! 'tain't your place. Stop and fish here as long as I like; and if ever I meet him anywheres I'll give him such a licking as'll make him squeal."

"You be off!"

"Shan't."

"Oh, you won't, won't you?" cried a gruff voice; and old Dan'l came from behind a laurustinus clump. "You, Peter—you go and get a basket full o' them brickbats from down by the frames, and we'll soon see whether he'll stop there."

"Yah! go on with your old brickbats. Who cares for you!" cried Bob. "Yah! look at him! Who stole the boat, and cried to go home again? Who stole the boat?"

"Oh, if I could only get across!" said Dexter, in a hoarse low voice.

"Would you give it him if you could!" said old Dan'l, with a grim laugh.

"Yes," said Dexter, between his teeth.

"Ay, he would, Dan'l," said Peter excitedly. "I wish he was over yonder."

"Yah! yah! look at the old caterpillar-killers," cried Bob. "Who stole the boat? Yah!"

These last were farewell shots.

"They won't bite here," cried Bob, moving off, "but don't you think you frightened me away. Come as often as I like. Yah! take him home!"

Dexter's face was scarlet as he watched his departing enemy, thinking the while of his own folly in leaving his friends for such a wretched young cur as that.

"Think he would?" said Peter.

"Ay, two on him," said Dan'l, after glancing cautiously up toward the house.

"Shall us?"

"Ay, if you like, my lad," said Dan'l. "Say, youngster, if we help you acrost will you go and start him outer the west medder?"

"Yes," cried Dexter excitedly.

"All right. Don't make a row."

Old Dan'l went off, and Peter followed, to return in five minutes with a great shallow wooden cistern across the long barrow, old Dan'l looking very grim as he walked by his side, and carrying the familiar clothes-prop.

"There, that's as good as a punt," he said. "Look here! You'd better kneel down on it; I should take off my jacket and weskit, and roll up my sleeves, if I was you."

Dexter's eyes sparkled as he followed this bit of advice, while Dan'l took one end of the cistern, Peter the other, and they gently launched it in the little river.

"Ain't scared of him, are yer!" said Dan'l.

Dexter gave him a sharp look.

"That he ain't," said Peter. "Look here, Master Dexter," he whispered, "don't let him hug you, but give it him right straight out, and he'll be down and howl in two two's."

Dexter made no reply, but stepped into the great shallow punt-like contrivance, seized the prop handed to him, and prepared to use it, but the strong steady thrust given by Peter sent him well on his journey, and in less than a minute he was across.

"Come on, Dan'l," cried Peter. "Don't I wish we was acrost too!"

They crept among the trees at the extreme corner of the garden, where they could hold on by the boughs, and crane their necks over the river, so as to see Dexter tearing along the opposite bank into the next meadow where Bob was fishing, in happy ignorance of the approach of danger; and, to further take off his attention, he had just hooked a good-sized perch, and was playing it, when Dexter, boiling over with the recollection of many injuries culminating in Bob's cowardly lies, came close up and gave a formal announcement of his presence by administering a sounding crack on the ear.

Bob dropped his rod into the river, and nearly jumped after it as he uttered a howl.

"Look at that!" cried Peter, giving one of his legs a slap. "Oh, I wish I was there!"

Bob was as big a coward as ever stepped. So is a rat; but when driven to bay a rat will fight.

Bob was at bay, and he, being in pain, began to fight by lowering his head and rushing at his adversary.

Dexter avoided the onslaught, and gave Bob another crack on the ear.

Then, trusting in his superior size and strength, Bob dashed at Dexter again, and for a full quarter of an hour there was a fierce up and down fight, which was exceedingly blackguardly and reprehensible no doubt, but under the circumstances perfectly natural.

Dexter got a good deal knocked about, especially whenever Bob closed with him; but he did not get knocked about for nothing. Very soon there were a number of unpleasant ruddy stains upon his clean white shirt, but the blood was Bob's, and consequent upon a sensation of his nose being knocked all on one side.

There was a tooth out—a very white one on the grass, but that tooth was Bob's, and, in addition, that young gentleman's eyes wore the aspect of his having been interviewing a wasps' nest, for they were rapidly closing up, and his whole face assuming the appearance of a very large and puffy unbaked bun.

Then there was a cessation of the up and down fighting; Bob was lying on his back howling after his customary canine fashion, and Dexter was standing over him with his doubled fists, his face flushed, his eyes flashing, teeth set, and his curly hair shining in the sun.

"It's splendid, Dan'l, old man," cried Peter, slapping his fellow-servant on the back. "I wouldn't ha' missed it for half a crown."

"No," said Dan'l. "Hang him! he's got some pluck in him if he ain't got no breed. Brayvo, young un! I never liked yer half—"

Dan'l stopped short, and Peter stepped back against the dividing fence.

"Beg pardon, sir?"

"I said how did that boy get across the river!" said the doctor sternly.

There was no reply.

"Now no subterfuges," said the doctor sharply.

Peter looked at Dan'l in dismay, but Dan'l spoke out—

"Well, sir, beg pardon, sir, that young cub come up to the side abusing Master Dexter, and calling him names, and he let us have it too."

"Yes; go on."

"Well, sir, Master Dexter was a-chafing like a greyhound again his collar, and Peter and me fetched the old wooden cistern, and let him punt hisself across, and the way he went into him, sir—boy half as big again as hisself, and—"

"That will do," said the doctor sternly. "Here, Dexter! Come here, sir!"

Dexter turned in dismay, and came faltering back.

"The moment he is home again!" said the doctor angrily.

"Yah! Coward! G'ome, g'ome!" yelled Bob, jumping up on seeing his enemy in retreat. "Come here again and I'll knock yer silly. Yah!"

"Dexter!" roared the doctor; "go back and knock that young blackguard's head off. Quick! Give it him! No mercy!"

Dexter flew back, but Bob flew faster to the hedge, where he leaped and stuck; Dexter overtaking him then, and administering one punch which drove his adversary through, and he got up and ran on again.

"Hi! Dexter!" shouted the doctor; and the boy returned slowly, as Peter stood screwing up his face to look serious, and Dan'l gave his master one of his cast-iron smiles.

"Well, yes, Dan'l, it was excusable under the circumstances," said the doctor. "But I do not approve of fighting, and—er—don't say anything about it indoors."

"No, sir, cert'nly not, sir," said the men, in a breath; and just then Dexter stood on the far bank looking anxiously across.

"Mind how you come," cried the doctor. "That's right; be careful. Give me your hand. Bless my soul! the skin's off your knuckles. We shall have to tell Miss Grayson after all."

Dexter looked up at him wildly. He could not speak.

"Better put that cistern back," said the doctor quickly; and then to Dexter—

"There, slip on your things, and go up to your room and bathe your face and hands. No, stop! I'll go on first, and shut the drawing-room door."

The doctor hurried away, and as soon as he was out of sight, Dexter, who had slowly put on his waistcoat and jacket, gazed disconsolately at the two men.

"What shall I do?" he said dolefully.

"Do!" cried Peter; "why, you did it splendid: he won't come no more."

"But the doctor!" faltered Dexter, with the spirit and effervescence all gone.

"What, master!" cried Dan'l. "He won't say no more. Here, shake hands, my lad. It was fine."

"Hi! Dexter! Here, my boy, quick!" came the doctor's voice. "It's all right. She has gone out."

"There!" said Dan'l, laughing; and Dexter ran in.

Chapter Forty Three
The Right Place for a Backward Boy

"Where's Dexter?" said the doctor.

"Down the garden," said Helen.

"Humph! Hope he is not getting into fresh mischief."

"I hope not, papa," said Helen; "and really I think he is trying very hard."

"Yes," said the doctor, going on with his writing. "How are his knuckles now? can he hold a pen?"

"I think I would let him wait another day or two. And, papa, have you given him a good talking to about that fight?"

"No. Have you?"

"Yes, two or three times; and he has promised never to fight again."

"My dear Helen, how can you be so absurd?" cried the doctor testily. "That's just the way with a woman. You ask the boy to promise what he cannot perform. He is sure to get fighting again at school or somewhere."

"But it seems such a pity, papa."

"Pooh! pish! pooh! tchah!" ejaculated the doctor, at intervals. "He gave that young scoundrel a good thrashing, and quite right too. Don't tell him I said so."

The doctor had laid down his pen to speak, but he took it up again and began writing, but only to lay it aside once more.

"Dear me! dear me!" he muttered. "I don't seem to get on with my book as I should like."

He put down his pen again, rose, took a turn or two up and down the room, and then picked up the newspaper.

"Very awkward of that stupid fellow Limpney," he said, as he began running down the advertisements.

"What did he say, papa, when you spoke to him?"

"Say? Lot of stuff about losing *prestige* with his other pupils. Was sure Lady Danby did not like him to be teaching a boy of Dexter's class and her son. Confound his impudence! Must have a tutor for the boy of some kind."

Helen glanced uneasily at her father, and then out into the garden.

"Plenty of schools; plenty of private tutors," muttered the doctor scanning the advertisements. "Hah!"

"What is it, papa!"

The doctor struck the paper in the middle, doubled it up, and then frowned severely as he thrust his gold spectacles up on to his forehead.

"I've made a mistake, my dear,—a great mistake."

"About Dexter!"

"Yes: a very great mistake."

"But I'm sure he will improve," said Helen anxiously.

"So am I, my dear. But our mistake is this: we took the boy from the Union schools, and we kept him here at once, where every one knew him and his late position. We ought to have sent him away for two or three years, and he would have come back completely changed, and the past history forgotten."

"Sent him to a boarding-school!"

"Well—er! Hum! No, not exactly," said the doctor, pursing up his lips. "Listen here, my dear. The very thing! just as if fate had come to my help."

The doctor rustled the paper a little, and then began to read—

"'Backward and disobedient boys.'"

"But Dexter—"

"Hush, my dear; hear it all. Dexter is backward, and he is disobedient; not wilfully perhaps, but disobedient decidedly. Now listen—

"'Backward and disobedient boys.—The Reverend Septimus Mastrum, MA Oxon, receives a limited number of pupils of neglected education. Firm and kindly treatment. Extensive grounds. Healthy situation. For terms apply to the Reverend Septimus Mastrum, Firlands, Longspruce Station.'"

"There! What do you say to that?" said the doctor.

"I don't know what to say, papa," said Helen rather sadly. "Perhaps you are right."

"Right!" cried the doctor. "The very thing, my dear. I'll write to Mr Mastrum at once. Three or four years of special education will be the making of the boy." The doctor sat down and wrote.

The answer resulted in a meeting in London, where the Reverend Septimus Mastrum greatly impressed the doctor. Terms were agreed upon, and the doctor came back.

"Splendid fellow, my dear. Six feet high. Says Mrs Mastrum will act the part of a mother to the boy."

"Does he seem very severe, papa?"

"Severe, my dear? Man with a perpetual smile on his countenance."

"I do not like men with perpetual smiles on their countenances, papa."

"My dear Helen, do not be so prejudiced," said the doctor angrily. "I have seen Mr Mastrum: you have not. I have told him everything about Dexter; he applauds my plan, and assures me that in two or three years I shall hardly know the boy, he will be so improved." Helen sighed.

"We had a long discussion about my book, and he agrees that I am quite right. So pray do not begin to throw obstacles in the way."

Helen rose and kissed her father's forehead.

"I am going to do everything I can to aid your plans, papa," she said, smiling. "Of course I do not like parting with Dexter, and I cannot help feeling that there is some truth in what you say about a change being beneficial for a time; but Dexter is a peculiar boy, and I would rather have had him under my own eye."

"Yes, of course, my dear. Very good of you," said the doctor; "but this way is the best. Of course he will have holidays, and we shall go to see him, and so on."

"When is he to go, papa?"

"Directly."

"Directly?"

"Well, in a day or two."

Helen was silent for a moment or two, and then she moved toward the door.

"Where are you going!" said the doctor sharply.

"To make preparations, and warn Mrs Millett. He must have a good box of clothes and linen."

"To be sure, of course," said the doctor. "Get whatever is necessary. It is the right thing, my dear, and the boy shall go at once."

The doctor was so energetic and determined that matters progressed very rapidly, and the clothes and other necessaries increased at such a rate in Dexter's room that most boys would have been in a state of intense excitement.

Dexter was not, and he avoided the house as much as he could, spending a great deal of time in the garden and stables.

"So they're going to send you off to school, eh, Master Dexter?" said Peter, pausing to rest on his broom-handle.

"Yes, Peter."

"And you don't want to go? No wonder! I never liked school. Never had much on it, neither; but I know all I want."

"Hullo!" said a voice behind them; and, turning, Dexter saw Dan'l standing behind him, with the first dawn of a smile, on his face.

Dexter nodded, and began to move away.

"So you're going off, are yer!" said Dan'l. "Two floggings a day for a year. You're in for it, youngster."

"Get out," said Dexter. "They don't flog boys at good schools."

"Oh, don't they?" said Dan'l. "You'll see. Well, never mind! And, look here, I'll ask master to let me send you a basket o' apples and pears when they're ripe."

"You will, Dan'l!" cried Dexter excitedly.

"Ay: Peter and me'll do you up a basket, and take it to the station. Be a good boy, and no more Bob Dimsted's."

Dan'l chuckled as if he had said something very funny, and walked away.

"Here, don't look dumpy about it, my lad," said Peter kindly. "'Tain't for ever and a day."

"No, Peter," said Dexter gloomily, "it isn't for ever."

"Sorry you're going, though, my lad."

"Are you, Peter!"

"Am I? Course I am. A man can't help liking a boy as can fight like you."

Matters were growing harder for Dexter indoors now that his departure was so near. Mrs Millett was particularly anxious about him; and so sure as the boy went up to his room in the middle of the day, it was to find the old housekeeper on her knees, and her spectacles carefully balanced, trying all his buttons to see if they were fast.

"Now I'm going to put you up two bottles of camomile tea, and pack them in the bottom of your box, with an old coffee-cup without a handle. It just holds the right quantity, and you'll promise me, won't you, Master Dexter, to take a dose regularly twice a week!"

"Yes; I'll promise you," said Dexter.

"Now, that's a good boy," cried the old lady, getting up and patting his shoulder. "Look here," she continued, leading him to the box by the drawers, "I've put something else in as well."

She lifted up a layer of linen, all scented with lavender, and showed him a flat, round, brown-paper parcel.

"It's not a very rich cake," she said, "but there are plenty of currants and peel in, and I'm sure it's wholesome."

Even Maria became very much interested in Master Dexter's boots and shoes, and the parting from the doctor's house for the second time promised to be very hard.

It grew harder as the time approached, for, with the gentleness of an elder sister, Helen exercised plenty of supervision over the preparation. Books, a little well-filled writing-case and a purse, were among the things she added.

"The writing-case is for me, Dexter," she said, with a smile.

"For you?" he said wonderingly.

"Yes, so that I may have, at least, two letters from you every week. You promise that?"

"Oh yes," he said, "if you will not mind the writing."

"And the purse is for you," she said. "If you want a little more money than papa is going to allow you weekly, you may write and ask me."

It grew harder still on the morning of departure, and Dexter would have given anything to stay, but he went off manfully with the doctor in the station fly, passing Sir James Danby and Master Edgar on the road.

"Humph!" grunted the doctor. "See that, Dexter!"

"I saw Sir James laugh at you when he nodded."

"Do you know why!"

Dexter was silent for a few minutes.

"Because he thinks you are foolish to take so much trouble over me."

"That's it, Dexter," said the doctor eagerly. "So, now, I'll tell you what I want you to do."

"Yes, sir?"

"Show him that I'm right and he's wrong." Dexter looked a promise, for he could not speak just then, nor yet when they had passed through London that afternoon, reached Longspruce station, and been driven to the Reverend Septimus Mastrum's house, five miles away among the fir-trees and sand of that bleak region.

Here the doctor bade him "Good-bye," and Dexter, as he was standing in the great cold hall, felt that he was commencing a new phase in his existence.

Chapter Forty Four
Peter Cribb sees a Ghost

Helen rang the bell one evening and Maria answered the summons.

"Papa thinks he would like a little supper, Maria, as we dined early today. Bring up a tray. There is a cold chicken, I think!"

"Yes, 'm," said Maria, and disappeared, but was back in a few minutes.

"If you please, 'm, Mrs Millett says there is no cold chicken, 'm."

"Indeed?" said Helen wonderingly. "Very well, then, the cold veal pie."

"Yes, 'm."

Maria disappeared, and came back again. "Please, 'm, Mrs Millett says there is no veal pie."

"Then tell her to make an omelette."

"Yes, 'm." Maria left the room and came back. "Please, 'm, Mrs Millett says there's no eggs, and it's too late to get any more."

"Ask Mrs Millett to come here," said Helen; and the old lady came up, looking very red.

"Why, Millett," said Helen, "this is very strange. I don't like to find fault, but surely there ought to have been a chicken left."

"I'm very glad you have found fault, Miss," said Mrs Millett, "for it's given me a chance to speak. Yes; there ought to have been a chicken, and the veal pie too; but I'm very sorry to say, Miss, they're gone."

"Gone?"

"Yes, Miss. I don't know how to account for it, but the things have begun to go in the most dreadful way. Bread, butter, milk, eggs, meat, everything goes, and we've all been trying to find out how, but it's no good."

"This is very strange, Millett. Have you no idea how it is they go?"

"No, Miss; but Dan'l fancies it must be that rough boy who led Master Dexter away. He says he's sure he caught sight of him in the dark last night.

Somebody must take the things, and he seems to be the most likely, knowing the place as he does."

"This must be seen to," said Helen; and she told the doctor. Consequently a watch was kept by the gardener and the groom, but they found nothing, and the contents of the larder continued to disappear.

"If it were a man," said the doctor, on being told of what was going on, "I'd set the police to work, but I hate anything of that kind with a boy. Wait a bit, and he will get more impudent from obtaining these things with impunity, and then he will be more easily caught."

"And then, papa?" said Helen.

"Then, my dear? Do you know that thin Malacca cane in the hall? Yes, you do. Well, my dear, the law says it is an assault to thrash a boy, and that he ought to be left to the law to punish, which means prison and degradation. I'm going to take that cane, my dear, and defy the law."

But somehow or another Master Bob Dimsted seemed to be as slippery as an eel. He saw Peter one day and grinned at him from the other side of the river. Two days later he was seen by Dan'l, who shook his fist at him, and Bob said—

"Yah!"

"Have you heard from Master Dexter, Miss!" said Mrs Millett one morning.

"No, Millett, and I am rather surprised. He promised so faithfully to write."

"Ah, yes, Miss," said the old lady; "and he meant it, poor boy, when he promised, but boys are such one's to forget."

Helen went into the library where she found the doctor biting the end of his pen, and gazing up into a corner of the room.

"I don't seem to be getting on as I could wish, my dear. By the way, we haven't heard from that young dog lately. He promised me faithfully to write regularly."

Helen thought of Mrs Millett's words, but said nothing, and at that moment Maria entered with the letters.

"From Dexter?" said Helen eagerly.

"Humph! No! But from Longspruce! I see: from Mr Mastrum."

The doctor read the letter and frowned.

Helen read it, and the tears stood in her eyes.

"The young scoun—"

"Stop, papa!" said Helen earnestly. "Do not condemn him unheard."

"Then I shall have to go on without condemning him, for we've seen the last of him, I suppose."

"O papa!"

"Well, it looks like it, my dear; and I'm afraid I've made a great mistake, but I don't like to own it."

"Wait, papa, wait!" said Helen.

"What does he say? Been gone a fortnight, and would not write till he had had the country round thoroughly searched. Humph! Afraid he has got to Portsmouth, and gone to sea."

Helen sighed.

"'Sorry to give so bad an account of him,'" muttered the doctor, reading bits of the letter—"'treated him as his own son—seemed to have an undercurrent of evil in his nature, impossible to eradicate—tried everything, but all in vain—was beginning to despair, but still hopeful that patience might overcome the difficulty—patience combined with affectionate treatment, but it was in vain—after trying to persuade his fellow-pupils one by one, and failing, he threatened them savagely if they dared to betray him, and then he escaped from the grounds, and has not been seen since.'"

There was a painful silence in the doctor's library for a few minutes.

"'Patience combined with affectionate treatment,'" read the doctor again. "Helen, I believe that man has beaten and ill-used poor Dexter till he could bear it no longer, and has run away."

"I'm sure of it, papa," cried Helen excitedly. "Do you think he will come back!"

"I don't know," said the doctor. "Yes, I do. No; he would be afraid. I'd give something to know how to go to work to find him."

"If you please, sir, may I come in?" said a pleasant soft voice.

"Yes, yes, Millett, of course. What is it?"

"Dan'l has been to say, sir, that he caught sight of that boy, Bob Dimsted, crawling in the garden last night when it was dark, and chased him, but the boy climbed one of the trained pear-trees, got on the wall, and escaped."

"Confound the young rascal!" cried the doctor.

"And I'm sorry to say, sir, that two blankets have been stolen off Master Dexter's bed."

There was a week of watching, but Bob Dimsted was not caught, and the doctor sternly said that he would not place the matter in the hands of the police. But all the same the little pilferings went on, and Mrs Millett came one morning, with tears in her eyes, to say that she couldn't bear it any longer, for only last night a whole quartern loaf had been taken through the larder bars, and, with it, one of the large white jars of black-currant jam.

Mrs Millett was consoled with the promise that the culprit should soon be caught, and two nights later Peter came in to announce to the doctor that he had been so near catching Bob Dimsted that he had touched him as he chased him down the garden, and that he would have caught him, only that, without a moment's hesitation, the boy had jumped into the river and swum across, and so escaped to the other side.

"Next time I mean to have him," said Peter confidently, and this he repeated to Mrs Millett and Maria, being rewarded with a basin of the tea which had just come down from the drawing-room.

It was just two days later that, as Helen sat with her work under the old oak-tree in the garden—an old evergreen oak which gave a pleasant shade—she became aware of a faint rustling sound.

She looked up, but could see nothing, though directly after there was a peculiar noise in the tree, which resembled the chopping of wood.

Still she could see nothing, and she had just resumed her work, thinking the while that Dexter would some day write, and that her father's correspondence with the Reverend Septimus Mastrum had not been very satisfactory, when there was a slight scratching sound.

She turned quickly and saw that a ragged-looking squirrel had run down the grey trunk of the tree, while, as soon as it saw her, it bounded off, and to her surprise passed through the gateway leading into the yard where the old stable stood.

Helen Grayson hardly knew why she did so, but she rose and followed the squirrel, to find that she was not alone, for Peter the groom was in the yard going on tiptoe toward the open door of the old range of buildings.

He touched his cap on seeing her.

"Squir'l, Miss," he said. "Just run in here."

"I saw it just now," said Helen. "Don't kill the poor thing."

"Oh no, Miss; I won't kill it," said Peter, as Helen went back into the garden. "But I mean to catch it if I can."

Peter went into the dark old building and looked round, but there was no sign of the squirrel. Still a little animal like that would be sure to go upwards, so Peter climbed the half-rotten ladder, and stood in the long dark range of lofts, peering among the rafters and ties in search of the bushy-tailed little creature.

He walked to the end in one direction, then in the other, till he was stopped by an old boarded partition, in which there was a door which had been nailed up; but he remembered that this had a flight of steps, or rather a broad-stepped old wood ladder, on the other side, leading to a narrower loft right in the gable.

"Wonder where it can be got," said Peter to himself; and then he turned round, ran along the loft, dropped down through the trap-door, and nearly slipped and fell, so hurried was his flight.

Half-across the yard he came upon Dan'l wheeling a barrow full of mould for potting.

"Hallo! what's the matter?"

Peter gasped and panted, but said nothing.

"Haven't seen a ghost, have you?" said Dan'l.

"Ye–es. No," panted Peter.

"Why, you white-faced, cowardly noodle!" cried Dan'l. "What d'yer mean?"

"I—I. Come out of here into the garden," whispered Peter.

Dan'l was going down the garden to the potting-shed, so he made no objection, and, arrived there, Peter, with solemn emphasis, told how he had gone in search of the squirrel, and that there was something up in the loft.

"Yes," said old Dan'l contemptuously—"rats."

"Yes; I know that," said Peter excitedly; and his eyes looked wild and dilated; "but there's something else."

Dan'l put down the barrow, and sat upon the soft mould as he gave his rough stubbly chin a rub.

"Lookye here, Peter," he said; "did yer ever hear tell about ghosts being in old buildings?"

"Yes," said Peter, with an involuntary shiver, and a glance across the wall at a corroded weathercock on the top of the ancient place.

"Well, my lad, ghosts never comes out in the day-time: only o' nights; and do you know what they are?"

Peter shook his head.

"Well, then, my lad, I'll tell you. I've sin several in my time. Them as you hears and don't see's rats; and them as you sees and don't hear's howls. What d'yer think o' that?"

"It wasn't a rat, nor it wasn't a howl, as I see," said Peter solemnly; "but something gashly horrid, as looked down at me from up in the rafters of that there dark place, and it made me feel that bad that I didn't seem to have no legs to stand on."

"Tchah!" cried the gardener. "What yer talking about?"

"Anything the matter?" said the doctor, who had come up unheard over the velvety lawn.

"Hush!" whispered Peter imploringly.

"Shan't hush. Sarves you right," growled Dan'l. "Here's Peter, sir, just seen a ghost."

"Ah! has he?" said the doctor. "Where did you see it, Peter?"

"I didn't say it were a ghost, sir, I only said as I see something horrid up at end of the old loft when I went up there just now after a squir'l."

"Squirrel!" said the doctor angrily. "What are you talking about, man? Squirrels live in trees, not in old lofts. You mean a rat."

"I know a squir'l when I see one, sir," said Peter; "and I see one go 'crost the yard and into that old stable."

"Nonsense!" said the doctor.

"Did you find it, Peter!" said Helen from under the tree.

"Find what?" said the doctor.

"A squirrel that ran from here across the yard."

Peter looked from one to the other triumphantly, as he said—

"No, Miss, I didn't."

"Humph!" grunted the doctor. "Then there was a squirrel!"

"Yes, sir."

"And you saw something strange!"

"Yes, sir, something awful gashly, in the dark end, sir."

"Bah!" cried the doctor. "There, go and get your stable lanthorn and we'll see. Helen, my dear, we've got a ghost in the old stable loft: like to come and see it!"

"Very much, papa," said Helen, smiling in a way that put Peter on his mettle, for the moment before he had been ready to beg off.

He went pretty quickly to get his stable lanthorn, and came back with it alight, and looking very pale and sickly, while he bore a stout broomstick in the other hand.

"For shame, man! Put away that absurd thing," said the doctor, as he led the way through the gate in the wall, followed by Helen, Peter and Dan'l coming behind.

"Go first with the lanthorn," said the doctor to the old gardener, but Peter was stirred to action now.

"Mayn't I go first, sir!" he said.

"Oh yes, if you have enough courage," said the doctor; and Peter, looking very white, led the way to the foot of the ladder, went up, and the others followed him to the loft, and stood together on the old worm-eaten boards.

The lanthorn cast a yellow glow through its horn sides, and this, mingling with the faint pencils of daylight which came between the tiles, gave a very peculiar look to the place, festooned as the blackened beams were with cobwebs, which formed loops and pockets here and there.

"There's an old door at the extreme end there, or ought to be," said the doctor. "Go and open it."

Peter went on in advance.

"Mind the holes, my dear," said the doctor. "What's that?"

A curious rustling noise was heard, and, active as a young man, Dan'l ran back to the top of the ladder and descended quickly.

"Well 'tain't me as is skeart now," said Peter triumphantly.

Just then there was a sharp clap from somewhere in front, as if a small trap-door had been suddenly closed, and Dan'l's voice came up through the boards.

"Look out!" he shouted, and his voice sounded distant. "There's some one up in the far loft there. He tried to get down into one of the hay-racks, but I frightened him back."

"Stop there!" said the doctor. "We'll soon see who it is. Go on, Peter, and open that door. That young larder thief for a guinea, my dear," he continued to Helen, as Peter went on in advance.

"Door's nailed up, sir," said the latter worthy, as he reached the old door, and held the lanthorn up and down.

"How came it nailed up?" said the doctor, as he examined the place. "It has no business to be. Go and get an iron chisel or a crowbar. Are you there, Daniel?"

"Yes, sir," came from below. "I'm on the look-out. It's that there young poacher chap, Bob Dimsted."

Peter set the lanthorn on the floor and hurried off, leaving the little party watching and listening till he returned, but not a sound broke the silence, and there was nothing to see but the old worm-eaten wood and blackened tiles.

"I've brought both, sir," said Peter breathlessly, and all eagerness now, for he was ashamed of his fright.

"Wrench it open, then," said the doctor; and after a few sharp cracks the rotten old door gave way, and swung upon its rusty hinges, when a strange sight met the eyes of those who pressed forward into the further loft.

Chapter Forty Five
A Startling Discovery

The rough loft had been turned into a kind of dwelling-place, for there was a bed close under the tiles, composed of hay, upon which, neatly spread, were a couple of blankets. On the other side were a plate, a knife, a piece of bread, and a jam-pot, while in the centre were some rough boxes and an old cage, on the top of which sat the ragged squirrel.

"There," said Peter triumphantly, as he pointed to the squirrel.

The doctor was looking eagerly round in search of the dweller in this dismal loft, but there was no one visible.

"Found him, sir?" came from below.

"No, not yet," replied the doctor. "Here, Peter, go up that other place."

There was no hesitation on the groom's part now. He sprang up the second ladder and went along under the roof, but only to come back shaking his head.

"No one up there, sir."

"Are you sure he did not come down!" cried the doctor, as Peter lifted a rough trap at the side, through which, in bygone days, the horses' hay had been thrust down.

"Quite sure, sir," shouted back Dan'l. "I just see his legs coming down, and he snatched 'em up again, and slammed the trap."

"The young rascal!" said the doctor; "he's here somewhere. There must be some loose boards under which he is hidden."

But there was not a loose board big enough to hide Bob Dimsted; and after another search the doctor rubbed his head in a perplexed manner.

"Shall I come up, sir, and have a look?" said Dan'l.

"No, no. Stay where you are, and keep a sharp look-out," cried the doctor. "Why, look here," he continued to Helen; "the young scoundrel has been leading a nice life here, like a Robinson Crusoe in an uninhabited island. Ah! at last!" shouted the doctor, staring straight before him; "there he is. Here, Peter, hand me the gun!"

Peter stared at his master, whose eyes twinkled with satisfaction, for his feint had had the desired effect—that of startling the hiding intruder.

As the doctor's words rang out there was a strange rustling sound overhead; and, as they all looked up, there came a loud crack, then another and another, and right up, nearly to the ridge of the roof, a leg came through, and then its fellow, in company with a shower of broken tiles, which rattled upon the rough floor of the loft.

The owner of the legs began to make a desperate effort to withdraw them, and they kicked about in a variety of peculiar evolutions; but before they could be extricated, Peter had climbed up to an oaken beam, which formed one of the roof ties, and from there reached out and seized one of the legs by the ankle.

"I've got him," he cried gleefully. "Which shall we do, sir—pull him through, or get the ladder up to the roof and drag him out?"

"Here, Daniel! Come up," said the doctor.

The old gardener came up eagerly; and one of his cast-iron grins expanded his face as he grasped the situation.

"Brayvo, Peter!" he cried. "That's the way to ketch a ghost. Hold him tight, lad!"

The doctor smiled.

"Don't let them hurt him, papa," whispered Helen.

"Oh no; they shall not hurt him," said the doctor quietly. Then, raising his voice—"Now, sir, will you come down quietly, or shall I send for the police to drag you out on to the roof?"

An indistinct murmur came down, after a vigorous struggle to get free.

"Woho! Woho, kicker!" cried Peter, speaking as if to a horse.

"What does he say!" said the doctor.

"Says he'll come down if I'll let go."

"Don't you trust him, sir," cried Dan'l excitedly.

"I do not mean to," said the doctor. "Will you come down quietly?" he shouted.

There was another murmur.

"Says '*yes*,' sir," cried Peter.

"Then, look here," said the doctor, "you hold him tight, and you," he continued to the gardener, "climb up on that beam and push off a few tiles. Then you can draw him down through there."

"All right, sir," cried Dan'l; and as Peter held on to the leg, the old gardener, after a good deal of grunting and grumbling, climbed to his side, and began to let in daylight by thrusting off tile after tile, which slid rattling down the side of the roof into the leaden guttering.

The opening let in so much daylight that the appearance of the old loft was quite transformed, but the group on the worm-eaten beam was the principal object of attention till just as Dan'l thrust off the fourth tile, when there was a loud crack, a crash, and gardener, groom, and their prisoner lay in a heap on the floor of the loft, while pieces of lath and tile rattled about their heads.

The old tie had given way, and they came down with a rush, to the intense astonishment of all; but the distance to fall was only about five feet, and the wonder connected with the fall was as nothing to that felt by Helen and her father, as the smallest figure of the trio struggled to his feet, and revealed the dusty, soot-smeared face of Dexter, with his eyes staring wildly from the Doctor to Helen and back again.

"Dexter!" cried Helen.

"You, sir!" cried the doctor.

"Well, I *ham*!" ejaculated Peter, getting up and giving his thigh a slap.

Dan'l sat on the floor rubbing his back, and he uttered a grunt as his face expanded till he displayed all his front teeth—a dismal array of four, and not worth a bite.

"Are you hurt?" cried Helen.

Dexter shook his head.

"Are either of you hurt?" said the doctor frowning.

"Screwed my off fetlock a bit, sir," said Peter, stooping to feel his right ankle.

"Hurt?" growled Dan'l. "Well, sir, them's 'bout the hardest boards as ever I felt."

"Go and ask Mrs Millett to give you both some ale," said the doctor; and the two men smiled as they heard their master's prescription. "Then go on and tell the builder to come and patch up this old roof. Here, Dexter, come in."

Dexter gave Peter a reproachful look, and limped after the doctor.

"Well, let's go and have that glass o' beer Peter," said Dan'l. "Talk about pickles!"

"My!" said Peter, slapping his leg again. "Why, it were him we see every night, and as swum across the river. Why, he must ha' swum back when I'd gone. I say, Dan'l, what a game!"

"Hah!" ejaculated the old gardener, wiping his mouth in anticipation. "It's my b'lief, Peter, as that there boy'll turn out either a reg'lar good un, or 'bout the wust as ever stepped."

"Now, sir!" said the doctor, as he closed the door of the library, and then with a stern look at the grimy object before him took a seat opposite Helen. "What have you to say for yourself!"

Dexter glanced at Helen, who would not meet his gaze.

"Nothing, sir."

"Oh, you have nothing to say! Let me see, now. You were sent to a good school to be taught by a gentleman, and treated as a special pupil. You behaved badly. You ran away. You came here and made yourself a den; you have been living by plunder ever since, and you have nothing to say!"

Dexter was silent, but his face was working, his lips quivering, and his throat seemed to swell as his breath came thick and fast.

At last his words came in a passionate appeal, but in a broken, disjointed way; and it seemed as if the memory of all he had suffered roused his nature into a passionate fit of indignation against the author of all the trouble.

"I—I couldn't bear it," he cried; "I tried so hard—so cruel—said he was to break my spirit—that I was bad—he beat me—seven times—I did try— you wanted me to—Miss Grayson wanted me to—I was always trying— punished me because—so stupid—but I tried—I took a bit of candle—I was trying to learn the piece—the other boys were asleep—he came up—he caned me till I—till I couldn't bear it—break my spirit—he said he'd break it—I dropped from the window—fell down and sprained my ankle—but I walked—back here—then I was—afraid to tell you, and I hid up there."

There were no tears save in the boy's voice; but there was a ring of passionate agony and suffering in every tone and utterance; and, as Helen read in the gaunt figure, hollow eyes, and pallor of the cheeks what the boy must have gone through, she turned in her chair, laid her arm on the back, her face went down upon it, and the tears came fast.

The doctor was silent as the boy went on; his lips were compressed and his brow rugged; but he did not speak, till, with wondering eyes, he saw Dexter turn, go painfully toward where Helen sat with averted face, look at her as if he wanted to speak, but the words would not come, and, with a sigh, he limped toward the door.

"Where are you going, sir!" said the doctor roughly.

"Up there, sir," said Dexter, in a low-toned weary voice, which sounded as if all the spirit had gone.

"Up there!" cried the doctor.

"Yes," said Dexter feebly; and without turning round — "to Mr Hippetts, and to Mr Sibery, sir. To take me back. It's no good. I did try so — hard — so hard — but I never had — no mother — no father — not like — other boys — and — and — "

He looked wildly round, clutching at vacancy, and then reeled and fell heavily upon the carpet.

For Mr Mastrum had done his work well. His system for breaking the spirit of unruly boys, and making them perfectly tame, seemed to have reached perfection.

With a cry of horror Helen Grayson sprang from her seat, and sank upon her knees by Dexter's side, to catch his head to her breast, while the doctor tore at the bell.

"Bring brandy — water, quick!" he said; "the boy has fainted."

It was quite true, and an hour elapsed before he looked wildly round at those about him.

He tried to rise, and struggled feebly. Then as they held him back he began to talk in a rapid disconnected way.

"'Bliged to take it — so hungry — yes, sir — please, sir — I've come back, sir — come back, Mr Sibery, sir — if Mr Hippetts will let me stay — where's Mother Curdley — where's nurse!"

"O father!" whispered Helen excitedly! "Poor, poor boy! what does this mean?"

"Fever," said the doctor gently, as he laid his hand upon the boy's burning forehead and looked down in his wild eyes. "Yes," he said softly, "fever. He must have suffered terribly to have been brought to this."

Chapter Forty Six
Fever works Wonders

Doctor Grayson's book stood still.

For many years past he had given up the practice of medicine, beyond writing out a prescription for his daughter or servants, but he called in the services of no other medical man for poor Dexter.

"No, my dear," he said. "It is my fault entirely that the boy is in this state, and if such knowledge as I possess can save him, he shall come down hale and strong once more."

So Dexter had the constant attention of a clever physician and two nurses, who watched by him night and day, the doctor often taking his turn to relieve Helen or Mrs Millett, so that a little rest might be theirs.

And all through that weary time, while the fever was culminating, those who watched learned more of the poor fellow's sufferings at the scholastic establishment, during his flight, when he toiled homeward with an injured foot, and afterwards when he had taken possession of his old den, and often nearly starved there, in company with his squirrel—his old friend whom he found established in the loft, whence it sallied forth in search of food, as its master was obliged to do in turn.

One night Helen went up to relieve Mrs Millett, and found Maria leaning against the door outside, crying silently, and this impressed her the more, from the fact that Peter and Dan'l had each been to the house three times that day to ask how Master Dexter was.

Maria hurried away, and Helen entered, to find old Mrs Millett standing by the bedside, holding one of the patient's thin white hands, and watching him earnestly.

"Don't say he's worse," whispered Helen.

"Hush, my dear," whispered the old woman. "Ring, please, Miss; master said I was to if I saw any change."

Helen glided to the bell, and then ran back to the bed, to stand trembling with her hands clasped, and her eyes tearless now.

The doctor's step was heard upon the stairs, and he entered breathlessly, and without a word crossed to the bed, to bend down over the sufferer as he held his wrist.

The silence in that room was terrible to two of the inmates, and the suspense seemed to be drawn out until it was almost more than could be borne.

At last the doctor turned away, and sank exhausted in a chair; and as Helen caught his hand in hers, and questioned him with her eyes, he said in a low and reverent voice—

"Yes, Helen, our prayers have been heard. Poor fellow! he will live."

Chapter Forty Seven
Convalescence

"Get out," said Dan'l, some weeks later. "Tired? Why, I could pull this here inv'lid-chair about the garden all day, my lad, and not know it."

"But why not rest under one of the trees for a bit?" said Dexter.

"'Cause I don't want to rest; and if I did, it might give you a chill. Why, you're light as light, and this is nothing to the big roller."

"I'm afraid I'm a great deal of trouble to you all," said Dexter, as he sat back, supported by a pillow, and looking very white, while from time to time he raised a bunch of Dan'l's choicest flowers to his nose.

"Trouble? Tchah! And, look here! master said you was to have as much fruit as you liked. When'll you have another bunch o' grapes!"

"Oh, not yet," said Dexter smiling, and he looked at the grim face of the old gardener, who walked slowly backwards as he drew the chair.

"Well, look here," said Dan'l, after a pause. "You can do as you like, but you take my advice. Peter's gone 'most off his head since master said as you might go out for a drive in a day or two; but don't you be in no hurry. I can draw you about here, where it's all nice and warm and sheltered, and what I say is this: if you can find a better place for a inv'lid to get strong in than my garden, I should like to see it. Humph! There's Missus Millett working her arms about like a mad windmill. Got some more jelly or blammondge for you, I s'pose. Lookye here, Master Dexter, just you pitch that sorter thing over, and take to beef underdone with the gravy in it. That'll set you up better than jelleries and slops."

Dan'l was right. Mrs Millett was waiting with a cup of calves'-feet jelly; and Maria had brought out a rug, because it seemed to be turning cold.

Two days later Dan'l was called away to visit a sick relative, and Peter's face was red with pleasure as he brought the invalid chair up to the door after lunch, and helped deposit the convalescent in his place, Helen and the doctor superintending, and Mrs Millett giving additional orders, as Maria formed herself into a flesh and blood crutch.

"There, Dexter," said the doctor; "we shall be back before it's time for you to come in."

He nodded, and Helen bent down and kissed the boy. Then there was the crushing of the wheels on the firm gravel, and Dexter lay back breathing in health.

"Thought I was never going to have a pull at the chair, Mas' Dexter," said Peter. "Old Dan'l gets too bad to live with. Thinks nobody can't take care of you but him. Let's see, though; he said I was to cut you a bunch of them white grapes in Number 1 house, and there was two green figs quite ripe if you liked to have them."

Peter pulled the carriage up and down the garden half a dozen times, listening the while till he heard the dull bang of the front door.

"They're gone," he said gleefully. "Come on!"

He went down the garden at a trot, and then carefully drew the wheeled-chair on to the grass at the bottom.

"Peter, did you feed the squirrel!" said Dexter suddenly.

Peter looked round very seriously, and shook his head.

"Oh!" ejaculated Dexter. "Why didn't you feed the poor thing?"

"Wait a minute and you'll see," said the groom; and, drawing the chair a little further, until it was close to the brink of the bright river, he turned round—

"Thought you'd like to feed him yourself, so I brought him down."

There, on a willow branch, hung the old cage, with the squirrel inside, and Peter thrust his hand into his pocket to withdraw it full of nuts.

But Peter had not finished his surprise, for he left the chair for a few moments and returned with Dexter's rod and line, and a bag of worms.

"Going to fish?" said Dexter eagerly.

"No, but I thought you'd like to now you was better," said Peter. "There, you can fish as you sit there, and I'll put on your bait, and take 'em off the hook."

Dexter fished for half an hour, but he did not enjoy it, for he could not throw in his line without expecting to see Bob Dimsted on the other side. So he soon pleaded fatigue, and was wheeled out into the sunshine, and to the door of the vinery, up which he had scrambled when he first came to the doctor's house.

A week later he was down at Chale, in the Isle of Wight, where the doctor had taken a house; and here, upon the warm sands, Dexter sat and lay day after day, drinking in the soft sea air, and gaining strength, while the doctor sat under an umbrella to think out fresh chapters for his book, and Helen either read to her invalid or worked.

Chapter Forty Eight
The Proof of the Doctor's Theory

Three years, as every one knows, look like what they are—twenty-six thousand two hundred and eighty long hours from one side, and they look like nothing from the other. They had passed pleasantly and well, for the doctor had been so much pleased with his Isle of Wight house that he had taken it for three years, and transported there the whole of his household, excepting Dan'l, who was left in charge at Coleby.

"You see, my dear," the doctor had said; "it's a mistake for Dexter to be at Coleby until he has gone through what we may call his caterpillar stage. We'll take him back a perfect—"

"Insect, papa?" said Helen, smiling.

"No, no. You understand what I mean."

So Dexter did not see Coleby during those three years, in which he stayed his terms at a school where the principal did not break the spirit of backward and unruly boys. On the contrary, he managed to combine excellent teaching with the possession of plenty of animal spirits, and his new pupil gained credit, both at home and at the school.

"Now," said the doctor, on the day of their return to the old home, as he ran his eye proudly over the sturdy manly-looking boy he was taking back; "I think I can show Sir James I'm right, eh, my dear?"

Old Dan'l smiled a wonderful smile as Dexter went down the garden directly he got home.

"Shake hands with you, my lad?" he said, in answer to an invitation; "why, I'm proud. What a fine un you have growed! But come and have a look round. I never had such a year for fruit before."

Chuckling with satisfaction, the doctor was not content until he had brought Sir James and Lady Danby to the house to dinner, in company with their son, who had grown up into an exceedingly tall, thin, pale boy with a very supercilious smile.

No allusion was made to the doctor's plan, but the dinner-party did not turn out a success, for the boys did not seem to get on together; and Sir James said in confidence to Lady Danby that night, precisely what Dr Grayson said to Helen—

"They never shall be companions if I can help it. I don't like that boy."

Over the dessert, too, Sir James managed to upset Dexter's equanimity by an unlucky speech, which brought the colour to the boy's cheeks.

"By the way, young fellow," he said, "I had that old friend of yours up before me, about a month ago, for the second time."

Dexter looked at him with a troubled look, and Sir James went on, as he sipped his claret.

"You know—Bob Dimsted. Terrible young blackguard. Always poaching. Good thing if they had a press-gang for the army, and such fellows as he were forced to serve."

It was at breakfast the next morning that the doctor waited till Dexter had left the table, and then turned to Helen—

"I shall not forgive Danby that unkind remark," he said. "I could honestly do it now, and say, 'There, sir, I told you I could make a gentleman out of any material that I liked to select; and I've done it.' But no: I'll wait till Dexter has passed all his examinations at Sandhurst, and won his commission, and then— Yes, Maria—what is it!"

"Letter, sir, from the Union," said Maria.

"Humph! Dear me! What's this? Want me to turn guardian again, and I shall not. Eh, bless my heart! Well, well, I suppose we must."

He passed the letter to Helen, and she read Mr Hippetts formal piece of diction, to the effect that one of the old inmates, a Mrs Curdley, was in a dying state, and she had several times asked to see the boy she had nursed— Obed Coleby. During the doctor's absence from the town the master had not felt that he could apply; but as Dr Grayson had returned, if he would not mind his adopted son visiting the poor old woman, who had been very kind to him as a child, it would be a Christian-like deed.

"Yes; yes, of course, of course," said the doctor; and he called Dexter in.

"Oh yes!" cried the lad, as he heard the request. "I remember all she did for me so well, and—and—I have never been to see her since."

"My fault—my fault, my boy," said the doctor hastily. "There, we shall go and see her now."

There were only two familiar faces for Dexter to encounter, first, namely, those of Mr Hippetts and the schoolmaster, both of whom expressed themselves as being proud to shake their old pupil's hand.

Then they ascended to the infirmary, where the old nurse lay very comfortable and well cared for, and looking as if she might last for months.

Her eyes lit up as she saw Dexter; and, when he approached, she held out her hand, and made him sit down beside her.

"And growed such a fine chap!" she said, again and again.

She had little more to say, beyond exacting a promise that he would come and see her once again, and when he was about to leave she put a small, dirty-looking, brown-paper packet in his hand.

"There," she said. "I'd no business to, and he'd ha' took it away if he'd ha' known; but he didn't; and it's yours, for it was in your father's pocket when he come here and died."

The "he" the poor old woman meant was the workhouse master, and the packet was opened in his presence, and found to contain a child's linen under-garment plainly marked—"Max Vanburgh, 12," and a child's highly-coloured toy picture-book, frayed and torn, and further disfigured by having been doubled in half and then doubled again, so that it would easily go in a man's pocket.

It was the familiar old story of Little Red Riding-Hood, but the particular feature was an inscription upon the cover written in a delicate feminine hand—

"For my darling Max on his birthday, June 30th, 18—.
Alice Vanburgh, The Beeches, Daneton."

"But you told me the boy's father was a rough, drunken tramp, who died in the infirmary."

"Yes, sir, I did," said Mr Hippetts, when he had a private interview with the doctor next day. "But it seems strange."

"Very," said the doctor.

Helen also agreed that it was very strange, and investigations followed, the result of which proved, beyond doubt, that Dexter Grayson, otherwise Obed Coleby, was really Maximilian Vanburgh, the son of Captain Vanburgh and Alice, his wife, both of whom died within two years of the day when, through the carelessness of a servant, the little fellow strayed away out through the gate and on to the high-road, where he was found far from home, crying, by the rough, tipsy scoundrel who passed that way.

The little fellow's trouble appealed to what heart there was left in the man's breast, and he carried him on, miles away, careless as to whom he belonged to, and, day by day, further from the spot where the search was going on. The child amused him; and in his way he was kind to it, while the little fellow was of an age to take to any one who played with and petted him. Rewards and advertisements were vain, for they never reached the man's eyes, and his journeyings were on and on through a little-frequented part of the country, where it was nobody's business to ask a rough tramp how he came by the neglected-looking, ragged child, who clung to him affectionately enough. The little fellow was happy with him for quite three months, as comparison of dates proved, and what seemed strange became mere matter of fact—to wit, that Dexter was a gentleman by birth.

All this took time to work out, but it was proved incontestably, the old nurse having saved all that the rough fellow had left of his little companion's belongings; and when everything was made plain, there was the fact that Dexter was an orphan, and that he had found a home that was all a boy could desire.

"There, papa! what have you to say now?" said Helen to the doctor one day.

"Say?" he said testily. "Danby will laugh at me when he knows, and declare my theory is absurd. I shall never finish that book."

"But you will not try such an experiment again?" said Helen laughingly.

Just then Dexter came in sight, bright, frank, and manly, and merrily whistling one of Helen's favourite airs.

"No," said the doctor sharply; and then—"God bless him! Yes: if it was to be the making of such a boy as that!"